THE KEY

SIMON TOYNE

HARPER

Harper
An imprint of HarperCollins*Publishers*
77–85 Fulham Palace Road,
Hammersmith, London W6 8JB

www.harpercollins.co.uk

This paperback edition 2012
1

A catalogue record for this book
is available from the British Library

ISBN 978 0 00 739162 2

Starmap image © the Trustees of the British Museum.
All rights reserved

Typeset in Minion by Palimpsest Book Production Limited,
Falkirk, Stirlingshire

Printed and bound in Great Britain by
Clays Ltd, St Ives plc

MIX
Paper from
responsible sources
FSC™ www.fsc.org FSC™ C007454

Find out more about HarperCollins and the environment at
www.harpercollins.co.uk/green

THE KEY

Also By Simon Toyne

Sanctus

To Roxy
(you can read it when you're eleven)

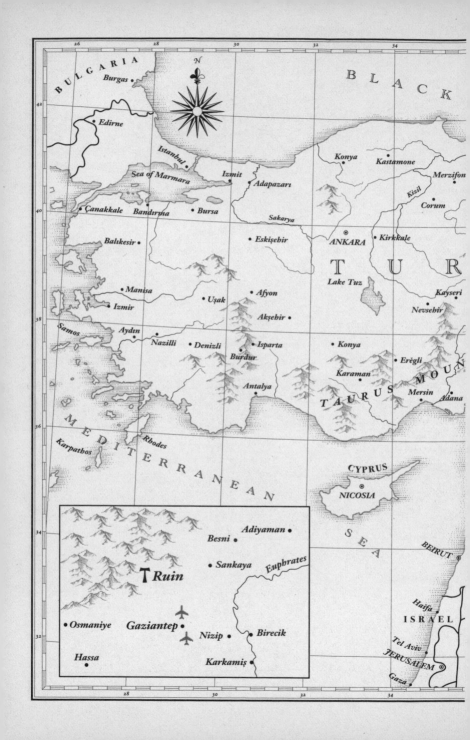

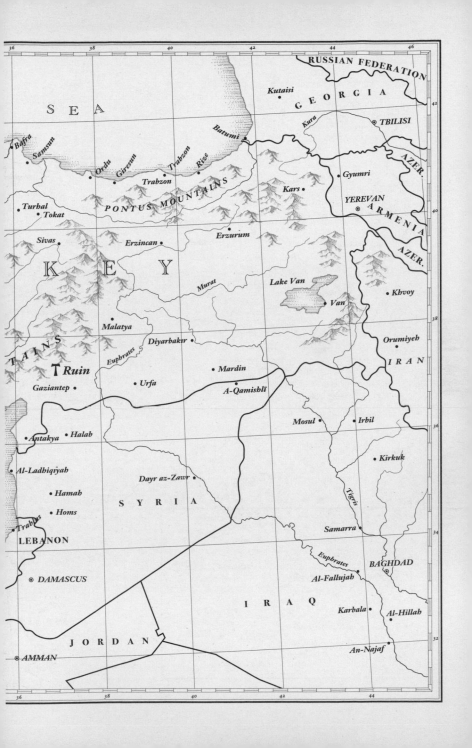

I

And suddenly there came a sound from heaven as of a rushing mighty wind . . . And they were all filled with the Holy Ghost, and began to speak with other tongues . . .

King James Bible Acts 2:2–4

1

Al-Hillah, Babil Province, Central Iraq

The desert warrior stared through the sand-scoured window, goggles hiding his eyes, his keffiyeh masking the rest of his face. Everything out there was bleached the colour of bone: the buildings, the rubble – even the people.

He watched a man shuffle along the far side of the street, his own keffiyeh swathed against the dust. There weren't many passers-by in this part of town, not with the noon sun high in the white sky and the temperature way into the fifties. Even so, they needed to be quick.

From somewhere behind him in the depths of the building came a dull thud and a muffled groan. He watched for any indication the stranger may have heard, but he kept walking, sticking close to the sliver of shade provided by a wall pock-marked by automatic weapon fire and grenade blasts. He watched until the man had melted away in the heat-haze, then turned his attention back to the room.

The office was part of a garage on the outskirts of the city. It smelled of oil and sweat and cheap cigarettes. A framed photograph hung on one wall, its subject appearing to proudly survey the piles of greasy paperwork and engine parts that covered every surface. The room was just about big enough for a desk and a couple of chairs and small enough for the bulky air-conditioning unit to maintain a reasonable temperature. When it was working. Right now it wasn't. The place was like an oven.

The city had been plagued for months by power cuts, one of the many prices they'd had to pay for liberation. People were already talking about Saddam's regime like it was the good old days. *Sure, people might have disappeared from time to time, but at least the lights stayed on.* It amazed him how quickly they forgot. He forgot nothing. He'd been an outlaw in Saddam's time and had remained one under the current occupation. His allegiance was to the land.

Another grunt of pain snapped him back to the present. He began emptying drawers, opening cupboards, hoping he might quickly find the stone he was looking for and vanish into the desert before the next patrol swung past. But the man who had it clearly knew its value. There was no trace of it here.

He took the photograph off the wall. A thick black Saddam moustache spread across a face made featureless by pudgy prosperity; a white dishdasha strained against the man's belly as his arms stretched around two shyly grinning young girls who had unfortunately inherited their father's looks. The three of them were leaning against the white 4x4 now parked on the garage forecourt. He studied it now, heard the tick of the cooling engine, saw the shimmer of hot air above it, and a small but distinctive circle low down in the centre of the blackened glass of the windscreen. He smiled and walked towards it, the photo still in his hand.

The workroom took up most of the rear of the building. It was darker than the office and just as hot. Neon strips hung uselessly from the ceiling and a fan sat in the corner, silent and still. A vivid slash of sunlight from a couple of narrow windows high in the back wall fell across an engine block dangling on chains that seemed far too slender to hold it. Below it, lashed to the workbench with razor wire, the fat man in the photograph was struggling to breathe. He was stripped to the waist, his huge, hairy stomach rising and falling in time with every laboured breath. His nose was bloodied and broken and one of his eyes had swollen shut. Crimson rivulets ran from where the wire touched his sweat-slicked skin.

A man in dusty fatigues stood over him, his face also obscured by keffiyeh and goggles.

'Where is it?' he said, slowly raising a tyre iron that was wet with blood.

The fat man said nothing, merely shook his head, his breathing growing more rapid in the anticipation of fresh pain. Snot and blood bubbled from his nostrils into his moustache. He screwed up his one good eye. The tyre iron rose higher.

Then the desert warrior stepped into the room.

The fat man's face remained clenched in expectation of another blow. When none came he opened his good eye and discovered the second figure standing over him.

'Your daughters?' The newcomer held up the photograph. 'Pretty. Maybe they can tell us where their *babba* hides things?'

The voice was sandpaper on stone.

The fat man recognized it, and fear glazed his staring eye as the desert warrior slowly unwound his keffiyeh, slipped off the sand goggles, and leaned into the shaft of sunlight, causing his pupils to shrink to black dots in the centre of eyes so pale they appeared almost grey. The fat man registered their distinctive colour and shifted his gaze to the ragged scar encircling the man's throat.

'You know who I am?'

He nodded.

'Say it.'

'You are Ash'abah. You are . . . the Ghost.'

'Then you know why I am here?'

Another nod.

'So tell me where it is. Or would you prefer me to drop this engine on your skull and drag your daughters over for a new family photo?'

Defiance surged up inside him at the mention of his family.

'If you kill me you will find nothing,' he said. 'Not the thing you seek, and not my daughters. I would rather die than put them in danger's way.'

The Ghost laid the photograph down on the bench and reached into his pocket for the portable sat-nav he had pulled from the windscreen of the 4x4. He pressed a button and held it out for the man to see. The screen displayed a list of recent destinations. The third one down was the Arabic word for 'Home'. The Ghost tapped a fingernail lightly on it and the display changed to show a street map of a residential area on the far side of town.

All the fight drained from the fat man's face in an instant. He took a breath and, in as steady a voice as he could manage, told the Ghost what he needed to hear.

The 4x4 bounced over broken ground alongside one of the numerous canals that criss-crossed the landscape to the east of Al-Hillah. The terrain was a striking mixture of barren desert and patches of dense, tropical greenery. It was known as the Fertile Crescent, part of ancient Mesopotamia – the land between two rivers. Ahead of them a line of lush grass and date palms sketched out the banks of one of them – the Tigris – and the Euphrates lay behind them. Between these ancient boundaries mankind had invented the written word, algebra and the wheel, and many believed it was the original location of the Garden of Eden, but no one had ever found it. Abraham – father of the three great religions: Islam, Judaism and Christianity – had been born here. The Ghost had come into existence here too, birthed by the land he now served as a loyal son.

The truck eased past a palm grove and bounced out into the chalk-white desert, baked to concrete by the relentless sun. The fat man grunted as pain jarred through his bruised flesh. The Ghost ignored him, fixing his gaze on a hazy pile of rubble starting to take shape through the windscreen. It was too soon to say what it was, or even how close. The extreme heat of the desert played tricks with distance and time. Looking out at the bleached horizon he could have been staring at a scene from the Bible: the same broken land and parchment sky, the same smudge of moon melting upon it.

The mirage began to take more solid form as they drew closer. It was much bigger than he'd first thought: a square structure, 'man-made', two storeys high, probably an abandoned caravanserai serving the camel trains that used to travel through these ancient lands. Its flat clay bricks, baked hard by the same sun almost a thousand years ago, were now crumbling back to their original dust.

Dust thou art, the Ghost thought as he surveyed the scene, *And unto dust shalt thou return.*

Blast marks became apparent as they drew closer, peppering the outer walls. The damage was recent – evidence of insurgence, or possibly target practice by British or American troops. The Ghost felt his jaw clench in anger and wondered how the invaders would like it if armed Iraqis started blowing lumps out of Stonehenge or Mount Rushmore.

'There. Stop there.' The fat man pointed to a small cairn of rocks a few hundred metres short of the main ruin.

The driver steered towards it and crunched to a halt. The Ghost scanned the horizon, saw the shimmer of air rising from hot earth, the gentle movement of palm fronds and in the distance a cloud of dust, possibly a military column on the move, but too far away to be of immediate concern. He opened the car door to the furnace heat and turned to the hostage.

'Show me,' he whispered.

The fat man stumbled across the baked terrain, the Ghost and the driver following his exact footsteps to avoid any mines he may try to lure them on to. Three metres short of the pile of rocks the man stopped and pointed to the ground. The Ghost followed the line of his extended arm and saw a faint depression in the earth. 'Booby traps?'

The fat man stared at him as though he'd insulted his family. 'Of course,' he said, holding out his hand for the keys to the truck. He took them and pointed the fob towards the ground. The muted chirp of a lock deactivating sounded somewhere beneath them, then he dropped down, brushing away layers of dust to reveal a hatch secured on one side by a padlock wrapped in a plastic bag. He selected a small key then wrenched open the square trapdoor.

Sunlight streamed down into the bunker. The fat man lowered himself on to a ladder that dropped steeply away into the darkness. The Ghost watched him all the way down from over the barrel of his pistol until he looked up, his one good eye squinting against the brightness. 'I'm going to get a torch,' he said, reaching out into the dark.

The Ghost said nothing, just tightened his finger on the trigger in case something else appeared in his hand. A cone of light clicked on in the darkness and shone into the swollen face of the garage owner.

The driver went next while the Ghost did a final sweep of the horizon. The dust cloud was further away now, still heading north towards Baghdad. There were no other signs of life. Satisfied that they were alone, he slid down into the dark earth.

The cave had been cut from rock by ancient hands and stretched away several metres in each direction. Military-style shelving units had been set up along each wall with thick sheets of polythene draped over them to protect their contents from the dust. The Ghost reached over and pulled one aside. The shelf was filled with guns, neatly stacked AK-47 assault rifles mostly, all bearing the scars of combat usage. Underneath them were rows of spam cans with stencilled lettering in Chinese, Russian, and Arabic, each containing 7.62mm rounds.

The Ghost worked his way down the shelves, pulling aside each polythene sheet in turn to discover more weapons, heavy artillery shells, brick-like stacks of dollar bills, bags of dried leaves and white powder, and finally – near the back of the cave on a shelf of its own – he found what he was looking for.

He eased the loose bundle of sacking towards him, feeling the drag of the heavy object inside, then unwrapped it reverently, with the same care he would use to peel dressings from burned flesh. Inside was a flat slate tablet. He tilted it towards the light, revealing faint markings on its surface. He traced their outline with his finger – a letter 'T' turned upside down.

The driver glanced over, his gun still on the hostage, his eyes drawn to the sacred object. 'What does it say?'

The Ghost flipped the sacking back over the stone. 'It is written in the lost language of the gods,' he said, picking up the bundle and cradling it as if it were a newborn. 'Not for us to read, only for us to keep safe.' He walked up to the fat man and glared into his battered face, his pale eyes unnaturally bright in the dim light. 'This belongs to the land. It should not be tossed on a shelf with these things. Where did you get it?'

'I swapped it with a goatherd, for a couple of guns and some ammunition.'

'Tell me his name and where I might find him.'

'He was a Bedouin. I don't know his name. I was doing some business up in Ramadi and he brought it to sell, along with some other bits of junk. He said he found it in the desert. Maybe he did, maybe he stole it. I gave him a good price anyway.' He looked up with his one good eye. 'And now you will steal it from me.'

The Ghost weighed this new information. Ramadi was a half-day's drive north. One of the main centres of resistance during the invasion and occupation, it had been bombed and shelled to rubble, and now had a cursed air hanging over it. It was also home to one of Saddam's palaces, now stripped clean by looters. The relic could easily have come from there. The late president had been a keen stealer and hoarder of his own country's treasures. 'How long ago did you buy it?'

'About ten days, during the monthly market.'

The Bedouin could be anywhere by now, roaming with his sheep across hundreds of square kilometres of desert. The Ghost held the bundle up for the fat man to see. 'If you come across anything else like this, you hold on to it and let me know. That way you become my friend – understand? You know I can be a useful friend, and you do not want me as your enemy.'

The man nodded.

The Ghost held his gaze for a moment then replaced the sand goggles.

'What about the rest of this stuff?' the driver said.

'Leave it. There's no need to take away this man's livelihood.' He turned to the ladder and started to climb towards the daylight.

'Wait!'

The fat man looked at him with confusion, puzzled by his surprising act of charity.

'The Bedouin herder, he wears a red football cap. I offered to buy it, as a joke, and he became offended. He said it was his most precious possession.'

'What team?'

'Manchester United – the red devils.'

2

Vatican City, Rome

Cardinal Secretary Clementi drew deeply on his cigarette, sucking the soothing smoke into his anxious body as he looked down on the tourists swarming across St Peter's Square like a plump god despairing of his creation. Several groups stood directly beneath him, their viewpoint alternating between their guidebooks and the window where he stood. He was pretty sure they couldn't see him, his well-stuffed black cardinal's surplice helping him to blend into the shadows. They were not looking for him anyway. He took another long draw on his cigarette and watched them realize their mistake then shift their collective gaze to the closed windows of the papal apartments to his left. Smoking inside the building was forbidden, but as Cardinal Secretary of the city-state, Clementi didn't consider the odd indulgence in his private office an outrageous abuse of position. He generally restricted himself to two a day, but today was different; today he was already on his fifth, and it wasn't even lunchtime.

He took one last long breath of nicotine-laced air, crushed the cigarette out in the marble ashtray resting on the sill, then turned to face the bad news that was spread across his desk like a slick. As was his preference, the morning papers had been arranged in the same configuration as the countries on a world map – the American broadsheets on the left, the Russian and Australian on the right, and the European ones in the middle. Usually the headlines were all different, each reflecting a national obsession with a local celebrity or political scandal.

Today they were all the same, as they had been for over a week now, each carrying more or less the same picture: the dark, dagger-like mountain fortress known as the Citadel that sat at the very heart of the ancient Turkish city of Ruin.

Ruin was a curiosity in the modern church, a former ancient powerhouse that had become, along with Lourdes and Santiago de Compostela, one of the Catholic Church's most popular and enduring shrines. Carved out of a vertical mountain by human hands, the Citadel of Ruin was the oldest continually inhabited structure on earth and original centre of the Catholic Church. The first Bible had been written within its mysterious walls, and it was widely believed that the greatest secrets of the early Church were still kept there. Much of the mystery surrounding the place stemmed from its strict tradition of silence. No one but the monks and priests who lived in the Citadel were ever allowed to set foot inside the sacred mountain and, once they had entered, they were never again permitted to set foot outside. Maintenance of the half-carved mountain, with its high battlements and narrow windows, fell exclusively to the inhabitants; and over time the Citadel had developed the half-finished, ramshackle appearance that had given the city its name. But despite its appearance, it was no Ruin. It remained the only fortress in all of history that had never been breached, the only one that had held on to its ancient treasures and secrets.

Then, a little over a week ago, a monk had climbed to the top of the mountain. With TV cameras capturing his every move, he had arranged his limbs to form the sign of the Tau – symbol of the Sacrament, the Citadel's greatest secret – and thrown himself from the summit.

The reaction to the monk's violent death had sparked a global wave of anti-Church feeling that had culminated in a direct attack on the Citadel. A series of explosions had ripped through the Turkish night to reveal a tunnel leading into the base of the fortress. And for the first time in history, people had come out of the mountain – ten monks and three civilians, all suffering from varying degrees of injury – and the newspapers had been full of little else since.

Clementi picked up the morning edition of *La Republicca*, one of the more popular Italian newspapers, and read the banner headline:

CITADEL SURVIVORS LATEST
DID THEY DISCOVER THE SECRET OF
THE SACRAMENT?

It was the same question all the papers had been asking, using the explosion as a pretext to dredge up every old legend about the Citadel and its most infamous secret. The whole reason the power base had moved to Rome in the fourth century was to distance the Church from its secretive past. Ever since, Ruin had looked after its own affairs and kept its house in order – until now.

Clementi picked up another paper, a British tabloid showing a shining chalice floating above the Citadel with the headline:

CHURCH ON ROAD TO RUIN
'HOLY GRAIL' OF SECRETS ABOUT
TO BE REVEALED?

Other papers concerned themselves with the more lurid and morbid side of the story. Of the thirteen people who had emerged from the mountain, only five survived, the rest having died from their injuries. There were plenty of pictures: harshly lit shots snatched from over the heads of the paramedics as they stretchered the monks to the waiting ambulances, the flash photography highlighting the green of their cassocks and the red of the blood that ran from the ritualized wounds that criss-crossed their bodies.

The whole thing was a huge PR disaster, making the Church look like a demented, secretive, mediaeval cult: bad enough at the best of times, calamitous right now when Clementi had so many other things on his mind and needed the mountain to hold its secrets tighter than ever.

He sat down heavily at his desk, feeling the weight of the responsibilities he alone carried. As Cardinal Secretary of State, he was de facto prime minister of the Vatican city-state and had far-reaching executive powers over the Church's interests, both domestic and international. Ordinarily, the executive council in the Citadel would have dealt with the situation in Ruin. Like the Vatican, it was an autonomous state within a state with its own powers and influence, but since the explosion he had heard nothing from the mountain – nothing at all – and it was this silence, rather than the clamour of the world's press, that he found most disturbing. It meant the current crisis in Ruin was very much his concern.

Reaching over the sea of newsprint, Clementi tapped his keyboard. Already his inbox was bursting with the day's business, but he ignored it all, clicking instead on a private folder labelled RUIN. A prompt box asked for his password and he carefully typed it in, knowing if he got it wrong the whole computer would lock and it would take at least a day for a technician to unlock it again. An hourglass icon appeared as his server processed the complex encryption software, then another mailbox opened. It was empty – still no word. Leaving the subject line blank, he typed into the body of a new message:

Anything?

He hit *send* and watched it disappear from his screen, then shuffled the newspapers into a neat pile and sorted through some letters that required his signature while he waited for a reply.

14

The moment the explosion had torn through the Citadel, Clementi had mobilized agents of the Church to closely monitor the situation. He had used Citadel assets to maintain distance from Rome, hoping that the executive council inside the mountain would recover quickly and take over responsibility for the clean-up. In his orderly politician's mind he saw it as deploying weapons to deal with an oncoming threat. He had never imagined he might be called upon to personally fire them.

Outside he could hear the chatter of the tourists drifting up from the square as they marvelled at the majesty and wonder of the Church, little knowing what turmoil boiled inside it. A sound like a knife striking a wineglass announced the arrival of a message.

> Still nothing. There is a rumour that a ninth monk is about to die. What do you want me to do with the others?

His hand hovered over the keyboard ready to type a reply. Perhaps the situation was resolving itself. If another monk died there would be just four survivors remaining – but three of these were civilians, not bound by silence and obedience to the mother church. They posed the greatest threat of all.

His eyes crept across to the stack of newspapers on the corner of his desk and saw their photographs staring back at him – two women and one man. Ordinarily the Citadel would have dealt with them swiftly and decisively because of the threat they posed to the long-held secret of the mountain. Clementi, however, was a Roman cleric, more politician than priest, a creature far removed from the trials of direct action. Unlike the Prelate of Ruin, he was not used to signing death warrants.

He rose from his desk and drifted back towards the window, distancing himself from his decision.

There had been signs of life inside the mountain over the past week – candles passing behind some of the high windows, smoke leaking from the chimney vents. They would have to break their silence sooner or later, re-engage with the world and tidy up their own mess. Until then he would be patient and keep his hands clean and his mind focused on the future of the Church and the real dangers that faced it, dangers that had nothing to do with Ruin or the secrets of the past.

He reached for the pack of cigarettes on the window sill, preparing to seal his decision with the sixth of the day, when the sound of shoe-leather on marble rose in the corridor outside. Someone was heading his way, in far too much of a hurry for it to be routine. There was a sharp tap on his door and the pinched features of Bishop Schneider appeared.

'What?' Clementi's question betrayed more irritation than he intended. Schneider was his personal secretary and one of the lean, career bishops who, like a lizard on the rim of a volcano, managed to live dangerously close to the white heat of power without ever seeming to get singed. His efficiency was beyond reproach, yet Clementi found it very hard to warm to him. But today Schneider's smooth veneer was absent.

'They're here,' he said.

'Who?'

But there was no need for an answer. Schneider's expression told him all he needed to know.

Clementi grabbed the cigarettes and thrust them into his pocket. He knew he would probably smoke them all in the next few hours.

3

Ruin, Southern Turkey

The rain drifted down like ragged phantoms from the flat, grey sky, swirling as it caught the fading heat of the dying day. It fell from clouds that had formed high over the Taurus mountains, pulling moisture from the air as they drifted east, past the glacier and towards the foothills where the ancient city of Ruin lay fringed by jagged crags. The sharp peak of the Citadel, rising from the centre of the city, tore at the belly of the clouds, spilling rain that glossed the side of the mountain and cascaded to ground level, where the dry moat stood.

In the old town, tourists struggled up the narrow lanes towards the Citadel, slipping on the cobbles, rustling along in souvenir rain ponchos made from red plastic to resemble monks' cassocks. Some were merely sightseers, ticking the Citadel off a long list of world monuments, but others were making the trip for more traditional reasons, pilgrims come to offer prayer and tribute in exchange for peace of mind and calmed souls. There had been many more than usual in the last week, prompted by recent events and the strange sequence of natural disasters that had followed: earth tremors in countries that were traditionally stable, tidal waves striking those with no flood defences, weather that was both unpredictable and unseasonal – just like the thick, cold rain that was now falling in this late Turkish spring.

They continued their slippery way upwards, rising into the

cloud to be greeted, not by the awe-inspiring sight of the Citadel, but by the ghostly outlines of other disappointed tourists staring into the mist towards the spot where the mountain should be. They drifted through the haze, past the shrine of wilting flowers where the monk had fallen, to a low wall marking the edge of the broad embankment and the end of their journey.

Beyond the wall, long grass moved gently where water once flowed, and there – just visible like a wall of night rising up from the edge of the mist – was the lower part of the mountain. It had the monumental and unnerving presence of a huge ship in a fog bank bearing down on a tiny rowing boat. Most of the tourists quickly headed away, stumbling through the luminous fog in search of shelter in the souvenir shops and cafés that lined the far side of the embankment. But a patient few remained, standing at the low wall, offering up the prayers they had carried with them: prayers for the Church; for the dark mountain and for the silent men who had always dwelt there.

Inside the Citadel, all was quiet.

No one moved through the tunnels. No work was being done. The kitchens were empty and so was the garden that flourished in the crater at the heart of the mountain. Neat piles of rubble and wooden props showed where tunnel repairs had been made, but those who had carried out the work had now moved on. The airlock leading into the great library remained shut, as it had done since the blast knocked out the power and disrupted the climate control and security systems inside. Rumour had it that it would open again soon, though no one knew when.

Elsewhere, there were signs that the mountain was returning to normal. The power was back on in most areas and prayer and study rotas had been posted in all the dormitories. Most significantly, a requiem Mass had been organized to finally lay to rest the bodies of the Prelate and the Abbot, whose deaths had plunged the mountain into a leaderless and unprecedented chaos. Every man in the mountain was heading there now, treading in solemn silence to pay their last respects.

Or almost every man.

High in the mountain, in the restricted upper section where only the Sancti – the green-cloaked guardians of the Sacrament – were permitted to tread, a group of four monks neared the top of the forbidden stairs.

They too walked in silence, trudging up the darkened stairway, each weighed down with the heavy trespass they were undertaking. The ancient law that bound them was clear: anyone venturing here without permission would be executed as an example to those who sought to discover the great secret of the mountain uninvited. But these were not ordinary times, and they were no ordinary monks.

Leading the way was Brother Axel, bristling like a brush, his auburn hair and beard a close match for the red cassock that showed he was a guard. Hard on his heels came the black-cloaked figure of Father Malachi, chief librarian, his stooped figure and thick glasses a legacy of decades spent hunched over books in the great library caves. Next came Father Thomas, implementer of so many of the technological advancements in the library, dressed in the black surplice of a priest. And finally there was Athanasius, wearing the simple brown cassock of the Administrata, his bald head and face unique among the uniformly bearded brethren of the Citadel. Each man was head of their particular guild – except Athanasius who was only acting head in the absence of an abbot. Collectively they had been running the mountain since the explosion had removed the ruling elite from their midst, and collectively they had taken the decision to discover for themselves the great secret they were now custodians of.

They reached the top of the stairs and gathered in the dark

of a small vaulted cave, their torches picking out roughly carved walls and several narrow tunnels that led away in different directions.

'Which way?' Brother Axel's voice seemed too big in the narrow confines of the chamber. He had led most of the way, surging up the stairs as though it was something he was born to, but now he seemed as hesitant as the rest of them.

Discovering what lay inside the chapel of the Sacrament was usually the pinnacle of a monk's life, something that would only happen if they were selected to join the elite ranks of the Sancti. But they were here on nobody's invitation and this group's deep-seated fear of learning the forbidden knowledge was both intoxicating and terrifying.

Axel stepped forward, holding out his torch. There were niches cut into the rock walls with solid wax oozing down where candles had once burned. He swept his torch over each tunnel in turn, then pointed to the central one. 'There's more wax here. It has been used more than the others; the chapel must be this way.'

He moved forward without waiting for confirmation or agreement, ducking to enter the low tunnel. The group followed, with Athanasius reluctantly bringing up the rear. He knew Axel was right. He had trod this forbidden floor alone just a few days previously and seen the horrors the chapel held. He steeled himself now to witness them again.

The group continued down the tunnel, the light from their torches now picking out rough symbols on the walls of crudely rendered women undergoing various tortures. The further they went, the fainter the images grew, until they faded entirely and the tunnel opened into a larger antechamber.

They huddled together, instinctively keeping close while their torches explored the darkness. There was a small, enclosed fireplace on one wall, like a blacksmith's forge, dark with soot and dripping ash to the floor, though no fire burned in it now. In front of it stood three circular whetstones, mounted on sturdy wooden frames with treadles to turn the wheels. Beyond them on the back wall a large circular stone with the sign of the Tau carved at its centre had been rolled to one side to reveal an arched doorway.

'The chapel of the Sacrament,' Axel said, staring into the darkness beyond the door. For a moment they all stood, tensed and nervous as if expecting a beast to come rushing out of the dark towards them. It was Axel who stepped forward to break the spell, holding his torch in front of him like a talisman against whatever might be waiting there. The light pushed away the dark, first revealing more dead candles inside the door, drowned in puddles of cold wax, then a wall, curving away to the left where the chapel opened out. Then they saw what the sharpening stones were for.

The walls were covered with blades.

Axes, cleavers, swords, daggers – all lined up from floor to ceiling. They reflected the torches, glittering like stars and carrying the light deeper into the chapel to where a shape rose up in the dark, about the same height as a man and as familiar to each of them as their own face. It was the Tau, symbol of the Sacrament, now transformed in front of them into the Sacrament itself.

At first it appeared like darkness solidified, but as Axel took a step forward, light reflected dully on its surface, revealing that it was made of some kind of metal bonded together with rivets. The base was bolted with brackets to the stone floor, where deep channels had been cut, radiating out to the edge of the room where they joined deeper gulleys that disappeared into the dark corners. A withered plant curled around the lower part of the cross, clinging to the sides in dry tendrils.

The group drew closer, drawn by the gravity of the strange object, and saw that the entire front section of the cross was open, hinged at the far end of the cross beam and supported by a chain fixed to the roof of the cave.

Inside the Tau was hollow and filled with hundreds of long needles.

'Can this be the Sacrament?' Father Malachi voiced what everyone in the group was thinking.

They had all been brought up on the legends of what the Sacrament might be: the tree of life from the Garden of Eden, the chalice Christ had drunk from as he was dying on the cross, perhaps even the cross itself. But as they stood now, confronted by the reality of this macabre object in a room lined with sharpened blades, Athanasius could sense gaps starting to open up between their unquestioning faith and the thing that stood before them. It was what he had hoped would happen. It was what he *needed* to happen in order to steer the Citadel away from its dark past and towards a brighter, purer future.

'This can't be it,' Axel said. 'There must be something else; something in one of the other tunnels.'

'But this is the main chamber,' Athanasius replied, 'and here is the Tau.' He turned to it, averting his gaze from the interior, where dark memories of the last time he had stood here were snagged on the sharp spikes within.

'It looks like it may have contained something,' Malachi said, stepping closer and peering at it through his thick glasses, 'but without the Sancti here to explain, we may never know what it was or the significance it held.'

'Yes. It's a great pity they are no longer here in the mountain,' Axel turned pointedly to Athanasius. 'I'm sure we all pray for their rapid return.'

Athanasius ignored the jibe. The Sancti had been evacuated on his orders, a decision he had made in good faith and did not regret. 'We have coped together,' he replied, 'and we shall cope together still. Whatever was here has gone – we have all borne witness to this – now we must move on.'

They stood for a while, staring at the empty cross, each lost in their own private thoughts. It was Malachi who broke the silence. 'It is written in the earliest chronicles that if the Sacrament is removed from the Citadel, then the Church will fall.' He turned to face the group, his glasses magnifying the concern in his eyes. 'I fear what we have discovered here can augur nothing but evil.'

Father Thomas shook his head. 'Not necessarily. Our old idea of the Citadel may have fallen, in a metaphorical sense, yet it does not follow that there will also be a physical end to everything.'

'Exactly,' Athanasius continued. 'The Citadel was originally created to protect and keep the Sacrament, but it has become so many other things since. And just because the Sacrament is no longer here does not mean the Citadel will cease to prosper or have purpose. One may remove the acorn from the root of a great oak and yet the tree will still flourish. Never forget, we serve God first, not the mountain.'

Axel took a step back and pointed his finger at Thomas and then at Athanasius. 'This is heresy you speak.'

'Our very presence here is heresy.' Athanasius swept his hand toward the empty Tau. 'But the Sacrament has gone, and so have the Sancti. The old ways no longer bind us. We have a chance to choose new rules to live by.'

'But first we must choose a new leader.'

Athanasius nodded. 'On this at least we agree.'

At that moment a noise rose up from the deeper depths of the mountain and echoed within the chapel, the sound of the requiem Mass beginning.

'We should go and join our brethren,' Thomas said. 'And until we have new leadership, I suggest we say nothing of what we have seen here – it will only lead to panic.' He turned to Malachi. 'You are not the only one who knows the chronicles.'

Malachi nodded, but his eyes were still magnified with fear. He turned and took a last long look at the empty Tau as the others filed out behind him. 'If the Sacrament is removed from the Citadel, then the *Church* will fall, not the mountain,' he muttered, too quiet for anyone else to hear. Then he quickly left the chapel, afraid to be left there alone.

4

Liv Adamsen burst from sleep like a breathless swimmer breaking surface. She gasped for air, her blonde hair plastered across pale, damp skin, her frantic green eyes scanning the room for something real to cling to, something tangible to help drag her away from the horrors of her nightmare. She heard a whispering, as though someone was close by, and cast about for its source.

No one there.

The room was small: a solid door opposite the steel-framed bed she was lying on; an old TV fixed high on a ceiling bracket in the corner; a single window set into a wall whose white paint was yellowing and flaking as if infected. The blind was down, but bright daylight glowed behind it, throwing the sharp outline of bars against the wipe-clean material. She took a deep breath to try to calm herself, and caught the scent of sickness and disinfectant in the air.

Then she remembered.

She was in a hospital – though she didn't know why, or how she had come to be there.

She took more breaths, long and deep and calming. Her heart still thudded in her chest, the whispering rush continued in her ears, so loud and immediate that she had to stop herself from checking the room again.

Get a grip, she told herself. *It's just blood rushing through your veins. There's no one here.*

The same nightmare seemed to lie in wait for her every time she fell asleep, a dream of whispering blackness, where pain bloomed like red flowers, and a shape loomed, ominous and terrifying – a cross in the shape of a letter 'T'. And there was something else in the darkness with her, something huge and terrible. She could hear it moving and feel the shaking of the earth as it came towards her, but always, just as it was about to emerge from the black and reveal itself, she would wake in terror.

She lay there for a while, breathing steadily to calm the panic, tripping through a mental list of what she could remember.

My name is Liv Adamsen.

I work for the New Jersey Inquirer.

I was trying to discover what happened to Samuel.

An image of a monk flashed in her mind, standing on top of a dark mountain, forming the sign of a cross with his body even as he tipped forward and fell.

I came here to find out why my brother died.

In the shock of this salvaged memory Liv remembered where she was. She was in Turkey, close to the edge of Europe, in the ancient city of Ruin. And the sign Samuel had made – the Tau – was the sign of the Sacrament, the same shape that now haunted her dreams. Except it wasn't a dream, it was real. In her blossoming consciousness she knew that she had seen the shape, somewhere in the darkness of the Citadel – she had seen the Sacrament. She focused on the memory, willing it to take sharper form, but it kept shifting, like something at the edge of her vision or a word she could not recall. All she could remember was a feeling of unbearable pain and of . . . confinement.

She glanced up at the heavy door, noticing the keyhole now and recalling the corridor beyond. She had glimpsed it as the doctors and nurses had come and gone over the past few days.

How many days? Four? Five, maybe.

She had also seen two chairs pushed up against the wall with men sitting on them. The first was a cop, the uniform a dark blue, the badges unfamiliar. The other had also worn a uniform: black shoes, black suit, black shirt, a thin strip of white at the collar. The thought of him, sitting just a few metres from her made the fear rise up again. She knew enough of the bloody history of Ruin to realize the danger she was in. If she had seen the Sacrament and they suspected it then they would try to silence her – like they had silenced her brother. It was how they had maintained their secret for so long. It was a cliché, but it was true – the dead kept their secrets.

And the priest standing vigil outside her door was not there to minister to her troubled soul or pray for her rapid recovery.

He was there to keep her contained.

He was there to ensure her silence.

ROOM 410

Four doors down the corridor Kathryn Mann lay in the starched prison of her own single bed, her thick black hair curled across the pillow like a darkening storm. She was shivering despite the hospital heat of her room. The doctors had said she was still in shock, a delayed and ongoing reaction to the forces of the explosion she had survived in the confines of the tunnel beneath the Citadel. She had also lost hearing in her right ear and the left one had been severely damaged. The doctors said it may improve, but they were always evasive when she asked how much.

She couldn't remember the last time she had felt this wretched and helpless. When the monk had appeared on top of the Citadel and made the sign of the Tau with his body she had believed the ancient prophecy was coming true:

The cross will fall
The cross will rise
To unlock the Sacrament
And bring forth a new age

And so it had happened. Liv had entered the Citadel, the Sancti had come out and now they were dying, one by one, the ancient enemy, the keepers of the Sacrament. Even with her damaged ears, Kathryn had heard the clamour of medical teams running in answer to the flat-lining wail of cardiac alarms all around her. After each alarm she would ask the nurse who had died, fearing it might be the girl. But each time it had been another monk, taken from this life to answer for themselves in the next, their deaths a portent of nothing but good. She had been kept apart from Liv so did not know for sure what had happened inside the Citadel, or even if she had discovered the Sacrament, though the steady deaths of the Sancti gave her some hope that she had.

But if this was a victory, it was a hollow one.

Whenever she closed her eyes she saw the body of Oscar de la Cruz – her father – lying broken and bloodied on the cold concrete floor of the airport warehouse. He had spent most of his long life hiding from the Citadel after escaping from within its walls and faking his own death in the trenches of the First World War. But they had still got him in the end. He had saved her life by smothering the grenade, thrown by a dark agent of the Citadel, meant for her and Gabriel.

It was Oscar who had first taught her about the Citadel, its sinister history and the secrets it contained. It was he who had taught her to read the prophetic symbols etched on the stone when she was still a girl, filling her with its meaning – a loving father telling dark stories to his blue-eyed little girl as later she had done with Gabriel, a mother passing the same stories to her son.

And when all this comes to pass – Oscar had always told her, *when the ancient wrong has been righted, then I will show you the next step.*

She had often wondered what private knowledge his words had hinted at – and now she would never know.

The Sancti had been unseated, but her own family had been destroyed in the process: first her husband; then her father – who next? Gabriel was in prison at the mercy of organizations she had learned not to trust; and she too had seen the priest, keeping steady watch just beyond her door, another agent of the same church that had already taken so much from her.

I will show you the next step – her father had told her. But now he was gone – killed just before his life's work had finally been realized – and she could see no step that might give her hope, or help save her, or Gabriel or Liv, from the danger they were in.

5

Vatican City, Rome

Clementi swept from his office with as much speed as his large frame could manage.

'When did they arrive?' he asked, his black surplice flaring out behind him like ragged wings.

'About five minutes ago,' Schneider said, struggling to keep up with his master.

'And where are they now?'

'They were escorted down to the boardroom in the vault. I came to fetch you as soon as I heard they were here.'

Clementi hurried past the two Swiss guardsmen, hoping His Holiness would not choose this moment to emerge from his apartment and enquire about Clementi's undue haste. As Cardinal Secretary of State, he had to work closely with the Pope – both literally and figuratively – discussing policy and getting his signature on important documents. The file in his hand did not contain any papal signatures or seals. His Holiness was not even aware of its contents or intent, something Clementi had worked hard to maintain.

He reached the end of the corridor and quickly barged through the door into the bare emergency stairwell beyond. 'Do we know which of the Group is present?'

'No,' Schneider replied. 'The guard wasn't sure and I didn't want to press him. I felt it better he remain vague on the details.'

Clementi nodded and descended into the gloom, brooding on what might await him at the end of this unscheduled summons.

The Group was a name he had given to the three as a means of turning them into a single entity, a mind trick designed to strike a balance of power in their arrangement: one of him, one of them. But it had not worked. They were far too powerful and distinctive to subsume into a homogenous whole and, try as he might, they remained as individual and formidable as when he had first approached them and laid out his scheme. The Group met as infrequently as possible, and always in secret, such was the delicate nature of their shared enterprise. With the calibre of people involved, arranging any meeting at all was a minor miracle of scheduling and they had not been due to meet again for another month; yet one or more of them was here right now, unannounced and unexpected – and there was only one viable explanation as to why.

'This has to be about the situation in Ruin,' Clementi said, arriving at a featureless metal door set into the wall of the first-floor landing.

He placed his doughy hand on a glass panel beside it, his cardinal's gold ring clinking against the glass, and a pale strip of light swept across his palm, casting pale, shifting shadows across his face that reflected in the polished metal of the door. Clementi looked away. He had always hated his appearance, his moon face with its fringe of curly hair – once blond, now white – making him appear like an oversized cherub. A dull *thunk* sounded inside the door and he heaved it open, hurrying into the dark and away from the sight of himself.

A narrow tunnel lit up in a flicker of neon as he moved down it, the walls turning from smooth concrete to rough stone as he passed from the Apostolic Palace into the stone foundations of the squat, fifteenth-century tower built next to it. After ten or so steps he reached a second door that opened into a small, windowless room, packed with shelves and crammed with box files.

'Go on ahead,' he said. 'Give my apologies and say I am cutting short another meeting and will be there directly. I will meet you in the lobby so you can brief me as to exactly who is there. I do not wish to enter a meeting of this importance without at least knowing who is present.'

Schneider bowed and slipped away, leaving Clementi alone with his churning thoughts. He listened to his chamberlain's footsteps receding, his eyes fixed on the crossed keys of the papal seal and the letters IOR that adorned every file in the room. He was in a section of the fortified tower of Niccolo V, built into the eastern wall of the Apostolic Palace, that now served as the headquarters and only branch of one of the world's most exclusive financial institutions. IOR stood for Istituto per le Opere di Religione – the Institute for Works of Religion – more commonly referred to as the Vatican Bank. It was the most secretive financial institution in the world and the prime cause of Clementi's present worries.

Set up in 1942 to manage the Church's huge accumulated wealth and investments, the bank had a little over forty thousand current account holders, no tax liabilities and the sort of unassailable privacy any Swiss bank would be proud of. As such, it had attracted some of the wealthiest and most influential investors in the world; but it had also courted more than its fair share of controversy.

In the 1970s and 80s the Institute had been used by the now disgraced financier Michele Sindona to launder Mafia drug money. After this Roberto Calvi, famously referred to as God's banker, had been appointed to take a tighter hold of the Church's vast resources; instead he had used the bank to illegally siphon billions of dollars from another financial institution, leaving the Church with an embarrassing and expensive moral responsibility when it eventually went bust. Calvi had been found dead a few weeks later, his pockets filled with building bricks and bank notes, hanging beneath Blackfriars Bridge in London. Much had been made of the ecclesiastical connotations of this location, especially in the light of Calvi's membership of a masonic lodge known as the 'Black Friars', but no one had ever been convicted of his murder. The long shadow cast by these scandals lingered on, and for Clementi the rehabilitation of the Vatican Bank had become a personal obsession. What's more, he had the perfect background to facilitate it.

As an undergraduate at Oxford he had studied history and economics as well as theology, discerning God's miracle at work in all three disciplines. In Clementi's eyes, the power of economics was a force for good, creating wealth so that people could be lifted from the evils of poverty and relieved of their earthly suffering. History had also taught him the perils of economic failure. He had studied the great civilizations of the past, focusing not only on how they had amassed their great wealth but also on how they lost it. Again and again, empires that had been built over hundreds, sometimes thousands of years, tipped from prosperity into rapid decline, leaving nothing behind but legends and ruined monuments. His economist's brain had pondered on what had become of their great wealth. Inevitably some of it passed to conquerors and became the seeds of new empires, but not all. History was littered with accounts of vast treasure stores that had vanished, never to be found again.

Once he had graduated and begun his rise within the Church, Clementi had served God in the best way he knew, by applying his learning and skill to update the Vatican's revenue streams so that money started flowing in where once it had only flowed out. He knew that economics now ruled the world where faith had once held sway and that, in order to wield the sort of power and influence it had once held, the Church would have to become an economic heavyweight again.

The further Clementi rose, the more influence he had, and

he used it to overhaul the outdated financial systems until finally his long service and deft stewardship was rewarded with the appointment to Cardinal Secretary of State and with it the keys to the main prize – the Vatican Bank itself.

His first act as Cardinal Secretary had been to amass all the bank's various confidential accounts and then personally audit them so he could see the exact state of the Church's finances. It was a task he didn't trust anyone else to carry out and it had taken him nearly a year to painstakingly sort the false records from the true and unpick all the subterfuge and false accounting to reveal the full picture. What he had discovered, in a room identical to the one he now stood in, had made him physically sick. Somehow, through systematic corruption and hundreds of years of appalling management, all the vast reserves of money that had been accumulated over the preceding two thousand years had evaporated.

Trillions of dollars – gone.

The Church still held a huge portfolio of property and priceless works of art, but there was no cash – no liquidity. The Church was effectively bankrupt, and, because of centuries of complex deception and false accounting, nobody knew it but him.

Clementi recalled the desolation of that moment, staring into the abyss of what the Church had become and what would surely follow when the truth came to light. If the Church had been a publicly listed company it would have been declared insolvent and broken up by the courts to pay what it could to creditors. But it was not a company, it was God's ministry on earth, and he could not stand by and allow it to be brought down by the mundane evils of greed and mismanagement. Instead he had relied on the things the Church had always fallen back on in times of need – its independence and its secrecy – and he had kept his discovery hidden.

Left with no choice but to carry on the dishonest practices bequeathed to him by his predecessors, Clementi had concealed the true accounts and set about maintaining the illusion of solvency by constantly moving around what little money there was and making what savings he could while he prayed for a miracle. But he did not despair, for even in the awfulness of his isolation and the great responsibility he alone carried, he could detect God's hand already working. For had He not bestowed upon Clementi the gifts to understand the complexities of finance and then blessed him with the position of Cardinal Secretary of State?

But the amounts of money lost were too colossal to be recovered by mere economies and financial restructuring. In addition to balancing the books, he needed to find a way to refinance the Church. In the end he found the solution in the most unlikely of places. The key to ensuring the Church's future, it turned out, was to look to its past – he had found his answer in Ruin.

Almost three years had passed since his moment of revelation, three years of carefully influencing world events by granting audiences and indulgences to presidents and prime ministers in exchange for favours only the Church could bestow. Like some papal legate of old, Clementi had nudged these modern-day Christian kings and emperors into war just so he could gain access to heathen lands the true church had once called its own. And now, just when his audacious scheme was on the verge of completion, it was being threatened by the same ancient and secretive place where the idea had originated.

He thought back to the newspapers on his desk, their headlines predicting the fall of the Citadel and salivating over the prospect of discovering what secrets lay within.

And one of those secrets was his.

If it were to be discovered, everything he had accomplished would be destroyed and the Church would be lost.

A sudden surge of anger welled up inside him and he cursed himself for his human weakness. He had delayed too long over the messy situation surrounding the Citadel. Wrenching open the door, he entered the blank corridor beyond, windowless and unexceptional save for its curved walls that followed the shape of the tower. He would demonstrate to the Group the true strength of his resolve by effectively signing four death warrants in front of them. Then they would see how committed he was; and they would be bound by blood, each to the other.

He burst through the door into the main lobby and stalked across the marble floor, past the ATMs that gave instructions in Latin, towards the steel-framed lift that descended to the vaults in the bedrock of the building.

The lift doors opened as he approached and Schneider jumped when he saw his master bearing down on him with fury in his eyes.

'Well,' Clementi said, stepping in and punching the button to take them straight back to the vaults. 'Which one of our esteemed associates am I about to face?'

'All of them,' Schneider said, just as the doors closed and they started to descend. 'The whole Group is here.'

6

Baghdad, Central Iraq

Dry dust clung to the evening air of Sadr City market, mixing with the smell of raw meat, ripe fruit and decay. Hyde sat across from the main market in the shade of a covered café, an imported American newspaper lying open on the table in front of him next to the sludgy remains of a small glass of coffee. Two flies were chasing each other round the saucer. In his head he placed a bet on which would take off first. He got it wrong. Story of his life.

He picked up the glass and sipped at the muddy contents, scanning the market from behind his scratched marine-issue Oakleys. He hated the coffee in Iraq. It was boiled and cooled nine times to remove all impurities and rendered almost undrinkable in the process. At least all the boiling meant there'd be no germs in it. Most Iraqis drank it with cream and a ton of sugar to mask the taste. Hyde drank it black to remind him of home, the bitter taste fuelling his hatred of the country he didn't seem able to escape. Black was also his favourite colour. Whenever life got too complicated and things started getting him down he would find a casino with a roulette table and bet everything he had on black, reducing his troubles to the single spin of a wheel. If he won, he would walk away with enough money to buy some peace of mind, never risking his doubled pot on another spin. If he lost, he literally had nothing left to lose. Either way, he would

36

leave the table changed somehow. He liked the simplicity of that.

He checked his watch. His contact was late so he waved the waiter over and watched him fill a fresh glass with the hated black liquid. He couldn't just sit with nothing to drink, he felt exposed enough as it was. His six-foot frame and white skin made him stand out, as did the redness of his beard, so he assumed he was being watched, though he couldn't see anyone. He picked up his paper and pretended to read, all the while surveying the crowd from behind his shades.

Sadr City was in the eastern suburbs. Before the invasion it had been called Saddam City and before that, Revolution. But none of that changed its inherent nature: Sadr City was a slum, quickly and cheaply built at the end of the 1950s to house the urban poor. These days there were even more people here, packed into houses and apartment blocks that had already been crowded when the concrete was still wet on the walls. And the market was where they all came to do their shopping. Right now was the busiest time, with everyone stopping by on the way home from work to buy fresh food, refrigerated through the heat of the day at someone else's expense. So many civilians crammed into one space made it an operational nightmare.

A few years ago someone had ridden a motorcycle packed with explosives straight through a sloppy evening checkpoint and blown himself up by the main entrance, taking seventy-eight other people with him. By the looks of the rickety buildings, they had simply dragged the bodies away, hosed the blood off the streets and carried on. You could still see craters in the walls where chunks of shrapnel had torn holes. But the thing that made this a suicide bomber's paradise also made it a preferred meeting place for his ultra-cautious contact: there was no better place to hide than in a crowd.

Hyde was cautious too. He had arrived early and claimed the best seat in the café for surveillance. It offered a one-eighty degree view of the street, with a solid wall behind making it impossible to approach without being seen. He'd bet himself that he could spot his man before he got to him. It was a game he liked to play every time he was sent on this particular detail. The contact was known for his ability to appear and disappear with ease. It was why he'd never been caught, despite the best efforts of several agencies on both sides of the political street. But Hyde had something of a reputation too. Back when he was in 8th Recon he had been the sharpest scout in his platoon. He'd prided himself on never letting anyone creep up on him, though his buddies had constantly tried; they'd even had a name for the game – Hyde and Go Seek. Now he was in civilian life, he had to work harder to keep those skills honed. He'd seen what working for the private companies could do to you; men who had been out of the army just two, three years, their muscle turned to flab, still trading on reputations they'd long since lost. That wasn't going to happen to him. Get sloppy in a place like this and pretty soon you'd get dead. So he pushed himself, treating every assignment as if it was a hot mission, just in case it turned out to be.

He started another sweep of the market, left to right, comfortable in his tactics. He had just reached the furthest point where the wall blocked his view when the scrape of a chair made him whip his head round.

'You have the money?' the Ghost said, settling into the chair on his blind side, his strangled voice barely audible above the noise of the street.

Goddamn – he did it again.

Hyde folded the newspaper and placed it on the table, trying not to appear rattled. 'What, no chit-chat? No "Hi, how's it goin'? How are the wife and kids?"'

The Ghost stared at him, his pale grey eyes cold despite the trapped heat of the day. 'You don't have a wife.'

'And how would you know that?'

'Nobody in your line of work has a wife – at least not for very long.'

Hyde felt anger catch light inside him. His fists clenched. He'd got the divorce papers from Wanda in the mail six weeks ago, after she'd hacked his Facebook page and found some messages she was not supposed to see. But this guy couldn't know that. He was just trying to push his buttons with a lucky guess. And it had worked. Right now he wanted to drive his fist straight through the middle of those freaky grey eyes.

The Ghost smiled, as if he was reading Hyde's thoughts and feeding off his anger. Hyde looked away and reached for his coffee, draining it to the thick gritty dregs before he'd even realized what he was doing. He'd met some hard characters in his time, but this guy was something else. He was taller than the average Iraqi and wiry with it. He also carried about him a sense of danger and physical threat, like a grenade with its pin pulled. The local crew said he was a desert spirit and refused to have anything to do with him. That's why Hyde always got these gigs. He didn't believe in spirits, he just did what he was told; old army habits died hard.

'It's in the bag under the table,' he said, staring out at the market crowds rather than engaging with the grey eyes again. 'Got my boot stamped down on the handle. You give me the package, I lift my foot.'

Something clunked down on the tabletop and a scrap of sacking was pushed towards him.

Hyde shook his head in exaggerated disappointment. 'Zero points for presentation.' He flipped open the sacking and examined the object inside. The stone looked incredibly ordinary. It could almost have been one of the chunks of masonry you found lining the streets in piles all over the city. He turned it over and saw the faint marks on its surface, just lines and swirls. 'Hell of a price to pay for a chunk of old rock,' he said, wrapping it up and lifting his foot off the bag containing fifty million Iraqi dinars, worth around forty thousand American dollars.

The Ghost stood up, the bag already in his hand. 'Make the most of it,' Hyde said, relaxing a little now the money wasn't his responsibility. 'Looks like the cash cow's about to get slaughtered.'

The Ghost hesitated then sat back down. 'Explain.'

Hyde savoured the look of confusion on his face. Now it was the freak's turn to be caught out. 'You really should stay more in touch with the burning issues of the day.' He slid his newspaper across the table. Above the fold on the front page was a picture of the Citadel of Ruin next to the headline:

WORLD'S OLDEST STRONGHOLD
ABOUT TO FALL?

'If the holy guys in the mountain aren't around to drive up prices, guess the bottom will drop right out of the market for bits of old stone.' Hyde trapped a greasy note under the empty coffee glass and hoisted the bundle of sacking under his arm as he stood to leave. 'This might be your last big payday my friend.'

'The Citadel has never given up its secrets,' the Ghost muttered, opening out the page and staring at the three photographs of the civilian survivors on the bottom of the page.

'Nothing lasts for ever,' Hyde said. 'Just ask my soon-to-be-ex wife.' Then he turned and walked quickly away, before the freak with the grey eyes had a chance to come back at him.

Hyde felt good as he left the dangerous buzz of the market behind and headed back to his 4x4. For the first time he'd got one over on the Ghost. He wasn't such a badass after all. He'd looked like he was going to puke when he saw the newspaper. He was just another hustler, trying to make a buck.

He squinted up at the deepening sky. Sun down was in an

hour and so was curfew. He needed to get across town and rejoin the rest of his crew at the hotel. They'd be heading out of town again at dawn, returning to the oilfields in the dusty badlands west of the city. He preferred it out there. Less noise. Less people.

He rounded another corner and saw the truck parked in the shade of a row of buildings, the red company logo on the door the only splash of colour in the drab street. Tariq was in the driver's seat, keeping guard to make sure no one stuck rocks up the exhaust pipe, or booby-trapped it in some way. Vehicles belonging to Western companies were always getting blown up or sabotaged.

Hyde waved to draw his attention. Tariq looked over and froze. Hyde spun away, sensing movement from his left, instinctively reaching for the automatic inside his jacket. He turned his head and found himself staring into a pair of pale grey eyes.

'You forgot this,' the Ghost said, draping the newspaper over Hyde's extended gun. He stepped closer, ignoring the gun pressing into his chest. 'These people,' he tapped the photographs on the cover, 'they may come here, searching for – something. If they come, let me know.'

Hyde glanced down and saw a satellite phone number scrawled beneath the three photographs. His lip curled into a sneer as he prepared to tell the Ghost where to go, but it was too late. He had already gone.

7

The Citadel, Ruin

The sound of the lament hit Athanasius like a wave as he and the other heads stepped into the cathedral cave and made their way to the front. It was the one space in the Citadel big enough to house everyone, and here everyone now was, united in their grief.

At the back were the numerous grey cloaks, the unskilled monks yet to be assigned a guild, separated from the higher orders by a vivid red line of guards. The brown cloaks came next – the masons, carpenters and skilled technicians who maintained the fabric of the Citadel – so tired after the work of the past week that Athanasius could see them swaying where they stood. In front of them were the white-hooded Apothecaria, medical monks whose skills elevated them above all but the black cassocks – the spiritual guilds, priests and librarians who spent their lives in the darkness of the great library, hoarding the knowledge that had been gathered in the dark mountain since mankind first learned to write and remember.

The sound continued to pulse from the congregation as Athanasius took his place at the altar and turned to face them all. It was traditional when the Prelate, the head of the mountain order, was gathered to God that the Abbot would deliver the eulogy and assume the role of acting Prelate until an election confirmed him in the position or chose someone else. But there were two bodies lying in state below the T-shaped cross at the front of the cave: the Prelate on the left, and the Abbot on the right. For the first time in its measureless history the Citadel had no leader.

As the lament neared its conclusion, Athanasius stepped up to the pulpit carved from a stalagmite and looked over the heads of the gathered monks to the raised gallery where the Sancti – the green cloaks – usually stood, segregated from their brethren to ensure the great secrets they kept remained so. There should have been thirteen of them including the Abbot, but today the gallery was empty. In the absence of an Abbot, or a natural heir drawn from the ranks of the Sancti, it fell to the Abbot's chamberlain to deliver the eulogy – it fell to Athanasius.

'Brothers,' he said, his voice sounding thin after the richness of the requiem, 'this is a sad day for all of us. We are without a leader. But I can assure you this situation will very soon be rectified. I have consulted with the heads of each guild and we have agreed to hold elections for the office of both Prelate and Abbot immediately.' A murmur rippled through the congregation at this news. 'All candidates must declare themselves by Vespers tomorrow, with elections to follow two days later. Such haste has been agreed by mutual consent because of the need to re-establish order coupled with the lack of a natural heir.'

'And why are we in this situation?' a voice called from the middle of the congregation. 'Who ordered the Sancti to be taken from the mountain?'

Athanasius looked towards the voice, trying to catch sight of the monk who had challenged him. 'I did,' he said.

'On whose authority?' Another voice, from further back in the massed ranks of grey cloaks.

'I acted on the authority of my own conscience and a sense of compassion for my brother monks. The Sancti had been struck down by some sort of haemorrhagic fever; they needed urgent medical attention and the explosion had cracked the walls to provide a quick means of evacuation. Modern ambulances were waiting outside. I did not think to question this providence. I merely thanked God for it and acted quickly to save the lives of my brothers. Had the Sancti remained in the mountain, they would now be dead, of that I feel sure.'

'And what *has* become of them?' A different voice now. Athanasius paused, fearful that the whole congregation was massing against him. Since assuming caretaker responsibilities, he had been privy to the Abbot's usual digests and communiqués from the outside world. By this method he had learned the fate of the monks he had sought to save.

'All have died – save two.'

Another murmur rippled through the crowd.

'Then we should await their return,' Brother Axel called out. The noise became a rumble of approval amid a general nodding of heads.

'I fear that is unlikely,' Athanasius replied, addressing the congregation rather than his challenger. 'The last remaining Sancti suffered the same affliction as the others and their condition is grave. We cannot rely on them returning or having the strength to lead if they do. We must look to new leadership. The elections are set.'

A new disturbance broke out and everyone turned towards it. A figure had entered the door at the back of the cave and was now moving steadily towards the altar, his approach accompanied by the hum of voices and a strange, dry hissing sound. It was Brother Gardener, his name earned from many years of service in the pastures and orchards that flourished at the heart of the mountain.

The dry whispering grew louder with each step and so did the murmur of voices until Brother Gardener reached the altar and grimly stepped aside to reveal the source of the noise. It was the branch of a tree, broken off at the thickest part, its leaves and blossom brown and withered.

'I found it in the orchard under one of the oldest trees,'

44

Brother Gardener said, his voice low and troubled. 'It's rotted right through.'

He looked up at Athanasius. 'And there're others, lots of others; mostly the older ones but some of the younger ones too. I've never seen anything like it. Something's happening. Something terrible. I think the garden is dying.'

8

Vatican City, Rome

Clementi emerged from the lift into the softly lit vault and headed to the same boardroom where the Group had last met. Everyone had been best of friends then. All the trickier elements of the plan had been carried out and the recovery team had been deployed in the field ready to find and deliver the great treasure Clementi had promised – but that was before the explosion in Ruin.

Clementi turned to Schneider. 'Make sure no one else comes down here until our meeting is concluded,' he said, then heaved against the heavy door and passed into the boardroom.

They were all present, as Schneider had warned him, the Holy Trinity of conspirators – one American, one British and one Chinese.

In a world obsessed with money and power their faces were instantly recognizable. At one time or another each had graced the cover of *Fortune* magazine as revered owners of some of the biggest companies in the world, modern-day empires whose assets and influence crossed international borders and set the political agenda in their own and other countries. In previous ages they would have been emperors or kings and worshipped as gods, such was the extent of their power. They had also collectively lent the Church six billion dollars, through private accounts managed personally by Clementi, to underwrite their joint venture and prevent the Church from collapsing beneath its colossal debt. But they had not been persuaded to do this out of a sense of duty or a love of God, it was purely for the potentially huge financial gains Clementi's proposition had promised, and, as in all such ventures, there came a time when dividends were expected – and that time was now.

'Gentlemen,' Clementi said, settling into a seat across the table from them, 'what an unexpected honour.'

No one replied. Clementi felt the skin tighten on his scalp, like a nervous candidate at a job interview. Reminding himself that *he* had invited them into his scheme, not the other way round, he tried to calm himself by reaching for a cigarette and lighting up. Xiang, the Chinese industrialist, was already smoking, the smoke from his cigarette making all three of them appear like they were smouldering. Despite their differences in age and nationality, each man carried the same dense gravity of absolute power and authority. At eighty-three, Xiang was the oldest; his suit, hair and skin as grey as the ash that dripped from his cigarette. Lord Maybury, the English media baron, was ten years younger, with unnaturally dark hair hinting at a degree of vanity and fear of getting old, and the sort of slightly shabby suit only centuries of good breeding could get away with. Pentangeli was the youngest at sixty-two. He was a third generation Italian-American who, despite the bespoke Armani suit and grooming, still carried a certain menace about him, something he had inherited from the grandfather who had arrived penniless from Calabria and fought his way to a fortune in the land of the free. Pentangeli was the only one of the Group who was a practising Catholic and, as usual, it was he who acted as their initial spokesperson.

'Do we have a problem, Father?' he asked, sliding a newspaper across the table. It was *USA Today*. On its cover were the familiar images of the Citadel and the three civilians, along with the question being whispered around the world:

DO THEY KNOW THE SECRETS
OF THE CITADEL?

'No,' Clementi said, 'there is no problem. It is unfortunate that this has happened now, but—'

'Unfortunate!' Maybury jumped in, his smooth privately schooled accent making every word sound condescending. 'Since time immemorial the Citadel has guarded its secrets. Only now, when one of its biggest directly affects our joint investment, does it start to look leaky. I would call that rather more than unfortunate.'

'No secrets have been revealed,' Clementi said, keeping his voice low and calm. 'This is merely the result of a few misguided terrorists making a token attack on the Church. I can assure you, from the moment they were brought from the mountain, the survivors have been isolated and monitored. Ruin is a city that owes its very existence to the Church. We have far-reaching influence there. They are being held in an old secure psychiatric wing in the main city hospital. A priest and a police guard have been watching them round the clock to prevent the press or anyone else getting close. All police interviews, all consultations with lawyers, all medical discussions with the patients have been recorded and passed to me. I can assure you that not one of them has shown any indication that they learned anything compromising to us during their time inside the Citadel.'

'Not yet,' Pentangeli said, flipping open his briefcase to retrieve a document with CIA stamped across the cover. 'You're not the only one with friends in high places.' He slid it across the table for Clementi to read.

It was the transcript of a confidential interview between a patient known as Liv Adamsen and a Dr Yusef Kaya, chief clinical psychiatrist at Davlat Hastenesi Hospital, Ruin. The final paragraph had been outlined in yellow highlighter.

. . . The patient displays classic symptoms of post-traumatic amnesia, possibly caused by a severe physical or psychological trauma. However, the patient is strong physically and her mind is otherwise lucid and unimpaired, so with time and therapy she should be able to fully recover her lost memories and return to continuous recall.

'She's a ticking time bomb,' Xiang said, in precise, smoke-tinged English. 'For myself I do not care whether this Sacrament is revealed to the world or not. Frankly, I think it is a myth – I am an atheist, as you know. What does concern me is that, if the Citadel cannot keep this, its biggest secret, might it prove unequal to the task of keeping ours?'

'And she's not the only concern,' Pentangeli added, pulling another document stamped *CONFIDENTIAL* from his case.

'Subject one: Kathryn Mann, forty-eight years old, half-Brazilian, half-Turkish, head of a global humanitarian aid charity with offices all over the world, including Ruin. Widow of Dr John Mann, US-born archaeologist and scholar, killed twelve years ago on a dig in Iraq along with the rest of his team after they reportedly discovered something in the desert around the location of Al-Hillah.' He looked up at Clementi. 'And you're not worried about that?'

Clementi said nothing.

'Subject two: Gabriel Mann, thirty-two, son of Kathryn and John Mann. Studied modern languages and economics at Harvard until his father was murdered, whereupon he joined the army. He rose to the rank of platoon sergeant in Special Airborne, saw combat in Afghanistan and was decorated twice before mustering out and joining the family firm working as a security advisor. In this capacity he worked on a number of projects in Iraq where he conducted his own investigation into his father's death. Three times he requested travel permits to Al-Hillah in Babil Province, and each time he was rejected because of ongoing insurgent activity and the perceived danger to civilian life.' He looked over the document at Clementi. 'Sounds like a man with unfinished business to me. Unfortunately, it's in an area where we also have some business interests. And that makes us very nervous.'

'We are all in agreement,' Xiang said. 'The risks these people pose is unacceptable to us. We have limited influence in Ruin, but, as you yourself said, through the Church you have plenty. We urge you to use it and use it quickly to protect your interests – and ours.'

Clementi held their collective gaze. An hour ago he might have hesitated, but standing in the file rooms of the Vatican Bank had reminded him of all he stood to lose. The survival of the Church was more important than anything, more important than his own soul. And if he burned in hell for what he was about to do, then it would be a sacrifice worth making. He reached forward and pressed a button on the desk phone in the centre of the table. Like everything in the room, the phone-line was as secure as most countries' national security network. It could not be traced and it could not be tapped.

He quickly dialled a number from memory, his fingers shaking from the adrenalin flooding his system. He left it on speakerphone so everyone in the room could hear the conversation he was about to have. He wanted them to witness it. He wanted them to be part of it. He studied their faces as the rapid beeps of the number turned into a ringing tone; then a click cut it off and a voice answered.

'Yes?'

'I am the light of the world,' Clementi said, 'whoever follows me—'

'—will never walk in darkness,' the voice answered, completing the security check.

Clementi licked his dry lower lip with a tongue that was

even drier. 'I want you to silence the witnesses, for the sake of the Church.'

There was a pause. 'All of them?'

'All of them; how soon can this be accomplished?'

In the background Clementi heard the squeak of rubber shoes on a vinyl floor. 'It will be done by morning,' the voice said. Then the phone went dead.

9

Room 406, Davlat Hastenesi Hospital

Liv grabbed a bulky remote-control unit from the table by her bed and fired it at the ancient-looking TV. She had been lying on her bed for long minutes, breathing slowly, hoping that her memory might return, when a single solid fact had surfaced: when she'd arrived in Ruin, however many days ago, her brother's death had been a big story. Maybe it still was; perhaps the news could plug some of the gaps she was having difficulty filling herself.

The set crackled and the sound faded up. Liv nudged the volume down so as not to alert the watchers in the corridor. The TV was old and the picture fuzzy, but whatever was feeding it a signal was modern enough and there were hundreds of channels available. Liv cycled steadily through them, searching for a news station. If she could just get a few solid facts to grab on to she felt sure she would be able to pull herself together. She continued through a parade of talk shows and daytime soaps until, finally, she found Al Jazeera, the Arabic news channel – but it wasn't what she was expecting.

At first she thought the station ident was wrong and she must be watching an extreme weather show. Horrific images of a tidal wave in Chile sweeping down a main street carrying people, cars and houses with it segued into a story showing a tearful farmer in the grain belt of Kansas, staring out on a huge field of wheat that had been battered to mud by hailstones the size of oranges.

'If you read your Bible,' the farmer said in a voice that wobbled with emotion, 'you might think Judgement Day was close at hand.'

A whispering static rose in Liv's head at the mention of this, bringing a vague nausea with it. She closed her eyes and breathed in through her nose and out through her mouth until it ebbed away. Whatever drugs they had her on were having some alarming side effects.

When she opened her eyes she received a fresh shock. The image on the screen had changed, this time to the one that had graced the cover of every newspaper in the world when Liv had first arrived in Ruin. It showed her brother, Samuel, standing on the summit of the Citadel, arms outstretched, his monk's cassock stretched taut, making the sign of the T-shaped cross with his body.

'It has been twelve days since the dramatic appearance of a monk on top of the Citadel in Ruin, and ten days since the explosion tore a hole in the base of it—'

Twelve days!

'Many believe these events in Ruin are in some way connected to the worldwide weather phenomena we have witnessed since, with various religious groups citing them as evidence of God's anger or signs of the oncoming apocalypse predicted in the Book of Revelation. They also suggest the deaths of the evacuated monks is God gathering his own, and just a few minutes ago, this death toll increased once again.'

The picture cut to a jostling image of a large bald man wearing a black moustache and a serious expression. A caption identified him as Dr Jemya, Chief Medical Registrar of Davlat Hastenesi Hospital, Ruin. He started to read the prepared statement and the sound dipped, translating the Turkish into English.

'Regretfully I am to announce to you, that at one

twenty-five p.m. local time, another of the persons removed from the Citadel lost their life. This brings the death toll to nine.'

The press pack boiled into rowdy life and started pelting him with questions.

What was the cause of death, was it the same haemorrhaging as the others?

'Yes.'

Do you know what's causing it?

'We're working on it.'

Is it a virus?

'No.'

Is it contagious?

He didn't answer, he just turned and ran up the steps to the sanctuary of the hospital.

'Thirteen people came out of the mountain. Now only four remain.'

The picture changed and Liv stared at her own photograph sandwiched between one of a dark-haired woman she vaguely remembered and another of a green-robed monk lying on a stretcher, blood streaming from uniform cuts all over his body.

'Of these, three are still in hospital, their condition said to range from comfortable to critical.'

Shaky news footage showed a dark-haired man being manhandled into the back of a police car.

'The fourth remains in police custody, where he is being held for questioning.'

The picture froze and Liv's heart rolled over as she recognized his face and a name surfaced in her mind.

Gabriel.

Seeing him brought a cascade of feelings and memories.

She remembered him smiling down to her in the darkness of the Citadel, and his arms holding her in the ER after he had brought her out, protecting her until the cops had come

54

to take him away. He had cradled her face in his hands and held her eyes with his.

If you get the chance, then go, he had said, *as far from the Citadel as you can. Keep yourself safe – until I find you.*

Then he had kissed her, full on the lips, until they'd pulled him away, leaving her alone in the screaming chaos of the hospital.

She touched her lips, remembering the kiss, wishing she could remember more. She had to get out of here, Gabriel's warning and her own instincts told her that. She needed to go somewhere safe to try to piece together the fragments of what had happened in the darkness of the mountain, far away from the dark influence of this place and the meds that were making her mind fuzzy. She needed to go home, she felt it with the sharpened instinct of the hunted.

Then, as if something had sniffed her fear and been drawn to it, she heard the squeak of a shoe on the vinyl floor outside. She stabbed the remote to silence the TV and, just as she settled back in her bed – the door began to open.

1O

The Citadel, Ruin

The rain lashed the mountain as Brother Gardener led the small delegation outside into the walled garden at the heart of the Citadel. It had been agreed that the heads and acting heads of the main guilds were the only people permitted to enter, until the condition of the trees had been properly assessed.

'There,' Brother Gardener said, pointing at the uppermost branches of an apple tree. 'See the discoloration in the leaves.'

Even Athanasius, who knew little about nature, could see the tree looked wrong. It appeared to be readying itself for autumn rather than bursting with the vigour of spring.

'When did you first notice this?' Axel asked, his policeman's demeanour sliding through the nasal drone of his question.

'Just yesterday. But I haven't been spending much time in the garden, what with all the clear-up work inside the mountain.'

'And before that there was no evidence of this . . . blight?'

'No.'

'So all this has come about since the explosion?'

'I suppose it has, yes.'

Father Malachi turned to face Athanasius. 'You see?' he said. 'You should never have allowed the Sancti to set foot outside the mountain. Something sacred has been upset by your actions. This is a clear manifestation of it.'

56

Athanasius stepped past to inspect the withering sections of the tree. 'Have you ever encountered anything like this before?'

Brother Gardener shrugged. 'From time to time.'

'And what were the causes then?'

'All kinds of things cause blight – drought, insect infestation, disease.'

'Might something like an earthquake cause it?'

'It might. If the ground shifts sufficiently, then roots get broken and the tree starves.'

'And would we all not agree that the shock of the explosion travelling through the mountain was similar to the effects of an earthquake?' He turned to Malachi. 'I realize we are all under tremendous strain because of what has happened here, but now is not the time for superstition and panic. Now is the time for clear heads and calm leadership.' He turned back to Brother Gardener. 'What would you suggest as the best course of action?'

The big man stroked his beard and surveyed the trees. 'Well, if it is as you say, then it won't get any worse. We can cut away the bits that are dead and dying to speed the trees' recovery. But if it is something else,' he cast a furtive glance towards Malachi, 'then it will spread.'

'And how might we stop it?'

He took a deep breath as if preparing to pronounce heavy sentence. 'We need to cut as deep as we dare and then burn everything we remove. It's the only way to make sure any disease has gone.'

'Very well, then I suggest at first light you assemble what men you need and carry out what has to be done. As for the rest of us, we should reassure our brothers that we have inspected the garden and it has sustained some damage from the after-effects of the explosion, but that Brother Gardener has it in hand.'

'And what if it turns out to be more than that?' came the nasal enquiry of Brother Axel.

'Then we will deal with that too. We are stretched thin as it is. I advise that we deal only with the real problems that face us, not the imagined ones that might.'

Axel held his gaze, giving no indication whether he was swayed by his reasoning.

'You are right.' It was Father Thomas. 'We are all tired and apt to jump at shadows. We should remember that, until the elections install new leaders, our brothers look to us for guidance. So we must steady the ship and seek to reassure rather than agitate.'

Athanasius had always been fond of Father Thomas. He spent many an evening with him discussing subjects ranging from philosophy to archaeology and everything in between. He found his company intelligent, rational and calm.

'The best way to reassure the brotherhood would be to re-instate the Sancti.' All eyes turned to Brother Axel. 'It would demonstrate a return to order and instantly calm the mountain's mood.'

'But who would elect them?' Thomas asked.

'We cannot address the issue of the Sancti until we have an Abbot to propose them or a Prelate to confirm their elevation,' Athanasius continued. 'Therefore any discussion of the Sancti must wait until after the elections.'

Axel switched his gaze between Athanasius and Father Thomas, as though tracing a fine thread stretching between them. He turned to Brother Gardener. 'I will post some of my men at the entrances to the garden in case any inquisitive brothers decide to take a midnight stroll. If there is anything else you need from me, let me know.' Then he turned and marched away.

Athanasius watched him go, feeling the chill of the rain more keenly. There were clearly two factions developing in the wake of the explosion: the rational and the fearful. And fear was heady fuel for those who might seek to exploit it; it was how the Sancti had exercised their dominance over the mountain for thousands of years. Although his decision to remove them had been born of compassion rather than political ambition, he couldn't help but admit in his private moments that he was glad they were gone and hoped never to see their return. He had felt a difference in the Citadel since the Sancti had left. It felt freer somehow; as if the air flowed more smoothly. But as he watched Axel reach the edge of the garden and disappear back into the mountain he realized their return could come about sooner than he had imagined, and that he had just stared a rival in the eye.

11

Room 406, Davlat Hastenesi Hospital

Liv watched the door swing inwards, revealing the darkened corridor and the shadow that stood there, the white slash of his collar glowing brightly in the gloom. She looked up at the priest's face. It was set in a practised mask of seriousness and compassion, like he was visiting a bereaved parishioner, or listening to a low-grade confession at the end of a dull Sunday. He seemed so normal, and yet she was terrified of him – terrified and full of an anger that rose up inside her, along with the detuned radio noise in her head. Her fists clenched on the bed, twisting handfuls of starched sheet. So complete was her focus on him that she didn't even notice the second figure enter the room until the door banged shut behind him.

He was bigger than the priest and several inches taller – though his bearish, stooping posture all but levelled them. His right arm was held tightly across his chest by a sling and his other held two black plastic evidence bags. A pair of intelligent eyes regarded her from above half-moon glasses that clung crookedly to an impressive nose. Liv broke into a smile, her anger melting in the warmth of his gaze. It was the detective who had first called her and alerted her to her brother's death.

'Arkadian!' The last time she had seen him was at the airport, in amongst the carnage when the agents of the Citadel tried to silence them all. She had seen him slammed backwards by the force of bullets. 'I thought you were . . .'

'Dead? Not quite. Obviously I've been better, but in the circumstances I'm not complaining.' He lowered himself on to the edge of her bed, his weight squashing the mattress and tipping her closer. His presence calmed her, almost as much as the priest's caused her distress. 'How are you?'

She wanted to blurt out everything that was going through her head, but instead her eyes flicked towards the priest listening in the corner of the room and she held back. She leaned in closer. 'Why is he here?'

'That's a good question.' Arkadian twisted round on the bed. 'What's your name, son?'

'Ulvi,' the priest said, looking like a schoolboy who'd just been caught smoking by the headmaster. He cleared his throat and straightened. 'Father Ulvi Şimşek.'

'Pleased to meet you, Father. Lady wants to know why you're here.'

The priest looked at Liv then back to Arkadian. 'It has been agreed that a member of the Church should be present at every interview.'

'But this isn't an interview. She's already given a statement, which I'm sure you've either listened to or read a transcript of.'

'I have to be here, as a representative of the Church.'

'And why is that exactly?'

The priest's face flushed at the continued interrogation. It made Liv feel better, seeing his obvious discomfort, but she still wanted him out of the room. 'The Church founded this hospital and still owns the land it stands on,' he said. 'It has been agreed that all persons who were brought from the Citadel will be monitored by a representative of the Church while they remain our guests.'

'Well then, how about we come up with our own agreement? You give us five minutes to have a little friendly catch-up and we promise not to tell your boss about it. Who's to know?'

The priest stared at Arkadian. 'God will know,' he said, as

if that put an end to the matter. 'I have been instructed to be present at every interview.'

'Yes, but you see – this isn't . . . oh, never mind.' He turned back to Liv. 'We're just going round in circles here. Why don't we agree to ignore him, like he's a butler or something?' He held up the evidence bags. 'I have something for you. They found it in the warehouse over at the airport. The tech guys have finished with it. Thought you might want it back.'

He dropped one of the bags on the bed. The plastic crinkled in her hands as she loosened the string around its neck. Inside was her battered holdall, the only piece of luggage she'd brought with her on the journey here. 'Thanks,' she said, closing it up again. She would wait until she was alone before going through it. She didn't want the priest's eyes roaming all over her private stuff. Then it occurred to her that he'd probably already seen it outside in the corridor, before it was allowed into the room. The thought made her feel trapped and helpless. She looked up at Arkadian. 'There's a cop outside in the corridor,' she said.

Arkadian nodded.

'Why?'

'Keep an eye on you and the others. Keep the press out.'

Liv smiled. 'I am the press.'

Arkadian smiled. 'Then I guess he's not doing a very good job. Fortunately for everyone concerned, you can't remember anything.'

'Yeah, lucky me.'

'You've been through a lot. These things take time.'

Liv glanced at the priest again, weighing up what he might know against what she might want to keep from him.

'What exactly *have* I been through?' Arkadian looked puzzled. 'Seriously. My memory is so patchy I can't work out what's real and what's not. It would really help if you could talk me through it.'

'What do you want to know?'

'Everything.'

Arkadian placed the second evidence bag down on the bed, took her hand and started to talk. He started with her brother's appearance on top of the Citadel, moved carefully through his death and what they found during the autopsy, and finished with the events at the airport where Oscar had died smothering a grenade meant for all of them, Arkadian had been shot and Liv had been knocked unconscious only to reappear a few hours later being carried out of the Citadel by Gabriel. When he had finished, Liv looked across at the priest. He didn't look back. Arkadian's carefully told history, delivered in the precise and methodical manner of a seasoned police detective, had blown the mist from almost every recess of her mind. She could now recall everything, all except the one thing she wanted to remember most – what had happened to her inside the Citadel.

'Thank you,' she said, squeezing Arkadian's hand.

'My pleasure.' He let go and reached into his pocket. 'They'll be letting you out of here soon.' He handed her a card. 'When they do, I want you to give me a call. Least I can do is drive you to the airport.' He looked down at his bandaged arm. 'Or get someone else to drive us both.' He leaned forward and kissed her on the forehead, reminding her of the way her father used to say goodnight when she was younger and the world was a safer place.

'You look after yourself,' he said, getting up and heading for the door.

'What's in the other bag?'

'Something for Mrs Mann,' he said. 'She's just down the hall.'

'Say "Hi" from me,' Liv said.

'I will.'

'And say "Hi" to Gabriel too – when you see him.'

'Oh, you can tell him yourself. They can't hold him for ever, and I'm not pressing any charges, even though he stuck an anaesthetic in me. I feel pretty sure he'll be out before you know it.'

12

Gabriel Mann was shoved head first through a fire door by the same stocky guard who had cuffed his hands behind his back a few minutes earlier. He was in the cell block beneath the main Ruin police building, a maze of low ceilings, uneven walls, and cramped corridors, cut hundreds of years previously from the bedrock of the city. Strip lighting flickered green against grey-painted walls, giving the impression that he was in the guts of a building that wasn't feeling too well.

Gabriel wasn't feeling his best either.

He had just left a meeting with his legal counsel who had outlined the charges against him. They had found three dead bodies in a hangar at the airport – a location the police could definitively place him at; two had been shot with a nine-millimetre pistol – his hands had tested positive for gunshot residue that matched spent cartridges found at the scene; he had been caught on camera at the city morgue at the same time as a body had been stolen; and he had assaulted a police inspector with a hypodermic needle loaded with Ketamine. It was this last charge that had undoubtedly ensured his charmless treatment at the hands of the silent sub-inspector. Most of the others would ultimately go away, but it would take time – and that was something he did not have.

He had replayed what he had witnessed in the Citadel over and over in his head, trying to make sense of it. He had no idea why he had been allowed to walk free, carrying the girl out with him, but he knew it was only a temporary escape. Whatever had happened to Liv at the top of the mountain before he had found her, whether she had discovered the Sacrament or not, was immaterial. The Sanctus monks sworn to protect the mountain's great secret would regroup and take steps to silence her. Liv was in mortal danger, so was his mother, and so was he, and he couldn't protect anyone while he was locked up in here. Escape was the only option – he just had no idea how he was going to do it.

He'd been checking the building as he'd marched through it, looking for possible means of escape. Every door they'd passed had opened into other cells; some had prisoners inside, most were empty. The interview room had been up a flight of stairs, which meant the cell block was in some kind of sub-basement. The only way in or out was through the automatic gate he'd passed through on his way down.

Gabriel began to slow as he approached his cell but another shove sent him stumbling straight past. He recovered his balance and kept on walking, his mind racing with the implications. He had been kept in solitary so far, which had suited him fine. A new cell could mean new cellmates. Not good.

They continued walking deeper into the maze. Paint bubbled on the walls where salts had seeped through the rock and nobody had bothered to fix it. There were fewer cells here and the ones they passed were all empty. It smelled mustier too. Unused. They reached the end of the corridor and another sharp shove sent Gabriel barrelling through a set of fire doors into a short tunnel chopped cleanly in half by a wall of bars. On the other side was a cell containing a steel toilet with no seat, a narrow bench built into the wall and a man so large he made everything around him seem as if it belonged in a child's nursery.

'Hands through the bars,' the sub-inspector ordered.

The giant took one huge step forward, covering the entire

width of the cell, and passed wrists as thick as sprinter's legs through the bars. His eyes never left Gabriel's face.

Gabriel was grabbed from behind and slammed sideways into the wall. 'Make a move and I'll stick you with the taser, understand?' The guard's breath smelled of coffee and cigarettes.

Gabriel nodded and felt the pressure ease as the guard turned his attention to the giant. It had surprised him when the stocky weightlifter of a sub-inspector had come alone to take him to his cell. Now he knew why: one cop meant less witnesses.

He glanced up at the smoke detector and closed-circuit camera bolted to the underside of the ducting that ran the length of the corridor, one of the old kind that produced a fuzzy black-and-white picture but no sound. The feed would be routed to the control room he'd passed on his way through the entrance gate. Another cop was probably watching now, ready to send in backup if anything went down. Except the camera wasn't pointing at the cell. So no one could see what was happening inside it; and once the sub-inspector had locked the door and walked away, no one would care.

His eyes returned to the hulking figure on the other side of the bars. The giant was staring straight at him with the cold-eyed menace of a cell-block challenge. Gabriel held his gaze, taking him in, knowing now that looking away would spare him nothing. The man's eyes were set deep in a flat face that was topped off by a surprisingly conservatively cut bowl of blond hair that he might've ripped off an insurance salesman to wear as a hat.

Gabriel held the bottomless eyes for another beat then took in the rest of him. He was immense; a caricature of a man sculpted from solid muscle by years of steroids and single-minded aggression. A cotton shirt strained to contain him, sleeves rolled up over meaty forearms. The handcuffs looked small and ridiculous on his thick wrists and, just above them, was something else that set alarm bells ringing in Gabriel's head. It was the blurry blue image of a jailhouse tattoo. Generally speaking, the larger the tattoo, the more time its owner had spent in prison. This one was huge. But it wasn't the giant's evident criminal past, or even his intimidating size, that caused Gabriel the most concern, it was what the tattoo depicted. The huge image – created by pouring ink on his arm and repeatedly sticking a pin into himself until it was fixed there for ever – was a cross. Somewhere in this steroid-fried monster's dark past he had found the light of God. And now the Church had found him, and clearly sent him on a mission to do their dark work.

Escape was no longer an option, it was a necessity. Once the guard had strolled away down the corridor Gabriel would be on his own, locked in the bowels of the earth, with this God-loving monster – and unless he did something fast, he would never get out of here alive.

13

Room 410, Davlat Hastenesi Hospital

Kathryn Mann stared at the object that had just slipped out of the evidence bag on to the hospital bed.

Arkadian had not stayed long. The memory of the last time they had met had hung too heavy over both of them, so he had made his peace offering and left.

'We found it among your father's things,' he had told her. 'There's a message for you in there. I thought you should see it.'

Inside the evidence bag she had found a book, bound in leather with a thong wrapped round a button on the cover to keep it closed. Just seeing it had misted her eyes. It was the same old-fashioned make of journal her father had always used. She reached to the bedside table to retrieve her reading glasses then carefully unwound the thong to loosen the cover and found the note written across the middle two pages in her father's neat hand:

My dearest Kathryn,

My love and light. I believe my work is over now and my return to Ruin will be for good this time. I hope I am wrong, but suspect I am not. No matter. I have lived long and you have filled those years with warmth and joy. If I do live, I will keep my promise and show you the next step, as I always said I would. If not, then you must discover it for yourself and decide whether to forgive me.

Know only that what I kept from you I did for your sake, and for the safety of my grandson.

Kiss Gabriel for me, and light a candle to my name so I may talk to you still.

All my love, for now and always,

Oscar de la Cruz

Every other page was empty. She reread his note, looking to see if she had missed something, but it remained as opaque as the first time she had read it. What had he kept from her? She had always thought they shared everything, that there were no secrets between them; only now, in death, had she discovered this was not so.

She remembered how, even when she was a small child, he had shared confidences with her, explaining that they were different from other people, that they were descendants of the Mala, the oldest tribe on earth, usurped by another who had sought to destroy them and bury the knowledge they kept. He had shown her their secret symbols, taught her the Mala language and revealed the mission they shared to restore rightful order to the world. But he had kept something from her so important that he had felt compelled to confess it from beyond the grave. Maybe she hadn't known him as well as she'd thought.

Even the note contained something that jarred with her memory of him. He had always been so particular about words, insisting on precision because they carried the most precious cargo of all – meaning. And yet here was a mistake: he had not asked her to light a candle 'in' his name, but 'to' it.

Then she realized.

It wasn't a mistake at all.

When she was a girl he had also taught her how their ancestors had kept their secrets. One method was to record messages on paper using lemon juice instead of ink. When the juice dried it was invisible, but the acids affected the paper so that a flame held against it would darken these sections first and reveal the hidden words on the page. When Oscar had written that he wanted her to light a candle 'to' his name so he might talk to her still, he had meant precisely that.

There was another message in the space beneath his signature. All she needed to read it was a flame.

14

Gabriel's body flooded with adrenalin as his mind ran through possible scenarios. If he ended up alone in the cell with the giant he would die. He had to do something in the next few seconds, before the guard locked him in. He glanced up at the low ceiling of the cell block, less than a foot above his head at the highest point. Not much room for manoeuvre. Fortunately the guard was short, which gave him a few extra inches, but he was also built like an Olympic weightlifter – and he was armed. As well as a taser he had a riot baton and a can of pepper spray clipped to his belt. At least he didn't have a gun.

A loud *clang* echoed in the cramped space as the guard unlocked the gate to the cell. Gabriel stepped slightly away from the wall, his back to the guard, the weight on the balls of his feet and his knees bending slightly to give him a light, central balance.

'One thousand lira if you put me in another cell,' he said.

There was a snort from behind. 'What you going to do, write me a cheque?'

Gabriel shook his head. 'Cash. Right now.'

He was banking on the cop being an old-school turnkey who wouldn't baulk at boosting his salary with a bit of free-lancing. Cash was a drug to a dirty cop and like any junkie he wouldn't care where it came from so long as he got a fix.

'Where you going to get a thousand lira?'

'My lawyer just slipped it to me. It's in my right pocket. Take me to another cell and it's yours.'

There was a pause. Gabriel could almost hear the cogs of the man's brain working.

He felt something press into the small of his back. 'Move and you get tasered, straight in your spine. And if that pocket comes up empty, I'm going to keep my finger on the button 'til you piss yourself, understand?'

Gabriel nodded. 'What about my new cell?'

'We talk about that later.'

Gabriel sank a little lower to the ground, focusing on a spot on the wall where the uneven surface jutted slightly. He felt the guard's hand frisking the outside of his pocket, then slip inside to extract what was in fact a business card his lawyer had given him.

As part of his military training, Gabriel had undergone several sessions of 'torture accustomization', which included being tasered to see how it affected him. Size or fitness didn't seem to have any bearing. Some of the bigger guys dropped like sacks of potatoes, while others recovered almost immediately. He'd been somewhere in the middle; not totally incapacitated, but pretty close, so he knew if he got this wrong he wouldn't get a second chance. A zap to the spine would disrupt his whole nervous system and by the time he recovered he would be locked in the cell with the blond gorilla. He focused on the electrodes pressing harder as the guard leaned down. Timing and speed would be everything. The guard leaned lower, his fingertips touched the business card at the bottom of the pocket. Gabriel sprang.

He threw his cuffed hands to the right, knocking the taser away from his spine. At the same moment he raised his leg, trapping the guard's hand in the folds of his pocket and kicked hard against the wall using the crevice for leverage. As he rose up, the loop of his arms slipped cleanly over the guard's perfectly positioned head and he squeezed as hard as he could just as the staccato crackle of the taser ripped through the small space.

Gabriel's right arm, now tight round the guard's neck, went

slack as 50,000 volts pulsed into it. He felt his grip weaken and pulled harder with his unaffected left arm, dragging the slack one tight where the handcuffs linked them and holding on with everything he had. They stumbled backwards and hit the wall, the jolt driving the electrodes deeper into Gabriel's flesh. His stronger arm began to slacken and the guard twisted his head away as he felt the pressure ease. He was getting free.

Gabriel let his legs crumple beneath him. They hit the floor hard, the guard getting most of the impact, and the taser jarred clear of his flesh. The moment the strength-sapping voltage was gone Gabriel squeezed with both arms, clamping hard on to the guard's thick neck. He rolled to his right, moving his weight over him as the dry crack of the charge started up once more. This time it made no difference. Gabriel's arm was now locked in place and every time the taser crackled it just turned him into a dead weight that pressed down harder on the guard's neck.

The human neck has three distinct areas of weakness that can be exploited by a chokehold: the carotid artery, the jugular vein and the windpipe. All three transport oxygen around the body. If one is cut off, for even a short amount of time, it leads to oxygen starvation and a gradual loss of consciousness. If all three are shut down, this happens in seconds.

It took about ten for the guard to go limp.

He sped things up by frantically stabbing the taser into different parts of Gabriel's body, but all this did was burn up what little oxygen he had left while Gabriel clung on, weathering the electrical storm, switching the tension to whichever arm was stronger during each attack until the guard stopped moving and the taser clattered to the hard floor. Gabriel glanced up at the giant, making sure it hadn't fallen where he could get hold of it. His face was a mask of eerie calm, his huge hands shackled in front of him as though praying. 'What's your plan now?' he asked in a surprisingly soft tone. 'What's your *in-ten-tion*? Hoping to make bail before he wakes up?'

Gabriel ignored him. He could feel the blood flowing back

into his fingers as fast as it would now be returning to the guard's oxygen-starved brain. He didn't have long. He grabbed the keys from the guard's belt, found the small handcuff key and fumbled it into the lock. His hands sprang apart with a mixture of pain and relief. He rubbed some life into wrists that were cut and sore then quickly started stripping the guard.

'You like boys?' The soft voice mocked from behind.

Gabriel pulled the guard's shirt off and fitted it over his own. 'I like freedom,' he said, buttoning it up then doing the same with the uniform trousers. They slipped neatly over his prison-issue jeans but were too wide in the waist and too short in the leg. He fixed them low on his hips, stuffed the tail of the shirt into the waistband and cinched the belt tight just as the guard began to stir. Gabriel grabbed him under the shoulders and rolled him over to the cell, being careful to stay out of range of the giant. He scooped the handcuffs off the floor, snapped one end on the guard's wrist and the other round the bars of the open cell door just as the guard woke up. His eyes rolled down, focused on Gabriel then he lunged forward. Gabriel sprang back and the handcuff caught on the lower cross bar with a loud clang, yanking the guard to a sudden stop. He looked down at what held him, then back up at Gabriel, just in time to take a face-full of pepper spray. A strangled wheeze squeaked from his constricting throat and he fell to the floor, choking and rubbing at his burning eyes with his free hand.

Gabriel stepped away from the cloud of spray and reached into the uniform shirt pocket for the guard's pack of cigarettes.

'Those things'll kill ya,' the giant said from behind the bars. '*Car-cin-o-gen-ic.*'

Gabriel pulled a disposable lighter out from inside the packet and clamped a cigarette between his lips. 'Ah, but that which doesn't kill you,' he said, flicking the wheel of the lighter to get a flame, 'just makes you stronger.'

He lit the cigarette, drew on it deeply, then tilted his head towards the ceiling and emptied his lungs at the smoke detector.

15

Officer Lunz jackknifed forward in his chair. He'd been daydreaming about fishing in his favourite pool in the Taurus foothills when the clanging bell had snatched him back to the control room. He scanned the bank of monitors, his heart thumping in his chest, looking for signs of what might have tripped the alarm.

The images were fuzzy at the best of times but with the sprinklers now filling the corridors with a fine spray, they revealed almost nothing. He could hear the muffled sound of banging and roars of complaint from the twenty or so inmates now being soaked in their cells. At least he hoped that was what the noise was about. He wondered how long it would take for the backup guards to get here. The system was always tripping itself, so response times had been getting slower. The cameras had started shorting out too. The whole system needed replacing, but the city didn't want to pay for it. Maybe the fact that the sprinklers had gone off this time might make them reconsider.

He reached over to silence the alarm then stopped when he saw a dark shape appear on one of the screens. It was a man stumbling through the spray, an arm covering his face. He was in D section, at the far end of the complex. Lunz pushed his glasses up on his nose and leaned into the screen. The figure left one screen and appeared on another, making its steady way towards him.

He glanced over at the closed door of the control room. Beyond it a gate of steel bars stood between him and whoever was now approaching. He unlocked a drawer in the desk, pulled it open and fumbled his holstered gun from inside. He felt its comforting weight in his hand and continued to watch the dark figure moving from screen to screen, drawing ever closer, while he waited for backup to arrive. The other screens remained empty. It obviously wasn't some kind of breakout. The figure was also dressed in dark clothes which meant he must be a guard. All the inmates were given light olive army surplus T-shirts to wear. He must have got caught in the spray. Lunz checked one last time that the other screens were empty, then rose from his chair and headed out into the corridor, taking his gun with him – just in case.

Outside, the hiss of the water was much louder. He squinted through the bars at the indoor rain until a uniformed figure appeared at the end of the corridor, stumbling towards him through the water haze. The man shouted something, but his voice was muffled by hissing water and the arm clamped across his face.

Lunz felt there was something wrong. He popped the thumb strap and slid his gun clear of the leather holster. 'You OK?' he shouted.

The figure continued to bump its way blindly along the wet walls, one hand feeling the way, the other rubbing his face. 'Pepper spray,' he shouted. 'Someone jumped me – grabbed my keys.'

Lunz stared past him towards the closed door at the end of the corridor.

They had his keys.

They'd attacked him with pepper spray.

It wasn't a false alarm – it was the real deal.

He gulped damp air, trying to clear his head. He pictured arms reaching through the bars of a cell at the far end of the block, fumbling various keys into the outside locks. How long before they found the right one?

The staggering guard stumbled the last few metres of

corridor and banged heavily into the gate, doubling over in a spasm of coughs. Even if they were out and already surging along the corridor, he would have time to open the gate, get him out and lock it again. He could do it. But it had to be now. He ducked into the control room, hit a button on the desk and was back out in the corridor as the gate slid open. The guard was still doubled over, coughing and wheezing, both hands on his face rubbing furiously at his burning skin. Lunz grabbed his arm and heaved him backwards as another loud noise rang in the corridor and a voice from behind made him jump.

'What happened?'

The backup team had arrived.

'Breakout in D block,' Lunz said, adrenalin running things now.

The two cops pushed past, guns drawn, but stopped short of where the water was coming down. 'Switch the sprinklers off, would you!'

Lunz dived back into the control room and hit a button to cut the sprinklers. He picked up the desk phone and punched a number. 'We got a casualty coming up from the cells,' he said, watching the two cops tearing along the dripping corridor on the monitors. 'Guard got a face-full of pepper spray. I'm bringing him up now.' He put down the phone just as the two guards passed into the main corridor. Still no movement on any of the other screens. Whoever had jumped the guard hadn't managed to break out of their cell yet. Lunz started to relax a little. He didn't see the figure rise up behind him or notice the faint smell of pepper until a jet of it squirted into his mouth and wrenched the breath from his lungs.

16

Room 406, Davlat Hastenesi Hospital

There were grey smudges on the handle and the side pocket of Liv's holdall, graphite powder traces of the forensic scrutiny it had been under.

Inside it was like a time capsule from a previous life: clothes, toiletries, pens, notebooks. She tipped everything out on to the bed, shaking her laptop free from where it had sunk to the bottom. It too bore traces of graphite powder and smelled faintly of the glue fumes they used to raise prints. She hit the power key but nothing happened. The police techs had obviously snooped through her hard drive and run the battery down in the process. She had a power cable, but it had a North American plug on the end, no good for Southern Turkish sockets. She turned the bag round and opened the side pocket. To her surprise, her passport was still inside. She took it out and stared at the scuffed blue cover with the Great Seal in the centre and the words *United States of America* written below. She had never considered herself to be especially nationalistic or sentimental before, but seeing it now made her want to cry. She so desperately wanted to go home.

The next two things she found did little to help her fragile emotional state. The first was a set of keys. She remembered locking the door to her apartment and dropping them into the bag as she dashed for the cab waiting to take her to the airport. The second was a paper wallet with *1-Hour Foto* written

78

on the side. Inside was a collection of glossy prints taken on a daytrip to New York. They showed a younger version of herself and a tall, blond man who looked just like her. It was the last time she had seen her brother Samuel alive. She stuffed them back inside the wallet before emotion overcame her and looked at the small piles of her old life spread across the bed, trying to shake their sentimental meanings and see them instead as a kit of parts to help her escape.

She had enough clothes but no cash, and her credit cards had been maxed out buying her plane ticket over here. Then there was the small matter of the priest and the cop keeping guard in the corridor. If she could create a diversion, she could maybe slip from the room while they were distracted. She thought about the medical staff that came by on their regular rounds. Perhaps one of them might help her, though with the ever-present priest in the room she wasn't sure how she was supposed to subtly broach the subject, let alone communicate some kind of workable plan. The staff had probably all been vetted anyway and told to report any clandestine contact.

She slid out of bed, careful not to tip her belongings on to the floor, and padded over to the window. The sudden brightness behind the worn blind made her squint, but what lay outside was no help. There was a sheer four-storey drop to the cobbled street below and a tantalizing view of a fire escape snaking down the building opposite. There was also the ominous and unsettling sight of the Citadel, rising above the rooftops and darkening the horizon like a watchful sentinel. She returned her attention to the room, taking stock again of everything it contained, weighing up each item for its possible value in helping her get out.

Apart from the TV and the bed there was very little else: a small table with a plastic cup and a jug of water on it; a row of switches above the bed, a plastic sleeve fixed to the wall containing her medical notes. An emergency alarm cord dangled from the ceiling with a red handle on the end, large enough for a flailing hand to grab. Liv considered what would happen if she pulled it. She had heard the response to other alarms in the last few days, voices and footsteps rushing to surrounding rooms. But although the noise and confusion might create enough of a smokescreen to distract the priest for a moment, all the attention would be on her, and it would be almost impossible to speak or pass a note to anyone without being spotted. She had to think of another way.

17

Police Headquarters

The stairwell leading to the cell block echoed with the thundering boots of cops responding to the alarm. Gabriel met them on the way up. Nobody gave him a second glance. They'd all caught the message that a guard had been sprayed in the face, so when they encountered one – struggling to breathe, eyes swollen shut, another guard helping him – they hurried on past to get at the bastards who'd done it.

Gabriel helped the guard along, his arm wrapped round him, his hand out of sight against the wall, pointing the man's own gun directly at his crotch to keep him quiet. Gabriel's other hand held a walkie-talkie that he'd grabbed from the control room and into which he maintained a one-sided dialogue to stop anyone striking up a conversation with him and also to cover up a good portion of his face.

They reached the top of the stairs as another pair of cops burst through the fire doors and started heading down. Gabriel slipped through the door after them into a short corridor. Ahead of him, through a square window set into a door, he could see the reception area. He kept the guard moving, jamming the gun harder into his pelvis to remind him it was there.

When they were a few metres short of the door he crooked the walkie-talkie under his chin, snatched the spray canister off his belt and gave the guard another blast full in the face.

He slipped the gun under his shirt and into the waistband of his trousers then burst through the door and into a room full of cops.

All heads turned as they entered the hall, drawn by the fresh coughing fit that accompanied their entrance. The two nearest uniforms rushed forward and took hold of the convulsing guard. Gabriel let them take him and spun away towards the exit. 'I've brought him up to the lobby,' he barked into the walkie-talkie. 'Where the hell's that ambulance?' Then he stepped out of the front door and was free.

He had no idea how long the guard's seizure would last, but he wouldn't have long. The cops in the basement must have worked things out by now. The road he was in was thinly populated, but the street ahead was busier. If he could make it to the corner and into the crowds he'd stand a chance. The corner was maybe six metres away. He kept the walkie-talkie clamped to his face and his eyes forward, resisting the urge to run.

He weaved in and out of what foot traffic there was, putting as many bodies between himself and whoever would shortly be following. The ground was wet from the recent downpour though it was no longer raining. It wasn't much of a break, but he'd take what he could get. It made his clothes, still drenched from the sprinklers, seem slightly less unusual.

He made the corner just as a siren started up behind him. Squinting against the glare of the bright sky, he matched his pace with the evening crowd and dropped the walkie-talkie into a bin. He had to get off the street as soon as possible. A wet cop wasn't the best disguise for a fugitive.

18

Davlat Hastenesi Hospital

The challenge of working out how to reveal Oscar's hidden message using the limited resources at her disposal had given Kathryn the greatest feeling of hope and purpose she had experienced in days.

From her fieldwork she knew you needed three basic things to start a fire: fuel, an accelerant and a flame. For fuel she had torn a couple of pages from the middle of her medical notes, not daring to risk taking any from the notebook, then shredded them to make a loose pile on one edge of the window ledge.

For the accelerant she'd had to think laterally. Roughly speaking it could be anything that would intensify a fire. She'd found what she was looking for in the hand sanitizer-gel dispenser by the door, the sort used in all modern hospitals. The label told her this particular brand was 40 per cent alcohol. Alcohol evaporated quickly to leave skin dry and had antiseptic qualities of its own. It was also a very effective accelerant.

She squirted a thick dollop into her hand, scraped it on to the sill then stacked the pile of shredded paper on top of it so it could start absorbing the flammable fumes as they evaporated. The longer she waited, the more saturated the paper would become and the better her chance of lighting it. But she still needed a flame, and for that she needed the sun to come out.

She lay on her bed, staring out of her window at the bright

band of sky between the passing rain clouds and the tops of the mountains. The last time she had lit a fire this way had been on the final trip she had taken with John. It had been one of those spur-of-the-moment things arranged, before Gabriel returned to college and John headed off to Iraq on the dig he would never return from.

They had spent the day off-season hiking along the Presidential Range in New Hampshire and got caught in a freak storm. By the time they made it to where they'd parked their hire car they were soaked to the skin, only to discover they had a flat battery. They headed back to a Ranger's hut they had passed on the path where some weekend walker had used up the firewood and not bothered to restock it. She and Gabriel had collected as many fallen branches as they could, but it was all too wet to light. They hadn't even noticed John had gone until he stepped into the cabin brandishing one of his socks on the end of a long stick, dripping with diesel from the car's fuel tank. They had piled the wet sticks on top of the sock and waited for the fumes to permeate the stack, the same way Kathryn was waiting now. Liquid diesel doesn't burn well, but the ether-infused sticks had burned just fine. They had spent the night there, huddling together, warmed by the fire – the last time they were all together. Kathryn smiled as she recalled it, remembering their closeness and their firelit smiles while the storm raged outside. Then she realized that the warmth was not in her mind, it was on her skin and flooding the room. The sun had come out.

She leapt out of bed and lunged towards the window. Sunlight was filling the street with warm afternoon light. It had dropped below the clouds and would soon fall behind the distant mountains. She needed to move fast.

She fumbled her reading glasses from the top of her head, and held them over the pile of shredded paper, the magnifying lenses focusing a pinpoint of light on to the top of it.

A tiny image of the sun appeared on the paper and she held

it as steady as her hand would allow. The bright dot darkened. It started to smoulder. The paper curled into ash around the dot, but it did not light. She moved the glasses, chasing the edge of the blackening paper with the bright dot, focusing the heat on the meagre kindling she had made. A curl of red glowed at the edge as the paper turned to ash but still it did not catch. She cupped her hand round it and blew gently across the top, trying not to disturb the pile or blow away the alcohol fumes trapped inside. She continued to blow, gentle and steady, focusing her attention on the red ember until her lungs were empty. Then, just as her breath was almost exhausted, it finally caught and flame started to devour the ripped-up paper.

She grabbed the diary from the bed and opened it to the centre pages, which she had marked with several more squares of torn paper. She had no idea how long the hidden message might be, but she only had a limited amount of fuel and the flame was burning quickly. She screwed up a square of paper, fed it to the fire, then gently offered up the first blank page to the flame.

The effect was almost instant. The heat darkened the paper wherever acid ink had soaked into it, creating swirls of symbols that steadily filled the page. The body of text, arranged to form the shape of an inverted Tau, was a mirror of the first prophecy she had grown up with and written in the same ancient script. Kathryn's eyes scanned the Malan symbols, the language of her tribe, translating them in her head as she read:

The Key unlocks the Sacrament
The Sacrament becomes the Key
And all the Earth shalt tremble
The Key must follow the Starmap Home
There to quench the fire of the dragon within the full
phase of a moon
Lest the Key shalt perish, the Earth shalt splinter and a
blight shalt prosper, marking the end of all days

She read it again, trying to dig meaning from the words. It seemed like a warning, but was too incomplete for her to understand.

There had to be more.

She grabbed another scrap of paper and fed it to the dying flame. The fire was burning faster than she had anticipated and smoke was starting to fill the room. She turned to the next page in the diary and held it over the flame.

More darkened text emerged, much more, but the fire was burning so quickly she didn't even stop to read it. She knew she was almost out of fuel and the smoke levels in the room were getting dangerously high so she kept moving blank pages over the heat, one after the other, feeding the flames until there were none left and the fire shrank to nothing and died in a final curl of smoke.

Outside she could hear footsteps approaching. In a few moments someone might walk into her room with the priest right behind them. She pulled open the window as far as it would go, scooping up the evidence of the fire and feeding it to the breeze. She left the window open in an effort to dilute the smell of smoke and scrubbed her hands with sanitizing gel while she cast around for somewhere to hide the diary. The room was bare. There were no hiding places. Kathryn lunged towards the bed and hid the diary in the only place she could see and undoubtedly the first place anyone would look. She hid it under the mattress.

19

Father Ulvi Şimşek sat in the hospital corridor, his fingers working the string of worry beads he always carried, still brooding about the earlier visit from the police inspector. He had been so dismissive and superior, questioning his presence there as if he were nothing.

If only he knew.

He counted the beads through his fingers, smooth stones made warm by the heat of his hand. There were nineteen on the black cotton string, each one made from a particular type of amber he had chosen because of its dark, reddish colour. Nineteen beads – nineteen lives, each one recalling a face. He counted in his head, his lips moving slightly as he remembered the names and how each had died.

Despite the priest's clothes, Ulvi's service to the Church was more specialized. He considered himself a soldier of God, trained by his country but now serving a greater sovereign lord. The beads reminded him of his own past – in the west of Turkey, close to the ancient borders with Greece – and while others of his faith said the Rosary to help purge them of their sins, he used the beads to remind him of where he had come from and what he had done. The dark stains on his soul were too deep to be cleansed in this world. And the world was imperfect. Only God was pristine. So he chose not to pretend that he could better himself here, or atone for what he had done. He was what he was, a darker instrument of the Lord's bright purpose. And God Himself had made him this way; He alone would judge him when the time came.

Ulvi reached the end of his roll call of remembrance and slipped the bracelet back into his pocket. He heard the clink as it snaked past his mobile phone and down to the ceramic knife beneath it, the blade as sharp as glass but invisible to the metal detector that had swept over him at the start of his shift. Elsewhere in his jacket was a hypodermic syringe with a nylon needle, a small bag of powdered flunitrazepam, and an ampoule of Aconitine poison. He had brought them with him every day since the cops had grown used to him and the routine checks had become sloppy.

He looked over at the policeman, slumped in his chair, his attention dulled and elsewhere. He was still reading the paper, working backwards from the sports pages like he did every day, slipping so far down in his chair that his chin almost touched the buttons of his uniform shirt. He was clearly cut from the same cloth as his boss. Arrogant. Dismissive. Stupid.

No matter.

A bored guard was one who could easily be dealt with. As the night shift wore on, and the hospital grew quiet, Ulvi would offer to make coffee to help keep them awake, and in the small staff kitchen down the hall he would slip the flunitrazepam into the cop's cup. He could imagine the look on the man's stupid face when he woke in the morning with a date-rape drug hangover only to discover that all three of his charges were dead in their beds. He'd like to see how that played out. He'd also like to see the look on that snotty inspector's face, but he would be long gone by then, off on another mission, serving God in his own dark way. He settled back in his chair, calmer now the waiting was almost over.

By tomorrow morning the message had said.

He wondered if there were others, agents like himself who had received the same message. The sensitive nature of his work meant he always worked alone so nothing could be traced to his masters if things went wrong. But nothing would go wrong, he was far too experienced for that.

Ulvi slipped his hand into his other pocket and gathered three loose beads into his palm, each like a solid drop of fresh blood waiting to be threaded on the black string of his rosary. He rolled them between his fingers, reciting the names in his head: Kathryn Mann, Liv Adamsen, Brother Dragan Ruja. He had been surprised when the remaining monk had been included in the mission. But it was not for him to question orders. The monk had already given his life to God anyway – Ulvi was just there to collect it.

He settled in his chair and reached for the novel he had brought to help pass the time. It was about the Knights Templar – warrior priests like him. He was about to start reading when he became aware of footsteps drawing closer. The cop heard them too and looked up from his newspaper as a nurse appeared round the corner and continued marching towards them. Ulvi checked his watch. It was too early for the evening rounds and she was walking with a sense of purpose and hurry. She must have been summoned by someone in the rooms.

The nurse arrived at the small table and picked up the signing-in sheet. She didn't acknowledge the presence of either of the men watching her. There had been tension ever since the hospital staff had been asked to clear out what few patients there were in the old psychiatric ward and stop the renovation work.

Be patient, Ulvi thought. *You'll have your building back by morning, I promise.*

He watched her write the time, her name, then '406' in the 'Room' column. Liv Adamsen's room. Ulvi picked up the keys from the desk and smiled at the nurse, but she gave him nothing in return.

So rude, these people, he thought as he walked ahead of her down the corridor. *The sooner I'm done here, the better.*

20

Liv was sitting up in bed, straining to hear the sounds outside in the corridor.

The footsteps had come from the right, so that was the direction she needed to head when she got out of the room. There was a loud, single rap on the door and she pulled the sheets tight around her neck as it started to open.

The priest stepped into the room and she immediately felt the dread expand within her. The nurse followed and walked over to switch off the call light that had summoned her. 'You OK?' she asked in accented English, automatically pulling a digital thermometer from her pocket and placing it against Liv's forehead.

'Yes, fine, I think – I just need to ask you something.' The nurse pressed a button to get a reading and the thermometer beeped. 'When I was admitted, what happened to all my stuff?'

'Personal items are stored in property office behind reception.' The nurse studied the display on the thermometer, then grabbed Liv's wrist to check her pulse.

'So how would I go about getting them back?'

'You sign when you leave.' She counted the heartbeats then let the wrist drop, looking into Liv's face for the first time since entering. 'Anything else?'

'Yes . . .' Liv glanced over at the priest, as if embarrassed about what she was about to ask. 'Can you tell me how I'm doing, you know – medically.'

The nurse plucked her notes from the wall holder and studied the file. 'Some hormone imbalance – oestrogen levels very high, but not dangerous. You have high temperature, nausea. Maybe you have some virus. Big concern is memory.' She flipped to the end and read through the psychiatrist's notes. Liv had tried to make them out for herself but they were written in Turkish. And much as she wanted to leave this place, there was no point in making a run for it if she was going to drop down dead a hundred metres from the door.

'Psychiatric report is good,' the nurse said. 'They only keep you here for observation.'

'What drugs am I on?'

The nurse scanned the notes and shook her head. 'No drugs. Just rest and observation.'

Liv was surprised at this and didn't entirely believe it. There was far too much weirdness going on in her head for her not to be doped in some way.

'So in theory, I could carry on as normal,' Liv said, watching the nurse's face for the slightest twitch of a professional lie. 'I mean, there's nothing I should avoid – going on a plane or scuba diving, for example?'

The nurse glanced at the priest and shrugged. 'You do what you like.'

'Thank you,' Liv said, the words coming out like a sigh of relief.

'Not a problem. Anything else?'

'Yes, there is one more thing,' Liv said, throwing the sheet off to reveal she was fully clothed. 'I'd like to discharge myself – immediately.'

Liv had already grabbed a bag from the floor and was halfway to the door when Ulvi's brain caught up with what was happening. Instinctively he moved to step in front of her, but she side-stepped him and squeezed through the open door.

Outside in the corridor the police officer rose from his seat and stepped towards her. 'Back in your room.'

'Why?' Liv said, looking calmly up into his face.

'Because . . . you're not well.'

'That's not what the nurse just said.' Liv glanced over her shoulder to where the nurse now stood. 'And I'm not under arrest, am I?'

The cop opened his mouth to say something then seemed to think better of it. 'No,' he said.

Liv smiled and cocked her head to one side. 'So would you step aside, please.'

He looked down at her, an internal debate raging in his head. He came to a conclusion and stepped aside.

'You must stay here,' the priest said, his words sounding like an order.

'No,' Liv said, already walking away. 'I really mustn't.'

She swung her bag over her shoulder and marched quickly away in the same direction she had heard the nurse arriving from.

Ulvi watched her go, weighing up his options. If he followed her now he could shadow her, wait until she was far away from the crowds, in a hotel room maybe: isolated; unobserved. It was tempting. But the other two targets were still here which meant so was the bulk of his mission.

He watched Liv reach the junction in the corridor and disappear round it.

In his mind he played back the events that had just taken place in the room, slowing them down, analysing them, then smiled as he remembered something Liv had said to the nurse.

She had asked if it was safe to fly.

He didn't need to follow her after all. He knew exactly where she was going. He hoped there were other agents in the field with him. His loss would be their gain. He pulled his phone from his pocket and carefully tapped out a text to his controller.

21

Kathryn Mann had heard the voices outside, but her damaged hearing had not allowed her to hear who was speaking or what they were saying. Whoever it was had gone away now and she listened to the silence until she thought it safe to retrieve the book from her feeble hiding place.

The pages whispered in the silence of the room, like hints of the secrets they kept. She slipped her reading glasses down from her hair, bringing the first page into focus.

Please forgive the elaborate form of this message, but you will see why I took pains to ensure only you might discover it. The text I have transcribed here is a copy of something I received several years ago. The origin of it, and the means by which it came to me, are the reasons I kept it from you all these years. I know we never had secrets. Let me explain why this remained the only one I ever kept from you, then hopefully you will understand why I sought to keep it so.

The original tablet that contained this message is lost. The only reason I know of its existence is because a photograph was sent to me from an anonymous source a few months after John was killed. On the back of the photograph was a hand-written note saying simply:

This is what we found. This is why we were killed.

How the person that sent it knew of my existence I have often pondered. Maybe John confided in them, or left it for someone to pass on to me in the event of his death, the same way I am now communicating it to you. I believe whoever sent it to me chose me deliberately because of my peculiar past. I was already dead in the eyes of the Citadel and so passing this dangerous knowledge to me would not put me at any risk. Even the vengeful Citadel would not seek to kill a man who was already dead.

Know that I often debated whether to share this information with you. I hated keeping a secret from you, but in the end I erred on the side of caution. If John was killed because he discovered this tablet then even a suspicion that you knew anything about it would place your life in danger. I knew that you would inevitably pass it on to Gabriel. So you see my dilemma. My desire to share this knowledge, weighed against the risk it might pose to the two people I hold most dear in the world. How could I take that risk? I couldn't - I didn't.

But now I sense the endgame is near. I return to Ruin in the hope that the words of this second prophecy will show us the way after the first has been fulfilled. And if for some reason I cannot pass this on to you personally, then I am writing it here so you may discover it for yourself.

If you are reading this then I am dead . . .

Kathryn broke off, the starkness of the phrase puncturing her emotional resolve and bringing forth the hot tears she had been holding at bay. She removed her glasses and wiped her eyes with the back of her hand. She could not bear to think of him writing this lonely note like a condemned man facing the prospect of his own death. She wiped her eyes again then replaced her glasses and continued reading.

. . . I hope the fulfilment of the first prophecy shines a light on this second so that it may now help you on your journey towards restoring the rightful order of things. I spent many evenings musing about the meaning of it, but without knowing what the Sacrament is, it always remained a riddle. For my part, there is one thing I can shed some light on.

During my brief time in the Citadel I chanced upon something that I think may be the Starmap mentioned here. It came into the library with the same consignment of relics as the fragments that formed the first prophecy. It too had the Tau symbol on it, as well as what looked like constellations and directions written in a language I could not understand. I intended to study it further and learn what language it was written in, but I never had time. Soon afterwards I learned that my presence was suspected in the Citadel so I stole the slate fragments and fled. I would have brought the Starmap as well, but it was too heavy. I knew if I tried to swim the moat with that weighing me down I would sink. So I did the next best thing. I hid it.

I didn't want the Sancti and their kind to benefit from whatever knowledge it contained so I put it somewhere they were unlikely to find it. My hope is that it rests there still and that with the first prophecy fulfilled you may now have free access to the Citadel yourselves and, by following the map I will outline, you will finally retrieve it.

Then the message ran out.

Kathryn looked at the next blank page. There had to be more here than she'd had time to reveal.

She flipped back to the first symbols she had revealed and read the first few lines again.

The Key unlocks the Sacrament
The Sacrament becomes the Key
And all the Earth shalt tremble
The Key must follow the Starmap Home
There to quench the fire of the dragon within the full
phase of a moon

The full phase of the moon lasted just over twenty-eight days. Assuming that the evacuation of the Sancti from the mountain marked the moment of release for the Sacrament, then ten days had already passed. She read the rest of the message with a growing sense of dread.

Lest the Key shalt perish, the Earth shalt splinter and a
blight shalt prosper, marking the end of all days

She wondered at the sickness that seemed to have struck the Sancti. Could this be the blight that was mentioned? In the chaos of the ER when she had first arrived at the hospital she had glimpsed what it had done to the monks – the blackened skin, the blood-red eyes, the bleeding. If that spread out into the world it would be like the darkest vision from the Book of Revelation, turning all men into the image of demons. She looked at the blank page, restless with a desire to know what else was written there. It would be a whole day before the sun swung round again and shone back through her window, a day she could not afford to lose. She felt the weight of what she had just learned and the frustration of knowing that it was locked in this room with her, with the clock already ticking.

Ten days gone.

Eighteen remaining.

22

The lift door opened and Liv experienced a surge of panic. After days locked up in virtual isolation the noise and volume of people milling around the reception area was overwhelming. She had found a baseball cap in her bag and pulled it over her head now to hide her face a little, then forced herself out of the lift and across the worn mosaic floor towards the reception desk. She scanned the signs crowding the walls, seeking one that might offer a clue, but they were all in Turkish.

'Patients' property?' she asked the receptionist.

A taloned finger pointed to a door by the entrance. She headed over, glancing outside as she passed the main door. It had been raining and the low afternoon sun shone off the wet pavement. A news truck was parked on the opposite side of the street, a cameraman and a reporter sitting in the cab smoking and talking while they waited for something to happen. She didn't want to be ambushed leaving the building and end up on the evening news again. She needed to stay under the radar – for the time being at least. There had to be another way out of here.

The patients' property office was tucked away in a dark cupboard with stacks of paperwork rising up from every horizontal surface and teetering precariously along the length of a narrow counter that cut the room in half. A young and bored-looking man sat behind it, steadily working his way through a large pile of folders with all the enthusiasm of a condemned man. Liv showed him the plastic tag around her wrist with her name and admissions number on it and he hefted a pile of folders under his arm and sloped off into the dark valley of shelves that stretched away behind him. Liv glanced at the door, listening to the muted sounds of the reception area beyond, ready to make a run for it at the first sign of marching boots. Her escape had been easier than she had expected. She had thought either the cop or the priest would have done more to stop her, but the surprise of her departure had clearly caught them both off guard. That didn't mean she was free and clear though. They would undoubtedly both have been straight on the phone to their superiors and might be looking to detain her again even now. She needed to be cautious.

The clerk returned from the dim archives carrying a cardboard container. She signed for it and pulled the lid off, recoiling at the sight of the clear plastic bag stuffed with her old bloodstained clothes.

'Rubbish over in corner.' The clerk pointed to a large portable waste bin with a yellow plastic sack bulging beneath it. Liv carried her box over and lifted the lid with her free hand. Inside were five or six other bags containing similarly blood-ruined clothing. She wondered why the hospital didn't just bin the stuff themselves. Then saw the disclaimer on the underside of the lid and understood. It was an insurance thing. It said if you threw away anything of value it was officially your fault. She added her bag of dried gore to the others and let the lid bang shut.

The only other thing left in the box was a creased white envelope containing some pieces of folded paper and a few hundred Turkish lira. She had no idea whether that meant she was rich or if it was merely enough to buy a cup of coffee. Either way, it was better than nothing. She stuffed the envelope into her holdall and left the box on the countertop. 'Thanks,' she said, fastening her bag and preparing herself for the outside world. The clerk said nothing, merely carried on rolling his boulder of paper uphill for all eternity.

Liv opened the door and scanned the people milling about in the reception area. The main entrance was out because of the news crew camped in front of it. Right now she needed to remain low key and draw minimal attention to herself. There had to be another exit. She locked on to a couple of guys in hospital greens walking away from her. There was something about their body language that caught her attention. It was relaxed, unhurried. One of them reached up to his breast pocket and she saw the telltale rectangle straining against the green material. She knew then, with the finely tuned instincts of a reformed smoker, that they were heading for a cigarette break. And, unless there was a smokers' room somewhere in the hospital, that meant they were heading outside.

She fell in line behind them as they passed through a set of double doors into a shabby corridor, matching her steps with theirs so they wouldn't hear her, but they were too preoccupied to notice the petite blonde woman following them. They reached a fire exit at the end of the corridor and leaned against the locking bar to open it, already fitting cigarettes into their mouths. Liv skipped along to catch up and slipped through the door after them. 'Hi!' she said, looking down an alley to where the main street was visible.

'Main entrance that way,' one of them grunted, pointing back down the corridor.

'I can get out this way though, yes?' Liv was already marching away towards the street. She didn't wait for a reply.

The alley opened up on to a wide street with two lanes of traffic all heading in the same direction. She walked against the flow, squinting against the glare and looking for a cab. At least the rain had stopped; cabs were always harder to come by when it was raining. She saw an empty one, waved it down and slid gratefully into the back seat.

'*Nereye?*' the driver asked.

'Airport,' she said, buckling herself in.

'Which one?' He switched to English with the ease of someone who made his living in a tourist town.

'The busiest,' she said, sliding low in the seat. 'Whichever has the most flights out of here.'

23

Ajda Demir squinted out of the fourth-floor window at the bright evening, holding her hand up against the reflected glare from the wet streets. The movement reflected in the glass, drawing her attention to the transparent version of herself hovering like a spectre in front of her. The story of the past week was written on her face: dark circles under her eyes, her forehead creased with worry, silver hair escaping from the usually immaculate confines of her scraped-back bun. She reached up and carefully smoothed it down, as if this small act could somehow return everything to order.

Turning from the ghost of herself, she surveyed the chaos that had been brought into her ordered world. The room she was in resembled a small classroom, with strip lights overhead and desks in lines that usually housed a mixture of fundraisers and aid workers who quietly ran one of the charity's larger projects based in central Sudan. Following the explosion at the Citadel, however, all that had stopped. Ortus accounts had been frozen worldwide pending a full enquiry into why the head of the charity had taken a truckful of fertilizer, donated in good faith by a large, well-respected conglomerate, and used it to try to blow up the world's oldest and most sacred monastery. For the past week a team of investigators had been camped out here, checking through the company accounts and records, searching for proof that the charity was a cover for a church-hating terrorist organization. They had found nothing, of course, but it didn't matter. The PR fallout had been immense. As well as fielding press calls and fending off reporters, Ajda had been busy compiling a steadily growing list of the various companies and funding bodies who were severing their ties with the charity. The towering heap of boxes before her, all of which needed re-sorting and filing away, was a physical manifestation of the huge mess the organization was now in.

But it wasn't the extra work that was making her soul heavy. It was the invisible cost, the unquantifiable ripples that this mess had caused. Through gaps in the piles of boxes she could see photos and maps pinned to the blank walls showing the projects that had been obscured by this investigation: a water sanitation and filtration system in the Sudan; a partially built new school in Sierra Leone; freshly ploughed fields in Somalia that had previously been sown with nothing but landmines. The people in these countries were the real victims. They wouldn't understand why their shattered lives were no longer being rebuilt.

Ajda felt the pressure of the day weighing upon her and listened out for thunder, hoping it might roll down from the mountains to clear the air. Instead she heard something that made her eyes widen and her skin go cold. It was the creak of a foot on a floorboard – there was someone in the building with her.

She listened for further noises, hoping for the call of a familiar voice or the sound of a conversation. But there was nothing. Everyone had gone for the day. She had locked the front door herself after the last person had left.

It came again: the creak of a floorboard, followed by a soft click.

It had come from somewhere above her, where no one was supposed to be. The first four floors of the building were taken up by offices. The fifth was the private apartment of Kathryn

Mann, whose family had once owned the whole building. These days she ran Ortus and 'lived above the shop', as she put it. But she was not in her flat, she was in hospital.

Another sound.

Softer now, like a drawer being opened.

Ajda stole across the floor on light feet, using the noises from above as cover for her own movement. She reached the door to the stairwell and looked up at the fifth-floor landing. One of the skylights was open.

The faint noises of activity continued to float down from above, too careful to be innocent, too loud to be ignored. Ajda crept up the stairs, keeping to the wall where the stair treads were firmer and less likely to creak. The door to the apartment was open. Beyond it a light was on. She paused for a second, uncertain what to do next. The sound of a filing cabinet ratcheting open overrode her fear. Whoever it was, they were going through private files, and that she wouldn't stand for. She strode up the final few stairs and crossed the landing to the door.

Inside the flat a uniformed cop was on his knees by a filing cabinet.

'Can I help you?' Ajda said, in a tone clearly meant to convey the exact opposite.

The cop removed something from beneath the drawer then stood up and turned round.

'Hello, Ajda,' Gabriel said, walking across to the large floor-to-ceiling bookcase.

Ajda had to fight back an uncharacteristic urge to rush over and hug him. 'I . . . I thought you were in jail,' she said.

'I was.' He squatted down, reaching for a black calfskin-bound copy of *Jane Eyre* on a lower shelf. 'And now I'm not.'

He pressed the spine of the book and the whole lower quarter of the bookshelf sprang open with a soft *click*. Ajda thought she'd known every inch of the office, but she had not been aware of the false panel and the cupboard concealed behind it.

A loud hammering from the ground floor made them both spin round.

'That'll be for me,' Gabriel said, unplugging a fax machine and lifting it out of the cupboard. 'Please don't answer it.'

The hammering continued in the sort of aggressive and persistent way that meant either police or debt collectors were outside the door. Ajda realized what must have happened and immediately felt fearful. Gabriel and his mother were good people. She'd worked with them both for long enough to know that much. A week ago she would have felt compelled to go and let the police in if they'd come calling. But after watching them trash her offices and trample underfoot the good names of those who worked there, she had changed her opinion. They could hammer until their fists bled: she would not let them in.

Gabriel laid the fax machine on the floor and turned it over. On the back were sockets for the phone line and power cable as well as a keyhole. Gabriel took a small key from the envelope he had found under the drawer, twisted it in the lock and lifted the top of the unit off. Inside, the electronics and working parts of a real fax machine had been squashed into about a third of the area. The rest was filled with stacks of different coloured passports and plastic bags containing bundles of currency in various denominations. Ajda saw dollars and euros as well as Turkish lira, Sudanese pounds and what looked like Iraqi dinars. There was also a thick stack of credit cards. 'What is all this?' she asked, her ordered world crumbling a little further.

Gabriel pocketed three of the passports and all of the cash. 'A lot of my work out in the field is under the radar,' he explained, quickly sorting through the credit cards. 'Many of the most needy people in the world are governed by the most corrupt. If we played by the rules, we'd never get anywhere, and the weakest people wouldn't stand a chance. I'm afraid I have to bend the rules from time to time in order to get things done.'

The hammering started up again downstairs, joined now by the sound of the reception phone ringing.

'I don't expect you to do anything you're not comfortable with,' Gabriel said, taking her gently by her shoulders. 'And if you want to go down and let them in, that's OK. None of this is your fight. But my mother's in danger and I want to help her, and you could help me.'

The hammering stopped as abruptly as it had started and the phone stopped ringing. Ajda looked up into Gabriel's earnest eyes and smiled.

'What would you like me to do?'

24

Davlat Hastenesi Hospital

Dusk brought the evening meds rounds in the hospital.

With one room now empty they were quicker than usual and Father Ulvi was eager to get them out of the way so he could concentrate on what else he had to do that night. He fiddled with the loose beads in his pocket as the nurse checked Kathryn Mann. Then they locked the door and headed to the last room at the end of the corridor.

The male nurse pushed the trolley slowly towards it, his large frame making surprisingly heavy work of the task. Ulvi knew it wasn't the bulk of the mobile drug cabinet that slowed his progress but a bone-deep reluctance to step into the room and face what it contained. He had to admit there was something about the monk's appearance that even he found unsettling. In the course of his own work he had witnessed some stomach-churning sights – savage knife attacks, burn victims, a whole freak show of human bodies warped beyond recognition by torture and violence – but even he had never seen anything like the patient in room 400.

Ulvi entered the room first, holding the door for the reluctant nurse to follow, being careful not to look at the bed until he had to. He could hear dry breathing, shallow and furtive, as though the thing lying there was stealing air. He closed the door, then turned to face the bed.

The sight never failed to shock him. The most striking thing about the monk was the colour of his skin. Where it was visible beneath the yellow stained dressings that covered most of his body, it was totally black, though Ulvi knew from his briefing notes that the man lying before him was a white Serbian monk named Dragan Ruja. He looked as though he'd been scorched or dipped in crude oil, so deep and dark was the colour of the skin hanging loosely on his shrunken frame. Whatever his disease was, it had gnawed him away, decomposing his living form until it was closer to that of a corpse. He resembled the mummified bodies they occasionally dragged from the mountains; climbers who had lost their way and slowly been desiccated over months or even years by wind and ice until nothing was left but a sunken, hollowed-out approximation of the living things they had once been. Except the mountain dead were brought to the morgue, not the hospital, and they did not watch you as you entered the room; or shrink away as cotton wipes dabbed at the rot that still oozed steadily out of them.

Ulvi studied the face, the long wild hair, sparse over parchment skin, the beard fringed around cracked lips, wasted like the rest of him and pulled back over a snarl of broken teeth made brown by bleeding gums. He looked as though he was howling, though thankfully he made no sound above the pant of his scratchy breath. The eyes – and thank God for this – were closed, for they were the things that unsettled Ulvi the most. If they were quick, maybe they could get out of here without waking him.

The nurse had clearly realized this too and was working swiftly. He took a fresh pair of nitrile gloves from a box, slipped them over his hands then swapped a new bag of plasma for the depleted one on the drip line. Next he laid out syringes loaded with Vitamin K and Thrombin to promote coagulation in the blood, as well as scalpels to cut free the pus-soaked dressings wrapped round his strange network of wounds. Then he made a mistake. He tore open a fresh package of dressings a little too eagerly and the sound of it ripped through the heavy silence. The thin, blackened lids instantly moved in response. Ulvi and the nurse watched, each hoping the eyes would settle and the thing would remain asleep. But it did not. The head rolled towards them and the lids parted, revealing the hellish eyes beneath. They were bright red, a result of all the blood vessels having burst and bled into the whites. Ulvi stared at them, transfixed by the sight of his brother monk and the demon thing he had become.

The light hurt.

Everything hurt.

When Dragan had first woken, here in this place, he had thought for a brief moment it must be Heaven; he was no longer inside the dark rooms and hallways of the Citadel, so therefore he must have died. But then pain had overwhelmed him, and he knew he was wrong, for Heaven could not contain agony such as this.

In the first few days, when he had realized where he was, he had waited for death – welcomed it even. He knew, through his agonies, that it had to be close – one way or another. Either his broken body would finally give up, or an agent of the Citadel would come.

The law was clear.

The secrets of the Citadel had to be protected.

And he was a Sanctus – a guardian of the Sacrament. There was no way they could let him remain in the world with what he held in his head. So they would bring him back, or they would send someone to silence him, as well as anyone else he may have spoken to.

But he had said nothing.

Not to the doctors, not to the police, not even to the priest who watched over him constantly, stealing into his room from time to time to whisper fresh news of what was happening outside and in the wider world. He wished the priest would leave him in peace. He didn't care for any of it. He just wanted to keep his soul pure so he could face his God knowing he had kept his oath and carried the secret to his grave.

And he had heard Death in the corridor, shuffling outside his door, teasing him with his closeness, then slipping away and into other rooms to claim other souls. Although he wanted it, yearned for it, Death left him alone.

So he endured, waiting his turn, which could not – praise God – be long. For despite the transfusions of the blood of others, and the drugs that stopped it from flowing straight out of him again, he could feel the life leaking from him, tickling and dripping in the dark wet places between the dressings and his blighted skin where the nurse dabbed and cleansed.

But now he felt differently.

Now he feared the whisper of death at his door. Earlier, when he had drifted out of agonized sleep from a dream where his body was whole and he was back in the cool tunnels of the mountain, he had discovered a dark figure standing in the room with him. At first he had thought the shadow was death, come to claim him at last. But as his ruined eyes cleared and the figure stepped forward, he saw it was just the priest, delivering fresh news.

Death had come after all, it seemed, but not to him.

You are the last, the priest had whispered. *The last . . .*

And as he lay pinned down by this news, he had felt strength flowing back into him along with the realization that death was no longer an option. Now he had to live. He did not know who in authority was left in the Citadel but suspected there was no one. Why else had he been left in the hospital to rot without a word? Why else had he not been silenced earlier, unless there was no one to give the order? If the old elite had been smashed, then he was all that remained. He was the only one who could rebuild it again.

He looked down now as the male nurse peeled away the

last sticky dressing to reveal his blackened, wasted body beneath. Seeing it was its own kind of agony; the ruined flesh, scored with his ceremonial scars, badge of his holy orders, red and swollen where blood and fluid leaked from him.

He had borne his suffering, as Job had done, and proved his worthiness for the task that had been reserved for him. He had been spared so he could restore the order once more. But a leader needed to be strong and there was only one place where his wrecked body could recover fully. If he were to live at all.

He had to get back to the Citadel.

II

None of us will ever accomplish anything excellent or commanding except when he listens to this whisper which is heard by him alone.

Ralph Waldo Emerson

25

Babil Province, Western Iraq

Hyde jammed his arm against the roof of the cab as they bounced over ruts in the road carved by recent floods. They had left the main road twenty clicks back and were now deep in the middle of nowhere. Out here there were no trees, no grass, no wind – nothing at all. Even the scrubby storksbill bushes that somehow managed to cling to the ground everywhere else in Iraq had been burned away by the slowly spreading eastern edge of the Syrian Desert. Whatever had once been here had been ground down by time and heat until it was reduced to just two elements – earth and sky – with a hazy smudge marking the place where the two met, as if the finger of God had been run along it, blurring the line between them.

Ahead of him was what he now called 'home', a sprawling collection of earth-coloured tents and prefabricated structures clustered together inside a razor-wire perimeter. Two huge earth movers trundled around inside the compound, kicking up dust as they dug a second storage lagoon even though the first one was still empty. At the centre of it all rose the dark, skeletal drill tower, sharp and slender like the spire of a church built to worship money. It reminded Hyde of the spindle of a roulette wheel and, as at every other low point in his life, here he was again, betting on how that spin of the wheel would end, hoping it would fall on black.

They reached the main gate, passed through the double perimeter and into the shade of the transport hangar. It was better equipped than anything he had ever seen in the army. When he had signed on he had been asked to put together a wish list of vehicles and equipment he might need. Being used to army quartermasters cutting any requisition list in half, he had padded the list, adding plenty of stuff he didn't really need. But he had got the whole lot. Money appeared to be no object for his new bosses, though with the drill still turning dry, he wasn't sure where the cash was coming from: not from the ground, that was for sure.

The truck stopped and he opened the door to the trapped heat in the hangar, stretching the kinks out of his back as he passed through a set of double doors designed to keep the heat out of the main building and the air-conditioning in.

The mess hall was half-full, men in desert lights eating dinner after a day on the drill. He knew they were coming off a shift because their bright white work clothes, designed to reflect the worst of the torturous sun, were now uniformly beige. He could feel heat radiating off them as he passed their tables, as if they were bricks that had been in the sun all day.

The air temperature dropped a few more degrees as he left the mess hall and entered the office complex, punching in the code to gain entry to his domain – the security nerve centre. The more important people had desks further down the corridor where the air-con stayed constant and you couldn't hear the noise from the mess hall, but he liked this just fine. In theory, it meant he could be up and outside much quicker if trouble arose – not that he was expecting any. The border with Syria was over seventy clicks away and the nearest town about the same. There were still pockets of *fedayeen* everywhere – the nationalist freedom fighters trying to kick out the Western invaders – and there were plenty of opportunistic criminals looking to kidnap key workers from the rich Western companies now flourishing in the unsteady peace; but Hyde doubted any of them would try anything here.

Most of his job as head of security had been done before they'd even stuck the first spade in the dirt. He'd deliberately driven all the construction trucks and armoured personnel carriers through the most populated places en route, to demonstrate the fire- and man-power they were taking into the desert. With the tactical capability of the compound an open secret, no one in their right mind would try to engage them – there were far too many softer and more easily accessed targets around.

Inside the control centre a bank of monitors cycled through strategic camera feeds from around the compound. At night the ones on the perimeter switched to heat and infrared frequencies, turning the dust-brown desert a ghostly green. Tariq, one of the locals he'd hired, was sitting in front of them, mesmerized by their unchanging monotony. He didn't look up.

Hyde collapsed in a seat by his desk, and threw the rolled-up copy of *USA Today* next to the bundle of sacking. He considered consigning the paper straight to the trash, but dropped it into a desk drawer instead – just in case. Jogging the mouse to wake his terminal, he loaded his email. The firewalls on the system were so good that he never got spam and the only way a message could drop into his inbox was if someone specifically addressed it to him and sent it from an approved IP. Hardly anyone had this configuration so he almost never got messages. He still found himself checking for emails from Wanda, but she hadn't sent him anything since the divorce papers. There was one message waiting for him, though. It was internal, from Dr Harzan – the big boss of the whole outfit:

We're just back from the desert.
Bring the relic to the ops room the moment you
return.

Hyde sighed and hauled himself to his feet. He didn't mind being ordered around – after sixteen years in the service, he was used to it – but it still irked him that he was being dicked about by a civilian. Grabbing the bundle of sacking, he headed out to the corridor.

When they had first interviewed him for the job he had been told one of his duties would involve ancient artefacts. At the time he hadn't given it much thought. Now he thought about it all the time. He'd figured if you were digging around in the ground, you might come across some old things that might be worth something, but he couldn't for the life of him work out what *buying* a bunch of overpriced archaeological relics on the black market had to do with drilling for oil. He'd asked Dr Harzan about it once. Harzan had told him that he wasn't being paid to think, just to do as he was told and keep quiet. So that's what Hyde did: he kept quiet about the relics; quiet about the compound and quiet about his strong desire to shove a live grenade up Harzan's ass and push him off a cliff.

He reached the operations room – at the cooler end of the corridor – knocked on the door and waited for a response. Even though he was security chief he didn't have a key to this room. The only people allowed inside were Harzan and his two assistants, Blythe and Rothstein, who spent their days out in the empty desert, digging holes in the sand like big, hairy, obnoxious kids and generally causing a massive security head-ache. Why they couldn't stay in the nice safe compound like everybody else was beyond him. Everyone referred to them as the three wise men – though not to their faces, as they didn't have a sense of humour between them. The whole facility was at their disposal, that much had been made crystal clear when he was hired. It was almost like the three wise men and their wild goose chases were more important than the oil they were drilling for. Hyde had peeked at their personnel dossiers once, to try to work out why they were so important. He'd hoped it would shed some light on things, but all it had done was confuse him. He had expected them to be hotshot geologists with long track records of finding oil where no one else had managed it, but all three turned out to be academics with PhDs in things like antiquities, theology and archaeology. He failed to see how any of that was going to scare up the golden goods from the ground. Yet again it seemed he'd bet it all on black, and the ball was going to drop down on red.

The door rattled as it was unlocked and Dr Harzan's bearded face appeared in a crack in the door, the dark rings around his eyes making him look like a panda.

'Bring it in,' he said, opening the door wide enough for Hyde to pass.

He headed on through and stopped by the table in the middle of the room. The other two weren't here but he could still smell them. They both smoked pipes and the odour clung to the air in the room. It was only the second time he'd been in here since the complex had become operational and it had got a lot messier since he'd last seen it. Scrolls of printout paper and seismic charts were piled up everywhere, spilling on to the floor in some places. A topographical map covered one wall, overlaid with a spider's web network of pins, Post-it notes and photographs of the night sky with various constellations marked out in chinagraph pencil lines. On the central table, state-of-the-art laptops sat side by side with old coffee cups and more chunks of stone tablet similar to the one he was carrying. They didn't even let the cleaners in here, that's why it stank worse than a frat boy's locker room.

'Let me see it,' Dr Harzan said.

Hyde handed the bundle over and watched Harzan unwrap it, eyes gleaming like a junkie unwrapping a rock of crack. His face fell when he saw what was inside.

'This is not what was promised,' he said. 'This piece is far too recent to be of interest.' He held it up for Hyde to see, as though he was a slow student who'd just flunked a test. 'It is written in Akkadian not proto-cuneiform and the symbols do not form the Tau.'

'I was sent to buy a relic,' Hyde said, keeping the anger from his voice. 'I bought a relic.'

'Well, you bought the wrong one. This one is no good.' He tossed it on to the table as if it were a paperback and turned away. 'Make yourself useful: one of the drivers was caught stealing petrol and selling it to nomads. He's in the brig. Go and deal with him – that should be more in line with your skill base. And shut the door on your way out.'

Hyde marched across the baking ground towards the tallest of the guard towers that doubled as a stockade, sweat dripping from his reddened face like his blood was boiling inside him. The Ghost had switched rocks on him and made him look like an idiot. He reached the door to the tower and practically kicked his way through it.

'Open it,' he said, nodding at the locked door of the brick cell built into the foundations of the tower. The guard obeyed.

Inside the cell was a twenty-something Iraqi lying on the wooden board that served as a cot.

'Grab his hand and hold it flat against the bed,' Hyde ordered. He didn't want to waste time with this petty thief; he had bigger scores to settle. The guard did what he was told. Hyde pulled his knife from his belt and slammed it between two of the prisoner's fingers. The man whimpered and stared at the knife with widened eyes.

'You stole from the company, yes?'

'No,' said the terrified man, in what could have been a plea or an answer.

'You stole from the company,' Hyde insisted, 'and thieving cannot be tolerated.' In a single swift movement he levered the knife down hard like a guillotine, snicking off the man's little finger with a soft crunch.

The prisoner screamed. Blood leaked from the cut, isolating the severed finger in a spreading crimson lake.

'Steal again and it's your hand,' Hyde said. 'Try to run and it's your life.' He turned to the guard, who looked as shocked as the prisoner. 'Clean him up and send him back to work.' Then he was out in the heat and brightness of the compound, wiping his knife against the leg of his fatigues.

Back in his office he wrenched open his desk drawer and pulled out the copy of *USA Today*. He grabbed his satellite phone from its charging dock and dialled the number written beneath the photographs of the three Citadel survivors. He'd like to do more than just snip a few fingers off the Ghost. He'd like to string him up and torture him slow, like they taught the black ops to do to put fear in the enemy.

The ringtone purred. Nobody picked up.

The Ghost had done it to him again.

26

Al Anbar Province, Western Iraq

Evening was coming, but the heat of the day remained trapped in the fringes of the Syrian Desert. It had been hammered into the rocky ground by the relentless sun and now radiated back up as though the world beneath the crust was molten. It was hard to believe anything could survive out here in this furnace heat and on this lunar landscape, but sparse tufts of grass somehow managed to struggle out of cracks in the earth and buckthorn spread across the gravel in whatever contours offered the tiniest amount of low shade – and the goats ate all of it.

The Ghost had a large network of men at his disposal, other *fedayeen* united in a common desire to protect the land and its people from the casual violence of dictators and invaders. He had spread word along the numerous goat trails that snaked out into the desert to the west of Ramadi, asking if anyone knew of a man who wore the red cap of an English football team. He wasn't hard to track down. He was called Ahmar, the Arabic word for 'Red'.

The Ghost found him crouched by the side of a muddy pool in one of the oases used by the herders, filling a canteen with water, surrounded by his goats. His faded red cap stood out vividly against the jostling backdrop of dusty black and brown wool. He had an AK-47 slung over his back and a Beretta sticking out of a leather belt that tightened the middle of his long white dishdasha.

Ahmar looked up at the sound of approaching hooves, eyes creased against the sun, his face a mass of leathery wrinkles. He could have been anywhere between thirty years old and a hundred.

'Nice gun,' the Ghost said, pointing at the Beretta.

The sound of the ruined voice triggered some recognition in the man and his face shifted into something between suspicion and fear. 'I didn't steal it,' he said, his hand drifting to the gun, more to hide it than use it. 'I traded it.'

The Ghost slipped from his saddle. 'I know,' he said, reaching slowly into his saddlebag. He produced a bundle of red material and unwrapped it, revealing the stone covered with symbols in the shape of the Tau. 'I want to trade too.' Ahmar hardly heard him, so mesmerized was he by the red cloth the stone had been wrapped in.

He reached out to touch the Manchester United football shirt, then stopped, suddenly fearful of what he might be asked to do in exchange for such a magical item. 'What you want to trade?'

'Just information. This stone – where did you find it?'

Ahmar considered the question then smiled broadly, revealing a mouth missing most of the teeth. 'I show you,' he said, kicking a goat out of the way.

He smoothed a wet patch of mud flat with his hand and snatched up a reed from the bank. With the point he made a series of fourteen dots to create the outline of what looked like a snake. Like all Bedouin, the goat herder navigated using the stars. The desert was ever-changing and there were no landmarks to steer by, but the stars remained constant. The Ghost steered by them too and recognized the constellation he had drawn. It was Draco, the watchful dragon, so called because it never set in the Northern hemisphere, but to the Bedouin it was known as the snake. Ahmar pointed at the square of four dots representing the head and traced his finger up along the line of its back until he was pointing at the horizon. 'Follow the snake,' he said. 'Keep to the left of the Billy Goat. Three days' grazing, a day on horseback – that is where I found this stone.'

The Billy Goat was the Bedouin name for Polaris, the North Star. By setting off to the left of it he would be heading north-west, following the sign of the snake deeper into the Syrian Desert. He had enough supplies in his saddlebags for at least a day, three maybe if he rationed himself and spared the horse during the worst of the heat.

Ahmar dropped down to wash the mud from his hand then wiped it dry on his dishdasha and held it out. The Ghost handed over the Manchester United shirt and watched him slip it over his head and rush to the main camp, calling out the names of other herders and holding his arms aloft as though he'd just scored a goal.

The Ghost remounted his horse and turned to the horizon. The sky was darkening to the east and the brightest stars already starting to shine. It would not be long before the western sky darkened too, where Draco lived, pointing the way into the desert, as it had since the beginning of time.

A day's ride – Ahmar had said.

The Ghost kicked his horse and they moved away from the smell of goats and the shade of the oasis.

With the moon's help, he might just make it before dawn.

27

Gaziantep is the larger of the two airports that service the city. Its position to the north places it closer to the Taurus mountains and closer to Ruin, therefore making it the destination of choice for most of the tourist traffic. At least, that was the gist of what the taxi driver had told Liv on their way here. As far as she was concerned, lots of tourists meant lots of flights, and that was all she was interested in.

She managed to buy a one-way last-minute standby ticket to Newark using most of the cash she'd found in the envelope. She used cash because she figured that if she was on some kind of watch-list then a credit-card purchase was more likely to trigger it. The desk clerk had made the booking and taken her money without a flicker of recognition. So far so good. But now she had to go through passport control.

The departure hall was pretty busy, thronged with tourists heading back home after having their souls cleansed. Liv checked out the lines and ended up opting for the longest one, purely because the customs officer at the head of it was grossly fat and looked as though he was about to fall asleep in the trapped, humid heat. She stepped in line and as the queue shuffled forward she watched him going through the motions of checking the passport against every passenger, gravity pulling his doughy face into an expression of perma-boredom. He barely glanced at anyone for longer than a second, so when it was Liv's turn to step forward she was feeling much calmer.

He opened her passport and glanced at the name of the bearer, checking it against the ticket. Then he looked up, his humourless eyes flicking between the photograph and her. Liv swept the baseball cap from her head and stared back, doing her best to maintain a neutral expression. She could feel his scrutiny crawling over her face, like the feelers of some giant insect. He was taking his time. Studying her. He hadn't taken this long on anyone else in line. The blood sang in her ears and she was sweating from a combination of stress and poor air-conditioning. His eyes continued to slide over her face, then dropped down to roam over her body. Ordinarily, Liv would have been outraged by this, but now she felt relief. He wasn't some crack border guard with a hidden agenda and heightened instinct for potential fugitives after all. He was just an ugly, overweight man who liked to stare at girls. So she let him stare, comforting herself with the knowledge that, if asked about her later, he would not remember her face.

After what seemed like several hours he finally snapped her passport shut and placed it on the counter. Liv grabbed it and hurried away, subconsciously fiddling with the top button of her blouse. She joined another line of people shuffling towards the final security check and breathed a little easier. She was nearly home and dry. The queue moved forward, voices pulsed around her, she started to relax. Then a loud crash at the head of the queue set her heart pounding again.

Liv looked up, fearing she would discover the fat customs officer surrounded by security guards and pointing directly at her. Instead she saw a woman dressed in full hijab, her heavily pregnant belly straining against the material of her gown. She had dropped her plastic tray and was scrabbling around on the ground while a man stood over her, shouting down in angry Arabic as she frantically scooped up the spilled items.

Then he hit her, with the back of his hand, as if he was swatting away a fly but deliberate and hard. The woman's head jerked to one side with the force of it, then she just carried on tidying the spilled items as if the blow had been nothing more or less than she was used to.

Liv didn't know whether it was the sudden focusing of attention or the outrage she felt at the man's hostility, but something happened inside her. It was like something giving way deep underground and rushing upwards. She could feel it flowing through her, almost lifting her off her feet as it rose, bringing the whispering with it, filling her head with its sound. It grew louder, roaring through her like steam through rock. Then she heard something else – something solid at the centre.

A word.

KuShiKaam

So stunned was she by this that everything else seemed to slip into slow motion. She watched with detachment as the security guard stepped forward and laid a hand on the arm of the man who had just hit his wife, his face reproving but not angry. The woman on the floor continued to gather the dropped contents and put them back in the tray. In the strangeness of all this, Liv's anger began to slip, the force of the whispering lessened and the word started to drift away. She snapped to attention, jamming her hand into her bag, burrowing through the jumbled contents in her frantic search for a pen. She feared the word would be lost, carried away down to the dark place in her head where her conscious mind seemingly could not follow. She found a pen and wrote feverishly on her hand in the absence of paper. But even as she did this the pen took on a motion of its own and instead of a phonetic approximation of the word she had heard, she inscribed a series of jagged symbols instead, looking like no language she had ever seen.

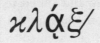

She studied what she had written and it shifted in her mind, first to the sound she had heard:

then to the meaning at its centre:

The Key

Liv looked up. The woman had now gathered her things and passed through the metal detector to join her husband. The security guards waved them through, ushering things back to normal as quickly as they could. They probably saw incidents like this every day, casual acts of domestic violence fuelled by stress and fatigue. Even so, they had stood by and watched a man hit a pregnant woman and done nothing about it. It made Liv sick to think of it, but there was nothing she could do. Starting a fight with a bunch of sexist pigs wasn't going to help keep her profile low. Even so the hissing noise in her head would not go away and she felt a surprising and intense violence towards the man who had struck his wife. She wanted to hurt him and humiliate him in front of everyone. She wanted to kill him even, grab a gun from one of the ineffectual guards and shoot him in the head. The intensity of her hatred surprised her. It seemed to feed into the sound in her head until it whistled like a boiling kettle. Her skin tingled too, pricking all over with pins and needles. It frightened her that she felt this way. It was as if there was something dangerous inside her that she didn't understand and couldn't control. She looked up and discovered people in the line were staring at her. A woman in front said something but she couldn't hear what it was through the noise in her head. She dumped her things in a plastic tray and stared in front of her, avoiding further eye contact as the line moved forward. What the hell was happening to her? She seemed to be losing her mind.

She passed through the metal detector and out into the concourse. It was bad enough she couldn't remember anything, now she was hearing voices too. It annoyed her – Liv Adamsen the razor-sharp reporter, the ultra rationalist, the cynical disbeliever of anything remotely New Agey – that something so 'out there' was now happening to her. She didn't like it and she didn't want it. She was still convinced she'd been drugged in the hospital and all of this was some hideous side effect that would pass as soon as she got some sleep and a couple of gallons of coffee inside her.

She glanced up at the departure board. Her flight was already boarding but she hesitated. Her instinct whenever anything didn't add up was to come at the problem from every angle until she had managed to make sense of it. Right now, her rational mind was telling her that the word she had scrawled on her hand must be something her scrambled mind had dredged up, some language she could verify and explain. She scanned the duty-free shops lining the walls of the terminal building and saw what she needed. It was in the opposite direction to her boarding gate. She hoisted her bag on to her shoulder and headed over. She'd have to be quick.

28

Gabriel glanced at the iPhone, the display bright in the dimness of the bar. He was in the mezzanine of the Sahnesi, the former theatre and opera house built for the European aristocracy who started arriving in Ruin en masse in the eighteenth century after it became a destination on the Grand Tour. These days it was a popular cinema and bar complex, and it had free Wi-Fi, which was the reason Gabriel had come here.

He pressed the browser icon on the screen and tapped HOSPITAL RUIN into the search window. Ajda had bought the phone from a secondhand tech store in the Lost Quarter specializing in all the stuff boosted from tourists. It had been expensive, but it came with a SIM card that could not be traced and gave him all the processing power of a laptop. The search came back with a phone number for the main reception which he dialled.

'Davlat Hastenesi Hospital.'

'Yes, I have some flowers to send to a couple of patients and am trying to find their room numbers.'

'Do you have the names?'

'The first is Mrs Kathryn Mann, the second, Liv Adamsen.'

He heard the tapping of fingers on a keyboard. 'Mrs Mann is being kept in room 410 in the secure psychiatric building. Miss Adamsen is in room 406 of the same building – no, wait a second. Actually Miss Adamsen was discharged today.'

'When?'

'It doesn't say. Only that her room is now vacant.'

'Did she have any visitors?'

There was a pause. 'What has this got to do with delivering flowers?'

'They have already been sent. I'm just checking to see if they got to her before she left.'

More tapping.

'The only thing on the system is a police visit this afternoon.'

'Thank you.'

Gabriel hung up, his mind racing with the implications of this new information. He switched back to the browser and typed RUIN POLICE FORCE into the search window. There was a hot-linked phone number under the first entry. He tapped it and returned the phone to his ear.

'Ruin Police Division.'

'Hello, could you please put me through to Inspector Arkadian in Homicide.'

'Inspector Arkadian is on leave at present.'

'Then could you patch me through to his mobile phone?'

'I'm afraid I can't do that, sir. Is there another member of the Homicide team who could help you?'

'No. I need to speak to Inspector Arkadian specifically. It's extremely urgent.' He cast around for anything that would give him some leverage. 'Tell him Gabriel Mann wants to talk. I escaped from police custody earlier today and I want to give myself up – but I'm only prepared to do it to him, and only if he calls me back within the next five minutes.'

29

The airport bookshop was filled with all the usual things catering for the average bored airline traveller. Liv made her way to a shelf of phrasebooks by the checkout desk and scanned the titles, picking out any with an unusual alphabet. She wanted to prove to herself that the word she had heard in her head was merely an echo of something she must have picked out in amongst the babble of voices. If she could just find out what language it was in then she could board her flight without worrying the whole way home that she was hearing voices and going nuts. By the time she reached the bottom shelf she had eight books in her hand. She opened the first, an Arabic phrasebook, and turned to the K section, looking for the word 'key'. She found it and compared the translation to the symbols on her hand. It wasn't even close. She did the same with the other seven books, working her way through Cyrillic, Greek, Chinese. None of them matched.

Dammit.

She jammed the books back and turned to go then stopped as something caught her eye on the next shelf. It was a book with a picture of a tablet on its cover with faint markings on its surface. They were not the same as the symbols Liv had written on her hand, but they were close. She took it down and opened it, only to discover that it was not a phrasebook – it was a history book. The inside flap provided a second shock. The photograph on the cover was of a five-thousand-year-old Sumerian tablet inscribed with a long-dead language. So she couldn't have overheard it in the departure hall. She flipped through the book in search of pictures of other ancient texts. She was about to give up and dash for the plane when she found something. It was a photograph of a carved stone cylinder with a hole through its centre. Beneath it was a broad strip of wet clay the cylinder had been rolled across, leaving a square of text behind made up of lines and triangles.

They looked exactly like the symbols on Liv's hand.

The caption identified it as a cylinder seal, an ancient method of reproducing messages. By inserting a rod or stick through the centre it could be rolled over wet earth or clay to reveal the writing inscribed on its surface. Often these were spells, laid on the edges of fields to bring forth bounty. The message on this particular seal, however, was unknown. It was written in a form of script known archaeologically as 'proto-cuneiform' or more poetically as 'the lost language of the gods' because of its great age and because its meaning had been forgotten in time.

Great, Liv thought, *now I'm hearing voices in a language that hasn't been spoken in nearly six thousand years; so much for putting my mind at rest.*

A tannoy announcement cut through the muzak calling for last passengers for Cyprus Turkish Airline flight TK 7121 to Newark.

She was out of time. She ran to the checkout, pulling the last of her Turkish lira from her pocket to pay for the book. She'd read it on the plane – always assuming she would still make it.

30

Brother Gardener threw another broken branch on to the fire and picked up the last, hoping this one might reveal something the others had not.

Following the earlier meeting he had organized a team of gardeners to scour the grounds and collect all fallen branches and leaves while there was still some light left in the day to see by. He knew from bitter experience that the only way to stop the spread of blight was to act fast and burn it out.

As each diseased branch was brought to him he had carefully dismantled it, like a pathologist examining a corpse, looking for clues that might reveal the cause of the contagion. He had found nothing. There was no fungus residue, no burrowing insects or weevils nor any of the other parasites that plagued a garden and spread disease such as this. He had never seen anything like it before. It seemed more like a dry rot than anything else, but he had never known it take hold so quickly in living wood. It was as if the life had just left it – the sap turned to poison, the wood to dry pulp.

He stamped on the last branch, poked through the dry splinters then added it to the pyre and stood staring into the flames. If anyone had asked, he would have explained away the tears in his eyes as smoke, but the truth was he loved the garden better than any person. He had tended it, nursed it and nourished it for over forty years, until his own name had been forgotten and he had become simply Brother Gardener.

And now it was dying, and he had no idea how he could stop it.

When dawn came the men would return and the surgery would begin. They would have to cut deep to make sure the disease could not spread. It was necessary, but no less painful for it. He imagined himself as a father on the eve of an operation where his child's limb would be sacrificed to spare its life. But his children were many, and there were no guarantees that any would survive.

So he stood in the dark, with smoke in his eyes, catching a strange whiff of oranges every now and again like a taunting memory of the orchard when it was bursting with health. He watched the fire until the bell rang in the mountain calling everyone inside for Vespers. It was the moment when the Citadel went to sleep for the night, a night he wished would never end, for he feared what the new dawn would bring.

31

Arkadian had just stepped through the front door when his mobile phone rang inside his jacket pocket.

'Do not answer that,' his wife hollered from the kitchen.

'Smells great,' he called back. 'What is it, Tocana?'

'I made it specially for my poor invalid husband to build up his strength, so if you want to eat any of it I suggest you switch off that phone and start acting ill.'

He took the phone from his pocket and peered at the caller display. 'It's work.'

'It's always work.'

'Arkadian,' he said, trapping the phone under his chin and shrugging stiffly out of his jacket to try to speed things up as much as he could.

'I have Gabriel Mann on the line,' the operator said. 'He insists on speaking to you. He says he wants to turn himself in.'

Arkadian snapped to attention, grabbing the phone and letting his jacket slide to the floor.

'OK, run a trace on the call and have a squad car on standby in case we manage to pin him down.'

'Already done, sir. Shall I put him through now?'

'Yes.' The line clicked and his ear flooded with the background sounds of a busy environment. Somewhere public, a bar probably. 'This is Arkadian,' he said. 'How can I help?'

'Sorry to ruin your evening.'

Arkadian glanced up at the empty kitchen doorway and heard angry stirring coming from beyond. 'Don't mention it. Where are you?'

'Somewhere much safer than jail. Listen, I need to ask you something. Have you been to visit Liv or my mother?'

'Yes.'

'When?'

'This afternoon.'

'And while you were there, did you talk to Liv?'

'Yes.'

'Did she say anything about leaving?'

Arkadian frowned. 'No. She's not going anywhere. They're keeping her in for observation.'

He heard a weary sigh on the end of the line. 'She's gone,' Gabriel said. 'She left shortly after your visit.'

'She can't have done. I'd have heard about it.'

'Why? She wasn't under arrest, and you're on leave.'

Arkadian flashed back through his visit. He remembered how small and vulnerable she'd looked in the bed as he got up to go. Then he realized something. 'I returned her bag to her,' he said. 'Forensics had finished with it, so I used it as an excuse to go and see how she was. It had her passport in it.'

'How quickly can you get hold of passenger lists from the airport?'

'I'd need a warrant.'

'Oh, come on, we need information, not a robust chain of evidence. Can't you pull some favours?'

'If she wants to leave the country, that's up to—'

'She left the country because she's in danger. I broke out of jail for the same reason. I was set up. There was someone waiting for me in a cell. I can give you a description, but I bet he's not there now and I doubt he'll show up on the roll call. The guard took me right to him. It was an inside job. The Citadel's woken up. It's making a move to silence us, which means Liv's in danger and so's my mother, just like before.'

Arkadian felt a twinge in his arm as he remembered the last time Gabriel had issued such a warning. He had been right then, and Arkadian had the bullet wound to prove it.

'It's up to you,' Gabriel said. 'Do what you think's best. I'll call you back in ten minutes.'

The sound of the bar cut off and Arkadian listened to dead air for a few seconds. From the kitchen he heard the sizzle of something juicy hitting a hot pan, then the phone clicked and he was automatically patched through to the tech guys. 'Any luck?'

'Not a chance. He was using an Internet phone. Very hard to trace, impossible to pin down quickly.'

'He's going to call back in ten minutes, might that help?'

'Not really. He could use a different phone, a different server, a different IP. Even if he used exactly the same setup, you'd have to keep him talking for a couple of hours to give us even a fighting chance. Internet calls can be routed anywhere in the world.'

'OK. Do it anyway.' He hung up and stared down at his jacket lying crumpled and abandoned on the floor, a symbol of the nice evening he'd had planned. He thought of Liv and the way she had watched the priest during their meeting. He'd sensed her fear – and now he knew why.

He opened the contacts on his phone and scrolled down looking for the name Yun Haldin. Yun was an ex-partner of his from way back who had quit the force to start his own firm. He now employed a large number of former cops and had contracts to run perimeter security at both local airports.

'You finished, or you going to go hungry?' his wife called from the kitchen, where the sweet-and-sour aroma of garlicky stew floated out.

Arkadian's stomach growled loudly in answer to his wife's question.

He found Yun's number and pressed the call button.

32

Gabriel exited the Skype application and Googled a travel comparison site. He entered details for flights from Ruin-Gaziantep (any) to New York (any) then looked around at the evening crowd as he waited for the information to load. He was sitting at a large table next to a group of tourists with his body angled to give the impression he was with them.

He swept his eyes across the room, looking for anything or anyone out of the ordinary. There were so many people tapping away on phones it was no wonder the Internet was slow in here. His eyes lit upon a TV screen in the corner of the bar broadcasting CNN with the sound muted. On screen a reporter was standing outside Ruin police headquarters. The picture cut and he found himself staring straight at his own mugshot.

He rose quickly from the table, scrutinizing his phone as an excuse to keep his head down as he moved towards the exit. Hardly anyone in the bar was watching the TV, but they could easily be getting the same news and photo on their phones. He'd make the morning papers for sure, perhaps the evening editions of the local ones. He had hoped for a little more time.

He stepped out of the main door on to the rain-glossed street and pulled a baseball cap from his pocket, jamming it on to his head and pulling the brim down low over his eyes while the flight comparison page finished loading.

There were plenty of flights from both airports. Too many. There would be no point in heading out to try to intercept Liv on the off chance he might pick the right one. He needed

Arkadian and his contacts, but it was too soon to call him back.

He started to move away down the street and opened another app that located free Wi-Fi spots. The reception was even slower now he had left the building's Internet footprint and it took a while for a map to appear on the screen. A blue dot pulsed at the centre showing his own location, then other icons started popping up around it. There was a hotspot in the direction he was heading, about two streets away, close to the hospital. He slipped the phone in his pocket and increased his pace. He wanted to be in position when the time came to call Arkadian. He also wanted to be nearer his mother. He knew it was the first place the authorities would look for him, which was why he had stayed away, but until he could figure out a way to ensure her safety he'd feel better being close – just in case anything happened.

33

It took Arkadian seven of the ten minutes he'd been given to get hold of his old partner and tell him what he needed. The rest was easy – too easy.

'She's on Cyprus Turkish Airline TK 7121 to Newark,' Yun said.

'What time's takeoff?'

'Five minutes ago.'

Arkadian felt oddly relieved. Maybe it was for the best. Liv had wanted to go home after all. 'Thanks anyway,' he said.

'No problem. The information was right there on the system the moment I accessed the database.'

Arkadian frowned. 'Why would that be?'

'Could be coincidence. More likely someone else had already put in the request.'

Arkadian's mind lit up with the implications. 'Is there any way you can find out who called up the information first?'

'Sure, hold on.' He heard the clatter of a keyboard and the background noise of planes. He wondered if one of them was Liv's. 'It's just showing a guest user ID,' Yun said. 'It came through on the blue channel though.'

'What's that?'

'The pre-authorized account for the Ruin Police Department. It would have come from one of the dedicated data terminals in your records office. Someone there will be able to tell you who asked for the info.'

It was an inside job.

The phone started beeping in his ear. 'Listen, Yun, I've got another call coming in. I owe you for this.'

'Just come work for me when you've finally had enough of the hours and the grief.'

'I'll do that.' He ended the call and returned the phone to his ear. 'Gabriel?'

'Any luck?'

'Yes and no.'

'Meaning?'

'You were right, and we have a big problem.'

34

Flight TK 7121

The thrust of the engines pressed Liv into her seat and made the raindrops slip from the window as the plane picked up speed. Beyond the lights of the airport she could see the broken peaks of the Taurus mountains rising up against an inky sky. She watched them until the cabin tilted backwards and the wheels lifted off the tarmac with a *bump*. At the same moment she felt a tightening in her stomach, as though something inside her was connected to the ground and was now being pulled unbearably tight as the plane accelerated away from it. She gasped at the sensation, doubling over and struggling to breathe. She was aware of the passenger next to her leaning forward, his face clouded with concern. The tightening increased until she felt that it might pull her through the floor of the plane; then something seemed to snap and she gulped air. A wave of nausea followed, along with the same intense pins-and-needles feeling over her entire body she had felt in the departure hall. The mild G-forces of the climbing plane didn't help. She turned and forced a smile for the person next to her, muttering something about nerves then closed her eyes and breathed deeply and slowly. She was really getting tired of all this. It was as if someone had a voodoo doll of her and was randomly sticking pins in it.

The plane started to bank and the delicate feelings inside her rolled with the movement. She continued to breathe until the sick feeling melted away and she felt safe enough to open her eyes again.

Outside she could see the stars beginning to prick the darkening sky and below them, shining like a bright stain, the lights of Ruin, nestling in the foothills of the mountain. She imagined each light as a person and one of them was Gabriel.

If you get the chance, then go, he had said, *as far from the Citadel as you can. Keep yourself safe – until I find you.*

Once she'd returned to Newark, got her head straight and her memory back, she would call him; then they could talk. She had so many questions, about what had happened in the Citadel, but also about him. She hardly knew him and yet, in the midst of all the darkness and strangeness of the past few weeks, it was to him that her mind had constantly returned. He shone through it all, like the lights she now looked down upon.

The plane shuddered slightly as the higher winds caught it and below her those same lights started to disappear, winking out one by one, as though the city was being switched off a block at a time.

She turned on her reading light. It made the dark symbols on her hand stand out against her pale flesh, mocking her again with their mystery. She pulled the book from the seat pocket in front of her and looked at the cover. It was called *The Mystery of Lost Languages*. Maybe she would find some answers in here.

Eight rows back a large man in a business suit sat jammed in an economy seat built for someone half his size. His eyes were fixed on Liv's blonde hair, glowing in the gloom of the cabin. She was looking down at something, reading. He wondered what it was. He liked books. They were full of words, and words were a kind of magic to him. It was how he had got his nickname during his first spell in prison: Dick, short for Dictionary. Sometimes people tried to make fun of his name, as if it meant something dirty, but not for long. He could tell which people said it properly and those who were calling him something else – a prick, a cock, a penis. That was the problem with language. It had such power, but it was slippery. You had to focus on the words and use them correctly to convey what you wanted. That's why he liked strong words. Pure words. Words that only had one meaning. The word he was currently savouring was one of these:

Ser-en-dip-ity

When the jailhouse hit had gone wrong, he'd been told his mission was over. Not his fault, just one of those things. He was too recognizable and the witness had got away. So he had been reassigned.

He'd gone to his hotel room, picked up his stuff and put on the baggy business suit that covered up all his tattoos and was specifically tailored to disguise his shape. Then he'd neatly combed his hair and headed off to the airport looking like any other nondescript, out-of-shape businessman on his way to who knows where. But God had known. He had made all this happen so that Dick ended up in exactly the right place at the right time. The perfect solution had presented itself, as if by accident.

Ser-en-dip-ity

If everything had gone to plan in the cell block he wouldn't have been at the airport and the girl would have got away. And she was the most important of the three targets. The girl was the most dangerous to the Church and needed to be silenced. And silence was the greatest power anyone could have over another person, the ability to take away their words. He'd learned that in prison. Whenever they had wanted to punish him, they had taken his books. But they could never take away the words in his head. Not unless they killed him. And he had such words inside him, the best words. They had been given to him by Isaiah – the name of a prophet and also of the old trustee who had wheeled the library cart round the corridors of E Wing.

'You like words,' he'd said one time as he'd shuffled past his cell. 'Well, take a look at this. All the words you'll ever need.'

Dick had never read the Bible before. It had never occurred to him. But he'd read it now, hundreds of times, until the words flowed through him like the blood in his veins. He had even scratched some of the more powerful ones on to his own skin, so he was like a book himself, anointed with spells to ward off evil when he was asleep and his tongue was still.

Deu-ter-on-om-y

Re-ve-la-tion

Ne-pha-lim

That's what he was – a Nephalim – one of the giants of legend, mentioned in Genesis. A creature of God. A watcher.

He was watching now in the dimness of the cabin, as the armrests dug into his legs and his knees rubbed against the seat in front. Once the girl was home, she would feel safe; and that was when he would strike.

That was when he would take away her words and silence her for ever.

35

Gabriel sprinted headlong down the street towards the hospital. The moment Arkadian had told him the passenger manifest had already been searched he knew. The Church's dark forces were making a coordinated move to tidy up their loose ends: first him, then Liv – next his mother.

He concentrated on the rhythm of his feet pounding the tarmac, driving him closer, step by step. He reached a corner and turned into Asklepios Street. Running through the streets like this wasn't the safest thing to do now his picture had appeared on the news, but he had to balance caution with haste. He reached a turning a third of the way down and rounded it, keeping tight to the houses. Ahead of him the street ended at a junction where the new extension block of the hospital rose up, shining with rain and reflected light. He scanned the upper windows, slowing as he neared the junction, wary of breaking cover into a main road that might have police patrols stationed on it. He stopped a few metres short and looked up from the safety of the shadows.

The main hospital building stretched along the full length of the street. At one end it joined the stone walls of the original building and at the other a covered walkway connected it to a smaller stone building that resembled a castle. This was the old psychiatric wing where the receptionist had said his mother was being kept.

A car swished past and he used the hiss of its tyres to mask his own splashing steps as he dashed to the other side of the street. The ground-floor windows were all boarded up along with a large doorway that had once served as the entrance. High up on the side of the building a scaffold platform jutted out. It was the sort of thing workmen used to hoist materials on to, but there were no ropes hanging down that might help him gain access, they were all curled up and secured to the scaffold poles. The windows to the side of the platform were mostly dark – but not all. Two glowed with light – one in the middle of the row and another at the very end – both on the fourth floor. The hospital receptionist had said his mother was being kept in room 410. His money was on the middle window. He continued to gulp air, relaxing slightly now he had at least located his mother.

Then he felt the vibration.

At first he thought it was thunder, rolling down from the clouds, but when the ground started to shake and a sound like trains in a subway rumbled up from beneath his feet, he realized what it was.

He stepped away from the nearest building, his legs unsteady on the quivering ground as the earthquake took hold of the city. He stopped in the middle of the road, away from any falling debris, his legs planted apart, and looked back up at the fourth-floor window. The shaking increased and the rumbling was joined by the high-pitched wail of hundreds of car and burglar alarms as the quake triggered them. Then, just as the noise and the tremors reached their peak, all the lights in the city went out.

Inside the hospital the sudden darkness was followed by frightened screams that echoed down the corridor from the main building.

Ulvi had managed to jam himself in a doorway and was hanging on to the edge of a wall that was trying to shake itself free from his grasp. There was a crash from way down the hallway as something heavy fell over in one of the partially renovated wards. Outside, car alarms shrieked through the streets like a beast on the loose. To Ulvi it was the sound of opportunity.

Once the earthquake ended, everyone would be busy and disorientated. No one would come running if an emergency alarm suddenly sounded all the way over here. And accidents happened all the time during quakes – falling masonry, broken glass, electricity sparking from severed cables. It was perfect. He just needed to get rid of the cop. He held on until the building finally shook itself still. The distant screaming seemed louder in the sudden quiet and it had been joined by the wail of alarms from various pieces of medical equipment throughout the building.

Ahead of him Ulvi saw the figure of the cop let go of a doorframe and step into the dust-filled corridor. He was looking towards a soft glow of light at the end of the corridor where most of the noise was coming from. The emergency power was clearly working in the main building, but the corridor remained dark.

'You think we should check out the lights?' Ulvi said, moving up the corridor towards the light. 'Someone must be able to get the power back on for us.'

'No,' the cop stepped ahead of him. 'You stay here and check the rooms. Make sure no one's hurt.'

Ulvi stopped and watched the cop march forward and disappear round the corner. He smiled. He had never seen him go into the room that contained the monk and had gambled on this small observation to give him his chance. If the cop had avoided it in daylight there was no way he would want to go in now in pitch darkness. Ulvi's offer to go and check what was happening with the lights had been calculated to make the cop volunteer instead. And he had, so now Ulvi was alone. He took the room keys from his pocket and used the light from his mobile phone to find the one with 410 stamped on it.

Ladies first, he thought, then moved through the darkness towards Kathryn Mann's door.

36

Gabriel stared up at the hospital building, listening to the sounds of distressed patients mingling with the thousand other fractured noises rising from the stunned city.

The main wing was illuminated from within by the dim orange glow of emergency lights, but the satellite buildings were dark. He fixed his eye on the square of black window that he believed was his mother's room, willing her to come to it so he could see she was OK. Behind him a car turned into the street, its headlights on full. Gabriel sank further into the shadows, his eyes still fixed on the dark window on the fourth floor. The car drew closer and swept round the corner, washing light across the darkened building ahead. In that moment Gabriel saw someone standing in the window on the fourth floor. It was too dark to see much but he had seen the white slash of a priest's collar and that was enough to set his own alarm ringing. He could have been there to check on the patients. The room might not even be his mother's. But he wasn't going to take the chance. The Citadel had tried to silence him earlier and he knew they were hunting Liv.

He leaped forward and sprinted across the rubble-strewn road towards the underground car park, all thoughts of caution and personal safety gone from his mind. He had to get to his mother, fast.

The barrier flashed past as he powered down the ramp, his way ahead illuminated by the fitful flash of hazard lights from all the cars parked there. He crashed through the doors to the stairs and launched himself up the first flight three at a time, grabbing the rail to slingshot himself round the curve. Already his legs felt tired. The sprint to the hospital had burned up most of his energy and he was running on fumes and fear. In his mind he pictured the scene that might be unfolding in his mother's room: the priest, turning away from the window, making his way over to the bed. The hospital was in chaos. She would be easy to subdue. No one would hear. The priest could take his time if he chose to, if that was why he was there.

Gabriel reached the ground floor and heaved himself up, using his arms to drag himself along the banister. His legs were burning, his breath ragged. It had taken him about ten seconds to make it up the first flight, but he was already slowing. Four more flights and then a dash across the connecting bridge and into the dark of the old psyche ward. His mother was a minute away at best.

One minute. Probably a little more.

Much too long.

37

Kathryn Mann watched the priest from the fragile fort of her bed as though he was a bear walking across her room. He was talking to her but her hearing was too damaged and the high-pitched whine of fear too loud in her head for her to make out what he was saying. His face was fixed in a kindly expression that didn't quite reach his eyes. He might be saying things to calm her after the quake, making sure she was all right – but she felt terrified.

She doubted she would have the strength to fight him or get away if it came to that. He looked so solid and strong and the quake had shaken her up, knocking her already fragile equilibrium. She felt weak and sick. The room was swimming, he was shifting in and out of focus as he moved closer to the bed. She felt a jolt as he shoved the bed back against the wall from where it had been shaken. Then he came round the side, still talking. He leaned forward, reaching for something behind her head and she caught snatches of what he was saying:

'. . . Don't worry. Soon be over . . .'

The room shifted as he slid a pillow from behind her head.

Her head lolled to one side and her gaze settled on the door. She was too weak to fight, or run, or even shout for help. She thought of Gabriel, and the pain of never seeing him again. She hoped he would come and find the diary, even if he was too late to save her. Her beautiful boy, so like his father.

Then, as if summoned by her need to see him once more – the door began to open.

* * *

Ulvi did not notice at first. He was focusing on the woman's neck, deciding whether to smother her or just break it for speed.

'Everything OK in here?'

He looked over and saw the cop.

Ulvi felt a surge of hatred. He had figured the idiot would be out of the way at least until the lights came on, but the damn irritating fool clearly wasn't even up to sorting out that simple task.

'All fine,' he said, adjusting the pillow that had almost become a murder weapon.

The cop regarded him from the doorway, his scrutiny switching between the woman and him. 'You checked on the monk?'

Ulvi's hatred continued to simmer. 'No, not yet.'

The cop nodded slowly as if the answer had revealed something. 'Well then, maybe you should.'

Ulvi felt such a desire to slit the man's throat it was almost unbearable, but in this room at least the policeman edged it on jurisdiction. The woman was under arrest and was therefore technically his charge. So he swallowed all the violent feelings he was experiencing and made his way out of the room without another word.

Outside, the corridor was still dark and he had to feel his way along the wall to where the monk's room lay. He reached it and looked back. The cop was there, watching him. He could see his outline against the distant glow of light coming from the main building. Why had he picked tonight to turn into a proper policeman?

No matter.

The monk needed dealing with too. He would kill him quickly then go back and finish what he had started. And if the cop was there, then he would have to die too. With the girl gone, Ulvi had a spare bead in his pocket.

38

The fear that had flooded Kathryn when the priest had been in her room was now curdling inside her.

'You OK?' the cop asked, stepping in from the corridor and closing the door behind him.

She nodded, forcing a smile that was lost in the darkness.

With the meagre light from the corridor now absent, the room was almost black. Since her hearing had suffered in the blast Kathryn had noticed how her other senses had expanded to fill the gap. She could smell the cop as his movement across the room displaced the air: coffee and fabric conditioner and some kind of disinfectant that had probably leached into the fabric of his uniform from sitting too long out there in the scrubbed corridor.

He appeared by the window, a silhouette against the night sky. A sliver of moon had risen over the rooftops, reminding her of the secret she carried. She felt the weight of it – as her father must have, carrying it alone for all those years. She sensed the air shift again as the cop stepped away from the window and came closer to her bed, bringing the smell of disinfectant with him.

'I'm not sure about that priest,' the cop said, almost to himself. 'That's why I came back – to make sure.'

A hand flew out of the darkness and clamped over Kathryn's mouth and nose, cutting off her breathing and preventing her from making any sound. He was wearing surgical gloves – the source of the antiseptic smell.

She tried to twist away, but he was already on her, straddling her body and pinning her to the mattress with his knees. She tried thrashing her head from side to side, hoping to dislodge his hand so she might scream, but the latex glove gripped her skin and held it fast.

He brought his face closer to hers.

'Shhhh,' he said, 'quiet now.'

He yanked her head sideways to expose her neck and she felt something sharp and cold on it. In a panic she threw every ounce of energy she had into arching her back and bucking against the hard hospital mattress, jolting him forward and making his hand slip from her mouth. She shrieked for half a second before the hand clamped down harder and the cop shifted position, grinding his whole weight painfully on to her arms to stop any further movement.

Her head was snapped round again, more violently this time, and she felt the pressure return, biting into her flesh. She had a sudden image of a vampire, feeding on her in the dark and she realized with certainty that she was going to die.

Kathryn thought of the secret she held in her head and wondered what would become of it. The cop – if he was a cop – would know the room would become a crime scene and anything in it would be scrutinized as evidence. The latex gloves showed he was being careful. If he found the book hidden in the bed, then she doubted anyone would ever discover its contents. Everything they had done, all the thousands of years of waiting for the prophecy to come to pass, would be for nothing.

Tears leaked out of her eyes at the injustice of it all. She cursed herself for being too weak to fight back, but destiny had always been stacked against them from the start. She regretted leaving Gabriel, but her father would be there on the other side, and so would John. She would see her husband again. She began to relax into her fate as she felt coldness spread through her neck as if death was already seeping into her.

Then the door to her room flew open and Gabriel surged through the darkness towards her.

39

Gabriel sprang at the shape on the bed, hitting it full on and driving it into the wall. The man was big and solid and undoubtedly armed, but Gabriel had landed on top, giving him the slightest of advantages.

He grabbed the man's right hand – the one most likely to be holding a weapon – and smashed his elbow hard into the wrist, shocking the tendons into release. There was a grunt of pain and something clattered away in the dark, too light to be a gun. Gabriel yanked the hand away and caught a glimpse of the man beneath him – not the priest but a cop. He grabbed for his holster, but the cop had got there first. His gun was already halfway out and angling up. Gabriel grabbed it and lunged forward with his head. He felt a wet crunch as the thick bone of his forehead connected with the soft cartilage of the cop's nose. His grip on the gun tightened reflexively in response to the pain – but there was no shot. Whatever make it was, the gun came with a safety catch, and it was still on.

Gabriel wrenched it more violently now he knew it wasn't going to fire, jerking it upwards in a series of sharp tugs to twist it away from the cop's grip. He drove his head forward again, drawing a fresh grunt of pain and feeling wetness on his forehead where blood was flowing from the first blow. With a final violent tug, the cop's finger snapped and Gabriel pulled the gun from his hand.

The cop cried out in pain and thrashed against the floor in panic, knocking Gabriel forward so his head hit the wall, dazing him slightly while the cop continued to buck beneath him in an attempt to get free. Gabriel had the gun now but was holding it by the barrel. Things were moving too fast to shift it into a firing position so he lashed out instead, using it like a hammer. His first blow glanced off the cop's head. Then a fist crashed into his side, bruising his kidneys and knocking the wind from him. He drew his arm back again but the cop kicked out and got lucky. He connected with Gabriel's arm and the gun went clattering away into the darkness.

Now neither of them had it.

The cop seized the opportunity and scrambled to his feet, vaulting over the bed and out of the room. Gabriel rolled after him, pausing by the door and ducking his head outside to scope the corridor, keeping it low in case the cop had a second gun. He needn't have worried. The cop's only intention was to get away. Gabriel saw him disappear round the corner leading back to the main building. He considered giving chase, but his legs were too tired from the sprint up the stairs and there was something more serious bothering him.

He pulled his phone from his pocket and used the light to locate the gun. It was a Beretta PX4 – not exactly standard police issue. He picked it up, checked the safety and slipped it into his waistband. Then he turned to the still figure of his mother on the bed. The thing that had been troubling him was her silence. She hadn't moved or said anything since he had flown across the room and knocked away her attacker.

'Hey,' he said, leaning in close. 'You OK?'

He shone the light of his phone into her face. She looked deathly pale, but her eyes were open. 'Gabriel,' she said, smiling up at him. 'I knew you would come.'

He took her hand and held it in his. Her eyes seemed to look straight through him.

He noticed something on her neck and moved the light over for a closer look. Blood leaked from a small, ragged puncture wound. Too small to be from a knife. The jagged edge suggested that whatever had made it had been torn free when he knocked the cop to the floor. He swept the light over the room and saw the syringe sticking out from under the bed, the plunger pushed most of the way in. He picked it up, sniffed it. There was no odour. The liquid inside was clear. It could be anything, anything that would render an adult instantly immobile.

He looked into his mother's face holding up the syringe. 'He injected you with something. I need to get a doctor. Find out what it is. See what they can do to flush it out. You just hang tight, OK?' He made a move to leave but Kathryn gripped his hand. 'Stay,' she said. 'It's too late. You'll never find anyone in time. I can already feel it working.'

Raw anger boiled inside him. He knew she was right. Even if he managed to find a doctor, the chances of persuading him to run an emergency tox test in time to administer an antidote were slender. But he refused to give in. There had to be a way. He was standing in a hospital and somewhere in this building there was something or someone that might save his mother's life. Then he realized exactly what it was.

He thrust the gun into her hand. 'If the cop, or the priest, or anyone else comes back to do you harm, then use this. I'll be right back. I promise.'

Then he kissed her on the forehead and darted from the room.

40

Gabriel knew that every mission relied on two things: objective and solution.

The first part he had already worked out. He needed to know what poison was coursing through his mother's veins and the only person who could tell him was the cop. The second part of the problem was finding him.

Casting ahead, Gabriel tried to anticipate the cop's next move so he could get there quicker. He would avoid the more populated areas so no one saw him, but he would also want to get out of the building as fast as possible before the main power came back on. The lifts were out, which left the stairs, and the first flight he would come across were the ones Gabriel had used, leading down to the underground car park – the perfect place for an ambush. If he could get there first.

He moved down the corridor and ducked through a door into a deserted ward room. Inside, the floor was littered with workmen's tools and materials, scattered by the earthquake. He spotted a pair of heavy-duty gloves amongst the mess and picked them up as he made his way to the window. It was sealed by a single piece of board that split with a single, sharp kick.

The cold night air hit him as he stepped on to the scaffold platform he had seen from the street. The whole thing rattled as if the earthquake had shaken it loose from the building. But now was not the time for caution.

He unhooked one of the lengths of coiled rope from the scaffold and dropped it over the edge of the platform. It was too dark to see but he heard it patter on the pavement, four storeys down. The other end fed through a pulley and was secured to the platform. Gabriel leaned back on the rope to test it then stepped over it, feeding it round his right leg, over his back and round his left arm.

Part of his special forces training had included hours of abseiling – down buildings, from helicopters, off bridges. Usually this was done with a full kit of harnesses and descenders, but he had also done it with just a rope, using his bodyweight as the brake. It wasn't comfortable but it was effective, and right now it was all he had. He jammed the gloves on to his hands, leaned back to create tension, and stepped off the platform.

The rope creaked and stretched as he started to descend. It was rough nylon cord, perfect for hauling up buckets of cement but not so great when it was digging into your flesh. With the correct gear he could rappel down four floors of a building in seconds, but if he tried that now he would take the skin off his hands, gloves or no gloves.

Gabriel turned his mind back to the cop, trying to gauge where he would be. Probably at ground level by now. He continued his careful descent, feeding the rope round his body as quickly as he dared until he sensed the pavement was near. He let go of the rope and dropped the last couple of metres, landing in a controlled crouch. He shook himself free, flicking the end of the rope out to see how much he had to play with.

Moving quickly to the ramp leading to the car park, he threw one end of the rope round the upright of the barrier-lifting mechanism and caught it with his free hand. He pulled it back across the space between the barrier and the wall, laying both lengths of rope flat to the ground and squatting by the outside wall where he couldn't be seen from the car park. The whole thing had taken only a few seconds.

Now he just had to wait.

All around were the sounds of a city in distress: distant

screams, raised voices, sirens of all kinds. He tried to zone it out and tune his hearing to the one specific thing he was seeking – the sound of someone running.

He wrapped both lengths of rope tight round his forearms to improve his grip.

Time stretched out. He thought of his mother lying alone in the dark, the poison spreading through her with every passing second. Leaving had been the only way to save her. He hoped to God he had made the right choice.

There was the crash of a door bursting open in the darkness of the car park and the hollow sound of boots pounding the concrete floor and heading his way.

Gabriel tensed. He replayed his own journey so he could judge the best moment to strike. He could picture the cop, his pace slowing slightly as he hit the upward slope of the ramp. He imagined his stride length. Gauged the number of steps it would take to reach the top.

Three.

Two.

One.

He yanked the rope upwards as a figure flashed into view. The cop's legs hit the rope and he tipped forward, hitting the ground hard, his arms shooting forward just in time to stop his face from breaking his fall.

Gabriel was already on him.

He jumped on to the cop's back, knees first, knocking the wind from him. Grabbing a handful of hair, Gabriel cracked his head down hard on the flagstones – too hard maybe – and had to stop himself from doing it again. Rage burned inside him now for what he had done to his mother, but he knew that killing the cop would be no kind of revenge: first he needed answers.

He shifted position and drove his knee into the small of the cop's back, grinding it against his spine until his hands reached back to stop him. Looping the rope round them,

Gabriel pulled it tight then reached into his pocket and brought his mouth close to the cop's ear.

'You forgot something,' he said, holding the syringe in front of his face so the cop could see it. 'You want to live?' He jabbed the needle into the cop's neck, making sure it hurt, and pushed the plunger all the way in. 'Tell me what this is and I'll get you the antidote.'

The cop went limp, the fight gone from him. Gabriel hauled him on to his back.

'Tell me what it is.'

The cop stared up at him, his face a mask of confusion and fear. 'Aconitine,' he said. 'One-way ticket. I hope you said goodbye to your mother.'

Gabriel wanted to beat the cop's head against the pavement until the brains spilled out, but it would be a waste of what little time he had left. His eyes swam as he looked up at the dark window on the fourth floor. He wanted to go back and sit with his mother, hold her hand, make sure she wasn't alone. He knew he should get away now before the lights came back on and someone found the cop. That would be the smart thing to do. That was what his brain was telling him. Instead he got up and ran back down the slope into the underground car park, heading for the stairs.

He couldn't remember exactly how he made it up the five flights to his mother's room. His legs were dead from the first run and his energy spent after the fight. He could feel the adrenalin curdling inside him, making him feel shaky and sick, but he kept reminding himself of the last thing he had said to his mother.

I'll be right back. I promise.

Kathryn raised the gun as he stepped into the room, angling it up from where it lay on the bed, her arm too weak to lift it.

'It's me,' Gabriel said, stepping towards her.

He took the gun and held her hand, struggling to find words

to tell her that there was nothing he could do, that he had failed. In the end he said nothing; he could see in her face that she already knew.

'Under the mattress,' she whispered. 'There's a book.' Gabriel slid his hand underneath and found it. 'It will show you the way. Your grandfather gave it to me in death; now, in death, I give it to you. You will know what it means. It's in your hands now. All of it is in your hands.' She took a deep breath that scraped in her throat, like a rope was tightening around it. 'Don't let them find you here. Take this knowledge and go – use it against them. Let that be your vengeance.'

Another breath howled through her throat like a dry wind, then flowed back out again, long and deep. She stared into his face.

'John,' she said, her face lighting up with joy, 'you came back. You came back for me.'

Gabriel swallowed his emotion at the mention of his dead father's name. 'Yes,' he said, going along with her hallucination, 'I came back for you.'

'I missed you, John,' Kathryn said, her eyes losing focus and her voice doing the same. 'I always wondered why you never said goodbye.'

Gabriel tried to think of something to say, but realized he was too late. Kathryn's eyes were still open but she could see nothing. He reached out with a nervous hand and pressed it into the still warm flesh of her neck.

There was no pulse. She was gone.

He felt a storm of anger rise up inside him again. The air flickered fitfully around him as if it was the raw power of his rage that was lighting up the night. The emergency lights had come back on again. In the golden glow of the low-wattage lighting his mother looked serene and beautiful, her dark hair framing her pale face, her skin smooth and unworried. The pain she had carried since his father's death had gone now. Gabriel leaned down and kissed her, tears dripping from his eyes and on to her cheek. He reached out and rubbed them away with his thumb.

Sounds drifted down the corridor. He took one last look at his mother then turned and left the room, slipping the book into his pocket.

Take this knowledge and use it against them, she had said.

There would be time enough for grieving when all of this was over. Right now was the time for revenge.

He moved across the hallway to the desk against the wall with the two empty chairs either side – one for the cop and one for the priest. The cop was down on the street dying or dead. The priest was still unaccounted for.

He checked the signing-in sheet and noted all the room numbers that had been visited earlier in the day. He saw Arkadian's name checked against room 410 – his mother's room – and 406, which must have been Liv's. The only other room number marked on the sheet was 400, the room where the last surviving Sanctus monk was being kept.

Pulling the gun from his waistband, he headed to the end of the corridor, counting down the room numbers as he went. The door to room 400 was partially open. He reached it and pushed it further open with the muzzle of the gun. The room was dark but he could make out a figure lying still on the bed, lit up by the spill of light through the door. From the twisted sheets and position of the body it looked as though the monk had not died without a fight, but the amount of blood pooling on the upper part of the bed and dripping to the floor suggested he had died nevertheless.

A sudden volley of voices echoing in the corridor snatched his attention. Someone was coming.

Don't let them find you here, his mother had said.

He turned and ran towards the voices, ducking back into the deserted ward just as a group of orderlies rounded the corner, making for the rooms where the dead awaited.

Gabriel stepped out on to the scaffold platform and wound

the rope around his leg, back and arm. Already the city was returning to life: streets were starting to re-emerge from the blanket of darkness where the power had come back on in random sections. Soon the whole city would be lit up and the cop would be discovered on the street below. He needed to get away while he still had darkness and confusion on his side and before his grief overwhelmed him.

In the distance the rising moon sketched the outline of the Citadel against the sky. It had reached out tonight with its dark tentacles, but had only succeeded in finding two of the four people it had sought to silence. He had escaped and so had Liv. And he vowed, as he stared at the mountain, that they would not get a second chance. He felt the hard edge of the book digging into him where he had tucked it into his waistband.

He would find Liv and then he would wreak his revenge. But for now he had to get away and he had to stay safe.

A scream in the corridor told him that the bloody remains of the monk had been found. He stepped off the platform and dropped down into the dark.

41

Flight TK 7121

The soft cabin light and subtly raised temperature conspired with the hum of the engines to send the passengers on Flight TK 7121 to sleep. All the airlines employed the same tactic: feed them quick then dim the lights and whack up the temperature. But Liv didn't trust herself to sleep. She was scared that her nightmare would return and she didn't relish the thought of waking up panicked and screaming at thirty thousand feet; so she drank coffee, and she read.

She began working through the book, searching for any other illustrations that matched the symbols she had written on her hand. The symbols on the Sumerian cylinder seal that had prompted her to buy the book were close, but not an exact match. She was hoping there might be further examples in the book, ones closer to the word she had heard. She wasn't quite sure what she would do with this knowledge if she found it, but she was used to dealing with facts, so facts were what she was seeking.

She found what she was looking for in the middle of a chapter called 'Lost Languages'.

It was on a page showing fragments of recovered stones from the ruins of various ancient libraries. Halfway down, tucked into the fold, was a picture of a broken tablet. Only the top half was visible, just three lines of swooping symbols. The very first ones jumped out at her. She held her hand flat against the page, comparing what she had written with the ones on the tablet.

They were identical.

She took her pen and carefully underlined the symbols on the photograph and wrote '*the key?*' in the margin next to it.

The caption told her the tablet was written in the same proto-cuneiform script that had first drawn her to the book. It had been found at the site of the ruined Library of Ashurbanipal in a place called Al-Hillah in modern-day Iraq. She underlined this too then turned to the beginning of the chapter and started scanning the text until she found further mention of the language.

Proto-cuneiform script is the oldest recorded form of writing and the precursor of all modern forms of written text. Sometimes referred to as 'Malan', after the tribe that originated it, or 'the lost language of the gods' because the ancients believed it was a gift to mankind from the gods themselves, it was used only by the high priests of ancient Sumerian society as a means of recording the most sacred of events. This restricted its spread and usage and ultimately proved to be its undoing. During the Elamite invasions around 2000 BC the Sumerian temples were destroyed and the priests put to death. Knowledge of the language perished with them and what few texts remain have proved insufficient to attempt any kind of comparative reconstruction of its meaning. Progress has further been hindered by the centuries-old system of acquiring and archiving many possibly useful examples of proto-cuneiform by the Institute of Ancient Writings based in the Citadel in the historic city of Ruin.

Liv felt a chill despite the superheated cabin. Even now, as she was flying away from the place at more than six hundred miles an hour, it seemed she still could not escape its influence. She flipped to the index and looked up 'The Institute of Ancient

Writings'. There was a whole chapter devoted to it. She turned to it and speed-read, hungry for the knowledge it contained.

The Institute of Ancient Writings was set up by the monks of Ruin in the fourth century BC, its origins coinciding with the first writing systems emerging from the ancient lands of Mesopotamia – 'the land between two rivers'.

An illustration on the opposite page showed a modern map over which the boundaries of Mesopotamia had been drawn. It stretched between the rivers Tigris and the Euphrates all the way up through Iraq and northern Syria to southeastern Turkey and the foothills of the Taurus mountains where the Citadel had stood even then.

The Institute's original mandate was to gather and collate all written knowledge so that it could be studied and preserved. The belief was that this knowledge, passed down by story-tellers through the oral tradition, had been gleaned by those closer to creation – and therefore closer to God – so its preservation was seen as a sacred duty.

As time moved on, however, and other ancient civilizations grew and prospered, they too wished to preserve knowledge as well as study and copy the works that had already been preserved. But the Citadel, ever known for its secrecy and silence, denied all access.

In response, the great emerging civilizations built their own libraries, starting with the Library of Ashurbanipal and progressing through the Royal Library at Alexandria, and the Library of Pergamum (see separate chapters). For a time these libraries grew and prospered, but as the civilizations that supported them crumbled and fell, so the libraries were either destroyed, looted by invading armies, or – in an ironic twist of fate – their contents acquired and transported back to the one library that still remained intact: the great library of Ruin.

Liv turned the page and discovered an eighteenth-century engraving depicting the Citadel's great library. It showed dark caves and tunnels lined with books and tablets stretching away while monks holding candles wove between stalagmites to study the things no one else was allowed to. Beneath the engraving was a quote from a Dr Parnesius, an eighteenth-century Oxford historian, quipping that 'while all roads lead to Rome, all books are read in Ruin'.

In modern times, as museums have become richer and the competition to house rare items has grown, the Guggenheims and Gettys have set up their own archaeological archive departments. As a result a competitive black market in ancient texts has flourished, enabling such treasures as the Dead Sea Scrolls to come to light and remain in it rather than be locked away in the mountain fortress of Ruin. And while these discoveries have helped broaden our understanding of our prehistoric past, the oldest languages, such as proto-cuneiform, and the knowledge they contain remain unsolved. The only hope of decoding them would be the discovery of a key.

Liv stared at this last word. Coincidence or omen? Ordinarily, she wasn't a strong believer in either, but nothing about her current circumstances could be described as 'ordinary'. She put it to the back of her mind and did what she always did – she followed the evidence.

Turning again to the index, she scanned the 'K' section. There were several page references for 'Key'. She turned to the main one.

The most famous 'Key' in the history of ancient languages is the Rosetta Stone. Prior to its discovery in 1799 by Napoleon's Commission des Sciences et des Arts our understanding of Ancient Egyptian hieroglyphics had faded from knowledge. Originally displayed within a temple, the stone was inscribed with a decree clearly intended to be read by all who passed. Carved in around 196 BC at a time when language was starting to proliferate, the decree was written in the three most commonly used languages of the time: Ancient Greek, Demotic script and Egyptian hieroglyphs. By comparing the known Greek it was therefore possible to work out the meaning of the other two 'lost' languages.

The discovery of these 'key' stones – carved on the cusp of changing world history – are now considered to be the holy grail of archaeological orthography. The most sought after being the so called Star-stone, or Imago Astrum, mentioned in the dynastic history of Ancient Babylon as being the key to understanding all ancient knowledge and whose loss to the world is believed to be referenced in the story of the Tower of Babel. As the stone was lost, so was our ability to understand the earliest of languages. Many believe the Imago Astrum found its way into the vast collection of the Institute of Ancient Writings in Ruin. Some even believe it may refer to the legendary Sacrament itself.

There was a picture reference at the foot of the page. Liv turned to it and found herself staring at the same broken tablet that contained the symbols she had scrawled on her hand. She looked at them again, their hidden meaning taking on a darker hue after what she had just learned. She felt a sudden urge to remove the marks from her skin, as though this might cleanse her of whatever madness was infecting her.

Unclipping her seat belt, Liv placed the book on her seat then walked quickly towards the bathroom at the front of the plane, scratching her hand as she went, as if the symbols were somehow infected.

Dick squeezed his legs up and out of the vice-like grip of the armrests. His body creaked as it uncurled itself from the tortured prison of the cheap seat and he stood slowly, feeling the pop and crack of joints stretching back to their natural shape. As he reached his full height, his hair brushed against the ceiling. Up ahead the girl reached the top of the aisle and disappeared through the door into the tiny bathroom. He was already moving forward before the 'Engaged' light came on.

He had spent his time in the flight musing about two things. The first was what sort of book the girl was reading, the second was trying to figure out if there was a way of killing her on the plane without getting caught.

The message he had received at the airport had told him that the girl represented a *clear and present danger* and needed to be terminated with *extreme prejudice*. Dick loved all this military jargon: the operatic quality of the words and lack of equivocation in them. But ironically it meant that, in order to execute his task as quickly and as efficiently as possible, he would have to wait. So in the meantime he would satisfy himself with answering the first question that had been running through his mind.

He reached her empty seat and glanced down at the book. It was open at a page of photographs. She had underlined something on one and written in the margin. His eyes lingered on the curve of her handwriting. It was elegant and compact, just like her. He pulled his phone from his pocket, checking that the other passengers in the row were asleep then took a photo of the page. He also memorized the title of the book and was pleasantly surprised when he saw what it was. He stretched again for the benefit of anyone watching, then returned to his seat, arching his back to give the impression he was merely stretching his legs. Maybe when the time came he would take her somewhere quiet, so they could talk a while first. Somewhere – *i-so-la-ted*.

It was rare to find a pretty girl who liked language as much as he did.

42

Arkadian set off on foot for Davlat Hastenesi Hospital with fragments of his conversation with Gabriel repeating in his head:

> *I was set up.*
> *Liv's in danger.*
> *So is my mother.*

He had heard about the deaths at the hospital via a wind-up radio tuned to the news and recalled the look on Kathryn's face after he dropped off the book, only a few hours ago. She had blamed him for Gabriel's arrest, he had seen it in her eyes and heard it in her silence. He thought she would soften once her son was released. But she didn't trust the system to protect him. And she had been right. Which was why he was walking through streets filled with dust and dazed people like a penitent sinner. He wanted to be there at the hospital – he *needed* to be there. The only way to make sure no evidence was overlooked or contaminated or accidentally lost was to be part of the investigation.

By the time he arrived police barriers had been set up, blocking off a section of the street running alongside the hospital. A solitary policeman was on guard, trying to keep back the surprisingly large crowd of reporters and television crews who had already gathered. Clearly not even an earthquake was enough to dislodge their interest in the story that had dominated the news for the past few weeks. Hooking his

ID card into his jacket pocket, Arkadian nodded a greeting to the cop, who recognized him and stepped aside to let him pass.

In the middle of the cordoned-off area a large square tent had been erected on the pavement. It glowed brightly from within, the lights powered by a small generator. One of the side flaps peeled aside as Arkadian approached and a paper-suited crime scene technician emerged. It was Bulut Gül, a senior member of the forensics team and also one of the guys Arkadian genuinely trusted within the department.

'Thought you were on leave,' Bulut said, nodding at the sling.

'So did I. I thought you might need a helping hand here – and I still have one that works.' He nodded at the tent. 'Who's in there?'

'According to the guard rota, he's called Nesim Senturk.' Bulut stepped over and opened the flap wide enough for him to see inside. 'He's one of the emergency draft. His service ID is missing, so we're not sure yet which district he came from. All the databases at the station have been knocked offline or otherwise fried by the quake. They're working on getting them back up again, but it's not exactly top priority; everyone with a pulse is out on the streets cleaning up the mess.'

Arkadian tilted his head to get a better look at the man's face. It was the same guard who had signed him in earlier when he had come to visit Liv and Kathryn. Following the explosion at the Citadel the police presence in the streets of Ruin had been raised significantly to calm the public and reassure the hordes of tourists that they were safe. In order to do this they had pulled in officers from several neighbouring forces, filling the main station house with unfamiliar faces. The dead guard was one of these.

'Where's his gun?'

'Haven't found it yet.'

'Cause of death?'

'Not sure. Don't think he fell though. Petersen is upstairs checking it out. My guess is he was tied up here and then injected with something. Look there on the side of his neck – puncture wound. We'll run a tox test when we get the bodies shipped over to the lab, but God knows when that's going to happen. The city's in chaos at the moment with all emergency services spoken for. There's broken gas mains and all sorts. At least we're nice and convenient for the hospital if we need to store them somewhere cold.'

'Where are the other bodies?'

'Two more on the fourth floor – both Citadel survivors, though I guess we shouldn't be calling them that any more.'

Arkadian felt a coldness creep over him. 'Same deal as here?'

'One of them looks the same, the other one's – a bit more messy.'

'Which one's which?'

Bulut looked up. 'You knew the woman, didn't you? I saw your name on the sign-in sheet. If it's any consolation, she wasn't the messy one.'

'Any suspects?'

'Only one. Gabriel Mann.'

Arkadian looked up in surprise. 'Gabriel! Why?'

'He's a fugitive.'

'Doesn't make him a murderer.'

'No, but he's connected to one of the victims, and we found his fingerprints in her room. A room that he is not supposed to have been in.'

Arkadian remembered how Gabriel had cut him off the moment he told him Liv's flight details had been searched. He could imagine him, sprinting to the hospital to protect his mother – getting here too late.

'How do you know they're Gabriel's prints if the databases are all down?'

'Petersen recognized them. If he says they belong to Gabriel Mann, that's good enough for me – for now, at least.'

Henrik Petersen was Ruin police force's top prints guy. He displayed an artistry with his brushes and graphite powder few could match. He could lift a print off almost anything and had a photographic memory. Less than two weeks ago he had applied his skills in the city morgue after the body of Liv Adamsen's brother had been stolen. He had found Gabriel's prints then. So if he said he'd found another print that matched then there was no doubt about it – Gabriel had been here.

'Mind if I go and have a look?'

'Be my guest.' Bulut turned back to the glowing tent. 'Plenty to keep me busy right here.'

As he made his way to the car park entrance, Arkadian glanced over at the press pack straining behind the police barriers. A news camera pointed his way and he turned his head away until he'd entered the quiet of the underground car park.

At the bottom of the ramp he stopped and pulled his phone from his pocket. Still no service. He needed to contact Gabriel. There was something rotten at the heart of the police department, something that went so deep that assassins could apparently be spirited into police cells and hospital rooms. It made him sick to think of it. He wanted to warn Gabriel that he had a murder warrant hanging over him now, but he had no way of contacting him. He had to hope that Gabriel would call him when the phones came back on. Until then, he would do what he had come to do: make sure the crime scene was processed properly, ensure that nothing was missed. He slipped his phone back into his pocket and walked over to the stairs that would take him up to the fourth floor and his own personal act of remembrance to the woman he had failed.

43

Gabriel stumbled through the broken city, tears streaking the stone dust that had ghosted his face, still clutching the book his mother had given him.

He could already feel the pain of her loss inside him, gnawing away at the part already worn thin by the death of his father. When John Mann had been killed, Gabriel had been consumed with anger. It had raged inside him, burning first for the murderers and then for himself. He felt guilty because he hadn't been there, fantasizing about how he could have made a difference if he had. It had caused deep cracks to appear in him and his pain and rage had bled into them and coloured the life that followed. The courses he had been studying seemed suddenly worthless, so he quit and joined the army, hoping to channel his anger and learn different skills. He wanted to equip himself with the practical tools that would enable him to bring the fight to those who had killed his father and armour himself so that, if danger ever came calling again, he could protect his family from it.

And danger *had* come.

And this time he had been right there.

But still he had been powerless to stop it.

All his combat training had proved unequal to the simple task of defending and protecting those he loved. Because his enemy was vast and intangible: it didn't stand up in front of him and level a weapon, it was everywhere, embedded in the faith of millions and the fabric of the very city he was stumbling through. It *was* the city.

Blinded by grief, he kept moving without knowing where he was going, intent on just putting one foot in front of the other and distance between himself and the hospital while avoiding the fire crews and anyone else in a uniform.

In the end, his survivor's instinct brought him to Melek Avenue, a wide, tree-lined street on the edge of the Garden District. It was an address unconnected to him and therefore unlikely to be visited by anyone seeking him out. It was also the home of the one person who knew more about the Citadel and its secrets than anyone outside the mountain. If the book his mother had pressed into his hands could be employed against the Citadel, then she would know how to use it.

Gabriel counted the houses until he reached the one he was looking for. He moved up the steps to the door, checking the street to make sure it was empty, then knocked loudly.

A siren was wailing at the far end of the street, one of the many burglar alarms the quake had triggered, but no one was coming to check. He heard footsteps inside the house and the sound of a drawer being opened in the hallway. The footsteps came nearer, a key twisted in a lock then the door opened sharply and he found himself staring into the beam of a hand-held torch and the cold, black eye of a gun barrel. He turned away from the brutal light, and started to raise his hands when a strident voice boomed from behind the light.

'Gabriel!' The gun vanished and the torch pulled back to reveal the owner of the voice. Even in the turmoil of the earthquake Dr Miriam Anata was impeccably dressed in her usual pinstriped suit with plain T-shirt. Her straight silver hair, cut in an asymmetric bob, gave her a stern appearance but her eyes were full of concern. Looking into them now made something inside Gabriel give way and he turned from her as his face crumpled in grief.

'What is it?' she asked, taking him by the arm and leading him inside. 'What has happened?'

'Kathryn,' he managed. 'My mother.'

He felt her arms around him, patting his back and shushing in his ear as though he were a child again. He was touched by this act of compassion, coming as it did from such a conventional and reserved person as Dr Anata. He tried to thank her and form words of explanation but none came. Grief had stolen his voice.

44

The Citadel hummed with noise and echoed with urgent voices in the aftermath of the quake. Most of the monks had been asleep when the tremors hit, shaking them out of their beds and into the corridors where they had ridden the worst of it out. Athanasius was one of them and he had spent much of his time since reassuring other monks that what they had experienced had been a tremor and not another bomb. The lingering smell of smoke from the garden had not helped his cause.

Some of the power had stayed on at least, so there had been enough working lights to quickly assess how much damage had been done. The answer was surprisingly little. It was as if the explosion ten days earlier had already pruned away the weaker parts of the mountain and the earthquake had merely shaken what was left to test how strong it was. A few rockfalls had been discovered here and there, and the library was being checked again to make sure no books had been damaged, but other than that the Citadel seemed sound and was getting back to normal. The rock piles were already being cleared away and many of the monks were returning to the dorms and chapels to continue sleeping or praying.

Athanasius was heading to his cell when he encountered Brother Axel coming down the tunnel towards him, fizzing like a lit fuse. 'This is your fault,' he said, pointing a finger at him. 'First the garden and now this. None of it would have happened if the Sancti were still here and the Sacrament safe.'

Athanasius checked behind him to make sure the tunnel

was empty then lowered his voice so it would not carry. 'This is superstitious talk and does you no credit as a leader of men. You of all people should be instilling calm at a time like this, not fear. We need order, not chaos.'

'We had order. For thousands of years we had it. And now it is gone in the space of a few weeks.'

'Order will return,' Athanasius said. 'Order *is* returning.'

'Indeed. You fancy that everyone sees things your way, but I think you are in for a surprise. In times of uncertainty people cling to tradition. And that is what I aim to offer. The elections will soon reveal which way opinion lies.'

Athanasius was about to respond when a sound made them both stop.

It was the Angelus bell echoing up from the tribute cave in the depths of the mountain.

Someone was outside, summoning the Ascension platform so they could be admitted.

45

Gabriel forced the story out, bit by bit, pushing it past his pain and grief until the details started to flow and his sorrow hardened back to anger. When he had told Dr Anata everything he handed over the diary and sank into the leather sofa, feeling utterly wrung out.

They were sitting in what had once been a grand reception room and was now a well-stocked library with books lining every wall and covering every horizontal surface. With the power still out, the space was lit only by candlelight, creating a sense that the room belonged to the past and not to the modern city wailing outside the heavy curtains draped across the high windows.

Dr Anata stared at the diary, her face white with shock. She had known Kathryn Mann for many years, working alongside her as an unofficial advisor, sharing knowledge and new discoveries on all things to do with the Citadel. She was Mala, like Gabriel's family, a descendant of one of the two most ancient tribes of men, the other being the Yahweh, the inhabitants of the Citadel who had stolen the Sacrament and used its power for their own ends.

Gabriel could see tears glistening around her blinking eyes as she turned the small volume over in her hands, the silver rings on her fingers catching the candlelight as they moved over the dark leather. Her lips formed silent words as she tried to phrase a question and, when she eventually managed it, her voice was brittle with emotion. 'Do you think they killed her for . . . do you think this is what they were after?'

Gabriel shook his head. 'If they'd wanted the book, the cop would've taken it. It felt like a clean-up operation to me, a coordinated move to silence anyone who had been inside the Citadel. Whatever is in the book, I doubt they even know about it.'

'Have you read it?'

He shook his head. 'I came straight here. I didn't know where else to go. I'm sorry if that was . . . inappropriate. I don't mean to bring trouble to your door. If you want me to leave, just say.'

Dr Anata tilted her head and glared at him through her half-moon reading glasses, giving Gabriel the sort of magnified look of indignation he had seen her dole out a few times before. The familiarity and honesty of it made him feel better somehow. She unwound the leather binding and opened the cover, angling the book towards the candle so they could both see what was written there.

Dr Anata had spent her life chiselling away at the myths of the Citadel. She had published more books on the subject than anyone living, knew all the legends and lore that surrounded it; so when she turned to the middle pages and saw the symbols forming the shape of the inverted Tau she gasped in shock. Gabriel recognized the heat-blackened writing from games he had played as a child when his mother had written secret messages for him to discover. He shook away the memory and focused on the text, translating in his head the Malan language she had taught him.

'What does it mean?' Gabriel asked.

'It's a myth – or so I always thought. It's called the "Mirror Prophecy", part of the lost knowledge of the Mala, the word of God recorded and passed down in secret by those who sought to preserve the truth.' She reached out and traced the symbols with her finger, following the inverted shape of the T. 'It is a companion piece to the prophecy that led you and Liv inside the Citadel. But if that was the Malan equivalent of the first book of Genesis, recording the truth about the beginning of things, the Mirror Prophecy is our version of the Book of Revelation. It speaks of the end.

'It was believed by the ancients to have been dictated by the gods themselves and recorded in the earliest form of human language as a warning to the future. This symbol, turned on its head, depicts the path we must travel and the choice we will face when we reach the end.'

She traced her finger down the central line of the T. 'See how the words describe the sequence of events that has already started to unfold:

> *The Key unlocks the Sacrament*
> *The Sacrament becomes the Key*
> *And all the Earth shalt tremble*

She turned and fixed him with her magnified eyes. 'The earthquake proves it. Liv *must* have released the Sacrament.'

Gabriel shook his head, remembering what he had seen at the top of the mountain. 'I'm not sure. The chapel seemed empty.'

Dr Anata hesitated at his words. She had spent her life chasing down the legend of the Sacrament, knew every theory of what it could be and had come up with several of her own. She had never dreamed that she might one day get to talk to someone who had actually been inside the Citadel, and only Gabriel's grief prevented her from bombarding him with the questions she had been burning to ask. 'Tell me what you saw,' she said, finally giving in to her curiosity.

Gabriel frowned. 'The Citadel's smaller than I imagined. Lots of cramped tunnels, like being inside a mine. The chapel of the Sacrament is high up at the end of a long flight of locked stone stairs. The walls are lined with blades, the Tau is at the altar end.'

Anata leaned forward. 'And what is the Tau?'

'It's . . . it's a coffin in the shape of a cross, maybe a metre and a half tall. When I got there, Liv was already in trouble. I thought she was dead. The front of the Tau was hanging open and the inside was hollow and filled with spikes like an iron maiden.'

'And there was nothing inside it?'

'Nothing.'

Anata nodded. 'Then she did free the Sacrament. You must have got there after it happened. It means the Mirror Prophecy is already coming to pass. When was the last time we had an earthquake here?'

'I don't know. Twenty years ago – maybe longer. It could just be a coincidence.'

'I don't believe in coincidences, not with everything that's already happened. I believe in fate and destiny. Think about the first prophecy: everything it predicted came to pass, line by line.' She dragged her finger down the new prophecy to where the line of the T split apart. 'And so will this one. We are already on the path leading to this junction – this choice – one way leading to the light, and the other to darkness.'

Gabriel read the last few lines, struck by the apocalyptic language they contained:

> . . . *Earth shalt splinter* . . .
> . . . *blight shalt prosper* . . .
> . . . *end of all days* . . .

'So how can we stop it?'

'We can't. All we can do is make sure, when the time comes, that we choose the right path.' She pointed to the middle section. 'It's laid out right here.'

Gabriel read the words, ignoring the more esoteric parts and zoning in on what he could understand.

The Key must follow the Starmap Home
There to quench the fire of the dragon within the full
phase of a moon.

'What's the Starmap?'

'Another myth. In ancient times, when the world was new and ever-changing, the first holy men were supposedly given the gift of language to record certain sanctified truths. One of the things they set down was the location of their most sacred and forbidden site, but because the earth was still shifting and settling they used the unchanging stars as their guide and created the *Imago Astrum* – the Starmap.

'The place it recorded was where the divine spark took hold – the original Home for all of us – the Garden of Eden. And because the Starmap revealed its location, it became the most coveted artefact of the ancient world. Possession of it was seen not only as an endorsement of a king's divine mandate to rule over other men but it was believed to bestow great fortune on whoever owned it. Some of the rulers who are known to have possessed it include King Solomon, King Croesus of Lydia and Alexander the Great – all legendary potentates famed for their immense power and huge wealth.

'As a tribute to the divine fortune the map brought them, each of these great rulers stored a portion of their wealth at the sacred site, believing it would not only please whatever power had brought it to them, but that a site so sacred and cursed would protect their treasure from those who sought to steal it. Certainly much of the huge wealth of these kings was unaccounted for after their deaths. If this location exists – and if it can still be found – it would be the greatest ancient treasure hoard in history. Gold, jewels . . . Priceless.'

'What happened to the map?'

'That's the question that has been asked by every emperor, scholar and treasure seeker for the past two and a half thousand years. In truth, no one knows. The last recorded mention of it is in the fourth century BC, when Alexander the Great died. His kingdom was divided and the Starmap lost. Some believe it was looted and taken to Persia, others that it was hidden away and ended up somewhere within the great library of Alexandria, built in Egypt in the dead king's honour. The Romans certainly thought so. Julius Caesar burned the library down in pursuit of the Starmap, but never found it. There is even a strong school of thought that the Starmap is the Sacrament, but this text clearly states that they are separate things; two things divided that must one day be united according to this prophecy. I wonder how Oscar came by this.'

She turned to the next page and found her answer. Gabriel read it too, his old anger flaring red when he read the words written on the back of the photograph:

This is what we found. This is why we were killed

They reached the end of the message and realized there must be more. Gabriel pulled the candle towards him, holding the next blank page over the flame and moving it across the heat until a drawing began to emerge showing a sprawling network of tunnels and caves that filled two pages of the diary.

'You wanted to know what it was like inside the Citadel,' he said. 'Well, here's your answer.'

Even in this crude drawing the scale and complexity of the Citadel was awe-inspiring. The map had been drawn in cross sections, showing different levels within the mountain, each getting smaller the higher up they got. On the smallest of these Gabriel saw an outline of a door with the words '*forbdn stair ldng to chapel of Scmnt*' written next to it. He had passed through that very door and climbed those stairs. He used it as a reference point and began tracing backwards down other tunnels he had walked, past the door leading out to the hidden garden and descending unfamiliar stairs and corridors to the lowest section of the map where, tucked away in a distant cave, a cross was marked with a skull drawn next to it, like a child's version of a pirate treasure map.

'There,' he said, 'that is where the Starmap is hidden.'

'But what's the significance of this?' Anata pointed to the symbol marked next to it – XIV – the number fourteen expressed in Roman numerals.

Gabriel stared at the cross and the Roman numerals and realized with a resigned weariness what he had to do. A little under two weeks after he had miraculously escaped from the one place on earth no man but his grandfather had ever got away from, he was going to have to break into the Citadel again to try to recover what Oscar had hidden.

46

The tribute cave had already attracted quite a crowd by the time Athanasius and Brother Axel got there. Monks were gathered in nervous knots, or clearing up stacks of spilled rice and tinned food that had been knocked from the storage shelves by the earthquake, moving them away from the great wooden spindle in the centre of the room that operated the lifting gear.

'Bring that up again!' Axel ordered, moving through the crowd towards the brown-cloaked Ascension monks straining against the spokes on the spindle. 'What were you thinking of, sending the platform down in answer to that bell? Is this the proper time to receive tribute?' He turned to Athanasius. 'See what happens when tradition is ignored? Everything starts to unravel.'

One of the brown cloaks kicked the brake into place and turned to Axel. 'We thought someone might be sending news or assistance following the earthquake.'

'And how do you know it was an earthquake?' Has anyone confirmed that? What if the disturbance we felt was another bomb, designed to flush us out further?' Axel stalked over to the wall and pointed at the small TV screen that usually displayed an image of whatever was below. It was still blank following the partial power failure. 'You cannot see who is ringing that bell and yet you are prepared to send the platform down to them. You could be hauling anything up here.'

Athanasius stepped forward. 'I think it's safe to assume that what we all experienced was indeed an earthquake.' He pointed through one of the slits cut into the outer rock of the mountain. 'See for yourself – the city is mostly dark. Their power must have failed also. If another bomb had been aimed purely at us, I doubt it would have affected the entire city. And the tremors we felt were long, not short and sharp like an explosion. I think we all know what an explosion feels like.'

Axel stared into the dark night where the bright city usually shone. There were only a few isolated patches of light to show there was anything out there at all. He turned back to the assembled crowd, his eyes darting from face to face as if he was mentally taking names. 'Very well,' he said, 'send it down, but I want this room cleared of all but essential personnel before you bring it up again. And do not start the ascension until I have guards in place. Earthquake or not, I do not want to take any chances.'

The Ascension monks took the strain and released the brake. The wooden platform settled on to the suspended ropes with a sailing-ship creak and slowly sank from view.

Though the Citadel had undergone many modifications and improvements over the years, the mechanics and operation of the Ascension platform had remained mostly unchanged. Tens of thousands of years previously, when tribesmen travelled from far and wide to give tribute to the holy men of the mountain, this was how they had been received. Gifts of food or other offerings were placed on the wooden platform and hoisted up by hand into what had come to be known as the tribute cave.

It was also how fresh blood entered the mountain.

The novices were hauled up one at a time in a ceremony known as the Ascension, which took place at the summer and winter solstice. The act of a man being elevated by the efforts of the monks inside the mountain was deliberately symbolic and the reason the system had never been updated. On some days, when the low cloud cut the top off the mountain, an ascending novice would literally rise into it and disappear as if he had gone straight to heaven. It was a spectacular piece of sacred theatre and one that still drew huge crowds whenever it was performed. So famous was the ritual that people would even gather to witness the weekly delivery of supplies, eagerly snapping pictures of sacks of flour and crates of live chickens rising up into the mountain on the creaky wooden platform.

Few, however, would be witnessing the Ascension today. The old town was deserted and the tribute cave had emptied rapidly following Brother Axel's orders. The only people remaining now were the heads of the guilds, two Ascension monks labouring at the wheel, and five red-cloaked guards who had emerged one by one from the dark and now stood by the edge of the loading bay, their hands tucked into the wide sleeves of their cassocks where their weapons were kept.

A piece of white cloth appeared on the main rope and spooled out from around the spindle, signalling that the platform was about to reach the bottom.

'Hold steady,' one of the Ascension monks commanded, taking the strain and slowing the wheel to ease the rope out ever more gradually until the marker drew level with a notch carved into the stone ceiling.

A hundred metres below them the platform touched down on the smooth flat surface of the offering stone. One of the brown cloaks pulled on the ratchet lever to lock the wheel in place then rested against the huge spindle and watched the summoning bell swing to a stop.

The silence in the cave was profound after the solemn clanging. Nobody spoke. Nobody moved. All eyes were fixed on the ropes snaking into the darkness, twitching slightly as something was loaded on to the platform below. Then a single loud clang rang through the cave, signalling that whatever was down there was loaded and ready to rise. The brown cloaks took the strain again, kicked the brake loose and started to haul the platform up the side of the mountain. 'It's not too heavy,' one of them said, heaving on the wheel with a well-practised rhythm. 'It'll be here in a couple of minutes.'

'Just bring it up, slow and steady,' Axel replied, his eyes fixed on the rectangle of night in the floor of the cave. He stepped closer to the edge, his hand reaching automatically into his sleeve.

Athanasius watched Axel, taking the opportunity to consider the man who had so recently challenged him and would undoubtedly do so again in the forthcoming elections. He was an authoritative presence, there was no doubt about that. Eight years as captain of the guards had gifted him the ability to deliver orders with supreme confidence and conviction. This quality would be attractive to many in the mountain who were used to strong command. But there was a chink in his armour.

Elections in the Citadel had historically been run to fill one vacancy – the position of Abbot. When the Prelate died, the Abbot automatically became acting head of the monastery until he was confirmed. This had always been a formality with seldom a challenge mounted – and certainly never a successful one. This time, however, it would be different. There was no automatic succession. Both the Prelate and the Abbot were dead and all their natural heirs – the Sancti – were gone. This time the men of the mountain would not only be voting for a new Abbot but a new Prelate as well, and between these two positions, the whole future of the Citadel would be decided. Because of this Athanasius had realized that, as in the American presidential race, success would depend on the combined appeal of both candidates, not the influence and standing of one. And Axel had no obvious allies. He had risen to his position through ambition and single-mindedness. He might be respected, but he wasn't liked. So if he ran for Abbot, who would be his Prelate? And if he ran for Prelate, who would serve directly under him? He might be able to convince one of the guards to stand as his running mate, but everyone would realize he was merely a puppet candidate whose sole purpose was to ensure that Axel achieved his long-held goal. And if Axel was elected, Athanasius knew he would re-establish the

Sancti in the name of tradition, slam the door on any reform and restore everything to the way it had been before. He was, after all, a soldier; strict orders and routine were what he trusted and understood. The old ways suited him perfectly.

There were of course others in the Citadel who would put themselves forward and stand a chance of election. Father Malachi, for example, was well respected and a definite candidate, but Athanasius felt sure he could forge some kind of alliance with him. As chamberlain to the previous Abbot, he knew the workings of the Citadel more than most and was therefore a useful ally.

But Axel was a different case. The best way to deal with him was to keep him isolated in his candidacy and hope his staunch adherence to the old hierarchy would alienate the large moderate faction within the mountain. The Sancti were gone, and there were many who did not mourn their passing and would relish their return even less. These were the people Athanasius would appeal to. These were the key to the Citadel's future.

'Hold steady!'

He looked up as the second distance marker rose from the darkness, indicating that the Ascension platform was nearing the top. Axel stopped pacing and stepped forward to peer over the lip of the tribute hatch, withdrawing his gun from his sleeve as he did so. Then he gasped and stepped away, levelling his gun at the darkness. The rest of the guards followed his lead, just as the supporting ropes rose, bringing the platform level with the floor.

Standing in the middle of the platform was a man, dressed in the apparel of a priest. Red eyes stared out at them from blackened skin and his lips curled in a parody of a smile as he regarded them coolly. 'Such a welcome for an old friend,' it said, in a voice that was ragged but familiar. 'Have I really changed that much?'

It was the syrupy Slavic voice that made Athanasius realize

who was standing before them. Brother Dragan, youngest of the Sancti, now returned from the dead and risen back into the mountain, his bloody eyes scanning the faces of the assembled men like Death seeking out the weakest.

'Fetch me my robes,' he commanded. A guard scuttled off, tripping in his haste to obey. 'And send word to the Abbot that I have returned.'

Axel cleared his throat. 'I'm afraid that will not be possible. Brother Abbot has sadly passed.'

Dragan shuffled forward stiffly and stepped off the platform on to the solid rock floor of the tribute cave. 'Send word to the Prelate then.'

'Again, that will not be possible. I regret that he too is no longer with us.'

'So who is the most senior monk remaining?'

Axel turned to look at the heads of the guilds, huddled by the spindle in the centre of the room. 'We have been running things democratically until such time as elections provide new leaders.' He turned back to Dragan. 'But now that God has seen fit to bless us with your return, you are the most senior monk in the Citadel.'

Dragan nodded and his lips curled in another ghastly smile. 'In that case, take me to the Prelate's quarters and spread the word throughout the mountain that, by the grace of God, a Sanctus has returned.'

And with that he walked past everyone into the darkness of the mountain, dragging Athanasius's dreams of reform with him.

III

Blessed is the one who reads aloud the words of the prophecy and blessed are those who hear and who keep what is written in it; for the time is near.

Revelation 1:3

47

Badiyat al-Sham, Al Anbar Province, Western Iraq

There was nothing on earth like being in the desert at night.

The same thin air that offered so little protection from the hellish daytime sun let in the absolute cold of space when darkness fell to steal the heat away again. And then there were the stars: billions of them, filling the sky with pinpoints of light and casting a microscopic glow over everything. The Bedouin used the stars to travel at night, their desert eyes accustomed to levels of light that city dwellers could never perceive. The Ghost used this skill now to pick his way over the stony ground and gravel paths, following the line of the dragon's back into the place the Bedouin called the land of thirst and terror.

The Syrian Desert was over half a million square kilometres of nothing. It spread across the land like a crusted sore, spilling out of Syria into northern Iraq, Jordan and Saudi Arabia. There were no settlements in the heart of it and no proper roads. During the Iraq War the insurgents had fallen back here, using the prehistoric brutality of the desert environment as their main defence against the technological might of the modern war machine. And it had worked; machinery broke down, dust storms grounded all air support, even hi-tech thermal-imaging systems could be rendered blind by the simple strategy of lying under a blanket on a warm rock. It was impossible to fight people when they had the land and nature on their side.

The insurgents had used the desert as their main base of operations, resupplying themselves with men and equipment that flowed over the leaky and unpatrolable border with Syria. It was only when the invaders had taken all the towns that they moved back to the cities to harry the new government with the more traditional terrorist tactics of roadside bombs and the ever-present threat of kidnap. So the desert was empty again – and yet, as the Ghost rode on through the night, he began to sense that he was not alone.

He saw the first signs of something out of place a few hours before dawn when the cold had chilled the air to crystal clarity and the moon began to rise. It was a dark shape, away in the distance, stretching across the otherwise flat horizon. Dismounting, he approached it on foot, keeping low to the ground so that any watching eyes with thermal-imaging scopes would not be able to see his hot outline against the cold sky.

As he drew closer he saw that the dark shape was actually a shadow, cast by the rising moon and a large mound of rocks and dirt that had been piled high next to a hole in the ground. He dropped lower and crawled towards it, stopping every now and then to listen to the empty silence broken only by the intermittent whisper of night breezes flowing around the jagged edges of the pile of rocks and earth.

The hole next to it was only a metre or so deep, far too shallow to account for the size of the pile that cast such a long shadow. In the middle of the hole a rock the size of a car had been partly excavated, then abandoned, as if whoever had been working there had suddenly lost interest. He moved to the spill pile and carefully picked his way up the side until he was high enough to have an elevated view of the surrounding terrain.

There were several other holes dotted around, each about the same size and depth as the first, each with a large rock semi-uncovered at the bottom. It was as if some huge beast had been digging around for something it had lost. One of the holes was significantly wider and deeper than the rest. He slid down and made his way over to investigate.

The hole was about one storey deep, with a ramp of earth spiralling to the bottom, wide enough for a horse to walk down. At the bottom of the pit was a ragged patch of blackness marking the entrance to a cave. It was one of the quirks of the Syrian Desert that large parts of it were honeycombed with extensive, subterranean cave systems, carved millions of years ago by water flowing through the sedimentary rock. You could hide whole battalions of men and equipment in the caves if you knew where they were. It was one of the reasons the Ghost had evaded capture for so long. If whoever had dug these holes was still around, this was where they would be, sleeping in the cave, away from the biting cold of the desert night.

He watched for a while, but saw no movement other than the creeping line of moonlight as the world slowly turned. There was no telltale tang of woodsmoke in the air to suggest people were there. Whoever had dug these holes, and for whatever purpose, they had gone. The Ghost skirted the edge of the crater then made his way down the ramp, his night-adjusted eyes probing the velvet blackness of the cave as he approached. Once inside, he listened to the deadened sounds, then took a penlight from his pocket and turned it on.

The tiny bulb lit up with all the force of a nuclear explosion and he had to shield his eyes against the light. The cave was empty – no sign of habitation, no sign of anything. It would have taken considerable resources and time to dig down to the cave and, as there was no obvious archaeological or mineral value to the site, there had to be another reason. The fact that the caves were empty suggested they had either been dug out so that something could be put in them, or something had already been here and now it was gone. He took a long last look then flicked off the torch and headed out.

The night seemed darker now and he blinked to restore his

night vision as he rose from the crater and studied the ground. He could detect faint footprints in the dirt, skirting the rim and converging on an area where deeper, rutted tracks led away and across the desert towards the eastern horizon, where dawn was already beginning to lighten the sky. He squinted towards it, and checked the stars. Something was wrong. At this time of year the sun rose directly into Gemini, but the patch of light was to the right of it. It was not the dawn but something else, something large enough to pollute the pure darkness of the desert.

And there was only one thing bright enough to do that at this distance. It had to be a settlement.

48

New Jersey, USA

It was three in the morning when Liv cleared immigration at Newark Liberty International Airport. She had somehow managed to stay awake through the twelve-hour flight using a combination of coffee and fear of what might happen if she slept. As a result, she was wired and scratchy and almost hallucinating with fatigue as she emerged into the headache-inducing brightness of the large and mostly deserted concourse.

A cleaner was pushing a large polishing machine across the hard floor in a slow, depressed waltz, while catatonic passengers looked on from the only coffee shop that was open, sipping wakefulness from paper cups. A few suited chauffeurs formed a welcoming committee, holding up cards with different names in a variety of handwriting. It gave Liv a feeling of déjà vu. When she had landed in Turkey over a week ago she had seen her own name amongst these greetings – the first time she had met Gabriel. She scanned the row of quizzical faces now, knowing the impossibility of his being there, but seeking him out all the same. Though she hardly knew him, she missed him.

She headed towards the exits, her lack of luggage allowing her to steal a march on other passengers. The night made dark mirrors of the glass doors and she hardly recognized herself as she approached them. She could see the dark circles under her eyes and the clothes hanging off her already skinny frame. It was as if she had left this airport as one person and returned as another. She took another step towards her strange self and the automatic doors slid open, removing her from sight and revealing the night beyond.

Dick had also beaten the crowd. He too travelled with hand luggage because he wanted to stay fluid. Some people who'd been inside surrounded themselves with tons of stuff once they got out. To Dick that seemed like building a new kind of prison. He preferred being able to walk out of anywhere at a moment's notice without worrying about who or what he was leaving behind – that was true freedom. He never gave much thought to other people's feelings, he wouldn't have been able to do his job if he did.

He drifted across the concourse, keeping a useful distance between himself and Liv. He kept tabs on her with his peripheral vision while checking his phone, looking like a flight-crumpled businessman chained to his BlackBerry. As she passed through the door, he picked up his pace. The time difference had landed them in Newark at the perfect time. Three in the morning was statistically the quietest time of the day, and less people meant more opportunity.

It was colder outside than he had anticipated, which was also in his favour. The cold drove people away and kept them indoors.

Ser-en-dip-ity

He scoped the area, checking for dark spots and possible witnesses. A few cab drivers were sitting in their cars with heaters on and engines running. The nearest one gave him a hopeful look then returned to his paper when Dick ignored him. He could see the blonde hair of the girl shining in the dark, made brighter by the sickly wash of the overhead sodium lights. She was moving away, heading towards the bus stop. If she got on a bus it might be a problem. He would have to get on it too to ensure he didn't lose her and she would most likely remember him from the flight. He didn't want to spook her, not yet at least.

He drifted past the line of parked cabs, still scrutinizing his phone though actually checking security. Since 9/11 all airport terminal buildings had become lousy with cameras. You couldn't scratch your nose without some security guard somewhere getting five different angles on it. Fortunately the girl had moved away from the entrance where most of the cameras were focused. It was as though she was offering herself up for sacrifice. He had hoped he might get her alone – talk to her – but the opportunist in him far outweighed the playful. His best opportunity was now. The taxi drivers all focused on the entrance, waiting for a fare, the cameras pointing elsewhere, no one else around. She stopped by the bus shelter and looked up the empty road. No bus. No one else waiting.

Dick made his decision.

He cut through a couple of parked cabs and headed across the road towards her, hoping to get it done before other passengers started to appear from the building. During the flight he had spent a long time watching the back of her head as she read her book, his eyes tracing the slender line of her neck, his hands opening and closing in his lap as he imagined them tightening round it. He had imagined the sound it would make as it broke: *Snap* – like a breadstick, or the stem of a wine glass.

He reached the central reservation and she looked up. She was so small compared to him that he figured he could stand in front of her and mask her whole body with his. No one would hear him ask her when the bus was coming, no one would see him snap her head back when she opened her mouth to answer. He was about to take the last few steps when she turned away and did something totally unexpected.

She waved.

Dick glanced down the street to where she was looking. A set of headlights was speeding towards them. Cars were not usually allowed in the bus lanes, but as it drew closer Dick saw why this one was. It was a police cruiser.

He raised his phone to his ear and walked right past her, heading towards the short-stay car park whilst fumbling for nonexistent keys in his pocket. Just another businessman returning from a badly scheduled trip.

49

Liv slid into the cruiser and slammed the door on the cold night.

'Jesus, Liv, you look like shit!'

She looked up into the doughy, moon-like face of Sergeant Ski Williams and smiled. It was the only thing she'd heard in days that she could truly believe.

'Sorry about the unholy hour,' she said, buckling herself in as he eased the cruiser away from the kerb. 'I didn't think about the time difference when I called.'

He waved away her apology and kept his eyes fixed on the road.

She'd known Ski Williams for close to ten years now. His real name was William Godlewski, but like many Polish cops he'd shortened and switched it around to avoid having to deal with his unpronounceable surname. He was one of the first cops she'd ever met on a proper assignment. He'd been a rookie too; maybe that's why they'd hit it off – two newbies trying to find their feet in a grown-up world. It amazed her that after all this time he still hadn't made it past sergeant. He was far and away one of the best cops she knew, but he was lousy when it came to the books. He had failed the detective's exam three times in a row. He was also terrible at kissing ass. Just couldn't do it. He was smart enough to know that it helped you get on, but if he thought a captain was an asshole he'd say so. There was something utterly uncompromising about him that was both infuriating and noble. It was why she'd called him from Turkey over anyone else to ask if he wouldn't mind picking her up. He was old school, like the Untouchables, and there was no one she trusted more.

'So, you going to talk to me or what? You've been all over the news for days now. When I saw you standing on the sidewalk there I didn't know whether to offer you a ride or ask for an autograph.'

Liv pulled her baseball cap lower to shield her face and hunkered down in her seat. It hadn't occurred to her that everything in Ruin would be news here. Foreign stories rarely got any airtime unless they were about a war where Americans were dying.

'What you heard?'

'Sounds like you got some kind of mediaeval curse hanging over you or something. Anyone you speak to gets offed. We've got two homicides that may or may not be linked to you and your little adventures overseas. I should get my head examined, letting you in the car. So what happened? Did you find out what they got in that mountain?'

'I don't know.'

'Oh, come on.'

'Honestly, I can't remember.'

She thought of the dream that frightened her so much she had chosen to stay awake for the twelve-hour flight rather than risk facing it. Her boss had been one of the two homicides Ski had referred to: killed merely because he had spoken to her. Maybe she was cursed.

'Listen, Ski. Just take me home and I'll tell you everything. Perhaps talking it through might jog something loose. Besides, I could use a shower and a change of clothes.'

'Take you home . . .' Ski said it flat and left it hanging.

Liv saw the troubled expression on his face. She'd seen that look before. His unbending streak of honesty meant he had the worst poker face of anyone she had ever met. It was the look he got when he had to tell someone some really bad news.

'Tell me,' she said.

Ski shook his head. 'Probably easier if I show you.'

50

Dick had intimidated his way to the front of the taxi queue and given the driver a story about how a buddy of his had been arrested. The driver's English was pretty sketchy, but he'd understood enough and they were now following the police cruiser at a safe distance. Dick glanced up from time to time to make sure it was still there, in between composing an email detailing everything that had happened so far. He knew from the girl's file that she worked as a crime reporter so he assumed her ride must be an acquaintance. It didn't appear to be a heavy-duty protection detail, it was much too casual for that. Maybe he was her boyfriend, in which case it was bad news for him. Dick had a schedule to keep and anyone who got in the way would become collateral damage. Whoever it was, he hoped he was taking her somewhere quiet, maybe somewhere with a basement – that would be best.

He finished the email and read it through, checking he hadn't missed any details. Then he attached the photograph he'd taken of the book the girl had been reading. It might not be important, but that wasn't for him to say. Finally satisfied, he hit *send* and watched until it had gone.

Up ahead, the police cruiser curved off the expressway on to McCarter Highway. There wasn't much traffic at this time of night and it was easy to keep tabs on them. He told the driver to ease back a bit. After a mile or so the taillights flared and the car turned off. The driver started to speed up, but Dick told him not to. He could see they were heading east into the Ironbound district and he remembered something from the girl's file that told him exactly where she was going.

'Welcome home,' he said, too quiet for anyone but himself to hear. 'Welcome home.'

51

Badiyat al-Sham

True dawn had started to show by the time the Ghost drew close enough to the cluster of lights to see what it was. He had worked his way into position using the contours of the land and the remains of the night to hide his approach. He was now lying on the upslope of a shallow berm and staring straight at the settlement through field glasses.

At first glance what he saw did not strike him as particularly remarkable. It appeared to be another of the thousands of oil drilling compounds that had spread like a contagion over large parts of the country since the end of the war. There was a thin drill tower in the centre, a collection of silver-sided buildings to house the workers, and a large transport hangar for vehicles and supplies. On the far side of the compound a flat, concreted area with a large painted 'H' showed where helicopters could land, though none were parked there at the moment.

Everything seemed normal – and yet there was something not right about it.

For a start, it wasn't on an existing oilfield. There were no other drilling operations for at least a hundred kilometres in any direction and the whole place was too clean. Exploratory drilling gear got moved around from site to site and usually bore the scars of oil grime and years of standing out in various godforsaken places being blasted by extremes of weather. The equipment here all shone with newness, as if everything had been shipped straight from the factory, taken out of its packaging and dropped into the desert like a theme-park version of a drill site. It was clearly operational, the drill was turning but there was no oil in either of the holding lagoons.

He remembered a government outfit seven or eight years back sinking a few wells out here. They moved on pretty quickly when they came up dry. All of this would be on record and it seemed unlikely that one company would now succeed where another had failed; especially with all the technology they used to sniff out oil these days. Down to a certain level you could pretty much see what was there using seismic readings, and beyond that it was too expensive to drill anyway.

The thing that really aroused his suspicions was the level of security. Iraq was still a dangerous place and any Western corporation had to have some protection, if only to dissuade opportunistic insurgents from kidnapping their employees and charging exorbitant ransoms. But the security levels at this place were off the scale. Two layers of razor wire formed a perimeter around the entire compound with two steel gates barring the only road in. There were guard towers positioned at the four corners, each with a shooting platform at the top and a gun visible through the slits in the side panels. They were M60 Mk43s, the US Army's heavy machine gun of choice. With an effective range of around a thousand metres and a fire rate of six hundred rounds a minute they were easily capable of stopping any approaching vehicle, even an armour-plated one, long before it reached the main gate. What they could do to a man was unthinkable. It didn't make sense that such heavy artillery was being used to protect what looked from the outside to be nothing more than a dry well. There had to be something else he was missing, something valuable enough to warrant this small, lethally equipped army.

The Ghost dropped down and moved in closer. Wary of the men in the towers casually scanning the land with their hands resting on their heavy guns, he went as far as he dared then crept back into an observation position.

He could hear noises now, drifting over from the compound: the clank of the turning drill; the hum of motors and air-conditioning units; voices speaking a mixture of Arabic and English.

A bunch of men in white overalls emerged from the main building and headed over to the drill where others were waiting to be relieved. Up in the towers the guard details changed too, staggered by a few minutes each time to ensure the compound was not left vulnerable by a simultaneous changeover. It was all very slick and professional, and all the more strange because of it.

The Ghost continued to watch, slowly building up an operational picture of the place. The sun would be up soon and he would have to slip away or risk being seen. He was about to switch position when the sound of diesel engines punctured the low-level operational hum of the place, and three jeeps emerged from the transport bay. They pulled up in front of the main building and waited.

More men emerged from the building and climbed into the vehicles. The men in front wore the same white overalls as the drill workers and carried an assortment of picks and spades. Those at the rear wore the desert camouflage of the tower guards and the jeep they climbed into had a flatbed at the rear and a roof-mounted M60. It was standard convoy protocol, expendable scouts in the front, security at the rear, VIPs in the middle. It was this group that the Ghost now focused on.

There were three of them, two Westerners and one Iraqi, dressed in a mixture of khaki and sand-coloured clothes that hung off their well-stuffed, out-of-condition bodies. Two of them had beards and long hair poking from beneath salt-stained sun hats. They were obviously civilians, and by the way they were carrying themselves and talking to the drivers, they were obviously in charge. The Iraqi seemed to be in overall command and there was something about him that seemed familiar, though the distance, combined with his beard, made it hard to get a proper look at his face. Then another man stepped out from the shadow of the building and a big piece of the jigsaw fell into place. He walked up to the leader of the group, spoke to him for a few moments, checked his watch and waved to the tower by the main gate.

The first of the two steel barriers rolled back and the convoy moved off, stopping in the no-man's land between the two rows of razor wire until the first gate was fully shut. Only then did the second slide open to release them back up the dirt track the Ghost had followed here. The man in the compound watched them leave then scanned the surrounding terrain. He paused as he looked at the Ghost's position and for a moment the two men seemed to stare at each other, though the Ghost knew he could not be seen. Then Hyde turned and walked away, disappearing into the shiny shell of the main compound building.

52

Newark, New Jersey

The first thing Liv saw when they turned into her street was the incident tape flapping in the road ahead. The wind that came off the river had torn it away at one end and was whipping it from side to side like a black-and-yellow snake. Ski pulled up to the kerb, trapping it beneath the wheels of the cruiser, then cut the engine. In the sudden silence the tape chattered against the underside of the car.

'We think the same guy who did the two homicides also did this,' Ski said. 'Good job you weren't home, huh?'

Liv didn't answer. She couldn't. She had been so desperate to come home to try to make sense of everything, but now she had finally got here all she found was more chaos and destruction.

Her home was gone.

The white clapboard sides of the building were scorched above every boarded window and the glass that had filled them lay in glittering drifts on the ground. She popped the car door and stepped out into the freezing wind. She could still smell ash and charred wood in the air. Ski got out and joined her on the sidewalk.

'What happened to the Da Costas?' she asked, nodding at the cracked windows on the first floor.

'They're OK. They were at work when it happened. Fire started around three in the afternoon. The building's been condemned. Everyone's staying with family or friends, waiting for the insurance to kick in.'

Another piece of incident tape stretched across a plank of rough plywood that had been nailed in place where her door had been. It also snaked along the fence enclosing the tiny square of garden that had made her want the apartment in the first place.

When she'd moved in, the yard had been covered in concrete stained with oil from the previous owner's Harley. She'd broken it all up herself, exposing the soil beneath and planting it with native seeds and shrubs, returning it to how it might have looked when man had first settled here. She had often laid on the patch of grass at the centre of her tiny garden, staring up at the sky – the ivy strategically blocking the view of one wall, the branches of the cherry tree the other – imagining she was lying in a long-ago forest, far away from her modern-day troubles.

Her apartment had been full of plants too, a remnant of growing up with an organic horticulturalist father who'd taught her to name all the plants at the same time as she'd learned her A-B-Cs. He'd always thought it weird that she'd ended up working as a big-city journalist, living in a concrete jungle when she had the earth in her soul. Maybe it had been her way of rebelling. Maybe she was just nosy. Either way, her apartment, with her plants and her flowers and the rich smell of earth and oxygen, was her sanctuary – her home.

And now someone had taken it all from her. She walked over and pulled some tape away, stepping through a broken gap in the fence and into her ruined garden.

Blackened pieces of furniture had been thrown in a large pile in the centre: a splintered table she had inherited when her dad died, some stubs of burned books, a mattress with a fitted sheet still clinging to it, and a few framed photographs, smoke-damaged but visible. She picked one up: it showed a vibrantly happy version of herself in a rowing boat on the lake in Central Park. Next to her was Samuel. For a moment she felt a rush of fury at him for bringing all this destruction upon her and leaving her alone in the world among the charred remains of her former life. But she was too tired to hold on to it for long. She was too tired to do anything and would have laid down right there in the mud had Ski not pulled her into a rough but well-meaning hug. She sobbed into his meaty shoulder, feeling wretched and alone, breathing in the comforting cop-car smell of him.

'Come on,' he said, stroking her back awkwardly, 'let it all go. You got someplace to go, someone you can call, 'cept me?' She shook her head. He held on and let her ride it out, working out what he might say that would make it better. Ski was no good at small talk at the best of times and this was far from that.

'I'd let you crash at my place,' he offered, 'but to be honest my ma would drive you nuts with all her questions. She's seen you on the news. You'd be like a celebrity. She'd probably invite her friends round and everything. Come on, let's get in the car. It's freezing out here. Crying ain't going to bring none of this stuff back. Let me see if I can't fix you up with something.'

53

Four in the morning in Newark, New Jersey.

Ten in the morning in Vatican City.

Reports of an earthquake had filtered through on the international news channels late the previous evening, along with rumours that some of the Citadel survivors had become casualties. Clementi had spent the evening and most of the night checking his secure communications, waiting for word, eager for confirmation that the threat to his enterprise had been removed. In the end exhaustion had driven him to bed with the question unanswered.

As soon as he had dispensed with his morning prayers and duties he had rushed to his office and logged in.

There were two messages waiting for him.

He read the first with a growing sense of unease. Despite his promise to the Group, only one of the four survivors had been silenced during the night. Of the other three, one was under surveillance but still at liberty in America, and the other two were missing. It had been a messy night. Two of the independent agents who had been watching the hospital were among the dead. He opened a picture attachment and winced at a crime-scene photograph showing the priest, wide-eyed in surprise and lying on a hospital bed with his throat cut and his blood pooling around him. The first news reports had wrongly identified him as the monk, but subsequent bulletins had corrected this. The monk was now officially missing, along with Liv Adamsen and Gabriel Mann, the one survivor the Group had seemed particularly concerned about.

He closed the first email and clicked the second, time-stamped several hours after the first, hoping for better news. It had been sent by the third agent and gave a detailed report of the surveillance of the missing woman. Clementi scanned through the details of what flight she had taken and how she had been met by a policeman upon landing. The message also contained a photo attachment under an explanatory note.

> The subject was seen reading this book throughout the flight . . .

He clicked it open and caught his breath when he saw the tablet, one of the few extant examples of the lost language not in the possession of the Citadel. The girl had underlined a line of symbols and written something next to it which made his skin go cold.

The key?

She had correctly translated a language only he, and a very few people in the world, could read and one that was central to his desire to restore the Church. He focused on her question mark. Did it mean that the translation was a guess, or that its significance was unknown? Then he saw what else she had underlined on the page and his mind was made up. It was Al-Hillah – the key to everything. She had to know something, and that made her very dangerous indeed.

The time for caution was gone. Yesterday he had agonized over his decision, now he didn't hesitate. He was much too far in to turn back.

Opening a new window, he typed a short reply:

> Silence the girl immediately.
> I expect to hear from you within the hour.

54

Newark, New Jersey

'This is you.' Ski pushed open the door with a flourish the hotel room beyond did not deserve.

It was stark and functional and not much bigger than the double bed it contained. A feeble amount of dawn light leaked in from a single window opposite and beyond was a prime view of a solid brick wall.

'It's perfect,' Liv said, stepping across the threshold.

Ski stayed outside in the corridor like a nervous date, digging around in his jacket pocket for something. 'Here,' he said, holding out a cheap-looking cell phone. 'It's got about fifty bucks' credit on it. You need to call anyone, use that. It's virtually untraceable.' Liv took it gratefully. 'I've put my number on there, in case you need to contact me in a hurry. You just take it easy for a while, OK?' He nodded, as if answering his own question, then turned and was gone. Ski wasn't one for big shows of emotion, but he had a huge heart, and that counted for more than anything.

Closing the door behind him, Liv twisted the lock until it wouldn't turn any more before checking out her surroundings. In many ways it wasn't dissimilar to the hospital room in Ruin. The décor was slightly better and the bed was a double, but other than that it had the same institutional blandness.

Ski had explained to her on the way over that the hotel was used to house key witnesses and jury members during big trials. He had checked her in using a dummy name and false details so that her own name and passport number wouldn't pop up on any databases. It would keep her off the radar, for a while at least, and that made her feel a little bit safer.

She took her laptop and charger from her bag and plugged them in by the countertop that served as a desk. At one end was a lamp with a mirror on the wall behind it, at the other a flat-screen TV. Liv switched it on and turned to a news channel out of long worn habit. She was about to start unpacking the rest of her things when the news anchor said something that made her head snap to the screen:

'The first quake occurred last night at eight p.m. local time in the historic Turkish city of Ruin. Though the tremors were not serious, they appeared to set off a chain reaction of other incidents that swept west across Turkey, and south and east into Syria and northern Iraq. Seismologists say this ripple effect has never been recorded before and they have been unable to give an explanation for what may have caused it.'

Liv stared at the map.

Her plane had taken off at precisely eight o'clock.

She recalled the lurch she had felt as the wheels had left the ground, like a cord being snapped inside her, then the lights blinking out below as the plane climbed into the sky. Were these things connected somehow? They couldn't be. They couldn't.

'So far, the only deaths appear to have been at Ruin Hospital. In an official statement, police confirmed that Kathryn Mann – one of the suspects in the recent bombing incident at the Citadel – is among the dead, although it is not known whether this was as a direct result of the earthquake . . .'

Liv stared at the screen, numb from the news.

'There are now only three remaining survivors from the Citadel bombing: the monk, whose whereabouts is unknown; Liv Adamsen, who it is believed discharged herself from hospital a few hours before the quake struck; and Gabriel

Mann, who escaped from police custody at around the same time.'

Liv felt the blood drain from her face and dry nausea rise up in her throat.

Kathryn – dead.
Gabriel – gone.

She wondered if he had really escaped, or whether something had happened to him too.

Still in a daze, Liv opened her laptop and Googled Ortus, the foundation where he worked. If anyone could make contact with him or tell her where he currently was, it would be them. She skimmed the homepage, found contact details for the Ruin office and reached for Ski's phone. Having copied its number on to a scratch pad, she dialled the number for Ortus, wondering how long fifty bucks would last dialling international on a no-contract tariff. A foreign ringtone purred in her ear, then someone answered in Turkish.

'Hi,' Liv said, powering through the language barrier, 'do you speak English?'

'Yes.'

'I'm trying to get a message to Gabriel Mann.'

A pause. 'He is not here.'

'I know, but is there anyone who might be able to contact him? I'm a friend of his, and I need to speak to him very urgently.'

'He is not here.'

Liv wasn't surprised at the stonewall reception, but it didn't make it any less frustrating. 'Can I leave a message for him, please? Just a message.'

'What message?'

'Ask him to call Liv. He'll understand. And thank you, it's very urgent.' She read out her phone number, thanked the woman again, then hung up. There was no way of knowing

219

whether her message would be passed on or simply dropped in the trash.

Frantically she ran through a mental list of the people she had met during her time in Ruin who might know something, but realized with a creeping sense of dread that most of them were now dead. Perhaps Ski was right about her being cursed. The history of the Sacrament was littered with curses and dire prophesies. Liv had been part of one herself. She remembered sitting in the shadow of the Citadel and discussing them with . . .

Opening another tab in the browser, she Googled 'Dr Miriam Anata'. In amongst the hits was a link to a website. Liv opened it and a picture filled the screen of the same formidable woman she had last met in the old town of Ruin. There was a contact page with publishers' details for all her books, a talent agent for public speaking engagements, and an email contact for the author. She clicked on the link and started to write.

Dr Anata,
This is Liv Adamsen. If you know how to contact G then please get him to call me urgently. I am safe and so is this number.

She copied Ski's cell into the message then sent it.

As she watched it leave the outbox a sense of uselessness and frustration settled on her. She was running out of options and had got precisely nowhere.

Flipping back to the Google results, she trawled through them in search of another number. In an hour or two she could call one of her colleagues at the paper and get them to dig out a home or mobile number for Dr Anata from the database, but she didn't want to wait that long, nor did she want to get caught up in a conversation with a reporter who would inevitably want details of everything that had happened to her in the last two weeks.

From somewhere down the corridor came the lonely sound of a door slamming, followed by footsteps hurrying away. It occurred to her that she could sit here all day, if she felt like it, until Ski came back to check on her and politely tell her that they needed the room and was there anyone she could stay with? But there was no one. Her family were all dead. Everything she had been was gone.

She wondered how many of this room's occupants had experienced the same feeling; key witnesses, preparing to burn down their old lives by giving testimony in big trials. Perhaps the room was somehow tainted by too many desolate thoughts of lost histories and uncertain futures. How easy would it be to give up, standing in a room like this with a brick wall for a view?

Unnerved by the dark dead-end route her mind was taking, Liv jolted herself into action. She emptied the remaining contents of her holdall on to the bed and started to fold the clothes, giving order to the few things she still possessed. She placed the history book on the nightstand along with her notebook and found the envelope that had contained the Turkish currency. She was about to drop it in the bin when it occurred to her that the few receipts it contained might hold some clue as to where she had been during her time in Ruin. Inside were a couple of taxi receipts, one for food, and a large piece of folded paper. She opened it up, hoping it might be an itemized hotel bill or something more informative. She was completely unprepared for what it turned out to be.

One whole side was smudged with charcoal where it had been rubbed against a stone relief. And where the charcoal was missing, symbols were revealed: the same symbols she had seen in the book. She turned it over and found a handwritten note:

This will not explain everything, nothing ever could, but it may be a start. I hope, having eased your escape from the mountain, things will change and we can talk of this further in person. But if the Citadel

remains closed, as well it might, know you always
have a friend here. To contact me, give confession at
the public church and ask for Brother Peacock. Any
sealed message you pass on will come to me unopened.
Yours
Brother Athanasius

The note jarred a series of fresh memories loose.

She remembered the monk, his smooth head glowing in
the dark of the chapel as he led them away through the smoke-
filled tunnels of the mountain and down to where the outside
world had broken in. He had helped them get away – he was
offering help still. She turned the page and stared at the
smudged symbols, so strange yet familiar. The main body was
in a solid block, but at the bottom they formed the shape of
the T. It was the biggest example of the lost language she had
seen – bigger than any of those pictured in the book.

As her eyes traced the outlines, the whispering in her head
began to rise in volume and her skin started to prickle. She
had been out of the hospital far too long now to write these
symptoms off as some kind of drug-induced side effect.
Whatever was causing them wasn't chemical; it had to be
psychological or something else she wasn't fully prepared to
consider.

Spreading the piece of paper on the desktop, she focused
once more on the symbols. Almost immediately the whispering
rose again, getting louder the harder she concentrated. It
swamped the hiss of traffic from the road outside, filling her
head while her skin crawled with tiny pinpricks. Liv rode it
out, forcing herself to bear it as if she were holding her hand
over a flame.

The whispering took form, becoming a voice in her head,
and the symbols before her eyes began to shift, revealing words
that explained everything . . .

55

Dick watched the hotel from a bus stop across the street, his crumpled businessman persona fitting in perfectly with the early-morning commuters who came and went with the steady stream of buses. The police cruiser had pulled away a while back with only the cop in the driver's seat. If he was a boyfriend then there wasn't much romance going on. A quick call to the hotel had established that there was no Liv Adamsen staying there – at least, not officially.

The fact that the cop had managed to check her in under a false name so quickly hinted at an existing system that everybody was familiar with and nobody questioned. Given that the hotel was round the corner from the main courthouse, Dick concluded it must be a safe house. Ordinarily this would be a major problem – safe houses were specifically designed to keep people like him out – but there was no squad car parked outside and probably no guards stationed in the corridors with their eyes sharpened by suspicion and too much coffee. The girl might feel comforted by the illusion of safety this place provided, but that was all it was – an illusion.

Dick liked this kind of calm surveillance, the cool-headed fact-finding before the heat of what was to come. Another bus pulled in and a posse of work zombies shuffled on, leaving him alone in the shelter. It was early enough in the year for it to still be gloomy at this time of the morning and he watched the lights coming on as the guests in the hotel woke up. It didn't seem to be that full.

His phone chirped in his pocket, telling him he had a new

message. He opened it and spotted two words that he usually savoured, but in this case tasted slightly sour.

Si-lence

Im-me-di-ate-ly

He deleted the message and headed for the entrance to the hotel, adopting the bearing of a weary businessman in search of a cheap room.

Once again, any notion of taking his time had been taken from him. Everyone was in such a hurry these days.

56

Liv grabbed her notebook and frantically transcribed the words running through her head, not trusting her fitful memory to keep hold of it for long. But even as she wrote she found things difficult to pin down or understand, the meanings shifting and slipping away within the whispering. It was as if whatever the symbols were trying to express was too nebulous or slippery to capture in language. When she had finished she collapsed back in her seat and breathed deeply, allowing the whispering to subside until she felt in full possession of herself again. She got up from her chair and stumbled into the bathroom, splashing water on her face before returning to read what she had written.

So they kept _her_ weak.
The light of God, sealed up in darkness,
For they dared not release her, for fear of what
 might follow,
Nor could they kill her, for they knew not how.
And as time passed the men became chained to
 their own guilt,
And their home became a fortress
Containing the only knowledge of the deed they had
 done,
Not a mountain sanctified, but a prison cursed.
With Eve still captive,
A holy secret - a Sacrament,
Until the time foretold when her suffering
 would end

Liv jumped up, knocking the chair over as if she had discovered a snake on the desk. She reread the last three lines, the key words pulsing in her head: Eve . . . a holy secret . . . a Sacrament.

Just saying them conjured clear memories of what she had seen in the Citadel. She remembered the Tau and the eyes inside it, green like hers, staring out at her. She remembered the front of the cross levering open, and seeing the frail girl inside with hair like moonlight and a body running with blood, ravaged by pinpricks and terrible wounds. She rubbed her own skin, remembering the prickles of her own recent experience. It was the same. She was the same. But it was not her experience she was remembering.

She looked back down at the notebook and read the rest of the translation:

> The one true cross will appear on earth
> All will see it in a single moment – all will wonder
> The cross will fall
> The cross will rise
> To unlock the Sacrament
> And bring forth a new age
> Through its merciful <u>death</u>

It was the prophecy that Gabriel had explained to her. And now she could see how it had all come true. Her brother had made the sign of the Tau – the one true cross – before he had fallen, and she had risen in his place, flesh of his flesh. She was the cross. She had unlocked the Sacrament.

More memories came. The knife in her hand, the spilt blood, hers and . . . Eve's, mingling on the floor. Their spirits joining as their blood flowed. She looked up at the mirror and stared at her eyes. Green eyes – hers, but not hers – like someone else was staring back. She reached out to touch her reflection but the sharp sound of a doorbell made her head whip round.

Adrenalin flooded through her. Who could be there this early in the morning? It rang again and she realized her mistake. It was just Ski's mobile ringing on the bed. She lunged for it, fearful it might stop and jabbed the button to answer it.

'Hello?'

There was the briefest of pauses – satellite delay – then he spoke.

'Liv. It's me. It's Gabriel.'

Never had she experienced such relief at the sound of somebody's voice. Liv felt the smile start somewhere deep inside her and radiate upwards like heat. So much had happened – so much to say. 'Hi,' she managed, her smile lighting up the word as though it was written in neon.

'Hi,' he said. He was smiling too. She could hear it in his voice. 'Where are you?'

'I'm . . .' She was about to say 'home', but the word stuck in her throat. 'I'm back in New Jersey in a hotel a friend sorted out for me.' She caught sight of the TV and remembered the news she had seen on it. 'How about you? I saw the news.'

'I'm OK,' he said, shutting down her question, the smile suddenly absent from his voice. 'We can talk about it later. Right now we need to get you safe before the Citadel finds you again. Have you got your laptop and access to the Internet?'

'Yes.'

'Have you ever used Skype before?'

'Of course.' Skype was every journalist's friend. Wherever there was Wi-Fi it could be used instead of a phone to make free calls. It also worked as a videophone and was increasingly being used to file news reports from difficult foreign locations. Liv opened up the application and copied Gabriel's Skype address. Then she clicked on 'new contact' to make the call.

57

The receptionist looked up at the man in the crumpled suit lumbering towards her and clipped on her corporate smile.

'How can I help you today, sir?'

'Well, you could have a word with my boss and tell him these early-morning flights are killing me.' He dropped his holdall to the floor and leaned heavily on the reception counter, glancing down at the computer screen.

'Do you have a reservation with us, sir?'

Dick took a deep breath and let it out slowly in a pantomime of weariness. 'No, I'm afraid I don't. What I do have is a court appearance later this morning and, after getting exactly zero sleep on the overnight from London, I need somewhere to rest my weary head for an hour or two, otherwise I'm not going to be much use to my client. I guess they don't call it the red-eye for nothing.'

He handed over a passport and a dummy credit card in the same fake name.

'Let's see what we can do for you, sir,' she said, taking the documents and pecking away at the keyboard.

'I don't need anything special,' he said, rubbing his eyes with the heel of his hand. 'Just a basic room where I won't get woken by the noise of the traffic or the morning crowd heading down to breakfast.' Her fingers continued to tap. He leaned in conspiratorially, the counter creaking under his weight. 'In fact, a lawyer friend of mine says they sometimes use this hotel to put up jurors and witnesses in key cases. I bet those rooms are nice and out of the way. One of those would be perfect.'

Her fingers finished tapping. She hit the return key, extracted a plastic card from a coding machine and slipped it into a cardboard wallet. 'Room 722,' she said, writing the number on the front of the card. 'Take the elevator to the seventh floor and it's at the end of the corridor to your right. Do you need a hand with any luggage?'

Dick took the keycard along with his passport and credit card and winked at her. 'No thanks,' he said, picking up his holdall and heading away across the lobby. 'You've been more than enough help already.'

58

The rapid beeps of a number being dialled fed through the stereo speakers of Liv's laptop. She was still in shock from the flood of memories the translated text had brought back. For all her scepticism and rationality what she had read there made a sort of sense. It explained why she could understand an ancient language she had never heard of or learned. It explained why she felt the sting of needles every time the whispering rose up. But it didn't explain what 'The Key' was, or what it had to do with her. The dialling tone switched to a ringing one. Liv cleared her throat and pushed herself up in the chair, suddenly nervous about seeing Gabriel again.

On screen the feed from Liv's webcam popped up, revealing a low-res version of herself, amplifying how tired and dishevelled she was looking. She fussed with her hair and rubbed at the dark circles under her eyes as if it was dirt that could be wiped away. She considered cutting the connection and splashing more water on her face first to try to make herself more presentable, but a click cut off the ringing sound and the main window expanded to display the incoming feed.

Gabriel's voice materialized first, much richer than it had sounded on the phone and just as deep as she remembered.

'Liv? Can you hear me?' Then there he was, gazing at her, his brow knitted with concern, his blue eyes burning from the screen. She reached out involuntarily to touch his face. 'Hey,' she said.

A smile softened his face and he reached out for her. It was the first time they had seen each other since the Turkish police had taken him away and he had told her to go somewhere safe, promising he would find her. And now he had made good that promise, though it was not quite the reunion either of them had envisaged.

'I need to show you something,' Liv said, reaching for the piece of paper she had found in the envelope. 'The monk who helped us escape from the mountain gave it to me. Let me know if you can't read it – turns out, I can!' She held it up to the screen and four thousand miles away in Ruin the symbols came into focus. She held it long enough for him to translate it. When she lowered it again Dr Anata had joined Gabriel on the screen. From the looks on both their faces she could tell that they'd both read it.

'Of course,' Anata said. 'What else would the Sacrament be but something of the original divine. It's the only thing old enough or powerful enough to make sense. The Sacrament is the earth goddess, trapped in darkness by envious men, and you have set her free. The prophecy has been fulfilled.'

Liv shook her head and let out a long breath. 'I have to tell you I'm having a lot of difficulty with all of this. A couple of weeks ago I would have laughed in your face if you had told me half the things I'm now taking seriously. Let's, for argument's sake, say that all of this is true, then why do I feel like crap? If some divine spirit has entered into me, shouldn't I be feeling fantastic? And why am I getting whispered messages that don't make sense? And how come those maniacs in the Citadel are still killing everyone? Doesn't feel like very much has been fulfilled to me.'

Gabriel and Anata exchanged glances.

'What?' Liv said.

'There is a second prophecy,' Gabriel said, 'the Mirror Prophecy, and it follows on from the first.'

He held Oscar's diary up to the webcam and this time Liv's screen filled with the familiar symbols. The whispering rose again as she stared at it and again she scribbled the translation into her notebook directly below the other. Even as she was transcribing she realized its significance. She had wondered what the key was and now she knew. It was her.

The Key unlocks the Sacrament
The Sacrament becomes the Key
And all the Earth shalt tremble
The Key must follow the Starmap Home
There to quench the fire of the dragon within the full
phase of a moon
Lest the Key shalt perish, the Earth shalt splinter and a
blight shalt prosper, marking the end of all days

She had been yearning for home ever since waking up in the hospital. At the time she had thought it was her survivor's instinct driving her to return to the familiar and the safe, back to America and away from the dark, threatening streets of Ruin. Now she realized it was something different. It had not been her own home she had been craving – and continued to crave – it was wherever the Sacrament had come from. 'The Key must follow the Starmap Home,' she repeated.

'Yes,' Dr Anata said. 'The Home referred to by the Mirror Prophecy is the original home for all of us, the place where the Sacrament first walked: Eden.'

Again Liv felt her rational self take a body blow.

'The Mirror Prophecy is clear,' Anata continued. 'The dragon is the symbol of fire and destruction. If you do not carry the Sacrament home to Eden in time, then the end of days will be upon us.'

'How long have we got?'

'Seventeen days – maybe less.'

'And if we fail?'

'The end of days is described in the Book of Revelation of Saint John the Divine. An antichrist will arrive on earth bringing plague, famine, earthquakes and flood. The oceans will rise up and swallow the mountains and the mountains will crumble to the sea. Cities will be destroyed. Life as we know it will end and the righteous will be gathered to God.'

Liv slumped in her chair.

Gabriel leaned forward until his face filled the screen. 'I'll arrange safe transport to bring you here. All the ancient biblical lands are close to Ruin and that's where we'll need to look. By the time you get here, I'll have worked out a way of getting into the Citadel.'

Liv snapped to attention. 'What?'

'That's where Oscar hid the Starmap. If we don't find it, we won't find Eden.'

Yet again the Citadel was pulling at her with its dark gravity. She had run as far away as she could and yet here she was, still shivering in the long shadow it cast, her destiny still tied up in the secrets it contained and now carried with her. Then a thought struck her. She reached for the sheet of paper, reread the note from Athanasius, then looked up at Gabriel and smiled. 'I think I know how you can get into the Citadel,' she said.

59

The elevator doors slid open and Dick stepped on to the blue-grey carpet of the seventh floor. He stood for a moment, scanning the long empty corridor, listening for any sounds through the early-morning quiet of the hotel. Turning right as the receptionist had instructed, and moving silently despite his size, he listened to each room as he went by.

He passed a tray covered with the gnawed remains of a room-service order, a couple of doors with 'Do Not Disturb' signs dangling from their handles, but other than that the corridor appeared to be unoccupied.

The hydraulic arm of a fire door hissed as he pushed through into the corridor furthest from the main stairwell. His own room was just inside, but he drifted past, drawn by sharp predatory instincts and the faint murmur of something at the end of the hallway. He followed the sound, barely more than a whisper, until he stood by the door it was coming from.

Dick reached out and touched its surface with his fingertips, feeling the tiny vibrations coming from the other side. Then he leaned forward, and pressed his ear to the door. It was fire regulated, which meant it was solid and therefore an excellent conductor of sound waves. Inside the room he could hear a TV tuned to a news channel and beneath it, softer and less distinct, the sound of two people talking.

He shifted his position, careful not to make any noise, and pressed his ear tighter to the surface. He had planned to improvise his way into her room under the guise of room service or housekeeping and break her neck the moment she opened the door. But another person put an entirely different complexion on things. He would have to wait a while longer.

For a brief moment he thought about kicking the door in with one mighty blow and taking his chances. It was what his old self would have done. But that was not the way he worked any more. He had learned to contain his violent exuberance and form his feelings into words. Words gave him control, and the word for this situation was clear:

Pa-tience

60

Liv stood under the hot shower feeling the tension she had been carrying around for the last few weeks running off and swirling down the drain with the dirty water. She was surprised by how calm she felt following her conversation with Gabriel. In effect, she had been given two weeks to live, and a near impossible task to complete if she wanted to change that, and yet her overwhelming reaction was one of relief. She had read that soldiers often experienced similar feelings when they were finally faced with combat duty. There was something comforting about knowing that your fate was in your own hands, even if the odds were stacked against you. She shut off the water and grabbed a bathrobe and a couple of thin towels from the rail.

The bedroom seemed particularly cold and gloomy after the glare of the bathroom and the steam followed her out like a vapour trail. Gabriel had told her to sit tight until he could work out the details of her transportation back to Ruin. From there she had no idea where they would go, but she would be with him, so that was something at least.

She packed her belongings and laid some fresh clothes on the chair, but didn't put them on. The travel arrangements were bound to take a while to sort out and she hadn't slept for more than twenty-four hours. Until Gabriel called back, she was going to try to sleep. After towelling herself dry, she wrapped the smaller towel round her damp hair and squirmed into bed.

The sheets were starchy and cool against her skin and the mattress was firm, but it felt like the finest feather down.

Outside she could hear the growing hiss of the morning traffic as people made their way into work. It struck her as odd that, here she was, lying in a nondescript corporate hotel room in New Jersey, contemplating a journey that would ultimately take her to the Garden of Eden. The idea seemed absurd, like calling up a travel agent and trying to book a flight to Mordor. In her rather vague religious upbringing she had assumed that the creation story and the Garden of Eden were legends. It had never occurred to her that they might be real.

She reached over to the nightstand and pulled open the drawer, curiosity outweighing her exhaustion. Sure enough, it contained a copy of the Gideon Bible, the only book you could find in every hotel room in America. She opened it to Genesis and scanned the first few pages, the onionskin paper feeling much too flimsy to carry the weight of the words printed on it. Then, in the tenth verse of the second chapter she came across something very interesting:

> *And a river went out of Eden to water the garden; and from thence it was parted, and became into four heads.*
>
> *The name of the first is Pison: that is it which compasseth the whole land of Hav'ilah, where there is gold;*
>
> *And the gold of that land is good: there is bdellium and the onyx stone.*
>
> *And the name of the second river is Gihon: the same is it that compasseth the whole land of Ethiopia.*
>
> *And the name of the third river is Hid'dekel: that is it which goeth toward the east of Assyria. And the fourth river is Euphra'tes.*

This legendary story was actually peppered with the names of real, modern-day places: Ethiopia, Assyria, Euphrates. She had always seen the story of man's fall as something of a parable, a metaphor for grander theological ideas. Now she read it straight, a true account of exile, a tale so rapid and terrible that man had already been banished from paradise before the end of the next chapter.

> *Therefore the Lord God sent him forth from the garden of Eden, to till the ground from whence he was taken.*
> *So he drove out the man; and he placed at the east of the garden of Eden Cherubims, and a flaming sword which turned every which way, to keep the way of the tree of life.*

Liv took her notebook and turned to a new page. She wrote down all the place names mentioned in Genesis that still existed, then studied the list. She added Al-Hillah, the place the tablet had been found, then Eden. She stared at what she had just written, still having difficulty comprehending that Eden might be a place every bit as real as the others. She added several question marks next to it before reading on, looking for further clues that might point her to where her destiny might lie. But in the end, the richness of the language and her own tiredness took hold. Halfway through chapter four, shortly after Cain slew Abel, her eyes drooped and the book slipped from her hand, her head full of columns of fire and modern rivers flowing out of an ancient land that was filled with gold and onyx.

61

Badiyat al-Sham

The Ghost followed the convoy across the desert at a safe distance, wary of the M60 and the heavily armed guards in the rear truck. It was easy to track them; the three vehicles kicked up enough dust to give away their position for miles and his horse was as swift over the rough ground as they were. After nearly an hour of driving the dust cloud disappeared, indicating that the convoy had stopped. He followed their tyre tracks until he felt he was getting close, then left his horse in the shade of a berm and covered the rest of the distance on foot. He had almost reached what he thought was their position when he heard the gunshot.

He slid his AK-47 from his back, shouldering it as he hit the ground. Scanning the way ahead, he saw a wisp of dust rising like vapour in the distance. From the sound, it had been a shotgun he'd heard – a close-quarters weapon – so it seemed doubtful that it had been meant for him. Even so, the Ghost kept low as he moved closer.

The trucks were parked in the shade of another spill pile, the byproduct of more hole-digging. One of the men in white overalls was crouched on the ground, de-rigging a broad tube that had been driven into the earth. It was part of a seismic refraction kit that fired a blank cartridge into the ground and measured the echo of the waves. Solid objects would reflect the waves back differently.

The three civilians in charge were hunched over a laptop, studying the findings. They seemed agitated about something. After some discussion, they pointed at a spot close to where the Ghost was hiding and started walking towards him. The white-overalled workmen followed, bringing their picks and shovels with them. The guards remained by their jeep looking bored.

The civilians reached a patch of ground about twenty metres away from the parked jeeps and pointed to the ground. Then they stood and watched as the workmen started hacking away at it. One of the bearded men pulled a bottle of water from a cool box and drank almost half of it in a single draught. Through his field glasses the Ghost could see the condensation on the side of the bottle and licked his own dry lips in response. The sun was only a third of its way up in the sky but was already starting to dry him out like a lizard on a rock. He needed to find better cover and take a drink himself, but the digging party was too close. His only option was to stay where he was until they got tired of digging their latest hole and moved on.

But they didn't.

After five minutes, a clear sound rang out from the hole drawing everyone's attention. The civilians rushed forward and the fattest of the three dropped down to clear away more earth with his hand. When he stood up he had a look of near exaltation on his face.

'Radio base and tell them to get the earth movers here right now,' he hollered over to the security detail. 'And tell them we'll need to set up a compound. We've found it!' He climbed out of the hole, smacking the dust from his hands. 'Praise God, we've found it.'

62

The Citadel

Dragan experienced a moment of pure panic as he entered the chapel of the Sacrament and saw the door hanging open, the needles exposed, the cross empty.

He fell to his knees before it, but not in any act of worship. After the exertions of his spectacular return to the Citadel he felt mortally weak. The single thing that had driven him on was his desire to be near the Sacrament again and resume the ritual of communion that suffused all those who partook of it with its sacred force and energy. Only the Sacrament could restore health and strength to himself and the mountain – but the Sacrament was gone.

As he looked around the empty chapel he caught sight of himself reflected in one of the shining blades on the walls. How could God taunt him so? How could He ravage his body like this and offer him the chance of salvation, only to pull it away again? Then he shook his head and felt ashamed. This was not the work of God. It was the Devil's doing he was witnessing here.

Dragan reminded himself of Saint Job and the trials he had endured after God removed his protection. Satan had taken away his prosperity, his family and his health to test his faith and make him curse the Lord's name. But Job had refused, cursing instead the day he was born. And had not Job been rewarded for this faith and ultimately been blessed with even greater prosperity and health than before? Dragan knew this was what he must do now. He had to keep his faith strong, though his body was weak and the way ahead uncertain. Only then would the Citadel be returned to its former strength.

Bowing his head, he prayed to the empty cross, confessing the sins he had committed since last he had stood here. He asked forgiveness for his lack of faith and for the strength to do God's bidding. Finally he said a prayer of remembrance for the departed soul of the priest who had been sent to take his life and had ended up losing his own. He believed that everything happened for a reason, that each step was pre-ordained and each man merely an instrument of God's greater will. As he thought now about the sequence of his own passage back to the Citadel, he began to see God's work even in that.

First he had sent him the nervous orderly, always in such a hurry to leave that one day he had left a scalpel behind. Then he had sent the priest who had died by the edge of that same blade as he tried to smother Dragan with a pillow. These things were not accidental; they had each been purposeful and ordained.

When he had finished his prayers he bent forward, lying full length on the cold stone of the chapel floor. He stretched his arms out either side, making the sign of the Tau with his body, abasing himself before the altar in an act of total subjugation and humility. He lay like this for a long while, praying that God might show him a sign to guide him further, until his aching body could stand it no more and a coughing fit forced him upright.

He stood stiffly, using his hands to brush away the dust that had collected on his cassock. A long, thin strand of gold twisted away in the air, caught by the flickering candlelight. He reached out and caught it in his hand, the fine gold thread standing out starkly against his blackened skin. He was surprised that such a thing was present in the chapel. Unlike the high church beyond the walls of the mountain, the holy men of the Citadel wore no ceremonial gowns of gold or silk. Even the Abbot and the Prelate wore the same rough cassocks as everyone else, so it was a mystery how a gold thread could find its way in here.

He held it up to the light, stretching it out to get a better look, then realized what it was. It was not a golden thread but a long strand of blonde hair, lighter at the tip and darker at the root. Bleached hair – female hair. He thought back to the woman who had been evacuated from the Citadel. He had seen her image on the news, even glimpsed her himself when they had first been admitted to hospital. Her hair was blonde too, the same colour and length as the strand he now held in his hand. She must have been here, inside the chapel. And she was a woman, a sacred vessel with the power to carry living things inside her.

Dragan turned and left the chapel with a renewed sense of purpose. He moved swiftly along the tunnel towards the top of the stairs then turned right into one of the ancillary passageways. A set of narrower steps carried him down a few levels to one of the deserted sections of the mountain where a series of abandoned cells fed off from the main tunnel. He entered the first door and saw what he was looking for, carved into the wall opposite. It was a loophole, a narrow window cut into the rock of the outer wall of the mountain; beyond it was a clear uninterrupted view of the sprawling city of Ruin.

He hurried over, reaching into the pocket of his cassock to pull out the mobile phone he had taken from the dead priest. Ordinarily, entrance by the Ascension Cave involved each new arrival stripping naked; a symbolic rebirth, but also a practical measure to ensure nothing from the outside world could be smuggled into the mountain. In the unusual circumstances of his own re-entry these customs had been ignored and the phone had remained undetected in his pocket.

He turned it on and the display lit up. As he had hoped, his elevated position and clear view provided him with a full-strength signal. His stiff black fingers moved over the keys as he navigated his way through the menu until he found the caller logs. There was only one number listed, with several calls in and out over the last few days. Text messages had also been received from the same number. He read through them, smiling as he came across the one that had ordered his own death. He selected the number it had come from and pressed the call-back button.

As he looked out over Ruin, waiting for the phone to connect, it struck him that he was standing in the same cell Brother Samuel had been taken to after he had failed his initiation. This was where he had escaped from and started the chain reaction that had led the Citadel to its current crisis. How sweetly ironic it would be if his sister's return completed the circle and put things back as they were. She must have carried the Sacrament out of the mountain. Only she could bring it back again.

The phone rang.

Dragan waited.

Then, just as God had ordained it, someone picked up.

63

Vatican City

Clementi had been pacing in his office, waiting for confirmation of his earlier order, when the phone rang in his pocket. He stubbed out his cigarette and answered it. 'You have news?'

'Yes.' The voice was thickly accented and unfamiliar. 'I have news from beyond the grave.'

Clementi said nothing, fearing a trap.

'Don't worry,' the voice continued, 'I am not angry that you ordered me killed. I understand better than most the need for these rules of absolute secrecy. I am only surprised you did not try it sooner. Unfortunately, the priest you sent did not manage to bring death to me, rather the other way round. By God's grace I am now back where I belong, inside the Citadel.'

He sounded Slavic. The personnel records Clementi had read indicated that the last Sanctus was a Serbian monk. It could be him, but he needed to be sure. He moved over to his desk and opened the top drawer where he kept the files relating to the crisis in Ruin. 'Tell me your name,' he said.

'I am Dragan Ruja. Born in the city of Banja Luka on the twenty-fourth of October 1964. I entered the Citadel in 1995 following the death of my family during the Bosnian War.'

It was him. No question. The facts checked out. 'I am glad you have found your way home safely,' Clementi said, a slight shudder running through him as he realized he was talking to someone actually inside the Citadel.

'Thank you for your concern. However I have returned here only to discover there has been a theft. Tell me, do you know where Liv Adamsen is?'

'Yes.'

'Good. I presume you have issued a similar silencing order regarding her.'

Clementi didn't reply.

'You must cancel it immediately. She is not to be killed. She is to be brought here to the Citadel as quickly as possible. She is to be brought here alive.'

'I'm not sure that will be possible.'

'This is not a request, this is an order. You are familiar with the Constantinian decree of 374, ceding the Church's power to Rome?'

'Of course.'

'Then you know that the Prelate of Ruin remains *de facto* head of the Church, even though the Pope is its public and temporal figurehead.'

Clementi swallowed drily. If he'd had any doubts as to the identity of the man he was speaking to they had now been entirely banished. Only the most senior clerics in the Vatican and the governing elect of the Citadel knew these secret edicts.

'I will do all I can,' Clementi said, 'but the field agent is close to his target and I may not be able to contact him in time. There is a very real chance that the girl may already be dead.'

There was a pause on the line and Clementi could sense the anger in it. 'I hope for your sake that she is not,' the Sanctus replied. Then the line went dead.

64

Newark, New Jersey

Liv woke gently from sleep.

Outside she could hear the low-level hiss and rumble of traffic on the street. Light filtered softly through the curtains showing it was still day, although she had no idea what time it was. She might have been asleep for a few minutes, a few hours or even a few days. She blinked and peered around the plain hotel room. Her laptop was where she'd left it, folded down and switched off; her jacket was draped over the back of the chair; the Gideon Bible lay open on the bed where it had slipped from her hand – nothing was out of place, yet something was different. It took her a long few moments to realize what it was. For the first time in weeks she hadn't had the nightmare. She had woken up, gently and unterrified, like any normal person. There was no whispering in her ears, no vision of T-shaped crosses or things terrible and unseen moving in the darkness.

All was quiet.

All was calm.

She took a deep breath and let it out slowly, feeling the tension in her shoulders melt away. She felt relaxed – at peace.

Then a loud knock split the silence like a gunshot.

Liv sat bolt upright in bed and stared at the door, running through the short list of people who knew she was here: Gabriel; Ski; Dr Anata. No one else.

The chances were it was Ski, checking up on her, but she was reluctant to call out and confirm her presence in the room until she knew who was there.

Another knock made her jump, loud and emphatic, still no identifying voice. Even room service would have announced themselves by now.

She slipped quietly from the bed, wrapping the discarded bathrobe round her as she ran through her options. There was nowhere to hide in the tiny room, nothing she could see that could be used as a weapon. Her room was a trap – one way in, one way out.

Slipping round the edge of the bed and keeping as far away from the door as possible, she scooped up Ski's cell phone from the desk and quickly copied the number of the main switchboard from the hotel stationery into it. If whoever was out there tried to get into her room she would lock herself in the bathroom and call for security, scream rape – anything to get them running. She started moving, then a voice called out that stopped her dead.

'Liv?'

'Gabriel?' She had spoken his name without thinking and, in the silence that followed, instantly regretted it.

Whoever was out there had only said one word and it had been muffled by the thick hotel door. Was it Gabriel? It couldn't be, she had not long spoken to him in Ruin, half a day's journey away. Unless . . . maybe she'd slept longer than she'd thought; she'd certainly been tired enough.

'Liv?'

The voice again – so like him.

'Hang on a second,' she said, realizing there was no point in further caution. 'How come you got here so fast?'

'I came on the first flight. You must have been sleeping all day.'

It *was* him. Liv felt a flush of heat on her skin and lunged for the door, opening it without a second thought.

Another blast of heat hit her from the corridor, hotter even than the air in her room.

Gabriel was standing a little way back from the door, his arms by his sides, looking slightly awkward. He was exactly as she remembered, his white skin made whiter by his black clothes and hair, the cold blueness of his eyes the only point of colour in the windowless corridor. She looked into his face and smiled – but he did not return it. A single tear ran down his cheek, as though the blue ice of his eye was melting in the heat.

'I'm sorry,' he said.

Then the whole corridor erupted in flame.

Liv was knocked backwards by the blast. She landed on the bed and covered her face with her arms. Through the roar of the flames the whispering filled her head like a warning. When she tried to look at the place where Gabriel had been, the heat and the brightness forced her eyes shut. She stood up and tried to get closer to the door, covering her face with the sleeve of her bathrobe, hoping that Gabriel might somehow have survived the furnace.

Then, as quickly as it had come, the fire vanished, and instead of a hotel corridor a desert landscape was now framed by the open door. It was flat and featureless and made up of night-time shadows and the soft glow of moonlight. Liv drifted towards it, drawn by its strangeness.

She reached the door and saw it – the beast – the source of the inferno. It squatted on the sand; a huge lizard thing made of spines and plate and fire. Its red eyes were staring straight at her, while its spear-like tail quivered and curled towards the night sky where a full moon shone.

The beast took a breath, sucking in the flame and smoke that circled its mouth, closing its red eyes as it savoured her scent. Then something flew through the night, striking her in the middle of the chest and skewering both flesh and spirit. She tried to scream but no sound came out. She could feel her blood coursing down her skin like a memory of her time in the Citadel. It felt almost cool against the heat of the desert night. Then the thing lifted her up, raising her towards its mouth on the spike of its tail. She could smell death on its breath and saw a mark on its neck – a cross in the shape of an inverted T. Then it let out a shriek so shrill that it ripped through her head, and fire poured from its mouth to consume her.

65

Liv jerked forward in bed, the shrill shriek of the nightmare still echoing in her ears.

The hotel room was a mess – the chair tipped on its side, bedclothes twisted from the bed, and pages of torn paper drifting over everything. She wondered whether she was still dreaming and this was part of a layered nightmare she would have to escape bit by bit. She drew her knees up to her chin, waiting for what terror might unfold next, but no one knocked on the door, the temperature in the room stayed normal, and no dragons appeared in the middle of strange desert vistas. What she was looking at was real, and all the more disturbing because of it.

She tried to rationalize what might have happened: either someone had broken into her room and done this while she slept, or she had done it herself in some kind of dreaming fit. Neither explanation gave her much comfort. Her laptop was folded shut on the side where she had left it. Surely an intruder would have taken it? The only sensible conclusion was that she had done it herself, or whatever entity she now carried inside her had done it while her conscious self slept.

She scooped up a handful of paper from the bed. They were pages of scripture, ripped from the Gideon Bible. The cover lay on the floor by the bed. She picked it up and it flopped open in her hand like a dead thing. There was one page remaining, from the Book of Revelation, and it had clearly not been spared by accident. Most of the text on the page had been crossed out by a jagged, angry hand, but there was one section left:

> . . . *and behold a great red dragon, having seven heads and ten horns, and seven crowns upon his heads. And his tail drew the third part of the stars of heaven, and did cast them to the earth: and the dragon stood before the woman which was ready to be delivered, for to devour her child as soon as it was born. And she brought forth a child, who was to rule all nations . . .*

She stared at the words, the shrill sound of the dragon's cry still splitting her head.

A loud rap on the door made her jump.

'Make your way to the stairs, please, quickly now.'

The man moved away down the corridor, banging on every door and repeating his order as he went. The wailing sound was not the continued roar of the demon in her dream, but a fire alarm.

She quickly pulled on the clothes she'd laid out and grabbed her bag.

The siren was louder outside in the hallway and she clamped her hands over her ears as she headed towards the stairwell. She wondered at the coincidence of the verses from Revelation describing her nightmare so exactly. Maybe she'd read it before falling asleep and planted the seeds of those images in her mind.

She reached the fire door and pushed her way through, wondering if Gabriel had managed to sort out her passage to Ruin yet. She couldn't believe she was actually looking forward to going back. Seeing him again had rekindled something inside her; something connected to him.

She was so distracted by these thoughts that she didn't hear the swish of the door opening behind her, or catch the sharp whiff of chloroform until the towel was already clamped on her face and held there by a hand as big as her head.

She tried to scream but the siren and the towel drowned it out. She tried to pull the huge hand away, but her arms were already wilting as the drug took hold. The last thing she remembered before the darkness rose to swamp her entirely was a sudden rush of fear as she noticed the image of a cross tattooed on the forearm of the man who held her.

66

Dick kicked the door closed and laid the girl down on the bed.

He checked his watch. Still ten minutes before he was due to report back. The hardest part was done. He had flushed her out, discovered she was alone and now she was his. All he had to do was snap her neck, then slip away. A 'Do Not Disturb' sign on the door would ensure no one discovered her body until tomorrow at the earliest, by which time he would be long gone.

Leaning in close to study her face, he caught the hint of hotel soap above the ethanol-tang of the chloroform. She had clear, almost translucent skin stretched over fine bones. Her lips were parted, and small white teeth shone in the moist darkness of her mouth. He leaned close enough to feel her warm breath against his skin and noticed a faint crease of concentration running between her closed eyes. He had one himself, forged over years in the furnace of self-education, mostly in prison libraries.

Seeing her holdall, he picked it up and rummaged inside for the book she had been reading on the flight. He always liked to keep something. A *sou-ve-nir*. There was hardly anything in the bag so he found it immediately. But he also saw something that soured his good mood.

He removed the Gideon Bible, handling the tattered remains as tenderly as if it were an injured bird. The cover fell open and he felt fresh disgust when he saw all the scribble on the one page remaining. She had taken the Lord's words in vain, destroyed them even, and in doing so had committed, in his eyes, the gravest of sins.

He looked down at her unconscious form. She no longer seemed pretty to him. All he wanted was to finish the job and leave.

Outside, the fire alarm cut out and the room fell silent. He would have to be quick if he wanted to use what confusion remained to aid his escape.

She had broken the spine of the Gideon Bible and now he would break hers. There was a certain Old Testament balance to this: an eye for an eye.

As he took hold of her head in his giant hands and tensed his shoulders ready to snap her neck, something chirruped in the silence of the room, the sound of a text message. He so wanted to hear the noise of her neck breaking, but instinct and experience told him to wait, and discipline made sure he complied. Pulling the phone from his pocket, he opened the message. It made his own frown line deepen. He read it twice then looked back down at her.

'You like words,' he whispered at her sleeping form. 'Well, I have a good one for you. *Re-prieve.*'

67

Ruin

The old town had remained closed all morning while the earthquake damage had been cleared away from the streets. When they finally did open the portcullis gates, a little after two in the afternoon, there were thousands of people waiting to climb up to the public church at the top of the hill to give thanks for their safe deliverance. Dr Anata was one of them.

She jostled along with the flow of packed bodies, noticing how everything in the old town appeared remarkably untouched. Some of the pilgrims remarked on this apparent miracle, but Dr Anata knew better: it had more to do with geology than theology. Earthquakes were like waves and so looser ground amplified them, whereas the solid rock the old town was built on had damped them down, rendering them less effective. The earthquake had been less intense here, that was the only difference.

It took her nearly forty minutes to make it to the top of the hill and pass into the cool, monolithic interior of the public church. It was packed with the penitent and hummed with the combined sound and nervous energy of all the tourists and worshippers who had gathered to offer up prayers of forgiveness, thanks or contrition. Dr Anata weaved between them all, heading directly across the flagstoned floor to the confessional booths in the furthest corner of the church. Gabriel had offered to go, but with normality returning to the city, and too many people on the lookout for him, she had gone instead, thrilling at the opportunity to play a small part in something as momentous as this. Her entire life she had read about history; today she was actually making some.

She arrived at the confessional and took a seat on the end of a pew lined with subdued worshippers, all staring resolutely at the curtained booths. The walls behind them were painted with an elaborate and vividly imagined mediaeval fresco depicting the day of reckoning. Dr Anata wondered if they would let her jump the queue if they knew she was here to try to avert the very thing they were all staring at. She doubted it. People were funny about queues – even when the end of the world was at stake – so she settled down for a wait. It took a further twenty minutes before she made the short walk of shame and closed the curtain behind her.

Inside, it was cramped and smelled of incense and fear. She perched on a wooden ledge, bringing her face level with the grille.

'Do you have something to confess?' a muffled voice prompted.

'I would like to pass a message to Brother Peacock.' There was a brief pause, then whoever had been sitting there promptly got up and left without uttering another word.

Dr Anata listened to the sound of retreating footsteps melting into the general hubbub of the huge church. She wasn't sure what she had expected, but this sudden and silent departure certainly wasn't it. She felt nervous in its wake. As an academic she was wholly unused to situations that placed her at risk and her mind was now in overdrive, imagining all sorts of scenarios involving security guards and brutal interrogation. Only the importance of the message she carried, and everything that hung on its safe delivery, prevented her from slipping away while she still had the chance. A moment later the hiss of the curtain on the other side of the grille told her it was already too late for escape. A different voice spoke, so close it made her jump.

'I am the emissary of Brother Peacock,' it said. 'Do you have a message for him?'

'Yes.'

'Tell it to me and I will make sure he gets it – in confidence.'

Dr Anata pulled a sealed envelope from her pocket. 'I have a letter for him.'

'Then bow your head before God and pray that he receives it.'

She did as she was asked. A small section of panelling slid open to create a hatch between the two stalls. She reached down and passed the envelope through it. There was a slight tug as it was taken from her, then the hatch slid shut as quickly as it had opened.

'When will Brother Peacock receive the message?' she asked. But there was no answer. Whoever had taken the message had already gone.

68

The fourth floor of the Ruin police building was as busy and chaotic as Arkadian had ever seen it. Raised voices and ringing phones filled the open-plan office and the whole place smelled of stewed coffee and stress. The major problem was looting. In the wake of the earthquake the usual opportunists had stalked through the darkness, sifting through shops and businesses cracked open by the tremors. It was only in the cold light of day, when everyone else stopped rejoicing that they were still alive and turned their attention to more temporal matters, that they discovered they had been robbed. The moment the power had come back on, and the phones with them, the robbery section of the Robbery and Homicide Division had been inundated.

Arkadian sat at his desk in the corner, doing his best to shut out the noise. Today he was one of the few people dealing with a body and not a break-in. Since returning from the hospital and regaining access to the databases, he'd been trying to discover where the dead police officer had come from. He'd found no mention of a Nesim Senturk in the service records from the surrounding districts so had spread his search wider, taking in all departments, anywhere in the country. His computer terminal was now busily crunching through all the data, looking for the needle of one single name in a haystack made up of years of accumulated details.

In the meantime Arkadian had been doing what he could to check up on Liv. A phone call to Yun had confirmed that her flight had landed a few minutes ahead of schedule at 3.05

a.m. local time. Arkadian had then called the security police at Newark International Airport and, after explaining who he was and undergoing a lengthy security check that involved giving out more personal details than he usually gave his bank, they put him through to the main control centre. Here the duty manager confirmed that Liv Adamsen's passport had been swiped through immigration eleven minutes after her flight landed and that CCTV showed her leaving the main terminal building a minute later and being picked up by a cop in a police cruiser; he even gave him the registration number. A further call to the New Jersey Police Department, and a slightly less stringent security check, and Arkadian had a name: Sergeant William Godlewski, currently off duty, though the desk sergeant promised he'd contact him and get him to call back.

Arkadian smiled for the first time in hours. Liv was OK. She obviously had an American version of himself looking out for her, and that made him feel a whole lot better. Moving down to the next item on his 'To Do' list, he punched in an extension number and covered his other ear to shut out the noise of the room.

'Cell-block security desk.'

'Suleiyman? It's Arkadian.'

'Hey, I thought you was off sick with lead poisoning?'

'Yeah, well, that didn't really work out. Half the city's been robbed, so who can sit at home watching game shows?'

'Better than the stuff I get to watch all day. How's the arm?'

'Hurts. Listen, could you call up the camera feeds around the time of the breakout yesterday so I can come down and take a look?'

'Er . . . no, actually I can't. We only just got the full systems up and running again, and several files are missing.'

'Which ones?'

'Everything from yesterday afternoon.'

Arkadian felt his cop's instincts tingle. 'Any chance you could restore them?'

'No. The files haven't been corrupted – they're not there. The backup system must have failed.'

'Has this sort of thing ever happened before?'

'No – first time.'

'Any idea what might have caused it?'

Suleiyman exhaled like a builder pricing up a tricky job. 'Could be lots of things: there was a load of water dumped in the cells when the sprinklers went off, that might have tripped something; the system's a piece of crap anyway and is always breaking down; plus we just had a major earthquake – take your pick.'

Arkadian suspected it was none of these. It was too convenient and the files that were missing too specific. 'OK, thanks, Suleiyman. Let me know if they show up.'

'Will do, but I wouldn't hold your breath.'

He replaced the phone and glanced up at the busy room, wondering if whoever had destroyed them was standing here now. A beep drew his attention to the screen. He had a match. The top sheet of a service record filled the screen with a photograph of a slight man in glasses in one corner. He didn't look anything like the officer Arkadian had seen lying dead on the street. The only things that did match were the name, the badge number, and the fact that both men were dead. The real Sub-Inspector Nesim Senturk had served in the main metropolitan district of the Istanbul police force and been killed in the line of duty over a year ago during a raid on a drug trafficker. Whoever was now lying on the slab in the Ruin city morgue was an impostor, slotted into the guard detail with a genuine name and badge number by someone with access to the police files. Whoever was behind all this was clearly knowledgeable, powerful and well connected.

The desk phone rang, cutting through the din of the room.

'Arkadian!' he answered, clamping it to one ear and his hand to the other.

'Yeah, this is Sergeant Godlewski from the New Jersey PD. I got a message to call about Liv Adamsen.'

Arkadian switched to English. 'Yes, thanks for getting back so quickly.'

'Do you know where she's gone?'

The question threw Arkadian. 'I thought she was with you?'

'She was. I dropped her off at a safe hotel a few hours ago, but I just got here to check she was OK and she's gone. All her stuff's gone too and the room is a mess.'

Then Ski told him about the pages torn from a Bible and Arkadian felt a coldness creep over him as he realized who had her.

69

The modified McDonnell Douglas DC-9 lifted off from Newark International Airport and began its rapid climb into the early-afternoon sky.

On the outside it appeared to be a regular charter flight, the only distinguishing markings being a light blue logo with a white dove on the tail that looked like a scrap of a better day, sliding across the flat, grey sky. Inside, it hardly resembled a plane at all. The seating section had been ripped out and replaced with a double layer of steel cot beds running almost the entire length of the plane. At the back a separate section was kitted out as a fully functioning operating room.

The DC-9 belonged to the White Dove Organization, a global, Church-run charity that flew extreme trauma victims and other civilian cases out of war-torn countries to be treated in state-of-the-art Western facilities. The plane averaged three round-trip flights a week with almost all the patient traffic being inbound. For the outgoing journeys it served as a transport plane, so for this flight all the bunks had been stripped of their mattresses and turned into large shelving racks that were stacked solid with boxes of medical supplies and other equipment.

The solitary patient was at one end, strapped to a lower bunk. Three seatbelts stretched across the knees, waist and chest, and thin arms stretched out either side of the body, mummified in bandages that also crept around the neck and wrapped the head. A gel mask covered the face, indicating that the patient had suffered some kind of severe facial trauma as well as extensive damage to the arms and torso.

The medical carnet detailing the patient's history was in a zip-lock bag tied to the side of the bed along with a passport that identified her as Annie Lieberman, a missionary from Ohio, who had been brutally raped and mutilated then set on fire and left for dead by rebel soldiers in Guinea, West Africa. The immigration officer who had come on board prior to their departure had checked the documents but hadn't bothered to unwrap the bandages or lift the mask. Burn victims never looked like their photographs anyway, so there was little point. Her notes said she had been receiving treatment at the Burn Center at Saint Barnabas in New Jersey and was now on her way to undergo genital- and breast-reconstruction surgery in a specialized clinic in Bangkok. He had blanched when he read the details and quickly signed the necessary paperwork to send them on their way.

The plane banked now as it broke through clouds, flooding the interior with slowly moving shafts of light as it levelled off and headed east. Part of the plane's modifications had been to add extra fuel tanks, giving it a much longer range than the standard factory model, but at seven and a half thousand nautical miles, the flight to Bangkok was still too far in a single hop. Consequently their flight plan included one re-fuelling stop at Gaziantep International Airport in Southern Turkey.

Liv lay in the cot bed, awake but not awake. She was aware of the hum and vibration of the engines. She could feel the pressure of the bindings holding her in place and there was also something on her face, pressing down on her skin. She tried to move her arm to feel what it was, but nothing happened. She tried to open her eyes, but they too remained shut. It was as if the communicating lines between her brain and her body had been severed, robbing her of all movement but leaving her mind alert. A sensory memory surfaced and she started to hyperventilate. She'd known these things before. Claustrophobia. Confinement. Pain. They were things so raw and familiar they felt like part of her. Yet even as she remembered them she knew they were not her memories. They belonged to the thing she now carried inside her, like a dark child she must deliver safely before time ran out for both of them. She remembered the dream of the dragon, and felt its presence nearby, waiting to consume the child, just as the passage in the Book of Revelation had predicted. Then something was lifted from her face and a voice whispered in her ear.

'Don't try to talk,' it said, 'and don't try to move: you won't be able to and it will only cause you distress. You've been paralysed by a drug called *Suc-cinyl-cho-line*. But don't worry, it will start to wear off pretty soon.'

She felt pressure on her eyelids as he placed his thumb and forefinger on them and gently prised them open. Bright light seared into her head and she found herself looking up not at some biblical beast but at the massive silhouette of a man. 'There you are,' he said. 'Soon have you home again, back where you belong.'

His words sank in and the panic returned. He continued to talk but Liv was no longer listening. All she could hear was the whispering noise rushing through her, drowning everything out like a scream, bringing images of the spike-lined Tau in the chapel of the Sacrament. Her skin prickled painfully at the memory of it and fear burned through her. She remembered the translation of the monk's note:

So they kept *her* weak.
The light of God, sealed up in darkness,
For they dared not release her, for fear of what
    might follow,
Nor could they kill her, for they knew not how.

They had kept Eve prisoner since the beginning of time and Liv had set her free, but not for long.

Soon have you home again, the man had said. They were both being taken to the Citadel to be sealed back up in darkness.

70

Brother Gardener moved through the cool, dark corridors of the mountain carrying the warmth of his recent work with him. He could smell the woodsmoke from the fire, still feel the heat of it licking his skin.

He had been up since before dawn, organizing his staff into a team of eight, each armed with saws and pruning shears. They had started at one end of the garden and moved through it, combing every tree and cutting as deep as they dared wherever they found the blight. At first it had seemed to be the oldest trees that were the worst affected, but as they progressed through the orchard they began to find signs of it creeping into the leaves and branches of younger specimens too.

Again he had taken it upon himself to organize the pyre on the firestone, studying each sacrificed limb in the hope that one might provide the key to understanding what had struck the garden. It had also given him the excuse to stay focused on something other than the systematic decimation of his beloved garden. Only when the last diseased branch had been dissected and thrown on the flames had he allowed himself to survey the devastation they had wrought. He had worked in the garden for over forty years, knew every plant and shrub. But he no longer recognized the crippled thing it had become. And when the pyre filled the firestone and raged with the heat of a burning fever he still had no clue as to what had brought the plague, nor what might drive it out again. Exhausted and distraught he had turned away, and sought refuge in the mountain where there was one thing left for him to try.

He stumbled along the corridor now, laying his hand on the uneven stone wall to steady himself, hoping he would not encounter anyone before reaching the sanctuary of the private chapels where he planned to pour all his pent-up emotion into a heartfelt plea to God to spare his garden. He reached the steps leading to the hall beneath the cathedral cave and almost lost his footing, so weary were his legs from standing all those hours. He felt like he might be sickening with something. He'd had a nose bleed a few hours back and he couldn't seem to shift the smell of oranges from his nostrils. At the bottom of the stairs was a short, narrow corridor lined on either side with wooden doors, each with a candle beside it, sitting in the congealed wax of thousands of predecessors. Most of them were lit, indicating that a chapel was occupied, but some were not. He headed to one, lit the cold candle from the sputtering wick of a neighbour, then fixed it in place and entered the room.

The chapel was little more than a cave cut from solid rock. It was lit by the votive candles of previous visitors, which wavered as he settled in front of them on a floor worn smooth by the knees of the faithful.

The heat continued to cling to him, even here in the cold dark heart of the mountain. He felt his skin prickle beneath his cassock as he knelt and gazed up at the small T-shaped cross resting on the altar stone.

His trees. His garden. Consumed by disease and then by flame, like a soul cursed by God. And there was nothing he could do to stop it.

He felt the emotion he had been bottling all day rising, expanding as it came until it exploded out of him in the form of a sob so raw it hurt his throat. He screwed his eyes closed and clasped his hands together, trying to focus his emotion into the prayer he wanted to offer up, but the sobs continued to wrack his body. He wrapped his arms tightly round his body, trying physically to get a hold of himself. He could still smell the smoke clinging to him and feel the heat of his body through his clothes. As he rocked himself back and forth on the hard floor, he buried his mouth in his shoulder to stifle the sobs so that no one in the neighbouring chapels would hear him.

The prickle of sweat beneath his robes started to itch and he rubbed at it through the fabric. Tears leaked from his eyes and dripped down his cheeks, but no matter how hard he cried nor how deeply he sobbed the desolation did not dissipate; instead it built inside him, expanding until he felt it might break him apart from within. As the pain of it grew, and the itching became unbearable, a sound emerged from his throat, a howl of lament so chilling and raw that he knew it would bring others.

He turned to the door in anticipation, wiping the wetness from his cheeks with the back of his hand as he tried to control himself. But the howl continued, louder and more desperate the more he tried to contain it. It was then that he noticed the wetness on his hand was dark in colour and his cassock was similarly stained wherever he had been scratching. In panic he tore at his clothes, shredding the front to reveal that the tickle of moisture he had felt was not sweat but a rash of boils that had erupted all over his skin. Wherever he had scratched they had burst and now wept a dark brown liquid. The urge to continue scratching was overwhelming. It was as if every atom of his body was itching and the only way to salve it was to scratch it all away.

He started tearing at his skin, the thick nails of work-hardened hands peeling away strips of flesh and bursting more of the pustules. The relief was immediate, far outweighing the pain that came with it. It was bliss. It was torture.

He heard the door open and looked up into the shocked face of a brother monk who visibly recoiled from the thing kneeling and rocking before him, its hands tearing frantically at pustulant flesh, its mouth a hollow from which the awful lament continued to wail, the eyes staring and desolate, weeping brown fluid instead of tears.

71

Arkadian felt the phone shiver and squinted at the display through the lower half of his glasses. The number was withheld. He stood up from his desk and moved quickly across the crowded room.

'Hello?' he said, pushing through the door and starting down the stairs to the exit.

'It's Gabriel.'

'Hey, I was just going to call you,' Arkadian cut him off before he could say any more. 'I'm leaving the office right now and my phone's about to die. Let me give you another number to ring. I'll be there in five minutes.' He read out the number of a landline he had written on his hand, then hung up before Gabriel could say anything else.

Gabriel listened to the disconnect tone in his ear, surprised at the brevity of the conversation. Arkadian clearly didn't want to talk, not on his mobile at least.

Five minutes.

He looked up at the wall of books lining Dr Anata's study. Maybe Arkadian needed five minutes to set up some kind of super trace. He'd read about new supercomputers, developed by the CIA as a weapon in the war on terror, that could chase down even the most complexly routed calls in seconds. The last thing he needed was to get caught and end up in another prison cell. Dr Anata should have delivered the message by now. Which meant he would have an appointment at the Citadel later that night, and there was no way on earth he could afford to miss it.

He opened the browser on his phone and tapped the number Arkadian had given him into the search window. A page of results appeared and he clicked a couple open. Both listed the number to a public phone in the Basilica Ferrumvia, Ruin's main train station. He frowned. It seemed an odd choice. Generic public phones were what people used when they wanted to talk anonymously to the police, not the other way round.

Gabriel glanced over to the TV flickering in the corner of the room. The time stamp in the corner of the screen increased by one minute: still four minutes left to decide whether to call back or not.

He had been watching the news channels for most of the day, keeping up to speed on what was happening in between making calls to various contacts and acquaintances in his bid to arrange safe passage to Turkey for Liv. He'd pulled in about every favour he had and she was now booked on a freightliner under a false name and with a false passport. He'd tried to call her to let her know, but she wasn't answering her phone. Maybe she was asleep. He hoped so. The clock ticked on the wall. On the TV a report about minor damage to several historic buildings ended and another about the deaths at the hospital began. A picture of his mother flashed up and he turned away. He looked at the time on his phone.

Five minutes were up.

He dialled the number.

Arkadian could already hear the phone ringing as he fought through the crowds in the huge glass-and-steel-vaulted expanse of the station building. It stopped just as he reached it. He swore loud enough to turn a few heads then pretended to fish around in his pocket for some change so he could stay by the phone. It rang again almost immediately.

'I'm here,' he said.

'What's with the new number, you got a better trace on this line?'

'No trace,' Arkadian said, catching his breath, 'quite the opposite. My phone is easier to tap – it's already set up for it – so I thought I'd go off the radar. That way we can talk in confidence. Listen, I'm very, very sorry about what happened at the hospital.'

Gabriel said nothing.

'I also checked on all the records relating to your escape from the police cells and you were right: everything's disappeared – CCTV footage, prisoner admissions logs, everything.'

'So if there's no evidence of my escape, I guess no one will be looking for me.'

'Oh, they're looking, all right. Only now they have a different reason to find you. They lifted your prints from the hospital. You're the prime suspect for all three murders.'

Gabriel let this sink in. It had not shown up on the news. The police were obviously keeping a tight lid on it, presumably because they thought he was still around and didn't want to scare him off.

'That cop was no cop,' he said, almost to himself.

'I know. I checked him out. I'm trying to find out where he came from, but so far I've hit a dead end. I don't know where you are, but you need to keep your head down.'

'Why are you on my side all of a sudden?'

'Because you were right; there's something rotten at the heart of all this. I feel terrible that I didn't do more to protect your mother. I should have realized the danger to her, to all of you. I'm going to do everything I can to make sure it doesn't happen again.'

'What about Liv? The same people are looking for her too.'

Arkadian let out a long breath. 'I think they may already have found her.' Then he ran through the conversation he'd had with the New Jersey cop.

'She's not dead,' Gabriel said when he'd finished. 'If they wanted to kill her, then the cop would have found her body in that hotel room. They're bringing her here. They must know that she's carrying the Sacrament, and they want it back.'

He looked at his watch, calculating the time in New Jersey. 'What time did you speak to this cop?'

'About twenty minutes ago.'

'And did he give any indication of how long she might have been missing?'

'He said he picked her up from the airport then dropped her off at the hotel around four in the morning. He checked up on her again around nine, after she didn't answer her phone. There'd been a fire alarm at the hotel just after seven. He wanted to see if she was OK, but she had already gone.'

'The fire alarm was a decoy. That's when they must have grabbed her.'

'I think so too. I checked immigration for any record of her passport showing up on outbound flights, but so far there's nothing.'

'They won't take her out under her own name. They'll ship her through on a charter or a private flight with false papers.'

'Then we need to intercept her this end.'

Gabriel's mind raced through the logistics. The two airports that served Ruin processed hundreds of flights a day. The first time Liv had flown into Ruin he had watched one airport and Kathryn the other. Now his mother was dead and if he set foot within half a mile of either airport he would be picked up by the security teams in a flash.

'Do you have anyone you can trust who could run a stakeout at the airports?'

Arkadian thought of Yun Haldin and his security company. He trusted Yun, but his operation was full of ex-cops and he couldn't vouch for all of them. 'Frankly, the way things stand, I don't trust anyone. And if she comes in as freight anyone running surveillance won't spot her anyway.'

Gabriel looked up at the TV screen, trying to think through their problem objectively. A reporter was standing by the Citadel, the caption beneath him read: WHERE ARE THE CITADEL SURVIVORS?

Then he realized he was staring at the solution. 'We don't need to stake out two airports,' he said, 'we just need to stake out the Citadel – that's where they'll be bringing her. Let's say they grabbed her sometime between seven and nine in New Jersey, then we have a two-hour window to work forward from. A direct flight here would take twelve hours. What's the time difference between Ruin and New Jersey?'

'Seven hours.'

'So, say she took off around nine. Add twelve hours – that makes it nine o'clock in the evening in the States. Four o'clock in the morning in Ruin.'

'The perfect time to bring someone into the Citadel without being seen.'

'Exactly. All we need to do is stake out the mountain in the small hours and ambush anyone who shows up.'

Gabriel frowned, suddenly realizing the flaw in this plan. He wouldn't be able to stake out the Citadel tonight, he would hopefully already be inside it. He thought of Arkadian with his arm in a sling, standing vigil on his own. He needed to draft in some help, but knowing who to trust made that risky and difficult.

The picture on the TV cut to the mayor, standing at the base of the mountain behind a podium weighed down with microphones from all the major news networks. Gabriel smiled for the first time since he'd spoken to Liv.

'I need you to make some calls,' he said.

72

News of Brother Gardener's breakdown swept through the Citadel, spreading like the virus everybody feared it might be. Rumours ignited in the refectories and deflected thoughts away from prayer and study, plucking at existing tensions and reawakening fears that, now the Sacrament had deserted the mountain, a biblical plague was about to descend upon them all.

Athanasius was in the Abbot's study when he heard of it. Ever since the explosion he had spent several hours there every day, trying to stay on top of the numerous communiqués, press clippings and memos that kept the Citadel informed of what was going on in the wider world outside. Lately they had made for gloomy reading.

He threw most of the cuttings away, balling them up as soon as he had read them and dropping them into a basket by his side that served the large fire that had stood cold since the old Abbot's death. He only came here for privacy. The basket was almost full and he made a mental note to tell the cooks to come and help themselves, as they always needed kindling for the refectory fires. He screwed up the last clipping and was about to rise and venture back into the mountain when a light tap on the door announced the arrival of today's dispatches.

The monk who brought them was Brother Osgood, a slight, nervy, rodenty monk who had only recently been promoted out of the grey cloaks of the novitiate to the brown cloaks of the Administrata. He crossed the room in silence, the muscles in his jaw tight with tension, and laid the stack of documents, bound with a single dark green ribbon, on the desk. Athanasius spotted the letter on top. It was handwritten and addressed to 'Brother Peacock'. He reached for it instinctively, eager to see what it contained, but stopped himself as he realized Osgood was still hovering.

'Something the matter?'

'Brother Gardener has been taken ill,' Osgood replied, one hand scratching the back of the other. 'Some say it is a form of plague that attacks the skin. He has been taken to the infirmary.'

'Thank you. I will go and see him when I have finished here.'

Osgood nodded but made no move to leave. He cleared his throat and stared down at his clasped hands. 'Do you think it could be? Plague, I mean. Only, with the blight in the garden and what happened to the Sancti, people are beginning to wonder.'

'What are they beginning to wonder?'

'They're beginning to wonder if we have displeased God in some way and are now being punished for it.'

Athanasius thought back to all that he had witnessed high in the chapel at the top of the mountain. 'Maybe we have.' He looked up and saw fear flit across Osgood's face. 'Don't worry,' he said. 'Brother Gardener is exhausted and deeply distressed about the blight. I'm sure whatever ails him has more to do with that than with God's displeasure. And I'm sure it isn't catching.' He nodded at Osgood's fingers, still nervously scratching. 'When others talk of fleas, one is apt to scratch. Go back to your duties and do not let gossip and rumour drive away your good sense. Here –' he nodded at the basket full of discarded paper – 'take this to the kitchen and give it to the hearth master. Never forget that today's news soon becomes tomorrow's firelighters.'

Osgood smiled, picked up the basket and hurried from the

room. The moment the door closed, Athanasius grabbed the envelope and ripped it open, moving across to the fireplace as he read the contents. Then he screwed it up, dropped it in the cold grate and set light to it, watching as the flame turned the dangerous words to ashes in the grate, before brushing them to dust with his hand.

Tonight the note had said.

He stood and quickly left the room, thinking about everything else it had said as he wiped the ash from his hand and headed to the infirmary.

73

Athanasius heard Brother Gardener before he saw him.

The sound of his low lamenting echoed along the hushed corridor leading down to the isolated caves of the hospital. There was something about the noise that made him want to cover his ears and flee, as if the moans of some poor, damned soul had leaked out of hell. It was a sound of torment and madness and it drilled into the most primal part of his brain where his deepest fears lived.

He reached the corridor where the wards and isolation rooms were located and found the right room simply by following the sound. Then he took a breath, swallowed drily and pushed open the heavy wooden door.

The first thing he saw was the ghostly figure of an Apothecaria standing vigil. Beyond him, the naked figure of Brother Gardener lay writhing on a bed. He had been stripped to his loincloth and bound to the metal frame by thick canvas straps the colour of bleached bone stained brown by something wet and oozing. His skin bubbled with boils and there were deep gouges and angry welts where he had clawed at them with such violence that it looked as though he'd been attacked by an animal. Even now his fists clenched and unclenched as if craving to scratch the terrible itch that drew the awful lament from his foam-flecked mouth.

The Apothecaria turned as Athanasius made to enter and held up a surgically gloved hand to stop him from coming further. As Athanasius withdrew to the corridor, he stepped forward to join him, closing the door and shutting out the worst of the noise. Only then did he remove his mask. It was Brother Simenon, one of the more senior of the medical practitioners. He pushed past without saying a word and started walking up the corridor.

'What ails him?' Athanasius asked, falling in step behind him.

'We don't know. At first I thought it might be the same thing that struck down the Sancti, but that was more like haemorrhagic fever. This is something different entirely. We've taken blood and samples of the discharged fluid from the pustules, but so far none of the tests have proved positive for any known diseases. There are symptomatic similarities with smallpox, which is why we've brought him here to the isolation wards, but it's not an exact match and I personally don't think that's what it is. There are also indicators of bubonic plague, but these diseases are extinct or extremely rare, so it's unclear how he could possibly have contracted either.'

'He was clearing the garden,' Athanasius said, remembering the last time he had seen him.

'Yes, the tree blight. I had thought of that, and it's the most likely cause. There are some forms of fungus and mould spores that can rapidly attack the human immune and respiratory system. These can provoke a massive allergic reaction that produces mycotoxins, or they cause mycosis, which is effectively a gross fungal infection. Because of the skin condition, I suspect what we have here is mycosis, though I've never heard of anything that can bring it on so rapidly. We're hoping we can find an example of the blight and test its toxicity, but as I understand the gardeners were ordered to burn all evidence of it.'

Athanasius nodded, thinking of the black infected smoke rising up into the clear air. 'What about the other gardeners?'

Simenon stopped by another large door. 'That's what I'm most concerned about.' He opened the door on to the largest ward in the hospital complex.

The room was narrow and vaulted, like a large cellar, with four beds lined up on each opposing wall – eight in total. Each bed contained a monk. They looked up in unison as the door opened and Athanasius saw the collective fear in their eyes. It was the entire garden detail, brought here under quarantine. Three more Apothecaria were in attendance, surgical masks covering their faces and blue nitrile gloves on their hands as they interviewed each monk in turn, looking for some early-warning symptom as well as taking numerous blood samples.

'We thought it best to isolate anyone who came into direct contact with the tree blight, until we can rule it out as the cause of whatever has infected Brother Gardener.' The wailing coming from down the corridor rose again, as if he had responded to the mention of his name. Everyone in the ward heard it.

One of the youngest monks, lying in a bed closest to the door, started weeping openly. He sank into the hospital sheets like a child hiding from the dark and stared through the open door towards the corridor as if the thing making the sound was coming for him next.

Simenon pulled the door closed and hurried back up the corridor, reaching into his pocket for a syringe and some sedative.

'And if it is the tree blight,' Athanasius asked, 'how soon before they start showing the same symptoms?'

'Brother Gardener was the first to come in contact with it and symptoms manifested themselves in less than twenty-four hours. So if the blight is the cause, and any of the garden detail have been similarly infected, then we will know soon enough.'

Simenon fixed the face mask back in place as he arrived outside the door. 'My prediction is that we will know within the next couple of hours. If the others are clear, we can literally breathe more easily and do what we can for Brother Gardener. If they have it, then what we have already done here will hopefully be enough to contain the spread. But there is a third potential outcome. If this thing proves to be something more virulent and contagious, some airborne pathogen that passes from host to host merely by proximity, then all of us in the Citadel, every last one of us, has already been exposed. We were all there, last night in the cathedral cave, when Brother Gardener dragged in the first infected branch and dropped it at the altar.'

Athanasius pictured the branch breaking as it hit the stone floor, the dry dust, caught in the light, rising from the crumbling wood like a wisp of smoke.

'Tell me,' Simenon asked, 'you were in the garden at the start of the clear-up operation. How many trees were infected? Was it just one or two? Was it confined to certain areas or certain types of trees?'

Athanasius shook his head gravely.

'It was everywhere,' he said, realizing the dark implication of Simenon's careful question. 'Almost every tree had been affected.'

IV

Then the LORD said to Moses and Aaron, 'Take handfuls of soot from a furnace and have Moses toss it into the air in the presence of Pharaoh. It will become fine dust over the whole land of Egypt, and festering boils will break out on men and animals throughout the land.'

Exodus 9:8–9

74

Evening brought the return of something approaching normality to the city of Ruin. There had been no aftershocks after the initial tremors, so the clean-up operation was rapid and unhampered. Most of the streets had re-opened with restaurant tables spreading over pavements that had been littered with broken glass only a few hours previously. There were plenty of people too, relaxing after the stress of the previous twenty-four hours. Into these crowds Gabriel emerged.

He ambled along, sticking to the more touristy streets, his face covered by the peak of his cap, heading through camouflaging crowds to the old town wall. He didn't need to be in position for another few hours, but any earlier and the daylight would have made him easier to spot, any later and his presence on the empty streets might arouse unwanted suspicion.

The old town itself was now closed to the public. Since the mid-nineteenth century, every building in the old town had been converted to commercial use. The official line was that the curfew was to keep the area quiet so as not to interfere with nocturnal worship within the mountain. In truth, there was an ancient covenant on all the land surrounding the Citadel that capped residential rents at mediaeval levels, whereas commercial rates were not controlled. The church had earned ten times more money from rental income after the ban had come into place. So no one was allowed in the old town at night. Every day at dusk, stewards swept the streets, shepherding tourists down the hill towards the public gates, ready for the portcullises to bang down and seal the place up for the night. Consequently, Gabriel's first challenge was to get inside.

He spotted Arkadian by one of the main public gates, loitering beside a metal door built into the old stonework. With millions of tourists and salvation seekers climbing the steep streets every year, there were almost daily incidents involving everything from twisted ankles to heat exhaustion. Most of these could be dealt with locally, but if something more serious transpired and they needed to get an ambulance up there fast, the emergency hatches came into use, operated and maintained by the ambulance service and the police.

Arkadian nodded at Gabriel as he approached and turned to the control panel to punch in the access codes. From somewhere inside the stone wall the sound of a motor began to purr and the metal screen started to rise. Gabriel slipped underneath without breaking stride. Arkadian followed, cradling his immobile arm as he crabbed underneath. He punched the same codes into another panel and the shutter juddered and reversed direction, sliding back down to the floor then banging shut with a percussive thump. The whole thing had taken less than a minute. They headed up the darkened streets in silence, keeping to the shadows.

The old town was lit by the yellowy glow of sodium lamps that cast a sickly light over the deserted buildings, making the whole place look diseased. They trod carefully, minimizing the sound of their footfalls on the hard cobbles, listening out for the sound of the clean-up crew. They heard nothing but the muffled noise of the night, and the sounds of people enjoying themselves beyond the old town walls.

Halfway up the hill Arkadian ducked into a narrow passage between two leaning buildings and unlocked a door to a small office with a counter running the length of it and posters on the walls giving advice about pickpockets in several languages. It was the old town police station, as good a place as any to wait until it was time to move. Gabriel checked his watch.

They had about four hours to kill, but at least they were in position.

Arkadian flipped the hatch on the counter and moved through to the back room, careful not to switch on any lights.

'You want a coffee?' he called out, already filling a kettle. 'It's going to be a long night, you'll probably be glad of the caffeine.'

'Thanks.' During all-night ops in Afghanistan, Gabriel and his troop had chewed on the caffeine pills known as Ripper Fuel, or sometimes emptied packets of freeze-dried coffee straight into their mouths to stay awake. It was the curious thing about combat: the thing that got to you most was the waiting. Boredom was at least as big a killer as the bullets. It made you crazy – reckless – and now, as then, he could afford to be neither. He should really try to get some sleep, but he knew it was impossible. He kept thinking of Liv, captured by the enemy and slowly heading this way. He couldn't help feeling that he had failed her.

'Here,' Arkadian held out a mug of black coffee, 'not exactly finest *khave*, but it should keep you awake.'

Gabriel took it and sipped the scalding liquid. 'Thanks,' he said. 'Thanks for everything.'

Arkadian shrugged. 'Just trying to make sure the good guys win. In the meantime, why don't you tell me exactly what all this is about?'

Gabriel thought of everything he had learned in the last few hours: the Mirror Prophecy, the end of days, the search for the true location of Eden. It was difficult to know where to start. He looked up into the intelligent face of the detective and it suddenly became obvious.

'It started twelve years ago,' he said, 'or it did for me at least. It began with the death of my father . . .'

75

The devotional day within the Citadel was divided into twelve different offices, with the four nocturnes breaking the night into quarters; the second of these was Compline. It began two hours after dusk and marked the moment when the mountain effectively went to sleep and the curfew began. No one was permitted to wander the tunnels, save for the guards who patrolled them, the monks on prayer rota on their way to or from the private chapels, and monks of a high enough rank to grant them exemptions from many of the rules that governed the rest.

Consequently, half an hour after Compline had begun, all was quiet – but not all slept.

Father Thomas was still awake, working alone in the library running endless systems checks to try to mend the faults in the security and environmental systems that had kept the library closed for so long. So far he had managed to fix the problems in the reading rooms and offices, but the main chambers, interlinked and vast, remained faulty – so he worked on.

On the broad stone balcony that formed part of the Prelate's staterooms and overlooked the walled garden at the heart of the mountain a dark and ragged figure in a green cassock was also stirring. Dragan paced. He could not sleep. The Sacrament was not due to return to the mountain until just before dawn, yet already he could feel it drawing closer, bringing its life force with it. It had been taken from the mountain by traitors and heretics, but he had been chosen to return it – and so he would. By the end of the nocturnes it would be back in the chapel and locked in the Tau, its human vessel a necessary captive of the divine process. Only then would his strength return and the mountain be healed. Once that had come about he would deal with the traitors.

On the other side of the mountain in a windowless cell cut into the rock by the Abbot's chambers, Athanasius was also awake. He had listened to the mountain quietening beyond his door, carefully folding and refolding his spare cassock to give his hands something to do. His senses felt keen, sharpened by adrenalin born of fear and apprehension. Soon he would have to leave the safety of his room and venture through the darkness. He had broken curfew before, but always on the Abbot's business. However there was no Abbot now. This time he was on his own, and the business he was about was fraught with danger. So he folded and refolded his clothes.

And he waited.

76

Beyond the walls of the mountain, in the streets of the old town, all was quiet. The cleaning crew had gone and the waning crescent moon was up. In the police station Gabriel and Arkadian ran through the various things they each had to do, then shook hands and parted. Arkadian stayed back, Gabriel slipped out of the door and made his way up the silent hill towards the Citadel. It was almost one o'clock in the morning.

He trod softly, listening to the night. Everything was quiet. Even the city had gone silent beyond the old town wall.

The public square, thronged with tourists by day, was now empty, and eerie because of it. Gabriel slipped through one of the presentation arches beside the public church, and looked up at the Citadel. He felt exactly as he always did before a combat mission: focused, coiled – and a little afraid. Fear was essential. It stopped him from being complacent, and there was much to fear in what he was about to attempt.

Skirting the darker edge of the embankment, he kept close to the buildings as he made his way towards the wooden bridge spanning the dry moat. Above him he could see the tribute cave, high up on the sheer face of the mountain. No light burned within it. The only indication that there was anything there at all was the thin line of a rope, barely visible against the side of the mountain, a straight scratch on the surface of the night leading all the way down to the flat tribute stone at the base of the mountain.

He reached the rope and carefully took it in his hand, being careful not to pull on it. It was thinner than he had hoped and made in the traditional way out of hemp – not the strongest of materials, but at least it had a rough surface that would give him something to grip. He took a pair of climbing gloves from his pocket and slipped them over his hands, scanning the embankment for any sign of movement. A drooping flag on the side of a building drifted in the hint of a breeze. A piece of litter the night crew had missed skittered over the flagstones. Other than that there was nothing.

Gabriel took hold of a section of the rope and tested it. It creaked as he pulled on it, stretching a little, but not much. It would have to do. He took a deep breath, flooding his body with oxygen then heaved down on the rope, leaning all his weight into it and bracing himself for a quick exit if a metallic clang sounded high above him.

Nothing happened.

The message had got through.

The Ascension bell had been silenced.

Straddling the rope, he swept it round the outside of his right leg and over the top of his boot. He reached up and gripped it, pulling himself up, feeding the rope over the top of his right boot then trapping it in place with the sole of his left, which acted as a brake, holding his weight in his legs and freeing his arms to reach further up the rope. It was a simple 'brake and squat' technique taught to every soldier in the US Army. It allowed you to inchworm your way up anything, so long as your upper body strength held out and the rope didn't break. The tribute cave was about a hundred metres above him. Gabriel tried not to think about the odds of there being a weak spot somewhere along the length of the rope.

Instead, he cleared his mind of everything and set into a steady rhythm.

Straighten legs.
Reach up.
Grip with hands.
Pull legs up.
Brake – Repeat

He was covering around a metre each cycle, a hundred reps before he reached the tribute cave. In battle training he had regularly done five sets of ten, though that had been on a thicker rope which had been easier to grip. At least he wasn't carrying his combat pack this time, just a gun and a copy of his grandfather's map.

He continued his steady rhythm, twisting in the night air as the rope tightened and creaked. The tendons in his wrists started tightening too, burning with each new grip. His rhythm slowed, but he continued steadily. He kept thinking of Liv, scared and alone, being brought here now by the people who had killed his mother. He would not let the same thing happen to her. No matter how much pain he felt, he would keep on going, for her sake.

It took him nearly ten minutes to reach the tribute hatch, by which time every muscle in his arms and legs was screaming in agony and his clothes and gloves were soaked with sweat. Most of the hatch was filled with the solid wooden structure of the Ascension platform. The bell rope ran alongside it and disappeared into a hole in the rock; big enough for the rope to pass through, but much too narrow for him. He inched up the final length of exposed rope until his head rose above the level of the cave floor.

It was empty.

There was no one lying in wait for him.

He needed to get closer to the lip of the cave or the wooden platform, both of which were just beyond his reach. He began to shift his weight back and forth, setting the rope swinging. The rope creaked as the swinging increased. He would only have one chance at this.

The rope swung out.

The fibres creaked.

The edge of the cave rushed back at him.

He let go at the top of the upswing and arced towards it.

The moment the rope left his hand he knew he was going

to land short. He could feel gravity dragging him down as if he had rocks in his pockets. He lunged desperately at the edge of the opening and hit it with a bone-crunching thud, jarring his ribs and knocking the wind from his lungs. His lower half dangled down into the dark, his arms the only thing stopping him from falling. He clung on, pain blooming in his ribs, circling his legs for something solid to kick against, but there was nothing there. The opening jutted out from the side of the mountain with nothing below it but a hundred-metre drop.

Gabriel focused his remaining energy into his shaking arms, willing them to pull him up, but the surface of the cave floor was like marble, worn smooth by thousands of years of traffic. Every time he tried to draw himself up, he lost a little ground, slipping back rather than inching forward. In the end he stopped moving altogether, locked in position, aware that if he carried on he would only keep slipping until he fell to his death.

But he had to do something.

Even just hanging there he could feel himself slipping, millimetre by millimetre. With a desperate effort he threw his right leg sideways, kicking it as high as he could. It caught the lip of the cave and stayed there. He wiggled his foot to gain more grip, the rubber of his sole squeaking its way across the slick surface. But for every inch of progress his foot made he could feel his arms weakening further. After the exertion of the climb there was no grip left in his fingers and nothing to hold on to. Hanging sideways, more off than on the rock platform, he knew his arms were most likely to give way first. With each second his sweat-dampened fingers were slipping. Soon he was going to fall head-first down the side of the mountain and he didn't have the strength to stop it.

Then a hand grabbed the back of his jacket and started to tug him upwards.

Gabriel pulled too, timing his efforts with the rhythm of whoever was trying to haul him up so that in five well-timed tugs he was up and over the edge of the cave and sprawling gratefully against the stone floor. His sweat-slicked skin felt cool against the cold rock and he lay there for a moment, basking in the glory of being alive. Had it been made of eiderdown it could not have seemed more comfortable or welcoming. He looked up into the face of the man who had saved him.

'We must hurry,' Athanasius said, 'we cannot be found here.' He held out a bundle of folded robes. 'Put these on and you will pass unnoticed through the mountain.'

Gabriel hauled himself off the floor, his shaking muscles complaining all the way, and pulled the scratchy woollen garments over the top of his own clothes. They would keep his aching muscles warm, which was good as he would need his strength again soon enough if he wanted to escape from the mountain. He looked up and held out his hand.

'Gabriel,' he said. 'Thank you for saving my life again.'

The bald monk looked slightly embarrassed. 'Athanasius,' he replied, shaking the proffered hand, 'or Brother Peacock, if you prefer. Your message mentioned something about a map.'

Gabriel dug a piece of paper from his pocket and held it out. It was a copy of the map Oscar had drawn in his journal. Athanasius took it and traced the outlines of tunnels and corridors with his finger, until it arrived at the symbol of crossed bones.

'It's the ossuary,' he said. 'Whatever you seek lies buried below the cathedral cave, along with the sacred bones of the prelates.' He lifted the oil lamp down from its niche in the wall. 'Pull your cowl over your head, keep a distance behind me and hide if anyone stops me to talk. No one should be abroad in the mountain this late. Let's just hope everyone else is obeying that rule more strictly than I.'

Then he turned and left the tribute cave, heading for the darker depths of the mountain.

77

Gabriel followed the glow of the oil lamp as it bobbed ahead of him in the darkness. It slid along the tunnels, picking out dark doors and wires that snaked along the walls like veins. Every ten paces or so a light fitting jutted out, but none were lit. He wondered if this was down to the recent earthquake or just to save energy. It was a thought that strangely unsettled him. For so long he had demonized the Citadel and all who dwelt within it that to find himself suddenly inside and struck by these trivial details seemed surreal. He reminded himself he was in the enemy camp and that he was here for a reason. Reaching into his pocket, he felt the reassuring weight of the gun, and kept his eyes on the light ten or so paces in front of him and his mind on his mission.

Sometimes the curve of the tunnel made the light vanish from sight for a second or two and he had to feel his way quickly along the rough walls to catch up. Other times it dropped to the left or rose to the right as Athanasius descended or climbed stairways to other levels. Gabriel tried to keep track of where he was, but it was impossible. He hoped his guide was taking him on this circuitous route to avoid the more populated areas of the mountain rather than to confuse him in a prelude to an ambush.

After ten minutes of walking, ducking beneath low lights and squeezing through tunnels so narrow only one man could pass at a time, they stepped through a grand doorway into a vista that took Gabriel's breath away. The cave was so vast he felt dizzy from the sudden space. Huge stalactites hung down from the distant ceiling and a massive window was cut high in the far wall. He could see the partial moon through it, reminding him of the ticking clock as it cast its silver glow through the antique glass, creating watery patterns on the stone floor below. They must have walked right through the centre of the mountain and arrived on the other side.

'This way,' Athanasius whispered, 'the ossuary lies beneath the cathedral cave.'

Gabriel followed him, past the looming shape of the Tau rising up from the altar to the far wall where a needling formation of stalagmites formed a natural screen hiding a small door studded with metal bolts. Athanasius twisted a key in the lock, the noise echoing in the huge space like the bolt-action on a rifle. Gabriel looked behind to check they were still alone before following Athanasius through the door.

They were at the head of a stone ramp descending into darkness. It smelled of death. Athanasius locked the door and headed down, the musty hint of decay growing stronger with each step. At the bottom of the ramp another door barred their way and the smell of dry, mouldering rot billowed out at them as it opened.

'The ossuary,' Athanasius said, stepping inside and holding up the oil lamp to cast its light into the chamber beyond.

There were rows of long niches cut into both walls, three-high, stretching away into the darkness in either direction, making the narrow chamber resemble a carriage on a sleeper train, but those who slept here would never wake. In each niche Gabriel could see bones sticking out of rotting cassocks that covered what was left of the bodies of the formerly great. In one of the recesses in front of him a skull had rolled clear of the cowl and stared sightlessly at them. Below it the letter X was carved into the rock.

Gabriel stepped forward. The location of the Starmap had been marked with an X on Oscar's map, but it seemed odd that he would hide it right opposite the door.

In the light of the lamp Gabriel could see something else carved next to it, partly obscured by the same gossamer layer of cobweb that covered most of the walls and openings. He wiped it away with his thumb and received a shock when he saw what it revealed: L I V.

He stared at the carvings for a moment, baffled by the presence of Liv's name in this secret crypt. Then he realized his error. Every niche had a symbol carved beneath it. The one above was XLIII, and to his left the sequence continued with XLII, XLI, and XL. They were Roman numerals. XLIV was simply the number 44.

He took Oscar's map from his pocket, remembering what was marked next to the crossed bones: XIV, the number 14.

'This way,' he said, heading left.

He hurried the length of the dank tunnel, counting down the numbers as he went, the flame of Athanasius's oil lamp casting a long, restless shadow before him. The lower the numbers got, the rougher the walls of the tunnel became. When they dropped below the thirties, the tunnel changed again. The cobwebs that had laced the walls were now gone, cleared away so that each opening yawned clean and dark. The bodies inside had also been tidied up, and the loose piles of dusty bones were now wrapped neatly in canvas bundles that had been placed in the centre of each recess with the skull resting on top.

'Here,' Gabriel said, drawing level with number 14. He produced a compact torch from his pocket and twisted it on so the white light of the tiny bulb flooded the darkness.

'What is it we are looking for?' Athanasius asked, holding up the oil lamp to add more light.

'Something like a piece of rock, or a section of a stone tablet with symbols etched on it; too heavy for someone to swim with, but small enough that they could smuggle it in here to hide.'

He swept the torch beam across the recess and felt his galloping hope trip inside him. Apart from the neat parcel of human remains in the centre, the niche was completely empty. He checked the neighbouring recesses: all empty save for the same neat parcels and grinning skulls that mocked him with their smiles. He examined the walls, the floor, the ceiling. All spotless and cut from solid rock, so there was no chance Oscar might have buried it.

He turned his attention back to the only thing remaining in recess XIV – the wrapped package of bones beneath the skull. He had initially ignored it because it looked too small, but having eliminated all other possibilities, it was the only place the Starmap could now be. He reached in and picked it up.

'Please,' Athanasius said, 'do not disturb the relics.'

Gabriel would happily have ignored him, but the moment he lifted the loose parcel he could tell it was far too light to contain what he was looking for. Whatever Oscar had hidden here, over ninety years earlier, was gone: someone else must have found it. He placed the bundle carefully back down on the shelf, and ran his hand over the cold, clean stone.

'Why is it so tidy here?'

'These are the oldest remains in the ossuary – the first prelates of the mountain. Their great age has caused them to crumble almost to dust, which can drift away on the slightest breath. It was decided by an order of council that their remains should be protected.'

'When was this?'

'Around ten years ago.'

Gabriel nodded. Ten years too late. 'Is there anyone else who comes down here?'

'Only the Sanctus novitiate. As part of their preparation for office, each apprentice spends time here, contemplating their position as the latest link in an unbroken line stretching back to the very beginning. These catacombs are effectively a giant reliquary and the bones of the prelates are relics themselves, sanctified by long proximity to the ultimate relic of all – the

Sacrament. As these are the remains of the very first prelates, the founding fathers of the Citadel, they are the most sacred of all. That is why the novices come here to pray.'

This explained how Oscar had managed to smuggle the Starmap here in the first place. He had been apprenticed to the order of the Sancti before he had escaped. He could have brought it here and hidden it during his silent devotions, safe in the knowledge that few others ever ventured here. Until they decided to tidy the place up.

'Would there be any record of these renovations?'

'All works are catalogued and kept in the archives of the great library. But the library is still closed. I could probably gain access, but not until after Matins at the earliest, and it won't be straightforward. The archives are huge.'

Gabriel let out a frustrated sigh, remembering the sliver of moon he had seen through the huge cave window, getting imperceptibly smaller with each passing hour. He reached into his pocket and pulled out his iPhone. 'Time is the one thing we don't have,' he said, tapping it and handing it over to Athanasius. The screensaver was a photograph of the page in Oscar's diary containing the Mirror Prophecy. Athanasius took it and started to read.

The air in the cathedral cave tasted sweet after the decay of the crypt.

'We'd better hurry,' Athanasius said, moving towards the main door, 'the devotional rota will be changing soon and the corridors will not be so empty. I'll take you back a quicker way.'

They retraced their steps through the winding maze of the mountain, cutting corners here and there, taking them past dormitories of snoring monks and private chapels where others prayed. Gabriel hung back as before, his head bowed low, his cowl covering his face, distancing himself from Athanasius in case they were stopped. They had almost made it back to the tribute cave when they both heard it – a low moan, rolling through the darkness like the tortured cries of a trapped animal. They stopped and listened to it rising in intensity before quickly ebbing away. Then they heard footsteps. In the echoing confines of the tunnel it was impossible to tell which direction they were coming from. Gabriel sank into the shadows of a doorway and felt for his gun as a figure in a red robe appeared behind him and swept past towards Athanasius.

'You must come with me,' the monk said.

'Come where?'

'The infirmary. Brother Simenon ordered me to find you. He says it's urgent.'

Another chilling moan rose up from somewhere deep in the mountain. 'Very well,' Athanasius replied. 'I was just on my way up these stairs to drop the new rota off at the tribute cave, but I suppose that can wait.'

Gabriel pressed himself against the upright of the door and watched the red-cloaked monk escort Athanasius away down the passage, taking the meagre light of his oil lamp with them. In the utter blackness he listened to their fading footsteps until they had melted into silence then stepped back into the corridor and carried on the way they had been heading. He palmed the torch from his pocket and twisted it on, smothering most of the light with his hand. Up ahead he could see a stone staircase branching off from the main tunnel, hopefully the ones Athanasius's cryptic instruction had alluded to.

After a few minutes of climbing he felt cold night air flowing from his left and followed it all the way to the tribute cave. He stripped out of the monk's cassock, left it folded on a low shelf and headed to the edge of the hatch. He hooked the bell rope with a length of construction timber stacked in one of the storage bays. His arms were still heavy and weak, but at least gravity would be on his side this time. He slipped the gloves back on and hauled on the rope to take the tension.

He had climbed up here hoping to find a map that would lead them to a sacred and ancient ending. He was leaving with nothing more than the slimmest of hopes that Athanasius might pick up the cold trail, somewhere in the archives. Gabriel looked out into the moonlit night, knowing that Liv was out there somewhere. He had promised he would not let her down, yet he had consistently failed. He had not been able to protect her, and he had not managed to find the one thing that might ensure her deliverance from the prophetic sequence she was locked in. With this thought weighing him down he wrapped the rope round his leg and stepped off the platform, slipping into the night like a man slowly being hanged.

78

By the time Athanasius reached the stairway leading to the infirmary, the sound he had heard in the upper section of the mountain had turned into a chorus of the damned. It grew louder with every step until it took all his nerve to continue his descent towards it. He could hear ragged words in the noise now, words of lament and pity, with 'forgive me' being the most repeated.

He was met at the bottom of the stairs by a guard wearing a white surgical mask that stood out against the raised cowl of his red cassock. Another masked guard stood by the door to the main ward – the place where all the noise was coming from. As Athanasius drew closer the guard held a mask out for him and watched in silence as he put it on. Only then did he step up to the door and knock on it loud enough to be heard above the din. There was the sound of a bolt being released from inside, then the door began to open.

The scene that greeted Athanasius was a depiction of hell. The eight beds he had seen earlier were now in complete disarray, strewn haphazardly across the floor where the thrashing occupants had shunted them with their violent contortions. Each monk had been stripped to the loincloth and bound to his bed as Brother Gardener had been. All displayed the same symptoms: dense rashes of boils over most of their skin, gouge marks where they had flailed at their flesh before being restrained, and the constant and woeful lamenting that accompanied their suffering.

The loudest cries came from a bed near the door whose

occupant had managed somehow to shrug off his restraints and was now clawing at his flesh with his freed hand, dragging his nails across a rash of boils that burst and bled, causing him to howl in a mixture of agony and relief. Two Apothecaria were attempting to pin him down, their blue nitrile gloves struggling to grip on to skin made slick by the brownish liquid that oozed from the burst pustules. A third aimed a syringe at the flailing upper arm, swaying in time to the movement until he finally managed to jab it home. The mask of twisted torment melted away as the sedative took effect, revealing the face of the young, frightened monk Athanasius had seen earlier.

He turned and met Brother Simenon's eyes, staring at him from the gap between his mask and cowl.

'All the trees, you said.'

Athanasius nodded. 'All the trees.'

'And has the blight returned to the garden?'

Athanasius shook his head. 'Not the last time it was inspected.'

'So you would agree that the containment worked.' Athanasius nodded. 'And you would naturally advocate a similar procedure to help contain the potential spread of the human manifestation of this disease?'

Despite the fevered heat of the room, Athanasius felt a chill as he realized why he had been summoned here. 'You think I should be quarantined?'

'Not just you. The only people who have contracted this sickness so far have been those who spent time in the infected parts of the garden and dealt directly with the diseased material. And you were there, as were the other heads of the guilds. You all stood in the garden, inspecting the rotten material, possibly even handling it, while you decided what to do about the blight.'

Athanasius thought back to the two silent guards who had greeted him outside. He had initially thought they had been posted there to keep people out. Now he realized the truth.

They were there to keep them in. 'But if I had been infected, surely I would be displaying symptoms by now?'

'Not necessarily. Your exposure was limited, so it could be working more slowly within you. These men all had extended and uncontained exposure; and quantity is a key factor in cases of acute mycosis. If there were any other way to do this I would suggest it, but we cannot risk this thing spreading further. All those who may have been contaminated must remain segregated for at least four days and under strict observation. Provided no symptoms present themselves within that time, we can safely assume that the infection has been contained. Otherwise . . .' He let the thought hang. 'If it makes you feel any better, I myself, together with my staff, will remain here too for the duration of the quarantine period.'

Athanasius saw the logic of this, but it presented a problem. The quarantine would mean a four-day delay before he could check through the records on Gabriel's behalf – always assuming he didn't end up strapped to a bed or worse. This thought raised another question and, though he feared the answer, he had to ask: 'How is Brother Gardener?'

'I'm afraid Brother Gardener died shortly after you last saw him. He suffered massive organ failure caused by his chronic infection. The pustules you see on the skin are also present internally. Violent physical activity bursts them and floods the body with toxins. When the levels get too high, the organs simply shut down.'

Athanasius looked again at the writhing bodies strapped to the beds and imagined the boils running right through their flesh, the same boils that might now be forming in his own body.

'And where are we to be kept? There is no room here and proximity to those already infected would surely negate the point of a quarantine.'

'The guards are making arrangements. Myself and the staff

will occupy the remaining isolation caves. I'm sure they will come up with something appropriate.'

Athanasius's mind raced ahead, seeing an opportunity in his imminent isolation. 'Might I make a suggestion? The library is close by and accessible without the need for passing through the more populated areas of the mountain. We could turn one of the reading rooms into a makeshift ward for the duration without too much disruption. No one is using it at the moment and its sealed nature and climate-control systems will ensure the air we breathe will not contaminate the rest of the mountain.'

Simenon nodded. 'I will propose it. In the meantime, you should leave this room and wait outside in the corridor. The other heads have been sent for. I wanted to talk to you first as I knew you would see the sense and logic of it and possibly help me convince the others.'

'Of course.'

As if on cue, the sound of someone pounding on the door cut through the moaning and Simenon opened it to discover a bewildered Brother Axel standing outside. Athanasius slipped from the room and put his hand on Axel's shoulder, turning him away from the terrible sights inside.

Axel shrugged free and stared into his face with thinly disguised anger. 'Do you see what you have done?' he said. 'You have brought a plague down upon us.'

'Let us hope not,' Athanasius replied. 'For both our sakes, let us pray it proves to be something else.'

79

Strong winds over the Atlantic had pushed the white dove on the tail of the DC-9 swiftly on its flight towards the furthest edge of Europe. It landed at Gaziantep International a little ahead of schedule at two fifty a.m.

At three minutes past three, a loader pulled up to the plane and raised its platform to the passenger door. Two things were loaded on to it: a box, roughly the same shape and size as a coffin, and a large, blond man dressed in black, who laid his hand flat on the box, as though he were making a pledge on an oversized Bible. The loader lowered them to a waiting van, its rear doors already open, the key in the ignition. Unassisted, the man slid the box off the loading platform and into the back of the van, then slammed the doors and headed for the driver's seat. He turned the key in the ignition and the robotic voice of the sat-nav gave him the first direction of the pre-programmed route. Four minutes later he was easing the van through the security gate and on to the service road that ran round the perimeter fence. It took him to the main road leading away from the airport and up into the mountains towards the city of Ruin.

He made it through the mountain pass and entered the outskirts of the city at exactly half past three. The flat voice from the dashboard guided him on to the great wide Eastern Boulevard then on to the inner ring-road that circled the old town and took him to the northeastern section, known as the Umbrasian Quarter. Nine minutes later he had reached his destination.

Dick eased the van into the warehouse built on the lower side of the old town wall, reversed it into a loading bay and cut the engine. Heavy vehicles were not allowed into the old town, so the tons of food and merchandise that had to be carted up to all the cafés and gift shops each day were delivered using the funicular. Resembling a large, slow rollercoaster, the funicular ran directly through the old town wall and up the side of the hill in a concealed stone tunnel that started in the main goods warehouse.

Checking the area was deserted, Dick slipped out of the driver's seat, grabbed a hand pallet truck and opened the back of the van. He slid the coffin-shaped box on to the truck and wheeled it over to the solitary carriage that had been left lined up by the entrance to the tunnel with its side door open and ready. When he'd loaded the box inside he wedged his large frame into the personnel section at the rear of the carriage and opened an email on his phone to reread the instructions he had been sent.

Flipping open the safety guard on the control panel, he punched the third of three red buttons. The carriage slowly started to move, pulled along the track by a ratcheted chain, the soft rubber tyres and electric engine making hardly any noise in the stillness of the night. It moved into the dimly lit tunnel then started to climb, all the way up to the third and final stop, right at the top of the old town where the embankment encircled the base of the Citadel.

The time was three forty-one.

Dragan clung to the rough wall of the tribute cave and looked down through the hatch like a ragged bird of prey. He saw no movement, only the sodium-lit streets of the old town spreading out below him like a luminous yellow stain.

He could feel the cold of the night seeping into his weakened flesh, but he could also feel something akin to the first hint of rain on the breeze or the sun coming out from behind cold clouds to warm him. Just as the ocean responded to the pull of the moon the cells of his body were reacting to the approach of the Sacrament.

Soon it would be back, flooding the mountain with its cleansing force and radiating through his body, restoring health to the pitiful thing he had become.

Behind him he heard the scuff of a shoe on the stone floor as the two red-cloaked guards waited by the great spindle of the lifting gear. He had played on their fears and appealed to their ambition by promising to elevate them to the ranks of the Sancti in exchange for their help.

Return the Sacrament, he had told them, *and everything will be restored to the way it was.*

The Citadel, the Sancti – and him.

80

Dick felt the automatic brakes engage and the carriage start to slow. Up ahead the faint glow of sodium light leaked into the tunnel from the embankment terminal.

Final destination.

He felt a sense of calm and contentment. Once the box was loaded on to the Ascension platform and he had rung the bell to raise it, his mission would be over.

It would be *com-plete.*

This was one of his favourite words, so perfect in its form and meaning. Even the act of saying it made the mouth perform a full workout of sounds and plosives leaving the lips stretched in a satisfying smile. It was how he had felt when he had first discovered the words of God in prison and filled the empty vessel of his old self.

The carriage rolled to a gentle stop and he stepped out on to the loading bay. It was the size of a double garage, with storage racks lining the walls and electric hand-carts parked to one side, plugged into the wall to charge overnight. The racks were all empty, everything having been distributed for the night. His footsteps echoed in the emptiness, bouncing off the walls and mingling with the insect whirr of an electric motor as he took one of the smaller carts and steered it over to the carriage. He dragged the box on to it and headed across the platform towards the exit.

The cool night air hit him as he emerged from the loading shed and headed up a shallow ramp to the embankment. The Ascension platform was directly across from him, accessed by a wooden bridge. He made his way towards it, enjoying the solitude and sense of satisfaction that his work was nearly done.

He had just stepped on to the bridge when everything went wrong.

The first thing he heard was hurrying footsteps, scuffing over the dry flagstones towards him – three or four people by the sound of it. Instinctively he spun round, his hand reaching inside his jacket for his gun, then an intense white light blinded him.

'James Harris, World News. What's inside that box?'

He saw the edge of a camera lens beneath the bright light and the spongy end of a microphone thrust in his direction. He considered shooting out the light and taking his chances with whoever was behind it, but his mind caught up and made him stop. The camera was probably sending a feed to somewhere else or even broadcasting live.

He thrust his hand back in his jacket, but not before the cameraman had seen the gun and zoomed in on it for a second.

'There is nothing in the box,' he said. 'You have no authority here. You should not be here.'

'They have my permission.' A new voice and the outline of a man, one arm in a sling, the other holding out a police badge.

Police and press. All wrong.

There was nothing for it but to abandon his mission and escape.

He took a step towards the camera, smiling broadly, his arms rising up in the beginnings of a gesture of surrender. The cameraman backed away, but not quite fast enough. Dick brought his arm down in a rapid swipe, knocking the camera to the floor. There was a shattering of glass as the top light broke and everything was plunged into darkness. Then he threw himself at the policeman.

Pain lanced through Arkadian's arm as the man ran through him, knocking him backwards on to the flagstones. He twisted round – bringing fresh, tearing agony to his shoulder – and reached for his gun, but the hulking figure was already disappearing round the corner of the loading shed. He was gone. None of the others were going to pursue him. They were too preoccupied with the main focus of the exclusive story he had promised them.

The cameraman had picked up the camera and was zooming in on the lid while the reporter prised it open, giving a running commentary as he did so.

Arkadian struggled to his feet. He wanted to go after his attacker, but was in no physical state to run, so he drifted over to the box, hoping to God it contained good news.

The lid pulled away and clattered to the ground.

Liv was lying on her side, wrapped in blankets and bandages like a Halloween mummy. The reporter was asking her questions, but it was clear she was drugged. At least he hoped that was why none of the preceding racket had roused her. Arkadian reached in and pressed his fingers to her neck.

There was a pulse.

She was alive.

Dragan watched it all play out beneath him like a helpless God. As soon as the bright light flashed and the large figure knocked it out and fled he knew it was trouble.

He watched the others surround the box, the lid slide off it, and felt something surge within him when he saw the figure curled inside. He was drawn towards it and had to grip on to the cave wall to stop himself from tipping down into the gap. So close that he could see it, too far for it to do him any good. He felt like weeping, or raging, or killing something. But all he could do was watch as the group departed, taking the girl with them.

81

Arkadian held on to Liv all the way down the bumpy streets of the old town, his good arm wrapped round her like a father comforting his child, his bad arm singing with pain at every bump.

They were travelling in one of the 'moon buggies' used to ferry the old and infirm up the mountain. Right now he felt he qualified on both counts. The reporter was driving, while the cameraman scanned the streets with his lens like a soldier on point. Nobody spoke, aware that the giant man they had accosted could still be out there somewhere, hiding in the shadows, waiting to ambush his ambushers.

By the time they reached the bottom, Liv was starting to stir, shaken awake by the juddering descent. Arkadian punched the exit codes into the emergency hatch and smiled when the rising steel shutter revealed that the second part of the rescue plan was waiting.

The reporter saw it too. 'What's that ambulance doing here?'

'I called for it. Wasn't sure what state the hostage would be in. Pull over by the rear doors and I'll have them check her out, make sure she's OK before you get to talk to her.'

The reporter steered over to the parked ambulance and hit the brakes hard enough to telegraph his annoyance. The deal he had done with Arkadian gave him exclusivity on the story and now he could feel it slipping away.

The driver's door of the ambulance opened and a skinny, pale man with shoulder-length black hair got out and moved towards them. He dropped to his knee and grabbed Liv's wrist.

'Pulse is weak,' he said after a few beats. 'BP is low.' He lifted one of Liv's eyelids and shone a bright penlight into it, switched eyes and did the same. 'Pupils are constricted but responsive. Looks like some kind of barbiturate poisoning. I need to put her on oxygen and a drip and shift her to the hospital immediately so we can find out what they doped her with and start flushing it out.'

He threw open the doors and dragged out a retractable trolley, the legs springing open and clattering against the flagstones.

'Give the man a hand,' Arkadian said. 'I would, but . . .'

'Keep filming,' the reporter barked at the cameraman before stepping forward to help lift Liv on to the trolley.

The long-haired medic strapped her down then manoeuvred the stretcher back to the ambulance, slotting it into place with a hefty shove.

The reporter turned to Arkadian. 'You said we could interview her.'

'And so you shall, just as soon as she's been given the all-clear from the hospital. You wouldn't want to endanger her health in the pursuit of a story would you?'

Behind him the ambulance shuddered to life and the two-tone lights on the roof began to spin their bright colours across the greyness of the old town wall. 'I'll keep the rest of the press away, I promise,' Arkadian said. 'In fact, I'll ride with these guys to ensure it.' He climbed into the passenger seat and slammed the door behind him. 'I'll meet you at the hospital, just ask for me at the desk – they'll tell you where to go.' The ambulance pulled away.

The reporter jumped behind the wheel of the news truck and started the engine. He jammed it in gear and stamped on the accelerator as soon as the cameraman scrambled inside. There was a bang from outside and the wheel jerked to the right. He fought to keep it straight for a few metres, then hit the brakes and jumped out of the cab to see what was wrong.

A small piece of wood was embedded in the flat front tyre. He hooked his fingers round the edge and wrenched it free, the nails sticking out of the wood catching the streetlights as it clattered away across the road. Sabotage. He looked up just in time to see the ambulance slip round the corner at the end of the road and disappear from sight.

'Is she really suffering from a barbiturate overdose?' Arkadian asked.

The driver shook his head. 'Unlikely. She may have been dosed up with a barbiturate of some kind, but not to any dangerous level: she was responsive and her BP is fine. Was I convincing? I'm not used to dealing with them when they're still breathing.'

The driver was Dr Bartholomew Reis, senior pathologist at the city coroner's office. He had worked hundreds of cases with Arkadian and was the only person he trusted who could borrow an ambulance at short notice and make a convincing medic.

'Where to now?' Reis asked, switching off the siren and lights and easing the ambulance through the empty streets of Ruin.

'Keep heading east and out of the city,' Arkadian replied, watching the hospital loom up ahead then slip past and disappear behind them. 'I'll tell you when we're near.'

82

Vatican City

Clementi was dragged from a troubled dream by the harsh sound of a phone ringing. He checked the clock by his bed. The numerals showed that it was a little after four in the morning; the worst of all times to receive a call. He reached for the phone in the dark and snatched it up to silence the ring.

'Hello?'

'How quickly can you log on to your secure server?' It was Pentangeli, the American member of the Group.

'Ten minutes,' Clementi said, instantly awake. 'I need to get into the office.'

'Do it faster. I've just sent you something you really need to see.'

The phone went dead.

Clementi could hear the phone ringing in his office when the elevator opened on to the fourth floor of the Apostolic Palace eight minutes later.

He stumbled down the hall, keenly aware that the Holy Father was currently sleeping in the room next door. His own apartment was in a different building, on the other side of the Sistine Chapel. He had run the whole way, or as close to running as his bloated body would allow. Fumbling his key in the lock, he fell into the dark room, knocking a pile of newspapers to the floor as he grabbed the phone to silence it.

'I'm here,' he said, his words more breath than substance.

'Are you looking at your email?'

Clementi collapsed in his chair. 'I'm just . . . accessing it.' He fought for breath, his heart hammering in his chest, fingers shaking as they pecked away at the keyboard. There were two messages in his secure email account, one with the location ID of the compound in Iraq and one with no subject line or sender. He guessed this would be from Pentangeli. He opened it and a pop-up window automatically started playing a video clip.

At first it was too dark and shaky to make out; then the picture settled and a bright light came on, surprising a huge blond man dressed in black pushing a large box. Clementi felt the ground fall away from beneath him as he realized what he was watching.

'What you're looking at is raw, unedited news footage, flagged up by one of my senior news producers. They were going to run it as an exclusive on the next news cycle, but I made them spike it. All the media has now been destroyed. The only evidence that this ever happened is the file you're now looking at.'

The footage steadied again and showed the lid being removed. The camera framed up the sleeping form of the girl curled inside then panned away and tilted up showing the Citadel behind it. It was as damning as it could possibly be.

'Shortly after this footage was taken the girl was taken away under police escort to Ruin City Hospital – only she never got there. She's disappeared. Again. I know you said you were "handling" this,' Clementi couldn't miss the mocking quote marks around the word, 'so could you mind telling me where she is now?'

Clementi thought about lying, making up some story about how she was under surveillance and would be silenced within the hour, but he had made so many of those promises in the last few days that he couldn't bring himself to say it. 'I don't know,' he admitted.

There was a long exhale on the line before Pentangeli spoke again. 'I don't know why you're having such difficulty sorting this mess out. Don't forget, if this whole thing goes belly up, you're the one who'll suffer most. Beyond lending you money, we have no evident connection to this whole business. And one way or another we will get our money back, whether it's in cash or commodities. Hell, the site of St Patrick's in downtown Manhattan has got to be worth a quarter of a billion in real estate terms. So if I were you, I would throw everything you have at finding these people, before they stumble on to something that could really do some damage. Between us, we own most of the news and TV stations in the world, but we don't own them all. Don't count on the story being spiked if you screw up again. It's time you got your house in order, Cardinal. Let me know when it's done.'

83

Liv was aware of sounds and movement breaking through the soft cocoon of her drugged sleep. They were different from before, no longer the drone of a jet engine but something quieter. She could hear the crunch of tyres and feel the gentle movement of a vehicle travelling slowly over an uneven surface. The crunching slowed then stopped. She heard a door open and felt the springs rock as someone got in with her. It was still dark outside, she could sense it even though her eyes remained shut. She could smell the night creeping in through the open door and hear night noises woven into it: the dry rasp of crickets; the click of cooling earth.

Whoever had got in was standing close now, looking down at her. She imagined the huge blond man preparing another shot to keep her locked inside her own body. She thought of springing up and running into the night, but knew her body was too limp to obey. She braced herself for the bite of the needle. Then he spoke.

'Liv?'

Her eyes struggled open and she tried to focus. The figure looming over her was backlit by the bright interior light, but she knew who it was.

Gabriel smiled as her eyes rolled open and, in her mind, she smiled back and reached up to touch his face, but in reality her arm remained flat against the mattress and her face remained a mask. Whatever chemical prison she was in, she wasn't free of it yet. And even as she savoured this moment, memories of the nightmare returned. The last time she had woken from a dream and discovered him there he had been consumed with flame. His image began to liquefy as tears welled up in her eyes but she blinked them away and kept her eyes open. She wanted to look at him for as long as possible, even if he was an illusion.

He reached down and wiped away a tear with his thumb, then leaned over to kiss her. Only when she felt his lips touch hers and the warmth of his breath on her skin did she know that it *was* real. He was there.

Keep yourself safe, he had told her the last time she had seen him, *until I find you.*

And, though she had dramatically failed to keep her half of that bargain, he had somehow kept his.

'You're safe,' he whispered, and the words felt like a spell that unlocked her from some dark enchantment. 'Try to sleep now. We'll talk more when you've rested.'

Then he took her hand and held it, staying by her side until her eyes closed again and she slipped back into the security of sleep.

84

Vatican City

Clementi swallowed drily, his eyes fixed on the darkness of his office, staring at nothing. He had promised to call Pentangeli back once he'd checked in with his field operatives and found out what was happening. The latest report lay open on his desk, filed from the airport in New Jersey. He had dialled the contact number on the cover sheet, but no one was answering. There was a bump next door and the scrape of a chair across the floor. His Holiness was awake, undoubtedly roused by the sound of the phone ringing.

Clementi put the phone down and flicked on the desk lamp, revealing the spill of newspapers across the office floor where he'd knocked them over in his hurry on the way in. He dropped to his knees and started tidying them up in case the Pope decided to pay an unscheduled visit. If asked, he would say it was something to do with the global financial market; His Holiness always glazed over when he started talking about money – therein lay a large part of the Church's problems.

As he placed the last newspaper back on his desk his eyes snagged on the front page. It showed two photographs, one of Liv Adamsen and one of Gabriel Mann. Above them was the banner headline: MISSING – PRESUMED MURDERED?

An overwhelming wave of pure hatred consumed him. How could these people, these nobodies, be causing him such trouble?

He looked back up at the computer monitor to check the time and spotted the unopened email from earlier. It had been sent by Dr Harzan, the operations manager at the desert compound. He had skipped over it because of the ringing phone and the pressing urgency of the other email in the inbox. He opened it now and read its short but wonderful contents. It was miraculous, like a ray of sun shining through storm clouds, or the answer to a long-held prayer.

We found it – and it's far, far bigger than any of us dared hope.

Clementi read and reread the note, all the stress of the last weeks – years even – melting away in the warm glow of those few simple words.

They had found it, buried in the desert of northern Iraq, hidden throughout history, only to be found again by him, for the greater glory of God.

85

It was light when Liv woke.

She'd had the dream again while she slept, only this time
it had been different. The Tau had stood, not in some featureless darkness, but in the middle of an empty desert at night,
a fingernail moon hanging low in a sky full of stars. It had
been a dream shot through with anxiety and dread, although
nothing had happened. She had just sat, staring up at the
dwindling moon as it sank towards the horizon, slowly disappearing in a drift of sand until, moments before it and she
disappeared entirely, she woke up.

She was lying in the lower bunk of a row of three in a
wooden dormitory room that reminded her of summer camps
she had gone to when she was a kid. It had the same smell of
wood and dust and sunshine. There was also coffee brewing
somewhere and her stomach growled in response. She tried
to sit up and, to her utter relief, her body obeyed. The drug
she had been given was losing its grip on her, but she still had
the cottonmouth dryness of the recently sedated.

Easing herself out of bed, she slowly got to her feet, testing
her balance and feeling the stiffness in her muscles. The room
shifted a little as she rose and she had to cling to the steel
frame of the bed until it steadied again. She could hear the
pulse in her head and feel the dark threat of a headache lurking
behind her eyes. Ordinarily she would have popped an Advil
and got back into bed, but the smell of the coffee lured her
on. She needed the caffeine and the rehydration: but most of
all she wanted to see Gabriel again.

She found him in the next room, sitting at a table opposite Dr Anata and Arkadian. They were all hunched over a fold-out map pinned flat by a leather-bound book and a laptop wired to a phone. Gabriel rose from his chair and walked over to her, hesitant and slightly nervous, as if he didn't quite know what he should do. Liv solved the problem for him by collapsing against him and squeezing him hard. He was wearing a pullover that felt soft against her cheek and held the same cedarwood and citrus smell of him that she remembered from before. She pulled back and looked up into his face. 'Just checking you're real,' she said, her voice raspy from lack of use. 'You've been popping up in my dreams – and not in a good way.'

Gabriel smiled. 'I'm real,' he said. He pulled a chair out for her and sat back down. 'You want some breakfast?' He said this as if they were on a weekend away with friends and she had slept in with a hangover.

Plates of bread and apples, and pots of honey and butter were set out on the table, and her stomach growled at the sight. It would all have been quite pleasant if the circumstances had been different. Gabriel poured coffee from a jug and stirred in a big spoonful of honey. She drank the sweet liquid, savouring the way it scalded the back of her throat and hit her empty stomach with the combined force of caffeine and sugar.

She looked down at the map on the table. It showed the eastern edge of Turkey and the brown expanse of Syria, Jordan and Iraq. 'So where are we going?' she asked.

There was a moment of awkward silence.

'We're not entirely sure,' Gabriel admitted. 'I . . . didn't find the Starmap. Someone else had got there first. The monk who helped me get inside the mountain, Athanasius, is going to check the archives and try to find out what happened to it.'

Even though Gabriel's words had mortal implications for her, Liv could hear the pain of disappointment in his voice and wanted only to reach out and tell him it was OK. 'So we wait,' she said brightly, trying to make it sound as if this was the best they could have hoped for.

Another awkward silence stretched across the table. Dr Anata broke it.

'We haven't got time to wait,' she said. 'I've been going through some research papers on ancient maps and other documents that I thought might point us in the right direction.' Her voice was low and measured in a way that disturbed Liv deeply. 'I discovered something, a couple of things actually: one that may be of use and one that – is less helpful.'

In her former life as a crime reporter, Liv had done a feature on what the police called 'Death Notices', the most hated part of any homicide detective's job. It referred to the visits they had to make to victims' families in order to break the painful news that someone they loved was never coming home again. In the course of her research, she had studied the specific changes in body language and the careful cadence of the voice as it shaped itself to deliver this most unwelcome of all news. Liv recognized those telltale signs now in Dr Anata.

'We'd been working on the assumption that the countdown started when you released the Sacrament. But having read up on ancient systems of measuring time, I realize we were wrong.' Dr Anata picked up the leather-bound book from the table and turned to the middle pages. 'The Mirror Prophecy says you must follow the Starmap Home *within* the phase of the moon. So far we have applied our modern, fluid notions of time to this, and treated it as a relative measurement. For us, a specific period of time can start whenever we choose because we have clocks to measure it by. But the ancients only had the fixed rhythms of nature, so time for them was always expressed as an absolute. Therefore the phrase *"Within the phase of a moon"* does not refer to a twenty-eight-day period that started when you released the Sacrament. It refers to the fixed period of celestial time during which all of these events must happen.'

Liv realized now why Dr Anata's tone and behaviour had been so horribly familiar. Like those detectives she had followed to unsuspecting doors, Dr Anata had been carrying the burden of death with her. Only this time it wasn't news of some victim in the morgue, it was the prognosis for her survival.

'How long have I got?'

'The current phase of the moon ends tomorrow night,' Gabriel said, his voice tight and controlled. 'We have two days to find the ancient site of Eden or the Sacrament will die inside you, you will die with it, and God alone knows what will happen to the rest of us.'

Liv looked out through a dusty window to a uniform line of trees stretching away from the shack. Blossom drifted down from them like snow and above them, low on the horizon, she could see the partial moon, curling like a fingernail in the lightening sky.

'You said you'd found two things,' she said, watching it melt away, as it had in her dream, which now made a terrible kind of sense.

Dr Anata reached over and turned the laptop round so Liv could see it. 'I found this,' she said.

On the screen was a browser window with a picture of a cracked clay tablet.

'This is the *Imago Mundi*, the oldest known map in the world, and part of the permanent collection of Babylonian artefacts in the British Museum. *Imago Mundi* literally means "map of the earth", and many – myself included – believe it was inspired by the Starmap.'

Liv leaned forward and studied the photograph. A section at the top of the tablet was crammed with strange symbols and below that were two perfect circles – one inside the other – containing another symbol that Liv recognized immediately as the Tau.

'I came to the conclusion that, if this was inspired by the Starmap, then the two would exhibit similar characteristics and principles. Maps are always designed to be uniform and stick to certain rules so that as many people as possible can interpret them. Modern maps, for example, always have north at the top, and the oceans coloured blue. And the one thing about this map that is consistent with every other from the same period is this.' She pointed at the T in the centre of the circle.

'It's always right in the middle and everything else is relative to it. In the past, scholars assumed it was the Tau and must refer to Ruin, because of the city's long associations with the symbol. But when cuneiform started to be decoded in the nineteenth century they discovered their mistake. The upright actually represents a river and the crosspiece a city, under whose walls that river flowed.' Dr Anata pointed to a symbol carved into the right-hand side of the crosspiece. 'Babylon. At one time it was the greatest city on earth and the centre of the civilized world. So naturally the very first map-makers placed it at the centre of everything.'

'And you think the Starmap will do the same?'

Dr Anata nodded. 'The route back to Eden will undoubtedly begin where all ancient journeys did, at the site where Babylon once stood.' She pointed a silver-ringed finger at a spot on the map. 'Al-Hillah – in the province of Babil, south central Iraq.'

Liv looked across at Gabriel, his face pinched in painful memory as he stared down at the point on the map marking the place where his father had been killed.

'We should load up the jeep and get going,' he said, rising from his chair. 'The border's a good few hours away. We don't have much time.'

V

And the Temple was filled with smoke from the glory of God . . . and no man was able to enter into the Temple, till the seven plagues of the seven angels were fulfilled.

Revelation 15:8

86

Vatican City

Clementi put the phone down and tapped his password into the secure server. He had been talking to Harzan for almost an hour, learning first hand everything they had found, and though the news had made him feel elated, he had ended the conversation feeling slightly anxious. It was more urgent than ever that the thorn in his side that had been bothering him since the explosion in the Citadel must be removed. For his grand scheme to be compromised by the inopportune investigations of a few terrorists would be tragic. Pentangeli's words kept echoing in his head:

. . . *throw everything you have at finding these people, before they stumble on to something that could really do some damage.*

During his lengthy conversation with Harzan, a new email had arrived. Clementi opened it now, eager for more good news.

It was a field report, filed by the one remaining active agent. Clementi skimmed through it. The agent confirmed what the news footage had already shown him: the girl had got away. There was no new information as to where she had gone. In the agent's opinion, the escape effort had been coordinated by the other survivor, Gabriel Mann, and the two of them were now on the run together.

Attached to the report were several photo files showing images of items found in the girl's luggage; her passport, the ruined Bible, and various pages from her notebook. One of the pages contained a list of place names:

Ethiopia
Assyria
Euphrates
Al-Hillah
Eden????

Clementi stared at the last three names.

They were getting close, much too close for comfort. If they managed to find the compound out in the desert then . . .

He paused.

Then what? Two people facing down a small, private army. He smiled. Pentangeli had it the wrong way round. Clementi didn't need to 'throw everything he had' at finding these people; they were clearly already on their way to find him, or the sacred spot in the desert at least.

He reached over, picked up the phone and dialled Harzan's number from memory. There would be no need to send out a search party – all he had to do was set a trap.

87

Babil Province, Western Iraq

Hyde stared out of his window at the brightening sky. He had already been up since a couple of hours before dawn, organizing the security and construction detail for the new site out in the desert. Outside he could hear the noise of trucks and other vehicles revving up ready to move out. He'd been all set to go with them, but now Dr Harzan had dropped this in his lap.

Sometimes he felt like a raw recruit, being handed all the crappy jobs no one else wanted. At least in the army there had only been one chain of command, so you knew who was above you and therefore which way the shit flowed. He remembered what the Ghost had said when he'd brokered the exchange for the relic.

These people may come here searching for something. If they come, let me know.

At the time he'd thought hell would ice over before he'd ask the Ghost for help. But with the three wise men draining his resources out in the desert, he figured he should swallow his pride and do the pragmatic thing. He would pay the man for his help, establish a power structure of master and servant. It wasn't his money after all.

He unlocked the lower drawer of his desk, pulled out the newspaper and dialled the number written in the margin. This time the Ghost answered.

'You have news for me?'

Hyde shook his head, already exhausted by the day. 'Would a simple "Hello" kill you?'

The Ghost said nothing.

Hyde pinched the space between his eyes, trying to massage away his headache. 'OK, let's cut the small talk then. Those people you spoke about, the ones you said would be coming to search for something in the desert? They're on their way.'

'How old is this news?'

'Fresh off the press, as far as I'm aware. I've been asked to find them quickly and you said you could help. You remember that?'

The Ghost said nothing.

Hyde continued to work at the spot on his forehead. 'Listen, if you're busy—'

'I can help you,' the Ghost said, then the phone went dead.

88

It hadn't taken much to convert the reading room into a makeshift infirmary. The desks had been moved aside to create space for four beds and the shelves that were normally packed with books were now crammed with boxes of syringes, sterile gloves, masks and strong sedatives. Another shelf was entirely filled with canvas straps, lying in readiness to restrain those who showed symptoms of what everyone was now calling 'the Lamentation'.

Axel was pacing, fuelled by frustration and fear, settling on his bed only fitfully before starting his circuit of the room again. Athanasius felt sorry for him. As captain of the guards, Axel was clearly feeling the stress and indignity of this incarceration more than the rest of them. He had also seen his life's ambition snatched away for a second time. He must have thought his elevation to Sanctus was guaranteed with the arrival back in the Citadel of Brother Dragan; then this had happened.

Father Malachi was dealing with the quarantine in a different way. He sat at one of the workstations, his face bathed in the green glow of a terminal screen, zoning everything out so he could disappear into his work. Unbeknown to the outside world, the vast majority of the millions of books and documents in the great library had been digitized and Malachi and his staff had been cataloguing and cross-referencing them for over a year. He therefore had enough to keep him busy for years to come, so long as he remained connected to his beloved library and unaffected by the disease.

Athanasius and Father Thomas crowded round the only other workstation in the room, tapping messages to each other on a blank document so that Axel and Malachi could not discover what they were discussing. Athanasius finished a summary of his fruitless search in the ossuary ending in the crucial question he hoped Thomas, architect of the library's database, could now help him with.

> Can you access the library inventory immedi-
ately following the ossuary renovations and see
if anything was added?

Father Thomas nodded, took over the keyboard and started tapping away. First he called up a general diary program and found the exact dates the ossuary had been renovated. It was listed in the general maintenance log over eight years previously. He copied the dates into a search facility on the main cataloguing program and hit return.

Pages of results filled the screen.

Athanasius felt weary just looking at them all. The Citadel was voracious in its acquisition of every publication, research paper or book that had anything remotely to do with the Sacrament. The number of new additions listed, even limiting the search to the weeks immediately following the restorations, ran into thousands. Sorting through them was going to take hours – days, maybe – and the inventory was far from detailed. Athanasius took possession of the keyboard again.

> Can you refine the search and look for
anything archaeological – specifically anything
etched on stone?

Thomas returned to the search window and tapped in a string of codes that meant nothing to Athanasius but clearly made sense to the program. This time only two items came back.

The results were laid out in a grid of four columns with a unique number on the left, a brief description of the item, a column detailing where it came from and a final column showing where it was now.

The first entry was described as a clay tablet written in proto-cuneiform script and incorporating Tau symbols in its design. It had come from Iraq after being acquired on behalf of the Citadel and was now stored in the Babylonian section of the library, along with several thousand similar examples acquired over nearly as many years.

The second item was more of a mystery.

It was described simply as a stone tablet with markings. The column showing where it had come from contained a dash and the final one, indicating where it was now stored had the letters ASV written in it, the number 2, and a date from three years ago. Athanasius assumed it must be more computer jargon, but when he pointed at it Thomas shrugged and shook his head, clearly as baffled as he was. He glanced up at the hunched figure across the room. 'Brother Malachi,' he called out. The librarian looked up in shock as if he'd forgotten there was anyone else in the room. 'I'm running some systems tests on the inventory database and I've found an anomaly. Could you take a look at it for me?'

Malachi rose unwillingly from his seat and shuffled towards them. 'What's the problem?' he asked, standing as far back as he could, as if fearful he might catch the Lamentation from being near them.

'This entry seems to have been corrupted in some way. Does it make any sense to you?'

Malachi peered through his thick glasses and huffed. 'It's not corrupted,' he said. 'The dash means it didn't come from outside the mountain. It will most likely have been transferred from a different department in the library, so there's no acqui-sition information to fill in.'

Thomas nodded. 'And the destination code?'

'That means it is no longer here.' He pointed at the letters ASV. 'That stands for *Archivum Secretum Vaticanum* and the date indicates when it was transferred there.'

Athanasius was shocked by the information almost as much as he was by the matter-of-fact way in which it had been delivered. 'But I thought nothing ever left the mountain.'

'It is rare, but it does happen. There were four transfers last century, for example – all to the Vatican Secret Archives.'

'And the number two,' he asked, pointing at the one part Malachi had not explained, 'what does that stand for?'

'It identifies the position of the person who made the request. Only the most senior clerics in the Vatican can authorize the transfer of material from our library and each of them is assigned a number. Number one refers to the Pope and number two is his second in command. This transfer was ordered by the Cardinal Secretary of State, Cardinal Clementi.'

89

Gabriel had done the journey to the border many times before, driving supplies down to the charity's various projects in Iraq. He told Liv about some of them as they drove – the schools they were building, the wetlands in the south they were re-flooding after Saddam Hussein had drained them to drive out the marsh Arabs who'd lived there for thousands of years. Gabriel talked and Liv listened, stoking the fire of his conversation with the occasional question while she leaned against the hot window and watched the dry, rocky countryside slide past.

The further they got, the more the green vanished and the desert took over. It reflected how she was feeling – as if some vital part of her was disappearing and slowly being replaced by dry dust. At first she tried to convince herself that it was just the residual effects of the sedative; but as the miles wore on and the feeling of emptying out grew stronger she started to think it might be something else. *Two days*, Gabriel had said; forty-eight hours – and they were going to spend at least half of it travelling, with no guarantees they were even heading in the right direction.

90

Athanasius got up from behind the workstation, stretched the kinks out of his back and made his way across the room to the small door leading to the washroom. Following their conversation with Malachi, he and Father Thomas had scoured the database for any other entries with ASV2 in the requisition line. They discovered Cardinal Secretary Clementi had submitted *seven* applications in the past three years – almost twice as many as in the whole of the preceding century – starting with the first item, which Athanasius was now convinced was the Starmap. It was the only one that remained unidentified. Of the other six, four were Mesopotamian maps and the remaining two were ancient accounts of travellers who claimed to have discovered the true location of Eden.

As a scholar, Athanasius had come across legends such as these; wild tales of trees that produced magical fruit and underground grottoes filled with vast hoards of gold. He had never seriously considered them to be anything other than allegorical or the fanciful imaginings of ancient storytellers. But, whatever his own thoughts, it was clear that the Cardinal Secretary of State in Rome believed them.

A light flickered on as he stepped into the washroom revealing a row of stone sinks facing a line of stalls. He stepped across to the furthest one and closed the door behind him.

The cubicle was little more than a square stall with a hole cut in the stone floor that led directly to the sewer. To one side was a bucket of water with a wooden cup floating in it that was used as a rudimentary flushing mechanism. There was no lock on the door, so Athanasius leaned against it and took the phone Gabriel had given him from his pocket. It lit up the dim cubicle the moment he touched the screen. He stared down at it, trying to remember the lesson he'd had on how to compose a message. He managed to call up a test message sent from Gabriel, hit the 'Reply' option then carefully transcribed a summary of everything he had discovered, working quickly, aware that the longer he was gone the more suspicion it would arouse, then he tapped the *send* button.

A small box opened up in the middle of the screen: 'Cannot Send Mail.'

He tried again and got the same message.

Outside, the door opened and someone walked to the sink and started filling it. He slipped the phone in his pocket, mindful of the light it gave off, and poured a cup of water into the hole before opening the door.

Father Thomas was splashing water on to his face when he emerged. Athanasius seized the moment and thrust the phone at him. 'It's not working,' he said, glancing nervously at the door.

Thomas took the phone and read the error message. 'There's no signal,' he said. 'We're too deep in the mountain.'

Athanasius felt instantly deflated. He was trapped in quarantine, for the next few days at least, in a location he had specified, buried deep beneath solid rock. He needed to get out somehow, or the information he had found would be useless.

Thomas held out the phone and Athanasius reached out to take it from him when the door behind them flew open.

Axel stood in the doorway. For a moment he stood looking at them both, his eyes switching from one to the other, seemingly oblivious to the glowing device being passed between them.

Then they saw the fresh blood dripping from his nose, just

as his face crumpled in anguish and he fell to his knees, his hands already clawing violently at the flesh beneath his red cassock.

'Help me,' he said, through ragged, mournful sobs. 'Please, somebody, help me . . .'

91

It took Liv and Gabriel eight precious hours to reach the Turkish–Iraqi border on roads that became increasingly worse. They knew they were getting close when they came to the first military checkpoint. Gabriel did all the talking and they were quickly waved on. The checkpoint was manned by Turkish soldiers, he explained as they drove away, and their primary concern was the PKK – Kurdish freedom fighters – not Western fugitives; the border would be a different story. He handed her a maroon British passport with a picture of a blonde girl in the back that looked a bit like Liv if you squinted.

'I borrowed it from one of the volunteers,' he said, watching the checkpoint disappear in his rear-view mirror. 'The border police never look too closely. They take photocopies for their files and I've already done some with the contrast whacked right up so you can hardly make out the picture anyway.' He reached over and gave her hand a squeeze. 'We'll be fine. I promise.'

Fifteen minutes later they crested a hill and saw the border crossing at Silopi, built on the side of a muddy river. It was little more than a delta-shaped concrete car park that ended abruptly at the river's edge. Liv's first reaction when she saw it was that she was going to die there. A road bridge extended from the centre of it, spanning the river and joining another complex of squat buildings on the Iraqi side: one bridge, one road, and literally thousands of trucks waiting to use it. They were parked in rows by the border-patrol buildings and in makeshift car parks on either side of the main road that snaked away through the dry land, choked with a solid, unmoving line of more traffic. If they had to wait in line it would take days to get into Iraq, days that they didn't have.

'Don't worry,' Gabriel said, reading her mood. 'That's the queue for road freight. We're going to join the one over there.' He pointed to a clear strip of road close to the bridge where a US Army Humvee was speeding towards a line of waiting taxis. It left the road, kicking up dust as it skirted around the parked cars and barely paused at the barrier before picking up speed again to cross the bridge into Iraq. On the far side of the river were more military vehicles and men with M4 assault rifles slung across their chests. They stood in the shade of a small arch that spanned the road. Above them was a sign written in Arabic with an English translation beneath saying 'Welcome to Iraqi Kurdistan Region'.

'We'll be on our way in no time,' he said. 'Trust me, I've done it many times before.'

Liv wasn't convinced. 'Have you ever done it with half the Turkish police force after you?'

He smiled and handed her a passport. 'They're not looking for me, they're looking for someone called Gabriel Mann.'

She opened the passport and saw his face staring back with someone else's name beneath it.

'Who's David Kinsella?'

'I am, when I need to be – all part of my glamorous existence as a charity worker. I got fed up with being thrown out of various countries for trying to help people the government were busy persecuting. Unfortunately, the deck is stacked heavily in favour of any regime who want to keep you out. All they have to do is stick your name on a list of undesirables and all normal methods of entry cease to work. So I got a little creative and stopped playing by the rules. Believe me, getting out of Turkey won't be a problem; it's what happens when we get into Iraq that worries me more.'

They drove along the road past the wall of lorries and parked next to the local taxis.

'This is where we might get held up a little,' Gabriel said, nodding towards the taxi drivers. 'They make a good living out of guiding tourists and travellers through all the red tape and don't take kindly to free agents who don't need them. We could plead with them, see if they'll let us queue jump, but I doubt any will, and we don't really want to cause a scene and draw attention to ourselves.'

Liv studied the line of taxi drivers and their passengers. There were around fifteen of them, all looking as if they were on a leisurely Sunday outing. Some were talking to the border guards, some were eating; most were smoking; a small group was even playing cards, but none of them seemed in a particular hurry.

'How do we know how many people are in front of us?'

Gabriel pointed at a blackboard with a number 12 chalked on it. 'You get a chit from the desk and wait until they chalk your number up.'

A wave of heat flooded the interior as he got out of the car and headed across to a uniformed man sitting behind a scratched Perspex window to get a number. Liv stared out of the window, jogging her leg up and down with tension. They couldn't afford to hang around here waiting patiently in line. Time was too short. They had to get to the front somehow, even if she had to kiss every driver to do it. She surveyed the level of male beauty on display. Stained shirts, vests and hairy shoulders. Maybe she'd try a different approach. She popped open her door, stepped out into the dry heat and headed over to join Gabriel.

'Twenty-six,' Gabriel said, showing her the chit he had just been given. 'I'm going to have to chat with some of these guys, see if I can't get us moved up the list.'

'Let me try,' Liv said, taking the chit and heading over to the four card sharks. 'Have you got any money?'

'A little.'

'Give me enough to grab these guys' attention. And translate for me, would you.'

She arrived at the upturned oil drum that served as a card table and smiled broadly. 'Hey, fellas. Any of you guys got a lower number than me?' She held up the chit while Gabriel translated. They each reached into various pockets and produced their own chits. Unsurprisingly, they all had lower numbers. She turned the full beam of her smile on to the driver holding up the number 14, a short, tubby man with a beard and the sort of glasses that went black in sunlight. 'How would you like to win some money?' she said. His face clouded with suspicion the moment Gabriel translated.

'Stick down twenty bucks' worth of dinars and ask him again,' she said to Gabriel out of the corner of her still-smiling mouth.

With the appearance of real money the man was suddenly interested. Liv scooped up three cards from the pile and held them up: a three of hearts, a seven of diamonds and the queen of spades. 'All you have to do is find the lady,' she said, flipping them over and mixing them up in such a way that it was easy to follow the queen. 'If you guess right, you get the money. If you guess wrong . . .' she held up the chit with 26 written on it, '. . . we swap numbers.'

Gabriel explained the rules. The man still wasn't convinced, but Liv was undeterred. 'OK, free go. No bets down.' She shuffled the cards some more. 'Find the lady.' The man hesitated then pointed to the middle card. Liv flipped it over to reveal the queen. 'Hey, we have a winner.' She handed him the cash.

'I thought there were no bets on that one,' Gabriel whispered.

'I can't see him complaining,' she muttered back. 'Stick some more money down while I've got the hook in him.'

Gabriel did as he was told while Liv shuffled the cards. Again she did it so slowly that following the queen was easy. 'OK,' she said. 'Your number against my bet. You want to take it?'

The man was staring at the card on the left and clutching the money he had just won. He nodded and laid chit number 14 down next to the cash.

'OK, then. Find the lady.'

He pointed to the card he'd been looking at. Liv flipped it over. It was the three of hearts. She scooped up the cash and the chit and shrugged. 'You can't win 'em all,' she said. 'But everyone gets a prize in this game.' She handed him the chit with 26 written on it and walked quickly back to the car.

Ten minutes later they were driving over the bridge and crossing the border.

Gabriel shook his head and smiled. 'Where on earth did you learn to do that?'

'Coney Island. I did a series of articles on classic boardwalk cons and an old-time grifter showed me how they worked. When all this is over, I'll show you how it's done.'

Gabriel's smile deepened. 'Deal.'

They passed under the sign welcoming them to Iraq and Gabriel parked in the shade of the arch ready to go through the whole process again with Iraqi customs and immigration officials. The office on the other side was almost identical to its Turkish counterpart – the only diffcrence being the uniforms. The patrol guards here wore drab green fatigues with military-style badges showing palm fronds encircling a sword and an AK-47. There were plenty of US military personnel around too. Gabriel had spotted a small enclosure of field tents set up off the road behind the main buildings. The Hummer they had seen earlier was parked in front of one and several other vehicles suggested there was a full platoon stationed here – thirty men at least.

The border guard studied their passport photographs, checked them against their faces, then handed them back. He finished his checks, stamped the vehicle documents and that was it.

'Welcome to Iraq,' he said.

It had been easier than Liv had thought. All they had to do now was drive for several hundred kilometres along some of the most dangerous roads in the world with no escort and no real idea of where they were going, to a place they hoped would lead them to the ancient site of Eden. It wasn't the most promising of missions, but even so, it felt like a minor victory to Liv as she pushed through the office door and back out into the blinding sun. Then she saw the welcoming committee.

There were three of them, all wearing the coffee-stain fatigues of the US Army. Two were inspecting their vehicle, the third faced them, his eyes hidden behind standard-issue Oakleys. 'Could I see your passports, please,' he said, his finger resting on the trigger of his cradled weapon.

'Is there a problem?' Gabriel stepped in front of Liv, as if that might protect her from what was happening. The soldier said nothing, he just continued to hold out his hand for the passports. Gabriel handed them over. The soldier didn't even look at them.

'Follow me, please. We need to ask you a few questions.'

92

Brother Axel was strapped to his bed and stripped to his loin-cloth. He lay moaning, his fingernails drawing blood from his palms as they worked away at the only bit of skin they could reach.

Athanasius, Thomas and Malachi were in the washroom, silently scrubbing their hands and faces with antiseptic soap in the stone sinks, wondering if the same poison that had claimed Axel was now working its way through them. It had taken all three of them to hold him down until the attendant Apothecaria had eventually managed to subdue him with a well-aimed shot of strong sedative.

They emerged from the washroom and were met by Brother Simenon, drawn here by the news that the contagion had claimed a new victim. He was hunched over the pustulant chest of Brother Axel, drawing a sample of fluid from one of the larger boils. When he finished, he handed it to an assistant then turned to the group, unsnapping his gloves and lowering his mask. The face beneath was drawn and hollow. He looked as though he hadn't slept in a month, though in truth it was only a few days.

'Well, at least this solves one problem,' he said, moving away from the bed to the far side of the room and perching on a reading desk. 'Brother Axel is not alone; there have been three other new cases of the Lamentation in the past few hours, apparently unconnected to the initial outbreak, which changes the game somewhat. I was wondering where we could put these new patients to keep them isolated; I might as well put them here. We can easily fit them in if we take more desks away and convert the second reading room. As you said earlier,' he nodded at Athanasius, 'the sealed nature of the library makes this a perfect isolation ward.'

'And what about us?' Malachi asked, his magnified eyes terrified and tearful. 'Are we to stay here too, sharing a room with the infected?'

'I see no reason to keep you. The purpose of your quarantine has now been negated by the fresh outbreak. I have recommended a new form of general quarantine within the mountain. From our studies of existing cases we have managed to identify a few early-warning symptoms. Anyone displaying these should be moved immediately to a containment ward. Everyone else should restrict themselves to their main area of work, and general movement throughout the mountain must be forbidden.'

'And has Brother Dragan sanctioned this?'

Simenon shook his head. 'Brother Dragan has locked himself in the forbidden stairwell and retired to the chapel of the Sacrament, advising everyone to pray for salvation.'

'Then who is in charge?'

'At the moment? Nobody.'

Athanasius's mind hummed with this new information. He turned to Malachi and Thomas. 'Then I suggest we three set up an emergency council to help implement Brother Simenon's suggestions. Between us, we can appeal to our guilds to remain steadfast, and quickly organize the logistics of a lockdown throughout the mountain. We can organize food distribution to the major stairwells, so no one need travel to the refectories, and keep the corridors clear for swift evacuation to the infirmaries in the event of new cases. Only by staying calm can we hope to see our way through this.'

Thomas nodded in agreement and Simenon brightened a little, as if someone had just removed a sack of rubble from his back.

'And where should we base ourselves?' Malachi asked. 'My main area of work is here in the library, and that is about to become a haven for the infected.'

Athanasius nodded as if considering this problem, though in truth he already had the answer. 'We could set ourselves up in the Abbot's chambers,' he said. 'For one thing, it is vacant, plus there's room for all three of us and it's well placed for coordinating efforts throughout the mountain.'

What he didn't say was that the Abbot's chambers, situated on the outside of the mountain with one of the few glazed windows in the Citadel, overlooking the modern city below, offered the best chance he was likely to get of picking up a phone signal.

93

The army tent was air-conditioned, but it was still hot enough inside to make Liv feel light-headed. The soldier led them down a canvas corridor towards a door that shook when he knocked on it.

'Yes!' The voice beyond the door sounded busy and officious.

The soldier opened the door and stood aside to let them pass.

Inside was an office with a desk, a military laptop, a phone and some aluminium folding chairs. There was also a lean colonel with a shining, shaved head and skin so black he could have been carved from ebony. He was sitting behind the desk reading an official-looking fax displaying two pictures: one of her and one of Gabriel. Liv's knees almost buckled at the sight of them.

The soldier stepped forward and placed their passports on the desk. 'Thank you,' the colonel said, 'that will be all.'

Liv heard the door close, and boots marching away. The colonel inspected the passports then finally looked up, fixing on Gabriel and shaking his head with the air of a disappointed parent.

'You should have stayed in the service,' he said.

Gabriel nodded, as if agreeing with him. 'And you should put some pictures up in here. Make it a bit more homely.'

A grin split the colonel's face and he was on his feet and crushing Gabriel in an embrace before Liv knew what was happening. Gabriel released the colonel from the bear hug and turned to her.

'Liv Adamsen, meet James Washington. We went through Special Forces training together when he was just a captain and I was a lowly grunt.'

'And now I'm a colonel in Military Intelligence and you're a civilian on the run from the law. Where did it all go wrong?' Washington stepped back behind the desk and handed over the fax. 'This came in through the wires a couple of hours ago. It's got a Homeland Security code on it, so you must have made yourself some pretty serious enemies.'

Gabriel skimmed through the fax and handed it to Liv. It was a rehash of the same information she had heard on the news in her New Jersey hotel room. The only new information was about her. It described her as a kidnap victim who needed to be located urgently to continue unspecified medical treatment. There was a number to call if they were spotted or apprehended.

'Have you checked this number?' she asked.

'I ran a router test on it. It's a dummy exchange that patches calls through to somewhere else. We can't get a location off it, if that's what you mean. The key thing is that it wound up on my desk, so whoever's looking for you knows you're heading this way.'

Gabriel nodded. 'Did you have any joy with any of the Iraqi police files?'

Washington nodded. 'You sure know how to milk a favour.' He pulled a folder from the top drawer of his desk and handed it over.

Inside were two collated bundles of official documents written in Arabic.

'They're copies of Ba'athist intelligence dossiers seized during the liberation of Baghdad. There may be more, but to be honest you didn't give me much time. It wasn't easy getting hold of them *and* hopping a lift out here. Next time, you might want to give me more warning.'

'I'll bear that in mind,' Gabriel said, flicking through the first sheaf of documents until he found a summary at the back in English.

It was a collection of military and police reports – dated 16 Sept 2000 – detailing investigations into an incident in the desert outside Al-Hillah in Babil Province. An archaeological dig had been attacked by unknown forces, leaving no survivors. A list of twenty names was attached to the report, mostly local but with a few Westerners mixed in. John Mann was top of the list. It confirmed what Gabriel had always believed: the incident had nothing to do with the Iraqi government. But there was new information in the file. At around the time of the incident a military base had picked up intermittent radar contact with an aircraft moving south from the Turkish/Syrian border. Its speed and flight pattern suggested it was a helicopter. The same aircraft had been detected again heading north from the dig site about twenty minutes later, but weather conditions had been poor and contact was lost. The report concluded that it had been a hostile incursion by Turkish forces, though it didn't speculate for what purpose.

But Gabriel knew.

The helicopter would have been full of agents from the Citadel, sent to retrieve the relics found at the site and leave no witnesses behind.

The second bundle of documents showed that they had botched it.

Someone had survived.

The top sheet was a patient's admission form for a psychiatric asylum on the outskirts of Baghdad. It was dated two weeks after the initial incident. The patient's name was Zaid Aziz. He had been found close to death, wandering in the desert, sun-blind and raving, with severe burns to his arms and legs. He told his rescuers that he had survived an attack from a dragon. Further interrogation had identified him as one of the missing workers from the dig near Al-Hillah. His burns tallied with what they had discovered there. Whoever had carried out the atrocity had piled the dead bodies up, doused them with kerosene and set them alight. Aziz also had a bullet wound to his arm and one to the head. His medical notes theorized that he had been knocked out by the head wound and must have appeared dead to whoever had thrown his body in with the rest. The pain of his burning flesh must have brought him round and saved his life. Unfortunately, by the time he was found, the trauma and days of dehydration and fever from the onset of sepsis had affected his mind. The dossier included a collection of interviews by police and psychiatrists conducted over a number of years, but nothing that shed new light on the incident. Aziz remained fixated on the same delusions: a fire-breathing dragon flying out of the night, and a ghost that had risen from the ground and drifted into the desert – something the psychiatrists interpreted as an obscure reference to himself.

Gabriel read through the notes with a growing sense of frustration. This man may have witnessed what happened to his father, but any knowledge of the attack appeared to have leaked from his cracked mind. It also slammed the door on one more avenue of enquiry. He had hoped the file would confirm that Iraqi Republican Guards had carried out the attack at Al-Hillah and shifted the relics to one of Saddam Hussein's many palaces. If they had, there might have been some chance of recovering them. But all the file had done was confirm what he already knew. Whatever his father had found was now locked inside the Citadel.

'Look at the date.' Liv pointed to the top of the last interview sheet. 'This interview took place less than six months ago.'

Colonel Washington nodded. 'Yep. He may be crazy as a bug, but he's clearly as tough as tin. I don't know if I would have survived twelve years in a Ba'athist mental asylum. Apparently the other inmates are scared of him. A year or so after he was admitted, he burned a man alive in a neighbouring cell. No one's quite sure how he managed it. The other patients believe he gained some of the powers of the dragon. So no one bothers him – not even the orderlies.' He checked his watch. 'Now, I hate to hurry you, but what are your plans for the remainder of your stay in this fair country?'

'We're driving down to Al-Hillah.'

'Are you nuts? Two unescorted Western civilians tooling down Highway 9 in a bright white pickup? Soon as you drop below Mosul you'll be killed or kidnapped – or both. No, I'm afraid I'm going to have to ask you to accompany me back to Command Centre in Baghdad. There's a chopper picking me up at fourteen hundred hours and I think I need to take you in for further questioning . . . before I realize, to my certain embarrassment, that you are not the people we're looking for and have to let you go. What you do after that is your own business.'

He handed Gabriel a scratchpad and a pencil.

'Before I return these files, you might want to jot down the address of that loony bin in Baghdad, just in case you're at a loose end. I'm sure Mr Aziz would be glad of the visit. I can't imagine he gets many.'

94

Hyde stepped out of the main building and into the heat of the day.

'Over there,' Tariq said, pointing east past the drilling tower.

Squinting into the sun, he saw the dust cloud rising up on the horizon. Sand and dust storms were a constant hazard in the desert. They could spring up out of nothing and turn day to night within seconds. They also did more damage to equipment than bullets or bombs, so he spent more time watching out and defending against them than he did against possible aggressors, saboteurs or kidnappers.

He walked swiftly over to the eastern perimeter and climbed the guard tower. Failure to react quickly to a sandstorm could shut down the whole operation for weeks. If sand got into an engine it would have to be stripped, cleaned and reassembled before it would work again. Guns seized when dust clogged the oil. Electronics shorted as microscopic grains of dust found their way into circuit boards. Even the men could go temporarily blind from tiny particles in the wind scouring away the surface of their eyes. Just another of the many, many reasons why Hyde loathed this country so much.

As soon as he got to the top of the tower he raised his field glasses to study the column of dust. Like a small mountain on the march, it billowed up from the ground as if the earth had started to boil. At the moment it was relatively small and still some way off, but it was definitely heading their way. If it didn't dissipate or change direction they would have to shut down until it had passed. Shutdowns cost money and time and the only reason he'd taken this job was because they'd offered him a profit share. So far, that equated to half a per cent of nothing.

Hyde glanced at the windsock by the helipad. The wind direction was northwesterly, yet the storm was coming from the east. Perhaps there was a crosswind out there somewhere, which would blow the storm off course before it reached them – or maybe it wasn't a dust storm at all.

As he squinted through the binoculars, focusing on the leading edge of the column of dust to try to make out some detail, he saw a flash of white, then another. Hyde smiled. He was right. It wasn't a force of nature at all, it was the Ghost, riding in with an army of horsemen spread out alongside him. The Bedouin always used this formation when riding at speed. It ensured they all breathed clean air and was an effective intimidation tactic, the rising dust cloud amplifying the presence of their approaching force.

He watched them draw closer, the riders visible now to the naked eye, points of white at the leading edge of the dust cloud, like the small, sharp teeth of a huge animal. There were nearly thirty riders, dressed in white dishdashas with their keffiyehs drawn across their faces. It occurred to Hyde that this scene would have changed little in thousands of years: the horses, the men, even the clothes had remained the same throughout history. The only difference was the weapons.

Hyde could hear the thump of hooves now, and something else, chopping its way through the air and getting louder. He turned and, in the blink of an eye, spanned the entire history of desert warfare. A helicopter gunship was skimming low across the ground and heading directly towards them. The guard started swinging his M60 towards it, but Hyde held up his hand and ordered the rest to do the same through his handheld radio. The chopper roared overhead and banked sharply, settling into a hover before dropping down to the helipad on the far side of the compound. The horsemen arrived at the perimeter fence at the same time.

Descending from the guard tower, Hyde made his way over to greet the new arrivals. He could see one of the riders separate from the rest and drift over to the main gate. He waved at the guard to let him in then carried on over to the helicopter.

It was a Bell AH-1W Super Cobra, or what the marines called 'the world's deadliest snake'. It was equipped with Hellfire missiles and a nose-mounted chain gun, slaved to the pilot's helmet. Whatever he was looking at, that was where the bullets would go, ten per second with a sound like the sky being ripped apart. It also had the latest Forward-Looking Infra-Red (FLIR) instruments on board, which could pick up radiation from heat and any number of other sources. Ground troops had learned not to wash their clothes with commercial detergent because the brightening additives effectively made them glow in the dark. The Cobra was a loaner from a local airborne division, courtesy of an earlier request he had made and the impressive political pull of his employers. The side door slid open as he approached and a huge blond guy uncoiled himself from the back seat and stepped out to meet him.

'Name's Dick,' the man said, thrusting out his hand and shooting him a cold smile that seemed like a challenge. He was more than a foot taller than Hyde and probably a hundred or so pounds heavier. 'I'm here to collect the girl and take her back, once she has been *re-ac-quired*.'

'Hyde,' he said, grasping the hand and embarking on a short hand-crushing competition that, if he was honest, he lost. The guy was a monster. He was also now in charge.

The giant let go of Hyde's hand and looked up just as the rider dropped down from his horse and unwrapped the keffiyeh from his face.

'You expecting an army?' the Ghost said, nodding at the idling helicopter.

'It's good to be cautious,' Hyde said, in no mood for his

particular brand of shit today. 'And it can find a target and kill it before it even knows it's been spotted.'

The Ghost looked the machine up and down then turned to Hyde and smiled. 'It never found me. I suggest I organize my riders into tracking parties. Maybe your whirlybird can cover the eastern section while we cover the desert to the west. Is there anything out there we should know about – anything of yours that might not be marked on the maps?'

Hyde looked into the pale eyes, knowing from the tone of his question that he already knew the answer. 'There're some excavation works left over from test drills about twenty or thirty clicks from here. There's also a smaller compound further out with temporary huts and security. You'll know it when you find it. They've been instructed to be aggressively defensive. I'll warn them you're in the area, but I still wouldn't get too close.'

'Sounds serious. Maybe you found something valuable out there.'

'Maybe.' Hyde turned and introduced the giant, partly to change the subject and partly to put the Ghost through the same hand-crushing ordeal he'd just had to endure. He watched the two men shake. The Ghost didn't flinch. He just stared into the big man's eyes and pulled him slowly down until his face was level with his. 'You need to cover up,' he said, his voice like fingernails on a blackboard. 'Out here, someone as fair as you can easily get burned.'

Then he let go of his hand and walked back to his men and his horses.

95

Baghdad

The asylum stood on the southern fringe of the city, isolated at the end of a street. It looked more like a derelict maximum-security jail than a hospital. Razor wire stretched round the squared-off roof of a solid concrete block, a thick coating of dust covered every surface and at first sight it appeared to be deserted. It was only as they drove past that Liv saw people moving in the shadows – wraiths in the dust with watchful eyes.

Washington had come with them. He said he had business in this part of town, but Gabriel doubted it. Either way, he was glad to have him along. Thanks to Washington's credentials and stone-faced military demeanour it took them less than ten minutes to gain access to the asylum. Promising he'd be back to pick them up within the hour, he departed for his dubious meeting, leaving them to follow a man in white overalls down bare concrete corridors that smelled of urine, faeces and desperation. An occasional ceiling fan turned lazily above them, just enough to mix up the smells but not enough to cool the air.

They progressed in silence, the state of the corridors and cells getting steadily worse the deeper they got into the stifling building. It was obvious that Zaid Aziz's lengthy stay here had not earned him any privileges. As they dropped down another level, what natural light there was disappeared entirely. The only illumination came from a string of low-wattage bulbs that had been switched on by the guard as he reached the bottom of the stairs. The patients down here – if 'patients' was the right word – clearly spent most of their time alone in the dark with their madness and their demons. The guard stopped in the middle of the corridor and waved his hand in the direction of the last cell on the left where the lights didn't quite reach. 'Aziz,' he said, in a way that sounded as if he was spitting. Then he turned and walked away, clearly unwilling to spend any more time down here than he had to. They listened to his boots scuffing away up the steps, leaving them alone with the remnants of men in the dark. The 'patients' heard it too and the basement steadily filled with shuffling sounds and filthy chuckles that slid down the darkness towards them. Gabriel turned to Liv, wishing he had not brought her here, but she just smiled and reached out to take his hand.

Then the corridor erupted in noise.

For a few seconds they stood there, gripping each other as the roar of voices engulfed them and the bars shook violently the entire length of the corridor. There was a loud crash nearby as a man ran at them from the back of his cell and collided with the upright of his door, gashing his head deeply and sending a spray of blood into the air. Opposite, another man had bunched his pants down to his knees and was thrusting his hips violently against the bars, his penis, covered in sores and scars from previous abuse, waving obscenely as he moaned in pain and pleasure. They didn't notice the figure behind them uncoil himself from the floor until an inhuman shriek split the gloom, instantly silencing the maniacal din and sending everyone scurrying back to the darkest corner of their cells.

Gabriel spun towards the sound and discovered a knife-thin man watching him from behind the bars. He was naked from the waist up and the entire right-hand side of his body was covered with thick scars that looked more like scales than skin.

They spread down his arm to a claw of a hand, up his neck and over the side of his head, robbing it of hair and tightening the skin so it pulled his face into a permanently quizzical look. And there was a smell coming off him that was very specific and very disturbing, given the man's history: it was the smell of smoke.

'Zaid Aziz,' Gabriel said, putting his hand to his heart and bowing his head in deference. 'My name is—'

'John!' the figure exclaimed with something close to wonder. His mouth twisted into a smile that became a snarl where his burns began. 'John Mann.' He stepped into the light, his right eye white and sightless, the left restlessly darting over Gabriel's face.

Gabriel took the scrutiny, feeling the steady pressure of Liv's hand like a lifeline to sanity.

'But I saw you die.' Aziz's voice was rusty from lack of use, and the ruined muscles around his mouth made his English sound strangely formal.

'I did die,' Gabriel said, playing along in order that he might utilize the bond of trust his father would have formed. 'Now I've come back and I'm looking for the people who did this to us. I want to pay them back.'

The man's face curled into another smile-snarl. Then his expression became guarded and he stepped closer to the bars. 'Then you must kill the dragon,' he whispered.

'Yes,' Gabriel replied. 'Tell me about the dragon.'

Aziz flinched and cowered on the floor, his white eye staring up as if seeing again the last thing it had witnessed. 'We heard it first, you remember? A roar in the desert, then the wings beating.'

'What did it look like?'

Aziz stamped his foot and glared at him. 'You SAW it!' he said, with the fury of a man who'd been telling the same story for twelve years to disbelieving ears. 'Don't *you* say it wasn't there. The others are fools, but *you* were there. *You* saw it.' The anger burned in his face then softened as confusion crept in. He reached up with the claw of his right hand and rubbed a raw knuckle against the molten flesh over his sightless eye. 'No,' he said, remembering more. 'You were down in the dig when the dragon came. You were in the library cave.'

'Tell me about the library – what did we find there?'

'So much treasure we found. You should remember.' He tapped his head. 'I remember. I remember everything. Sometimes they try to steal my memories with kicks and fists. Sometimes they try to steal them with the electric. But I keep them still. And I remember.'

'Tell me what you remember. Did the dragon kill everyone?'

Aziz shook his head. 'It was not the dragon that brought death. It was the white devils, born of its belly. They brought the fire and the fury. They laid us low and burnt everything. Tents. Vehicles. People. It was one of our own who betrayed us. I hid from the dragon and saw him showing the other devils where to look. He was the one who took them to the cave where you were. He was the one who killed you.'

'Did you see who it was?'

'He was a white devil, like them.'

'A Westerner?'

Aziz shook his head. 'A ghost. They were all ghosts. Only ghosts can ride a dragon. The ghost went inside the cave, brought out boxes and fed them to the dragon, stealing the treasure we had found. Then the earth shook and the cave was gone. You never came out. A white devil saw me and struck me down.' His hand rose again to the side of his head. 'The fire woke me when the dragon was gone. The sand made the fire go away. The desert saved me, see –' He held out his arm. Grit was embedded beneath the skin. 'I am part of the land now and the land is part of me. Ashes to ashes, dust to dust.'

'And after you put out the fire, what did you do then?'

Aziz shook his head. 'Everyone was dead. Everything was

burning. I was afraid the fire might touch me again. I feared the dragon's return, so I ran. I ran into the desert. But the dragon knows I live still. It wants to finish me – I can feel it.' He stepped forward and gripped the bars. 'Find the dragon, John Mann. Kill it for me so I can be free of this place. Only you can tame the dragon now – for you are a ghost too.'

96

Athanasius sat in the Abbot's private washroom, his back to the door, his face illuminated by the glow from the phone. Outside he could hear Father Thomas engaging Malachi loudly in a conversation designed to draw his attention while Athanasius slipped away.

He opened the message and pressed *send*. This time there was no error alert. Even so, he watched it until the screen went black then tapped it again to make sure. The screensaver was back in place, showing the photograph of the Mirror Prophecy. Ever since Gabriel had first shown it to him in the darkness of the ossuary he had been thinking about the possible meaning of the last few lines.

The Key must follow the Starmap Home
There to quench the fire of the dragon within the full
phase of a moon
Lest the Key shalt perish, the Earth shalt splinter and a
blight shalt prosper, marking the end of all days

A blight.

It was what Brother Gardener had called the disease when it first appeared in the garden; and now something was stalking through the corridors of the mountain and striking people down. And the earthquake that had shaken the mountain: was that not the earth starting to splinter?

It all suggested the prophecy was true, which meant the best way to stop the spread of the disease was to help the girl find her way home to Eden. And yet Brother Dragan believed only the restoration of the Sacrament to its place inside the chapel would cure the mountain. He was trying to bring her back here. Maybe *he* was the dragon mentioned in the prophecy and the fire of his zealous beliefs the thing that needed quenching. He needed to talk to him. Maybe if he could just show him the Mirror Prophecy he could convince him of its wisdom.

Father Thomas was still arguing with Malachi when Athanasius burst from the washroom and virtually sprinted across the room to the Abbot's desk.

'We need to talk to Dragan,' Athanasius said, pulling open the upper drawer where the old Abbot kept the key to the forbidden stairs. 'I think I know how we can cure the Lamentation.'

The Abbot was one of only two monks in the Citadel permitted to pass both in the upper, restricted section of the mountain reserved for the Sancti, and the lower parts where the general populace lived. The only other monk granted these privileges was the Prelate. Dragan had ventured up to the forbidden section through the Prelate's staircase; Athanasius now intended to do the same using the Abbot's. He grabbed the key and headed to the bedchamber.

A large wooden bed filled most of the space, draped with thick fabrics to keep the occupant warm. The only other thing in the room was a vast tapestry with the sign of the Tau embroidered upon it in green thread. Athanasius pulled it aside to reveal a door hidden in the wall.

'What are you doing?' Malachi called after him. 'You are not permitted to go through that door.'

Athanasius turned on him, all the frustration and stress of the last few weeks spewing out in his answer. 'What difference does it make? You've seen for yourself there's nothing there. Whatever secret we have pinned our past to, it's gone. We would be fools to fix our future to it as well. Brother Dragan is clinging to a dream, and it's a dangerous one that might kill us all.' He twisted the key in the lock and stepped through the door. 'I must find him and persuade him that, for all our sakes, he needs to let go.'

Malachi moved to try to stop him but Athanasius was too quick. He slammed the door behind him and locked it so no one could follow or try to stop him.

97

Washington was waiting for them when they emerged from the dingy hell of the asylum. They got into the cooled interior of the 4x4 – Gabriel in the front, Liv in the back – and drove away without saying a word.

'That bad, huh?' Washington said after a few kilometres of silence.

Gabriel shook his head, still trying to process the bizarre story he had just heard. 'I don't know, he seemed pretty lucid to me. I think he was telling the truth, or something he believed to be true. He said a dragon destroyed the camp and a ghost killed my father. I'm sure these must be abstract or metaphorical terms for something else, but his burns are real enough, and his experience was clearly traumatic enough to splinter his mind.'

Washington went quiet. 'Did he say "a ghost" killed your father, or "the Ghost"?'

Gabriel stared out of the window at the bleached streets as he tried to recall.

'It was "a ghost",' Liv answered.

Washington frowned. 'There's an insurgent – not a major league threat, so he's low down on the priority list – but he's caused us some problems in the past. He's known as Ash'abah – "the Ghost".'

'Is he still around?'

'Oh yeah. He's been around for ever. He's a proper old-school *fedai*, fighting anyone who comes along for the freedom of his land. Apparently he was a pain in the ass for the former regime too, so you've got to give him some credit. A lot of the locals see him as a kind of Robin Hood figure, which has made it hard for us to gather any useful intelligence on him or find out where his base is. All the most successful insurgents tend to live out in the desert. Most reports of the Ghost's activities come from south of here, in Babil Province.'

'Around Al-Hillah.'

'Exactly. The other thing worth mentioning is that he deals in ancient relics, selling them on the black market for premium prices. But he only ever sells to well-funded Christian organizations and occasionally to museums. Some people think this is because he is actually a Christian himself with roots stretching back to biblical times before Islam pushed the Christians out.'

'Any idea where we might find him?'

Washington shrugged. 'Not really. They don't call him "the Ghost" for nothing. The locals seem to view him with a mixture of fear and respect. Many of them think he actually *is* a ghost. He's supposed to have this big scar on his neck and a strange way of talking, like stones being rubbed together. If he was the one who sold out your old man, I would advise you to proceed with caution. He's pretty serious people out here – very well connected – and you're just a stranger in a strange land with no clue about how you're going to get to where you want to be. Fortunately for you –' he pulled over and pointed to a jeep parked on the forecourt of a battered-looking garage – 'it turns out that you too have friends with influence. I booked it through one of the dummy corporations we use. It's handy, being involved in covert work; they're a lot less particular about expenses. It's in your name, or at least the name in that phoney passport you're travelling with. Consider it a belated leaving present from Uncle Sam for all your hard work and early starts.'

Gabriel turned to him with a look.

'Don't you even think about giving me some weak-assed

civilian hug, Mann. I know you've been out for a while, but that's still no excuse for going soft.'

Liv leaned forward from the back seat and kissed him lightly on the cheek. 'Thank you,' she said.

Washington smiled. 'Now from you I'll take it all day long.' He turned to Gabriel, the sternness back in his face: 'But you disappoint me, soldier, you really do.'

Less than ten minutes later they were pulling out on to the dusty blacktop and heading south towards the edge of the city. They'd had to sign a whole bunch of disclaimers against explosives or small arms damage, but other than that it had been just like renting any car. Washington had sent them off like a nervous father, giving them his desert survival pack, a Glock 17 with the serial number filed off that he handed over with a wink, a spare clip and a lecture on never travelling first thing in the morning when the roads had been freshly mined.

Gabriel drove through the outskirts of Baghdad, glancing nervously out of his window at the first hints of dusk darkening the sky to the east. They drove in silence, both knowing they were heading into a hostile desert with only the sketchiest of ideas of what they were looking for. They were going to a place where ghosts and dragons roamed, and they both knew that the coming night was all the time they had left.

When dawn came it would all be over – one way or another.

98

Arkadian sat in a busy Internet café on the great Eastern Boulevard. Following the email he'd received from inside the Citadel, he had bought two hours of terminal time on a cheap, anonymous computer and got to work. It was rapidly becoming clear that the Vatican Secret Archives were not called 'secret' for nothing. You couldn't just call up a web page and browse the contents. You couldn't gain any kind of access at all without first going through a lengthy and prohibitively complex process of presenting your credentials and requesting a specific text, which would then be considered by a panel of bishops who only met once a month, and then – maybe – you might be allowed an hour in a reading room to study the document before it disappeared back into the dry darkness of the archives. He'd had to borrow an academic research ID from a lecturer friend of his at the University of Ruin just to access the website at all. From this he had at least ascertained that there was a whole section on ancient maps in the archive, but there was no information on any of them. Athanasius's message had given him exact transfer dates of the documents but without any detail there was no way of cross-referencing them. In frustration he typed *Imago Astrum* into the search box and hit return. He was immediately locked out of the site and further attempts to re-access it were blocked.

Next he looked into the man who had requested the transfer. If he could find something on him that he could use as leverage, he might be able to get him to reveal what the relics he had requisitioned were or what their significance was.

He had heard of Cardinal Clementi before and recognized him the moment he saw his picture in a news item; a fat, white-haired man in cardinal's robes shaking hands with the Chancellor of Germany. He was described in the article as a force for reform in the Church, the *éminence grise* behind the recently elected Pope. Several more articles said pretty much the same thing. They painted a picture of a man on a mission to place the Church back at the centre of world events. Judging by the calibre of politician he was pictured with, it looked as though he was succeeding: there he was, all pink flesh and smiles, shaking hands with the British Prime Minister, the President of France, the President of the United States. The political commentators all agreed that his easy acceptance at global power tables was down to one thing: money. After decades of mismanagement and scandal, Cardinal Clementi had apparently restored the finances of the Church almost overnight. And it was this, more than anything else, that set Arkadian's detective instincts bristling.

After almost twenty years wading through the darker waters of the human condition, Arkadian had learned that money was pretty much the root of all evil. Crimes of passion certainly happened, but not nearly as much as TV shows and crime fiction would have you believe. His experience had taught him that if you wanted to catch a criminal then, nine times out of ten, you had to follow the money: it was a cliché, but only because it was true.

He checked the dates when the relic was requisitioned against the news stories. All the ones charting the improvement in the Church's financial standing came after the transfer. Prior to this there was hardly a mention of the Cardinal in the news, and all economic reports relating to the Church were dire. Something significant had happened to change the game, and it had happened astonishingly quickly.

Arkadian logged on to the secure Interpol site and keyed in a series of codes to gain access to the companies directory.

It contained details of every registered business across Europe along with their tax returns and names of the directors. One of the main problems in running a lucrative but illegal business was how to spend the vast amounts of money being made without drawing attention to it. The most popular method of laundering money was to run it through the books of a legitimate business, which was why Interpol had set up this database.

Arkadian typed 'Clementi' into the search box. Hundreds of matches came back.

Because of his position and the Church's extensive investment portfolio he was personally linked to companies all over the world. Arkadian set to work sifting through them, looking for anything that might generate the sort of money that could refloat an organization as huge as the Catholic Church. If the legends were true and the relic was indeed a map showing the way to vast buried hoards of treasure, then the most obvious way to hide its discovery would be a gold-mining operation. Ancient treasure would be hard to turn into cash but pretending you'd struck gold and melting that treasure down into bullion would solve the problem instantly. A gold mine would also provide the perfect cover for the purchase of mineral rights as well as all the equipment to dig things out of the ground and smelt it. Only there was no gold mine.

He started cross-checking each company's tax returns for anything that looked profitable enough to explain the Church's sudden change of fortunes. Again there was nothing. After over an hour of searching, the only company he had highlighted as a potential candidate was an oil exploration company.

On paper it was wrong. It was running at a huge loss and was drilling in an area that had been tested before and come up dry. But, of all the companies listed, it was the only one that might legitimately dig around to see what it could find, and – most crucially – it was in the right place. The registered head office of Dragonfields SPA was in Vatican City, but they had office space in Baghdad and a compound operating under licence in the Syrian Desert. The licence gave coordinates marking out the broad patch of wilderness that was now theirs for the plundering.

He clicked on Google Earth, input the co-ordinates and within a minute found himself staring down on a brown patch of nothingness. He zoomed out until he picked up a road then scrolled eastwards along it until he finally found a sprawling grid of buildings the same colour as the earth. The image settled and Arkadian almost punched the air when the name of the other place popped up on the map. It was Al-Hillah.

99

Liv and Gabriel found the site where John Mann had died just as the moon rose above the horizon and the wind picked up. It was about ten kilometres outside Al-Hillah, past the huge mounds of bricks that were all that remained of the ancient city of Babylon.

An American garrison was stationed there now, camped in the shadow of the once great walls in lines of temporary tents surrounding a section of ground that had once seen the triumphal procession of King Nebuchadnezzar and more recently been bulldozed flat to accommodate squadrons of Apache and Cobra helicopters. The ground crew were busily anchoring the aircraft to the deck with securing cables as they drove by, wrapping the engine cowls with heavy-duty covers against the worsening weather. Gabriel took note but said nothing. It didn't matter how bad the weather got, they had no choice but to press on.

A few kilometres further along the main road they had found a goat track running north into the desert and followed it until the read-out on the jeep's sat-nav told Gabriel he had finally arrived at the coordinates where his father's life had ended. He had memorized them twelve years ago, always knowing that he would end up here one day, often running through them in his head like a mantra or a spell to keep his father's memory alive.

He switched off the engine and stepped outside, surveying the flattened dish of desert. He wasn't sure what he had been expecting, but it wasn't this. There were no graves to mark the site, no structures remaining to show there had ever been anything here other than rock and dust.

He'd often wondered how he would feel when he eventually got here. He had thought that coming here might make sense of the anger and abandonment he'd felt for most of his adult life. But standing here now he felt nothing. If anything, it served to emphasize how powerless he was against the merciless flow of the universe. His father had died out here and Gabriel had not been there to save him; now he was here with someone else who needed saving and he had no idea how to do that either.

Hearing the sound of the jeep door opening behind him, he turned away so Liv would not see the tears brimming in his eyes. He didn't want her to show him any pity when he deserved none. He had failed once and was failing again.

But instead of joining him, she walked away, up the bank of the wadi towards a spot on the horizon, her eyes looking up towards the stars.

'Liv?' he called out, but she didn't answer. She kept walking, her gaze fixed on the sky. 'Liv!' He moved across the sand and stepped in front of her, grabbing her shoulders to snap her out of her trance.

She blinked and looked at him as if she had just been shaken awake.

'Where are you going?'

She pointed up at a snaking line of stars hanging low in the sky. 'The dragon,' she said. 'I was following the dragon.'

Gabriel followed the line of her extended arm, recognizing the constellation she was pointing at. She was right – it was Draco, the dragon. The dragon was everywhere, it seemed: in the prophecy, in the madman's account of how his father was killed – and now even in the sky.

'Let's get back to the jeep,' he said, aware of how cold it was getting and how she was starting to tremble. 'We can follow the dragon in that. It will be quicker.'

'That way,' she said, pointing back up at the sky.

'Whichever way you want,' he said, steering her back to the car. He was losing her, he could feel it. Things predicted in the prophecy were coming to pass.

As he helped her into the passenger seat he heard a sound like a bird cheeping in the night. Gabriel climbed back in behind the wheel, slamming the door against the night wind. The noise had been his phone and he checked the caller ID before answering. It was Arkadian.

'I think I've found something,' he said before Gabriel even had a chance to speak. The detective revealed what he had discovered about the oil operation called Dragonfields, then supplied map coordinates. Gabriel fed the information directly into the sat-nav and set it to calculate a route.

Another dragon, Gabriel thought. *Coincidence or destiny?*

When the sat-nav finished its calculations, it answered the question for him. An arrow on the screen showed the direction the coordinates lay in, pointing in the exact direction Liv had been walking.

The oil operation was less than thirty kilometres away, somewhere in the wastelands of the Syrian Desert, following the constellation of the Dragon.

100

Athanasius had always hated the dark. When he had given his life to God and first entered the Citadel it had never occurred to him that he was also consigning himself to a life of darkness. The tunnels had been vastly improved during his time there, with electric lighting now used throughout most of the mountain, but the forbidden upper sections he now stumbled through had changed little in hundreds of years. In his haste to get here he had not brought a torch and was having to use the glow from the phone screen to guide him. It struck him as apt in many ways that the bright photograph of the prophecy was lighting his path towards the one man trying to thwart it.

He reached the upper section breathless and perspiring and held the screen to his chest to cut out the light. For a moment his eyes were blind, but as they slowly adjusted he could see a glow ahead of him. It was coming from one of the smaller tunnels to his left, not the one leading to the chapel of the Sacrament as he had expected. He followed the telltale light, keeping his own covered and feeling his way along the wall until he came to a forgotten, dusty corridor dotted with piles of rubble that showed how poorly it had been maintained. The glow was coming from a partially open door halfway along it. There was also a breeze, sweet-smelling after the trapped air of the stairwell, and it drew him towards the door.

The source of the glow was a flambeau that had been slotted into a niche in the wall. It guttered in the night breeze that flowed through a loophole cut in the outer wall. In his mind, Athanasius had imagined he was at the heart of the mountain.

It had not occurred to him that the higher he climbed, the narrower the mountain became and the closer to its edge he would be.

Dragan was standing by the opening with his back to the door. At first Athanasius thought he must be praying, but then he turned and he saw the phone clutched in the black, leathery grip of his hand.

'What are you doing?' Athanasius asked, realizing from his own experience the significance of his position by the open window.

Dragan snarled, his spare hand reaching for the wooden T-shaped crux in his belt. He pulled it clear, revealing the ceremonial dagger inside and lunged at him. Athanasius spun away, grabbing the burning torch from the wall and holding it out in front of him to keep him back. Dragan regained his footing and kicked the door shut, sealing the room. They circled each other, neither one advancing or retreating, clear in the knowledge that only one of them was going to leave here alive.

'I am trying to put right all the things you have ruined,' Dragan said, 'by returning the Sacrament to the mountain. The moment it was removed, everything started to die: first the Sancti, then the garden, and now everybody else. The Lamentation will strike you too; do not think you will be spared. I am trying to save your life too by doing this.'

'And what about the girl, what about her life? Is she an acceptable sacrifice?'

Dragan scoffed. 'The Bible is full of sacrifice made for the greater good. Christ himself sacrificed his own life.'

'Christ gave his life for the benefit of everybody.'

'And the restoration of the Sacrament to the Citadel will do the same. Look around you: earthquakes, disease . . . look at me –' He pulled up the arm of his cassock to reveal his withered, blackened arm. 'All of this has come about since the Sacrament was released.'

'Not true. There have always been earthquakes. There has always been famine, and drought and global epidemics. Shutting an innocent girl into a mediaeval cross full of needles to trap the divine spirit she carries inside her is nothing that we, as men of God, should be party to – whatever the cost to ourselves. I have read the Heretic Bible. I know the true history of the Sacrament and I know the true history of this mountain.' He held out his own phone, showing the photograph of the Mirror Prophecy, and placed it on the ground between them. 'I know you believe in what you are doing. But there is another way. We have a chance to put things right. Read what it says and see for yourself.' He stepped back and put the flaming torch to one side.

Dragan edged forward and picked up the phone.

Athanasius watched him read the words of the Mirror Prophecy. 'We have a chance here to restore balance to the world – but not by repeating our old mistakes.'

Dragan shook his head. 'You are wrong. All this does is prove the wisdom of what I seek to do. If the girl is carrying the Sacrament, then this *is* her home.' He started rubbing at the material of his cassock. 'She must return here or she will die anyway.' The rubbing became more frenzied and his voice rose to a shrieking wail. 'We will all die with her,' he howled, as his scratching became frenzied and the Lamentation overwhelmed him as swiftly and powerfully as it had all the rest.

101

Gabriel had managed to cover twenty of the thirty kilometres towards the Dragonfields compound when the shamal hit. He had felt the wind steadily strengthening, battering the jeep with increasingly powerful gusts, but he had not been able to see the telltale mountain of dust until it swallowed the stars overhead, and the headlamps suddenly lit up a wall of sand moving along the riverbed to meet them.

Moments later it enveloped them with a soft hiss as millions of particles of dust began to scour the outside of the jeep. Liv sat up in her seat, responding to the sound and to the sudden electro-static charge in the air that made the fine hairs on their skin stand up and the air around them crackle.

'It's OK,' Gabriel said, laying his hand on hers and experiencing a small electric shock as his skin made contact. 'We're nearly there.'

The hissing grew louder as the dust in the air thickened. Gabriel was having trouble seeing, the headlamps so smothered by dust that all they managed to do was create a ghostly glow in front of the jeep. He slowed his speed to little more than a crawl but still kept hitting the larger rocks he had previously been able to see and avoid. He checked the display on the sat-nav. The gentle curve of the wadi had turned them round and they were now heading in the wrong direction.

'We're going to have to stop,' he said. 'Keep a lookout and see if you can spot anywhere that might give us a bit of shelter. It won't be for long, I promise: just until the worst of the storm passes.'

They carried on for a few hundred metres, picking their way through the blinding dust cloud, flinching every time another rock banged against the bumper or scraped along the underside of the car. Gabriel knew if they stopped out in the open then microscopic dust could find its way into the engine, and it might not start again. Even a little bit of cover would help minimize the damage. They continued to crawl along, listening to the wind outside and the shushing sound of the sand punctuated by the spatter of grit carried by the stronger gusts.

'There!' Liv pointed at a large, dark patch of riverbank slipping through the gritty fog outside her window. Gabriel threw the wheel round and steered towards it, the headlights shaking free of the dust's grip long enough to reveal the smooth walls of a sizable cave. He eased the jeep into it, as far as he could manage before the ceiling sloped down, halting their progress. The back half of the jeep was still sticking out into the wadi, but the engine block was sheltered. It was as good as they were going to get. Gabriel cut the ignition so as not to flood the cave with exhaust fumes and switched off the headlights to save the jeep's battery.

With the engine noise gone, the howl of the storm seemed louder. Liv reached into the back and felt around for the desert survival pack Washington had bequeathed them. Inside she found the small Maglite used for map reading and signalling and twisted it on. She kept on twisting until the whole of the top came off, turning the focused, directional beam into a softer, general light that lit everything like a lamp. 'Come on,' she said, pulling the drawstring tight on the pack and slipping it over her shoulder, 'let's go and see how deep this cave is. The air inside will be cleaner to breathe.'

Gabriel followed, marvelling at her spirit in the face of everything, and joined her in the main body of the cave. She linked her arm through his and they set off into the darkness.

Like many of the caves that honeycombed the soft rock

beneath the desert, the one they had found was deceptively large. It twisted through channels cut by the steady flow of water when the land around had been rich and fertile. The further they moved, the quieter the howl of the storm became until it disappeared entirely and all they could hear was the crunch of their own footsteps and the echoing whisper of their breathing. It reminded Liv of the rushing sound the Sacrament made inside her, though she hadn't heard it since they had left Baghdad. The rapturous lightness it brought had also gone and she feared what that might mean. So far she had avoided thinking about the implications of not fulfilling the prophecy, but now, with time so short and nature having turned against them, she had to face facts. The wording of the prophecy was clear: if they didn't find Eden before daybreak, she was going to die.

Maybe she had been foolish to think that she alone could make a difference in the face of these immutable universal laws. She had always known she was going to die one day, just as she knew the world would end. Given enough time what once was green and living always ended up as dust. It was the way of things: everything had to die, everything had to end. Here was as good a place as any.

She stopped walking and her arm slipped from Gabriel's as she sank to the floor and felt the smooth rock against the palms of her hands. Gabriel dropped down beside her. 'Are you OK?'

She smiled at him. 'I want to rest. There's no point in going any further.'

Gabriel glanced over his shoulder at the cave. 'I guess not.' He slumped down beside her and fished out a thermal blanket from the survival kit. He spread it over her and bunched up the bag for her to rest her head upon.

She watched his face, pinched in concentration, and reached up to touch it. 'I meant there's no point in going any further on this trip. It's over. Even if the storm ended now, we don't know if we're heading in the right direction or how far away it might be.'

'It's only ten more kilometres. The sat-nav will take us right there.'

'Take us where though? To a place we're only guessing might have something to do with any of this.'

He opened his mouth to say something then stopped and looked away. She could feel the disappointment and pain, radiating off him like heat. She understood that he would never give up. He had lost his entire family in the pursuit of fulfilling this prophetic sequence and felt the burden of his responsibility probably even more than she did, who carried the weight of the Sacrament inside her. Her one regret, if death came to claim her, was that she had not had the chance to spend more time in the company of this strong, sweet man. They had both lost so much in the brief time they had been together, and shared so much, that it was as if a whole extra-ordinary lifetime had been distilled into a few weeks. And now their time together was running out.

She sat up and took his face in her hands, turning it towards her and seeing the tears on his cheeks. She leaned forward and kissed them, tasting the salt of his sadness. Then she held his face in her hands and stared into his eyes. 'It's not your fault,' she said. 'You've done everything you could to try to bring me to safety; no one could have done more. And I've felt more secure with you these past couple of weeks, even with the constant threat of death hanging over me, than I have ever felt in my life before. You did that for me – and I will always love you for it.'

Then she leaned in close and kissed his mouth. The static crackled in the air all around them as he kissed her back, their hands pulling urgently at each other's clothes in their hunger for each other, never once breaking the kiss for fear of what would follow.

VI

And there appeared another wonder in heaven; and behold a great red dragon, having seven heads and ten horns, and seven crowns upon his heads.

And his tail drew the third part of the stars of heaven, and did cast them to the earth: and the dragon stood before the woman which was ready to be delivered, for to devour her child as soon as it was born.

Revelation 12:3–4

102

The storm had lessened a little, but not by much, when the Ghost rode out from the compound at the head of his column of men. The dust still thickened the air and haloed the sliver of moon hanging low in the dirty night sky. Two armoured personnel carriers filled with security troops followed them out. Hyde was at the wheel of one of them with the giant frame of Dick filling the seat beside him. The combination of dust and darkness made it hard to see anything, but the Bedouin eyes of the Ghost and his men could see enough to ride by, and so they led the way. It had also been one of the Ghost's outriders who had spotted the faint glow of a vehicle's lights, moving stealthily across the desert to the south just before the dust cloud had swept over the land and obliterated everything.

Hyde was happy for the Ghost to be on point. If the inter-lopers were the hostiles they were looking for, he was hoping that there might be a bit of armed resistance and the freaky-eyed, gravel-voiced asshole might catch a stray bullet. It might even come from Hyde's own M4: stranger things had happened in the heat of battle.

By the time they reached the mouth of the dry wadi the dust had thinned enough for the stars to reappear and the horizon to become visible to the north. The Ghost halted his caravan and rode up to Hyde's vehicle.

'You should let us go in alone,' he said, his voice as dry as the desert air. 'These trucks are loud enough to rouse the dead. They've probably heard us already and are busy loading rifles and lining up grenades.'

Hyde looked at the track leading to the wadi. It was too narrow for the trucks to travel down safely; they could easily get caught in an ambush with little room for manoeuvre. Even so, he wasn't about to let the Ghost go off on his own where he couldn't keep his eye on him.

'I'll ride with you,' the blond giant said, opening his door and stepping from the truck.

The Ghost looked him up and down. 'I don't think anyone will want to lend you their horse. You'll probably kill it just by sitting on it.'

Dick surveyed the ring of riders. 'This one,' he said, pointing to the sturdiest-looking mount.

The Ghost nodded at the rider, who reluctantly slipped from the saddle and handed over the reins.

'Thank you,' Dick said, hopping on to the back of the horse with surprising grace. 'Whatever happens, the girl is to be spared. My instructions are clear.'

'What about the man?' the Ghost asked.

'He can die, for all I care,' Dick said, spurring his horse down into the mouth of the wadi. 'The girl is the only thing that matters.'

103

Gabriel and Liv lay side by side on the floor of the cave, their hands entwined, their arms touching, their heads so close they could hear each other breathing. It was so profoundly dark that it was easy to imagine they were far away from everything, floating in space, disconnected. It was such a seductive thought that neither of them moved or spoke for a long time, holding on for as long as possible before the real world burst back in.

Gabriel was up and moving the moment he heard the sound.

It had come from the direction of the cave entrance. Something solid banging against the side of the car, only lightly, but hard enough that the sound had travelled into the cave. It could have been a rock falling from the roof, but Gabriel's instinct told him otherwise. He found his discarded jacket in the darkness and pulled out the gun Washington had lent him – the untraceable Glock with a seventeen-round clip. He dropped to a crouch and edged back to the entrance, gun first.

The punch caught him squarely in the stomach, so fast and hard it was as if he had been hit with a shovel. He tried to react, but his body was already caving in on itself through lack of oxygen. An elbow crashed down on his forearm, knocking the gun from his grip.

Then a lamp flickered on.

'Hello again,' Dick said, slipping the night-vision goggles from his head. 'Remember me?'

Gabriel tried to move but was paralysed with pain from the brutal punch. He looked back over at Liv. Another man was standing over her, dressed in the loose desert clothes of a nomad, his sand goggles and keffiyeh covering his face and making him seem more alien than human. He had an AK-47 slung over his back and a pistol in his hand pointing directly at Liv. Gabriel held his hand out towards her but a huge foot caught him under the ribs and kicked him on to his back so he was staring up at the grinning giant, now holding the Glock that he had dropped.

'No more escapes,' the giant said. The gun looked vaguely ridiculous in his huge hand, like a toy. Gabriel watched the oversized thumb stroking the side of the gun and realized he was about to die.

There is no safety on a Glock – he thought, bizarrely grateful for his executioner's mistake as it gave him a half-second more of precious life. He looked back over at Liv one last time and smiled.

Then a gunshot boomed in the confines of the cave.

Hyde heard the gunshot echoing down the channel of the dry river and away across the desert. Some of the horses nickered at the sound then fell silent. He listened for any more sounds, other gunshots that would suggest the ambush had gone wrong or was being met with armed resistance. There was nothing, just the whisper of the dying wind.

He felt slightly deflated. The single gunshot meant Gabriel Mann was dead and the girl had been captured. It was over before it had even begun. He started up his engine and eased the truck forward into the wadi, no longer worried about the possibility of an ambush. All he wanted to do now was pick up the girl and get back to the compound.

104

Dick wavered where he stood, his right eye a mass of broken blood vessels from where the bullet had entered his temple and blown apart everything behind it. He stood like that for a moment, as if an invisible thread held him suspended from the ceiling, then he started to fall. Gabriel rolled away just before he hit the ground. Over by Liv, the *fedai* was still pointing his pistol at the spot where Dick had stood. He tucked it into his holster and held out his hand to help Liv up. 'Quickly,' he said. 'We must go quickly before the others come.' His voice scraped across the air – *like stones being rubbed together*.

Gabriel moved to get up, swept Washington's Glock from the giant's dead hand and pointed it at the Ghost. 'Get away from her.'

The strange insect eyes of the sand goggles angled down towards the gun. 'You have to trust me.' That voice again.

'Like John Mann trusted you?'

The Ghost shook his head slowly. 'Whatever you think happened. Whatever you think I did. You are wrong.'

'Tell me then. Tell me what happened. And if I believe any of it I might not shoot you where you stand.'

The Ghost looked over at the tunnel leading to the cave entrance. 'We really should hurry.'

Another gunshot boomed in the cave and shards of rock pattered down from the spot above the Ghost's head where the bullet had hit. 'Next one's your leg,' Gabriel hissed through his teeth. 'Tell me what happened.'

The Ghost nodded and in his eerie voice he started to talk.

'I was in the main chamber when the helicopter came. We had unearthed part of the lost library of Ashurbanipal, looted and hidden when Babylon fell. It was filled with treasures – the Mirror Prophecy was only part of it. There were accounts dating back to creation and books of spells passed down from when the gods walked the earth.

'We tried to keep our discovery a secret, knowing the danger if the Citadel found out, but there was a spy in the camp. Soldiers came dressed as Iraqi army but they looked wrong; they had no proper markings on their uniforms and the helicopter they flew in on was Russian – a huge Sikorsky gunship.'

Gabriel remembered the strange testimony of Zaid Aziz. He was familiar with these huge helicopters from his time in Afghanistan, left over from the Russian occupation. Everyone referred to them as Sea Dragons.

'They rounded everyone up, accused us of spying and made us pack all the relics into crates. They had guns and numbers so we did what they said. But once everything had been loaded into the helicopter they started shooting anyway. We heard the slaughter down in the main dig chamber, but by then they had already tied our hands behind our backs and were discussing what they were going to do to us. In the end they strung us up by our necks from one of the ceiling beams and rolled grenades in after us. The explosion actually saved my life. It released the rope from around my neck, though not before it had done this to my voice.

'When I came to, I was in darkness. I dug my way out to discover that everyone was dead. I salvaged what I could, including the camera containing the picture I sent to your grandfather. I was searching for water, but they'd taken it all. If I hadn't been found by desert scavengers, drawn by the smoke, I would have died. They looked after me and tended to my wounds. The woman who nursed me called me the Ghost because I had been dead and she had brought me back to life.'

'So why, if the Citadel sent men to kill you, have you been selling relics to them for years?'

'It suited me to keep them close and let them think I was their friend. It allowed me to stay in the desert and keep looking for what had been lost. I only ever sold them things that were not useful.'

Gabriel shook his head and levelled the gun at the Ghost's head. 'I don't believe you. I think you are working for them now, just as you were back then.'

'No,' the Ghost began to unwrap the keffiyeh from his face. 'The Citadel is my enemy, and always has been. And I did not betray your father, nor did I cause his death.' He removed the sand goggles from his face to reveal that he was telling the truth. The Ghost could not have betrayed Gabriel's father – the Ghost *was* Gabriel's father.

Gabriel stared. Shocked. Disbelieving.

'I'm sorry,' John Mann said, his shattered voice stretched thin with emotion. 'The Citadel killed us all to keep what we'd discovered a secret. They thought I was dead. If I'd returned home they would have come again, and this time they would have killed Kathryn and you, just in case. But as long as they believed the knowledge had died with me, you were safe: I stayed dead so that you might live.'

Gabriel shook his head and felt the old anger rising up. 'But we could have stayed together and hidden away as a family.'

'And what kind of life would that have been? Always looking over our shoulders, always wary of talking to anyone in case we gave something away?'

'Better than a life of not knowing. You were alive all this time and we never even knew. My mother died – did you know that?'

John Mann nodded. 'You cannot imagine the pain I have felt at not spending my life with Kathryn. But it was only my love for her that kept me away. One day I hope you will understand this.'

Outside, muffled gunfire rattled the night.

'Now we really need to get going. We have only a few hours left before dawn and it'll take us at least forty minutes to get there.'

'Get where?'

'You've read the Mirror Prophecy. You know what's at stake. We need to get you to the ancient site of Eden before the sun rises. And I think I know where it is.'

105

At the sound of automatic gunfire Hyde stamped on the brake to bring the armoured personnel carrier to a slithering stop.

'Form a perimeter,' he shouted, throwing himself from the cab.

Another volley crackled in the night, this time from a different source. The sides of the wadi reflected sound so it was hard to tell where the shots had come from. Behind him the men poured from the back of the carrier and started fanning out, circling the parked vehicle and moving up the dry banks. More sporadic fire rippled across the desert from a couple of new sources. It had the distinctive rattle of the AK-47, favoured weapon of the local insurgents. It was coming from everywhere.

Hyde made it to the top of the bank and surveyed the desert over the top of his M4. His night scope made the barren landscape glow green. He spotted the incandescent flash of gunfire about a hundred metres from his position. It was one of the Ghost's men, looping around in circles and shooting into the sky.

'It's the Bedouin,' he shouted to his men. 'They're drawing our fire. Stay here and engage them.'

He threw himself down the bank of the wadi, signalling for a couple of men to follow and took off on foot down the riverbed just as bursts of M4 fire started to respond to the AK rounds. He followed the hoofprints in the dust until he spotted the back end of a white jeep sticking out of a cave up ahead.

Hyde approached the cave in a low crouch, leading with

the barrel of his rifle. He ducked his head round the edge of the cave, scoping inside with his night-sight.

'Stay here,' he whispered. 'Make sure I'm the only one who comes out.'

He crept forward, quartering the darkness with his night vision, making sure nothing was ahead of him. He was happier going in alone. An enclosed and possibly hostile environment was the worst place to be with people you didn't know and didn't trust.

He found Dick's body sprawled massively on the floor of a small chamber, a single bullet hole in his temple, his eyes open and reflecting green in the infrared beam of Hyde's night scope. He scanned the space and found a footprint in the dust, heading deeper into the cave. He moved towards it, then stopped. There was something too perfect about it, too deliberate. He thought back to where he'd left the two soldiers and realized his mistake. Dick and the Ghost had ridden there. But when he'd arrived there had been no horses.

106

John Mann led the way with Gabriel and Liv sharing the bigger horse. They had followed the line of the wadi for a few hundred metres then cut across to another dry riverbed that sliced through the land in a different direction. Behind them the sound of gunfire rapidly melted away until all they could hear was the night air rushing past their ears and the thud of hooves on the dust.

Liv clung on to Gabriel partly just to feel him close but also to give him comfort. The revelation in the cave had been so sudden and shocking, she couldn't imagine what it must have been like for him. She was glad it had happened though. She hated the thought that, if she did die, Gabriel would be alone in the world with all his family gone. Now he had someone, and she was glad for that.

She looked up and saw the snaking line of Draco pointing to where the moon hung low, only the merest impression of it remaining in the lightening sky.

Not long now, she thought. *One way or another, not long now.*

'It's me,' Hyde called out as he neared the cave entrance. 'Don't shoot.'

He scrambled up the side of the wadi, scoping the landscape with his night-sight. There was still too much dust hanging in the air to see very far and the dust kicked up by a couple of horses would be a lot less than a vehicle. They had at least a fifteen-minute head start, but couldn't have gone too far. He slid back down the bank and ducked into the cab of the personnel carrier. The radio squawked as he plucked it from the dashboard.

'Base, this is Point One, do you read?'

'Copy that.'

'We have need of immediate air assistance for a search and discover. Get that Cobra airborne and tell it to turn on every instrument on the dash. I want it to light up this desert like a Christmas tree.'

107

They had almost reached the dig site when they heard the sound of chopper blades in the distance. They had been riding hard for the last ten or so kilometres, putting distance between themselves and the armed force that was now stepping up the search for them.

When they got within a couple of hundred metres John Mann reined in his horse and slipped from the saddle. Gabriel did the same, following him up a low berm to get a better view.

The compound had beefed up its security considerably in the twenty-four hours since John Mann had last seen it. It now resembled a mini version of the main one: same double perimeter wire, same guard positions, same guards leaning on the same heavy-duty automatic weapons.

'And how do you know this is the right place?'

'They've been digging all over this area of desert for weeks and this is the first spot they've got really excited about. Just look at the security.'

Gabriel was doing exactly that. He realized trying to muscle their way in was out of the question.

'If I create a diversion, you could possibly get closer,' John said. 'We're only looking for a general location, not a specific spot. I've spent the last twelve years reading everything ever written or discovered on the legends of Eden. I told you I sold the useless relics to the Citadel and kept the best pieces for myself. The Sacrament will be reunited with the earth the moment the flesh of the host makes contact with the hallowed dust of home. Getting her close might be good enough. It's probably our only chance.'

Gabriel nodded. 'Attacking it would be suicide. But we need to get inside the perimeter and as close to that hole as possible.' He turned to his father. 'I think we need to give ourselves up.'

The guard had only just received the message about the missing fugitives when he spotted two horses walking towards him out of the desert. He could see a white man and woman on one of them and the other rider looked Arabic. He was waving his keffiyeh above his head in a sign of surrender.

The guard got straight back on the radio and hailed Major Hyde.

'They're here, boss,' he said. 'Riding out of the desert with their hands in the air.'

He listened to his instructions then waved at the sentry on the gate. 'Let them through,' he said. 'Take their weapons and hold them until I get there.'

John Mann had loosely tied Liv and Gabriel's hands behind their backs and taken off Liv's shoes so she was barefoot. All she had to do was step off the horse and on to the ground to fulfil the prophecy.

The guards came to meet them, relieving them of their weapons before leading them in through the gates and into the main compound. Work lights glared all around the large hole, turning the ground daylight bright, but whatever was in the hole was below ground level and not visible from where they were standing.

From somewhere out in the desert, the angry chop of heli-copter blades started to build. One of the guards signalled for them to dismount. Gabriel slipped from the saddle and held his arms up to help Liv down.

She fell into Gabriel's embrace and he began to lower her, the point of her bare foot moving towards the earth like an arrow. She could feel the coolness of the night radiating off the ground, then she touched it and her foot settled on the dust.

Nothing happened.

Her other foot joined it. The night remained unaltered. As did everything in it.

The chopper noise grew louder and the guard pointed to a patch of bare ground by one of the temporary huts. They moved across the compound, passing close to the edge of the excavation site. When they were almost upon it John Mann looked down and realized his mistake and the enormity of its consequences. This was not the right place. The thing that had been uncovered, buried in the desert, was not some ancient treasure stored by the great potentates of history, nor was it evidence of a primordial forest, it was the wreckage of the Sikorsky Sea Dragon. A side section had been cut open so it now resembled a disembowelled beast. White-overalled workmen congregated around it like fat maggots, removing relics from the smashed crates inside. As John gazed down at his ruined past, the man in charge looked up and their eyes met. It was the same man he had watched through the binoculars when they had first found the helicopter. Only this time he was closer and he recognized him.

'Harzan.'

The man smiled and rose up the side of the pit to join them. 'John Mann,' he said. 'I have often wondered if the Ghost might be you. You are a hard man to kill, it seems.'

John nodded at the white-overalled people down in the pit. 'Do these people know how well you treat your co-workers?'

Harzan smiled. 'These people do not seek to use the past to threaten the Church's future.'

'Neither did any of my men, but you killed them anyway.'

Harzan shrugged. 'Oh, come, come, you know as well as I do that history is full of people who were in the wrong place at the wrong time. Some make a positive habit of it.' He looked at Gabriel. 'Your son looks just like you. It's a pity he takes after you in other ways too. Enjoy your time together. Father-and-son time is so important, don't you think? No matter how brief.'

108

Hyde spotted the Ghost as the Cobra descended to the compound. He was sorely tempted to open up with the chain gun just to see him ripped to bloody pieces, but he doubted he would be able to persuade the military pilot to oblige. He had to return the girl alive anyway and the gun was a bit too lively to risk it. Besides, he didn't want to take out Dr Harzan – not until he'd been paid, at least.

The skids touched down and the guards hustled the prisoners over. Hyde would take particular pleasure in killing the Ghost. For so long he'd had the impression that the insurgent looked down on him. He wondered if he would feel the same way after he had dropped him in the middle of the Syrian Desert and shot him in both legs. Gabriel he would merely shoot in the head: he felt no animosity towards him, he was just a job.

The three prisoners arrived at the chopper and were bundled inside by two guards who kept their sidearms trained on them. Hyde gave the pilot the thumbs up and they lifted off. The Cobra would take them back to the main compound then return to base. The rest of the journey would be made in the company chopper and, as the pilot was on the payroll, he would be a lot less squeamish about the unscheduled stops Hyde planned to make. He would fly to Turkey via the most inhospitable, godforsaken piece of desert he could find and make sure, once and for all, that the Ghost finally lived up to his name.

109

Liv was fading fast by the time the helicopter tipped forward and started racing east towards the main compound. It frightened her how quickly it had come upon her. She'd felt fine in the cave and on horseback. Now it was as if someone had pulled a plug out and her life force was rapidly draining from her. She raised her eyes to Gabriel, sitting opposite her in the cramped cabin. The expression on his face told her she must look as bad as she felt.

Through the window behind him she could see the sky beginning to lighten and the thin sliver of moon fading away, just as she was. When the sun rose, both of them would be gone, she felt sure of it. She was resigned to her fate. It gave her some small comfort to think that at least she would not make it as far as Ruin and be locked back in a cycle of torture and pain, imprisoned in the darkness of the mountain.

She could feel the thing she carried, curled up and still in the pit of her stomach, its dead weight pulling her down the way a star collapses to create a black hole that sucks everything into it including light. Maybe that's what would happen to her. Maybe that was what the end of days meant.

Below her the dusty desolation of the desert stretched away, and a memory surfaced that she knew was not hers. It was of the world when it was young and the land beneath her, green and fertile – and she walked free upon it. There had been a man there too and she looked up at him now and felt the warmth of his being and his strong arm around her. And he was here still, smiling down at her now: Gabriel.

'I'm sorry,' he said, but the helicopter was too loud for her to hear.

She shook her head and the vision of him dissolved in tears. There was nothing to forgive. She knew he understood the pain of separation and she was going to make him feel it again soon. She had loved him too late and for too short a time, but her destiny was not hers to choose.

The helicopter banked and began its descent to the desert floor. Through the window the sky and the earth tilted like a preview of the end of the world.

Then she saw it, squatting on the desert floor, its long black neck stretching out from a body of spines and plate with fire coming out of its mouth.

It was the dragon of her nightmares: the dragon of the prophecy and the Book of Revelation – waiting to devour her and the Sacrament inside her – and they were dropping down towards it.

110

Hyde had seen it too out of the pilot's window, burning in the desert before them like an early sunrise.

Goddamn, he thought, *they did it.*

He called ahead on the radio and managed to get hold of the operations manager. The man's excitement was clear, even through the emotion-stripping narrow band of the military frequency.

'We punched through a layer of capping stone,' he said, 'and there it was. It's huge. We're well-testing it now, that's why there's all the gas burn off. So far the figures are off the scale. It's high grade, sweet crude and there's an ocean of it down there. I've never seen anything like it. We drilled a world record depth of hole and found a world record amount of oil at the bottom of it!'

Hyde took it all in, imagining his profit share and all the things he could do with it. He'd love to head back to Austin and drive by his old house in some ridiculous car so Wanda would realize she'd given up on him right before the slot machine paid out. He'd bet it all on black and it had paid off: not on the spin of a roulette wheel, but on the turn of a drill.

They circled the compound, avoiding the thermals created by the burn-off, then started to drop to the helipad. The moment the skids touched down, Hyde was out of his seat and moving to the side door to start the transfer of the prisoners. He wanted to get this done as quickly as possible so that he could start concentrating on spending his money.

* * *

Liv was paralysed with fear. Through the window she could see the beast, huge and demonic. The door of the helicopter was yanked open and she felt its heat and heard its roar. It was calling for her, wanting her.

'Out!' a man with a gun shouted. John Mann went first and Gabriel followed. Liv stayed where she was, rooted by fear. Gabriel turned to look at her. He was framed in the doorway in exactly the same way as he had been in her dream – moments before the flames had engulfed him. In her delirium this memory seemed real and she leapt forward to save him from the dragon, hitting him in the chest and knocking him backwards. She was outside now, sprawled across Gabriel and the concrete floor. She could feel the heat on her back and imagined the beast watching her, drawing the breath that would flow out as flame and engulf them both. She didn't mind for herself, her life was already over, but Gabriel deserved to live.

She rolled away from him, scrabbling across the concrete to draw the fire down on herself alone and spare Gabriel from it. Pushing herself to her feet, she turned to face the beast, staggering backwards in an instinctive desire to get away. Her foot reached the edge of the concrete, stepped backwards on to the dry desert then everything became fluid and slow.

All sound cut out.

Except one.

The whispering.

Rising inside her.

The solid thing that she carried within her began to uncoil and grow. It became heavier as it expanded, pulling her to the earth. The ground felt alive wherever she touched it. She was on her knees now, sagging with the colossal weight of the thing she carried. The whispering was all around her, rushing through her like a hurricane or a river choked with spring ice-melt. Wherever she touched the ground she could feel it flow, passing through her into the earth and giving her relief from the pain of its containment. She fell forward, spreading herself out so that every part of her touched the dust. The effect was immediate. It was like a dam bursting inside her. She felt it pouring out of her and into the ground. And as it flooded out, she heard something else, a low rumbling rising up to meet it. Then the ground began to tremble.

At first she thought it might be the beast, shaking the ground as it walked. She turned to look at it towering over her, the flame still pouring from its open mouth. There was a sign fixed to its tall neck, a logo showing an oil derrick rising above a red line of earth. To Liv's terrified eyes it looked like an upside-down Tau. An alarm sounded high on the platform in a high-pitched shriek and the nightmare vision from her dream was complete.

She waited for the flames, knowing they were next, as beneath her the rumbling continued to build.

From deep inside the beast there came a tortured groan, like metal being twisted out of shape. As the noise grew, the fire sputtered and coughed until it flickered out entirely and a cloud of steam hissed from the vent where the flames had roared. Then the steam was gone too, smothered by water that shot from the vent under pressure so great it arced over the compound and split into an atomized spray that fell to the earth like rain.

In the holding lagoons, the thick black lake of oil that had already been collected began to bubble, and the rank, decayed deposits of long-ago forests clarified into something pure. Even the helicopter, idling on the hardpan, stuttered and seized as the fuel in its tanks turned to water.

Liv looked up at the spray spewing from the dragon's mouth, remembering the lines from the prophecy:

> *The Key must follow the Starmap Home*
> *There to quench the fire of the dragon within the full*
> *phase of a moon*

She had done it.

As quickly as it had overwhelmed her, the whispering left, sinking away, returning to the home it had once known; and Liv fell with it, on to the dust of the desert, and everything went black.

111

In all the confusion and chaos, the soldiers were no longer watching the prisoners. Some were staring up at the rig as their profit shares washed away. Others looked out into the desert at the approaching dust cloud, kicked up by the remnants of the victorious riders whose horses, unaffected by the miracle of fuel turning to water, had won the battle with Hyde's mechanized forces.

Gabriel scrambled over to Liv and checked the pulse in her neck. It was very weak. He picked her up and ran towards the nearest building, hoping a compound this large would have a proper medical facility.

Hyde caught the movement out of the corner of his eye. He was still in shock, trying to work out what the hell had just happened. One moment he'd been imagining the life he had always dreamed of, the next he was standing in the rain as poor as ever. He didn't understand it, but he knew it had something to do with the man and the woman who were running away from him. And he hated them for it.

He stepped across to the helicopter, pulled his M4 from behind his seat and sighted along the barrel, aiming for the broad back of the retreating man. He tracked his movement, settling on a point where the bullet would pass straight through him and maybe take the girl out too.

His finger tightencd. He pulled the trigger. The Ghost appeared in front of him – silent and unannounced as always – and took the bullet instead.

Hearing the shot, Gabriel looked over his shoulder and saw his father fall forward, knocking Hyde to the ground.

All the scenarios from his youth when he'd imagined what he would have done to save him flashed through his head. In the end it had been his father who had saved him.

He saw Hyde roll his father's inert body off him and bring the weapon back to bear. Then a blur of movement flashed across him as a rider galloped straight through Hyde, the horse kicking the gun away as it fired, trampling him beneath its hooves.

Gabriel didn't wait to see if he got up again. He kept on running, straight through the doors of the nearest building, carrying Liv to safety.

112

Inside, the building was deserted. The only sounds came from the great arc of water pattering down on the roof and the hum of air-conditioning.

Gabriel found the sick bay at the end of a long corridor and kicked the door open. Gently he set Liv on an examination table, feeling her neck for any improvement in her pulse. It was steady but still low. Her eyes rolled open but failed to focus. Her mouth formed words that were barely whispers. 'Did we make it?'

'I think so. Just hold on.'

The words of the prophecy prickled in his mind: . . . *within the full phase of a moon, Lest the Key shalt perish.*

He opened a cupboard-full of dressings and sterile gloves. Gabriel was field-trained in combat first aid, which was mostly about pain relief and stopping blood loss, neither of which applied in this situation. The next cupboard was locked. Obviously where they kept the good stuff. He raised his leg to kick it open just as the door opened behind him.

Gabriel spun round ready to fight and saw a medic standing in the door.

'Help her,' he said, grabbing the man's elbow and steering him towards Liv.

The man slipped immediately into doctor mode, checking pulse, temperature and reflex response in the same time it would have taken Gabriel to find and unwrap a Band-Aid.

'She's dehydrated and appears to be suffering from shock,' the medic said. 'Nothing serious. I'll put her on a drip and keep her mildly sedated.'

Gabriel nodded. More footsteps outside in the corridor, heading their way. He palmed a scalpel from an instrument tray and tensed his muscles ready to fight. His father was still out there, probably bleeding out from the bullet wound. He needed to get back to him.

The door to the sick bay opened and he saw he was too late: the same rider who had trampled Hyde to the ground was now carrying his father's body in his arms. Gabriel felt a twist of guilt: it should have been him, not this stranger.

The rider laid John Mann down on the second examination table and stepped aside as the medic took over. He cut away the blood-soaked shirt clinging to his chest and revealed a neat bullet hole that sucked and bubbled each time he breathed. This was the sort of injury Gabriel was more familiar with. The sucking meant the bullet had punctured the lung. It would gradually be filling with blood, effectively drowning and suffocating him. The colour was draining from Mann's face, and his lips were already turning blue. The medic grabbed an oxygen mask and held it over his gasping mouth. Gabriel stepped forward and took over, leaving the medic free to clean the wound and prepare an occlusive patch to try to re-inflate the lung. He leaned in low over his father's face, saw the eyes flicker open and focus on him.

'I'm sorry, my son,' John Mann said. 'One day you will understand. One day I hope you will forgive me.'

The grey eyes closed and the wheezing stopped. Gabriel looked at the chest wound – no longer sucking air, no longer moving at all. The medic grabbed the oxygen mask and held it tightly over his face with one hand while the other clamped down on the wound. The chest inflated and air hissed from around his hand, but when he took it away it sank again and all the air rushed out. The lungs had stopped working. He was gone.

The rider who had brought him in turned to Gabriel. '*Ab?*' he asked.

Gabriel nodded. 'Yes. He was my father.'

'He was good man.'

'Yes,' Gabriel replied. 'Yes, he was.' He looked across at Liv. She was still unconscious, but there was colour in her cheeks and she was breathing deeply. He moved to her bedside and kissed her forehead. Her skin was cool and her breath warm on his face. He turned to the rider, pointing at the AK-47 slung across his back. 'Could I borrow that?'

The rider handed it over without question.

'Thanks. Stay here and watch over them – both of them. I'll be right back.'

As it turned out, the rifle wasn't necessary.

Outside in the compound all resistance had been abandoned. Everyone was too distracted by the miracle they had witnessed to do anything other than marvel at it. They were gathered in circles, standing around the fountain of water gushing from the oil well. To the east, the sun had begun to peep over the rim of the earth and was filling the air with rainbows.

Hyde was staring too, but he saw nothing. He was lying on his back with both eyes open, the left one bloodshot and dilated below the deep dent in his skull where the horse's hoof had caught him. Gabriel looked down at him and felt nothing. He had always wanted to find the man who had killed his father, and imagined the pure righteous rage that would fuel his vengeance. Now that he had found him, he felt empty. His father was not the man he had imagined him to be – and neither was his end. He had grieved for him too long on a false assumption and now death had come for real there was nothing left to give – nothing except forgiveness.

He took Hyde's M4, slung it over his shoulder then gazed at the surreal desert scene playing out around him, the water rising up from deep in the ground and falling back down as rain. This dry scrap of desert, marked by a map that kings and emperors had waged wars to possess.

The last piece of the puzzle.

It didn't take him long to find the locked door of the operations room. He stood back, fired a short burst into the lock from the M4 then kicked the door open and stepped inside.

There was a large topographical map of the area pinned to the wall with various markers showing all the dig sites and a table in the centre covered with seismic charts and old fragments of ancient tablets. There were also copies of the same Iraqi military intelligence documents Washington had shown him. But none of this was what he was looking for.

The Starmap lay in a drawer of its own, nestled in a solid block of foam rubber cut to fit its irregular shape. It was black granite, cracked and chipped at the edges, but the symbols on it were still solid and clear. Dr Anata had been right. At the centre of it was the same T shape he had seen on the *Imago Mundi* from the British Museum. The central reference point was the same: the ancient city of Babylon near modern day Al-Hillah. Everything else was relative to it. He studied the markings, recognizing the dots that outlined the constellation of Draco. They pointed the way to a simple cluster of symbols denoting where the garden stood: a tree, some markings he assumed must relate to distance, and a simple stick figure of a human.

Gabriel lifted the stone, feeling its weight. It was no wonder his grandfather had been unwilling to jump into the moat with it. He could also feel more symbols on the back and turned it over. The reverse of the stone was filled with dense text in what looked to be two distinct languages, neither of which he recognized. It was surrounded by clusters of dots showing other constellations.

He produced his phone from his pocket and took photographs of both sides. He also took pictures of the room, the maps and the documents on the table. Finally he took a picture of the Dragonfields logo, then bundled the whole lot into a file and attached it to an email. Then he stepped outside where the signal was strongest and waited until the message had been sent.

Over by the lagoon a horse dipped its head to drink from a pool that had started the day as a pit full of oil. It was a scene he could have witnessed on any given day since the dawn of time. In the sky the moon was now gone, wiped away by the brightness of the coming day. He breathed deep, filling his lungs with the moist air. It didn't even smell like an oil drilling platform any more. It smelled natural and fresh, like oranges.

. . . *within the phase of a moon* – the prophecy had said. And by God they had done it – but only just. No one knew what had just been averted . . . or almost no one.

He shielded the phone from the misting rain and dialled a number.

113

Athanasius was in the Prelate's quarters, rinsing out a fouled dressing, when he felt the phone vibrate in his pocket. He looked over at the figure strapped to the bed. Dragan had been delirious since the Lamentation overtook him. Even so, the Sanctus still had moments of clarity, when all his hate came bubbling forth. He would have to be careful.

He set aside the cloth and moved quickly across the room towards a window that overlooked the walled gardens. The gardens remained out of bounds so there was no one there to see him. The inhabitants of the Citadel were either attending to the numerous sick wards that had been set up throughout the mountain, or lying strapped to a bed, trying to break free so they could scratch themselves to death. Even so, Athanasius scanned the orchard for any sign of move-ment before taking the phone from his pocket and finally answering it.

'Hello?'

'She's home,' Gabriel said.

Athanasius closed his eyes in relief. It was over. 'Thank God,' he said. 'I feared when I failed to find the map all might be lost. Tell me. What does Eden look like?'

'Nothing like you would imagine.'

'But you're sure it's the right place?'

'I'm positive.'

A wail echoed through the room as Dragan strained against his bindings.

'What was that?' Gabriel asked.

'A poor soul struck down by the blight.'

There was a pause on the end of the line. 'What blight?'

'It's some kind of . . . infection. The first case was reported about forty-eight hours ago. There have been new ones almost every hour since. So far, no one has survived it. We have attempted to contain it through quarantine. We now know that an infected subject only becomes infectious themselves after the first symptoms have manifested. By this method we have managed to isolate those who have become infected and slowed the spread of it. But now the Sacrament has been returned. So, according to the words of the prophecy, the blight shalt no longer prosper. It will stay here, locked in the Citadel.'

'What are the symptoms?'

'Every victim reported a strong smell of oranges followed by a sudden and violent nosebleed.'

Silence stretched out on the other end of the line.

'Hello?' There was no answer.

Athanasius looked at the phone. The screen was blank. The battery had died. He slipped it into the pocket of his cassock as another moan drew him back to the bed.

Dragan was dreaming, his eyes moving beneath the blackened lids. He seemed to be whimpering, saying something in his sleep. Athanasius leaned down to try to catch what it was. He recognized snatches from the Lord's Prayer, repeated endlessly in a pitiful chant.

. . . forgive us our trespasses . . . as we forgive those . . .

. . . forgive us our trespasses . . . as we forgive those . . .

Athanasius took a damp cloth from a bowl by the bed and laid it across Dragan's hot forehead. 'I forgive you,' he said.

The red eyes sprang open and focused at the sound of his voice. 'You,' Dragan said, 'always you. The Sacrament will return – then we will see.'

Athanasius shook his head. 'The Sacrament has returned to

its rightful home,' he said. 'It will never again return to the Citadel.'

Dragan stared up at him, then his face crumpled. 'In that case it's over,' he groaned. 'You have done for us all. The end of days is upon us.'

114

Gabriel stared out through the drifting rain, running through the details of his phone conversation.

First case reported forty-eight hours ago.

He had been inside the Citadel much more recently than that, after the blight had already taken hold.

He remembered the chilling cry that had risen up from the depths of the mountain and how Athanasius had hurried away to tend to it.

He wondered now if his bone-deep tiredness and aching body might be the result of something more sinister than fatigue, and all that he touched might be tainted too.

He looked back at the main building and pictured Liv inside, lying on the examination table: fragile and vulnerable.

Was he infected? Had he infected her?

Every part of him wanted to go back in there and sit by her bed, hold her hand until she woke, but he knew he could not. He had to put her safety first – he had to put everyone else's safety before his own.

We have attempted to contain it through quarantine, Athanasius had said, *an infected subject only becomes infectious after the first symptoms have manifested . . . a strong smell of oranges followed by a sudden and violent nosebleed.*

He wiped the back of his hand across his nose. There was no blood, but the smell of oranges was almost overwhelming. But he had only just started smelling them. The symptom was fresh, so there was still a chance of containment.

Without pause for thought, Gabriel walked directly to the

transport shed, giving everyone he saw a wide clearance. He grabbed a couple of canteens of water and a ration pack from the cab of a truck, and headed back out to the holding lagoon.

The horse looked up as he approached. He held out his hand and stroked it, talking softly as he loaded his few supplies into the saddlebag and fitted Hyde's M4 into a saddle holster. He thought of his father, lying on the bed next to Liv in the sick bay, and finally understood the sacrifice he had made. He hoped one day Liv would forgive him too for what he was about to do, just as he now whispered his own belated forgiveness to his father.

The horse splashed through the mud and pools of water until the dry earth began.

Gabriel fixed his eyes on the horizon. He did not look back. He did not trust himself.

He kept riding north, the smell of oranges following him, until he disappeared into the desert.

115

Arkadian was back at his desk on the fourth floor of the police building. He knew that everything he had been working on would soon be public knowledge, so he saw little point in continued caution. He finished his report and read it through.

Gabriel's email had provided all the missing links. He could now connect the Church with Dragonfields, the map with the ancient location of Eden and the timing of the huge loan to the Church that had underwritten the whole covert venture. They had been seeking buried treasure after all, but not the legendary hoards of Alexander the Great and King Croesus. They had been looking for more modern riches. All underground oil reserves start out as prehistoric trees and shrubs that decay over millions of years to become carbon-rich crude. Because of its size, its age, and the secrecy that had always surrounded its location, the Garden of Eden had become, over time, the largest, most enriched untapped oil reserve on earth. The Church had not been trying to locate Eden for any sacred reason but so that it could mine its past – everybody's past – in order to safeguard its own future.

Arkadian attached the report to a mailing list he had prepared including the addresses of as many news outlets as he could find – large and small, local and international – as well as several independent political blogging sites. The list also included Interpol, the press offices of a number of governments – and the Vatican. He had left the addressees visible so that each one would know who else it had been sent to and those who were already compromised would realize a cover-up was impossible. It was his way of casting the seeds as widely as possible so they could take root wherever they found purchase. He liked the biblical implications of this.

Finally he emailed his report to the entire Ruin City Police Department, copied it on to a flash drive that he slipped into his pocket, then grabbed his jacket from the back of his chair and went home to his wife.

VII

And the earth helped the woman, and
the earth opened her mouth, and
swallowed up the flood which the
dragon cast out of his mouth.

Revelation 12:16

116

She was in a dream of darkness, like before, but this time she did not fear it; this time she knew what the darkness contained. Waking from the dream, she reached out for Gabriel, as she had in the cave, expecting her hand to find his solid form, but he was not there.

Liv opened her eyes.

She was in some kind of medical room, but, though it was unfamiliar to her, she felt she belonged here, as if she was – home.

There was another bed. It was occupied by John Mann, resting at last. She could tell that he was dead, but she could also feel his peace. Slipping from her bed, she moved across to stand beside him, laying her hand on his. She felt anxious for Gabriel, wondering where he was and why he was not sitting vigil beside his father, whom he had found and lost again in the space of a few hours. Now he truly was alone in the world – like her. But he was not alone. He would never be alone. He had her, and she him.

Liv drifted out into a corridor, drawn by the noises from outside. The building seemed deserted, all sounds coming from the compound beyond. She moved down the corridor and spotted the door at the end with the splintered frame.

The Starmap was lying on the table where Gabriel had left it. Her eye traced the constellations marked on the surface, recognizing Draco, Taurus, and the Plough. She noticed an extra star in the last one, cut deeper than the rest, with a line drawn from it to a section of the text. There was no whispering sound to herald the arrival of a translation; this time she found she could just read it.

> *The Sacrament comes Home and The Key looks to Heaven*
> *A new star is born with a new King on Earth to bring*
> *order to the end of days*

It was as if some of the substance of the Sacrament had permanently rubbed off on her. She picked up the heavy tablet and turned it over, hoping there might be more on the other side. What she found was a note.

My darling Liv,

Nothing is easy, but leaving you is the hardest thing I have ever done. I know now what pain my father must have felt when he had to leave us. I hope to return when I can. In the meantime, do not look for me, just know that I love you. And keep yourself safe – until I find you again.

Gabriel

117

Dr Harzan paced around the rim of the pit where the Sikorsky lay buried.

Most of the relics had now been retrieved and were ready to be shipped to Turkey where they would finally enter the great library, as they should have done twelve years earlier. The sense that this long-unfinished business was about to be resolved gave him huge satisfaction.

And yet . . .

They had all heard the distant gunfire coming from the direction of the compound. Since then he had been unable to raise anyone on the radio. All he got was a whispering static. It made him uneasy. Maybe their radio was faulty; the damned sand got into everything. His encounter with John Mann earlier had also unsettled him. It was a potent reminder that history could return to cause trouble, even when you were sure it was dead and buried. These relics, with their alternate telling of the stories enshrined in the Bible were solid proof of that. The sooner they were locked away, where no one else could get them, the better.

His head recoiled as the round hit him in the eye and took away most of the back of his head. He toppled over and slid to the bottom of the pit, coming to rest against the metal fuselage of the dead dragon just as the sound of the gunshot caught up with the M4 round then echoed away across the desert.

118

Cardinal Clementi was at his desk, staring at his computer screen. His phone was ringing but he didn't seem to notice. He was slumped in his chair, his head sunk down almost to his chest, his shoulders loose and sloping as if the great bulk of his body was pulling everything down. A cigarette dangled from his marshmallow lips, almost an inch of ash hanging from the end. On the screen was an opened email sent by Pentangeli:

> We are calling in our secured loans as of start of business on Wall Street tomorrow. Should you fail to honor these debts here is a facsimile of tomorrow's city edition of the *Wall Street Journal*.

Beneath the text was a mock up of the front page with the splash headline:

CHURCH BANKRUPT

Through the constant sound of his ringing desk phone he heard footsteps approaching, hurrying towards him down the marble corridor, several people by the sound of it. The first arrived and started banging at the door. Clementi flinched at the sound and the ash finally fell from the end of his cigarette, spilling down the black expanse of his cardinal's robes. The handle twisted but the door remained shut. At least he'd had the presence of mind to lock it. Not that it would keep them for long. It was designed for privacy not a siege. They would break through soon enough.

He reached forward and deleted the email, as if that might remove the news it contained, then levered himself out of his chair and walked over to the window.

There were already crowds gathering below in St Peter's Square, looking towards the Apostolic Palace. But these were not crowds of the faithful, hoping to catch a glimpse of His Holiness, they were news crews, setting up cameras and equipment, ready to catch the breaking story – and this time they *were* looking for him.

Behind him the door continued to rattle and the phone continued to ring, but Clementi carried on smoking his cigarette and stared out at the view, as if it were a normal day. Despite everything that had happened, he still believed it had been a good plan. If he had gone public with the discovery of the site of Eden, the Church would have just ended up with another shrine in the middle of a country that now worshipped a different religion. What good would that have done them? The oil was different. It was a fluid commodity that could have flowed into the withered veins of the Church and changed everything. It could have been God's gift to His mission on earth; a modern miracle – a myth turned into money. But, for whatever reason, it was not to be.

Clementi took a final puff on his cigarette then placed it carefully in the marble ashtray, leaving it to burn down to the filter. He stepped up on to the high ledge of the window-sill and looked down at the gathering crowds, hearing the gasps as they spotted him. He thought of the monk who had climbed to the top of the Citadel, over two weeks ago now, and started the unravelling of everything. He held his arms out in the shape of a cross, just as he had, and stood like that, head bowed, until he heard the doorframe splinter behind him.

Only God will understand, he thought as he tipped forward, his weight pulling him down to the marble courtyard four storeys below him.

And only God can forgive.

Epilogue

The sun began to rise over Ruin, casting the deep, dark shadow of the Citadel across the tables and chairs that were steadily spreading out from the cafés and restaurants lining the embankment. The tourists hadn't arrived yet, but the bell in the public church was tolling, meaning the portcullises at the foot of the hill would now be raised and the pilgrims and sightseers were on their way.

Yunus clattered the last fold-out chair down on to the broad flagstones and resisted the urge to collapse on to it. He was sweating, despite the chilled morning air, and every muscle in his body ached. He'd been holding down two jobs for over a month now, salting away what cash he could to pay for his place at Gaziantep Üniversitesi, starting in September. He figured a solid summer season would pay for a big chunk of next year, provided he didn't lose any more days to explosions or earthquakes or any of the other crazy stuff that had recently shut down the old town and kept paying customers away. At least the closures had given him a chance to catch up on lost sleep, so he supposed they hadn't been all bad.

Stifling a yawn, he headed back inside the café where Auntie Elmas was pouring cardamom pods and coffee beans into the grinder.

'You look tired,' she said, her eyes still sharp in her weathered walnut face.

'I'll be OK – just need some coffee.'

He reached for one of the *khave* glasses stacked on the countertop, misjudged it and sent it tumbling to the wooden floor. It bounced and rolled away, miraculously not shattering.

'Go lie down before you break something,' she hissed, looking over her shoulder to check none of the other staff was listening. 'I give you a shout when we get busy.'

Yunus began to protest, but thought better of it. Auntie Elmas wasn't the sort of person whose mind was easily changed and right now he didn't have the energy. Maybe a quick power nap was what he needed. He picked up the glass, placed it on the counter and ducked through the streamer curtain leading to the stairs up to his illegal lodgings.

It had been Auntie Elmas's suggestion that he stay here after he had landed a job on one of the night clean-up crews. She clocked him out on the café staff sheet and his shift boss clocked him in so, on paper at least, he left the old town every night at the end of his shift and came back again in the morning. In truth he hadn't set foot outside the old town for nearly a month now, even during the evacuations. He got meals as part of his café wage and there was a washroom on the first floor for all his other needs. It was perfect and saved him a fortune in travel. He also took pleasure in the notion that, apart from the monks of the mountain, he was possibly the first person to live here in over a hundred and fifty years. At the university he was going to study history and tourism, so things like that appealed to him.

Yunus reached the attic room at the top of the building and collapsed on the bedroll hidden behind a wall of cardboard boxes. His room was an eight feet square cell filled mostly with non-perishable café supplies. Above him was a skylight the size of a paperback that let in negligible amounts of air and light but also afforded a view of the Citadel, if he stood on tiptoe. Sometimes, in the dead of night, if the wind was in the right direction he could smell smoke coming from the mountain and hear sounds of life from inside. He liked that too, it made him feel part of something ancient and mysterious – though lately the noises he'd heard had been unsettling. They had sounded like tormented moans and wails of pain. He hadn't liked that, all alone in the dark of the deserted old town.

Closing his eyes, Yunus tried to rest. It felt hotter than usual in the room. He generally slept between two and six, the coolest time of day, and the rest of the time he was working. He wondered how hot it would get in the height of summer. He could always move out if it got unbearable, or try sleeping on one of the lower floors. Until then, he'd stick it out and get some earplugs to block out the strange sounds in the night.

He breathed in the dusty smell of the ancient building mingling with aromas of food drifting up the stairs from the café. He could smell coffee being roasted and the scent of fresh oranges being squeezed, so strong it was as if they were in the room with him – which was impossible, because Auntie Elmas didn't sell fresh orange juice in her café.

It must be coming from somewhere else, carried on the breeze through the tiny crack of the skylight; maybe it was coming from the Citadel . . .

Acknowledgements

If you read the acknowledgements for *Sanctus* you may recall how I described the whole process of writing a first book as being like throwing a huge party and having no idea if anyone will come. Well praise be and hallelujah people came, so firstly I'd like to bow deeply and doff my cap to all those who read *Sanctus* and occasionally lifted my day by contacting me on Twitter or Facebook to tell me how much they'd enjoyed it. In fact if you ever feel an urge to contact a writer and are feeling a little shy or worried that it might be an imposition, just do it. We spend much of the year locked up inside our heads in small rooms and so messages from readers are like chinks of sunlight in our dark, uncompromising prisons.

Second books, I have now discovered, are also like throwing parties. Only this time you are labouring in the shadow of the last one you threw, constantly hoping that the same people who came to that one will also come to this and not leave early. In preparing this one I have to particularly thank my incomparable agent at LAW, Alice Saunders, who is agency in all the right ways and non-agency in all the rest, as well as Mark Lucas and Peta Nightingale for that well-timed lunch at Ping Pong. I also owe a huge debt to everyone at ILA who, quite literally, spread my words to the rest of the world – as well as George Lucas at Inkwell Management who keeps the fires blazing in America.

At HarperCollins I am very lucky to have two smart and lovely editors in my corner in the shape of Julia Wisdom in the UK and David Highfill in the US, as well as a genius team of editorial staff, designers, marketers and sales folk who put the right looking book in the right people's hands.

I also want to thank all the international publishers who bought *Sanctus*, many of whom I have met and all of whom I want to meet so I can buy them a drink and grin at them like a drunken fool.

Finally, and most importantly, I want to thank my inspirational children, Roxy, Stan and Betsy Bean, and my wife Kathryn for all the love and support, without which none of this would be possible and everything would be pointless anyway.

COMING SOON

SPRING 2013

BOOK THREE

of Simon Toyne's

bestselling series

Read an exclusive preview

NOW . . .

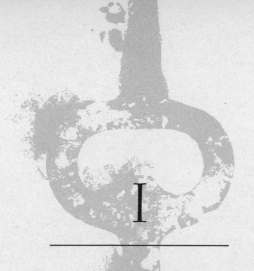

I

All things are full of gods
Plato

1

Merrifield looked up at the bank of screens.

Something was wrong.

He glanced behind him though he knew he was alone in the control centre. Everyone else was at the inter-departmental party they threw each year to mark the start of the Christmas holidays. Merrifield wasn't big on parties. He didn't drink and couldn't do small talk so he'd volunteered for the caretaker watch to garner some points and bag a little heavy-duty processor time to crunch a chunk of deep space data he was working on for his PhD. It was theoretical stuff, creation models for the so-called Eden systems, the first galaxies created following the Big Bang. He hoped it would impress his bosses – the Lords of the Skies – and push him to the front of the queue when they started putting together the James Webb Telescope control team.

He leaned forward in his chair and cocked his head to one side, listening to the chatter of the hard-drive. Some people could listen to a car engine and tell you what was wrong with it, others might hear one bum note in a symphony played by a sixty-piece orchestra. Merrifield knew computers – and this one definitely sounded hinky. There was a hitch in the processing tone, like a broken tooth on a clock wheel or a fresh scratch on one of the classic 45s he liked to collect. He stroked his knitted tie nervously as he considered what to do. Unlike the other techs at Goddard, Merrifield was strictly old school. He wore a tie every day, along with pressed trousers, horn-rimmed glasses and neatly combed hair – just like his boyhood heroes, the Houston mission controllers of the sixties and seventies. He also liked rules and order. He didn't like it when things went wrong.

A tap on his keyboard banished the Pillars of Creation screensaver, the most famous image taken by the telescope currently orbiting Earth 600 kilometres above his head. He ran through the standard checklist of the latest telemetry: temperature normal, speed steady, all systems green, no fluctuation in the solar wind – nothing abnormal in fact. He typed in a string of commands and the big screen on the wall flashed up an updated image from the main reflector feed. It showed the luminous swirl of COSMOS-AzTEC6, 13.4 billion light years away – the furthest system ever observed from Earth.

The processor crunched, making Merrifield visibly wince. The screen blinked and an application auto-loaded on to his desktop, one that he'd never seen before. It was a large box covering three-quarters of the screen, filled with numbers. Instinctively Merrifield's fingers hit the keys, typing in a search code to try and isolate the rogue program.

'Virus,' he said, almost to himself. 'We have a virus!' louder now, just in case anyone else was around.

The box remained on screen for less than a second then disappeared, locking Merrifield out. He tapped the keyboard and shook the mouse.

Nothing.

He kicked back, rolling his chair away from the desk and across the carpet tiles to another workstation. Same thing here: frozen screen, frozen keyboard. The processors chattered feverishly as they continued to feed on whatever digital poison had somehow found its way into the pristine system.

The main screen flickered, drawing his eye as the image started to shift and pixelate. He checked the telemetry again and felt the blood drain from his face as he realized what was happening. The telescope was moving. Whatever had locked him out was now taking control of the guidance systems and there was nothing he could do but watch.

He fumbled for a desk phone, knocking the receiver to the floor and pulling it up by the cord as he stabbed a button marked 'Dr Kinderman – cell'. On the screen the image continued to disintegrate as the eye of the telescope turned. In his ear the ringing tone began, and somewhere down the hall a Marimba tune rang in synch with it.

Kinderman was here.

Merrifield dropped the phone and launched towards the exit, sending his chair careening across the floor and into the wall. Outside in the corridor the ringing was louder and coming from Kinderman's office. He was in charge of the whole program. He'd know what to do. There must be some emergency override or reset that Merrifield wasn't aware of.

He made it to the door, knocked once out of deferential habit then barged in.

The state of the office came as a complete shock: wrenched-open drawers, papers everywhere, books all over the floor. The cell phone shimmied across the desktop a couple of times then stopped. For an awful moment Merrifield imagined Dr Kinderman lying on the other side of his desk, bleeding and unconscious. He launched himself into the room, waded through the drifts of paper and rounded the desk to discover with relief that there was no one there. The crunching of the pernicious code drew his eyes to the screen of the desk terminal. It was blank but for a simple box. But instead of numbers, this one contained a message:

MANKIND MUST LOOK NO FURTHER

2

When Gabriel Mann pointed the horse towards the horizon and away from the compound his only wish was to get as far as possible before he died.

He headed northwest, into the empty heart of the Syrian desert, with the heat of the rising sun on his shoulder and the scent of oranges strong in his nostrils. He tried not to think about all he was leaving behind because it only made it harder for him to go, and that was what he had to do.

He had to leave her.

Instead he tried to focus only on staying alive long enough to be far, far away when the disease took him. He didn't want to risk infecting others or fall where circling buzzards might draw human scavengers who would steal his clothes and weapons and risk carrying away something far more deadly. He needed to die where no one would ever find him, somewhere the desert sun could dry and purify his flesh and the wind could scatter his dust over the sterile ground where nothing grew and everything perished and was forgotten.

He travelled for nearly four hours before the fever struck. The heat had been building for some time, though it was hard to tell how much of it was coming from the sun and how much from him. He was in the scant shade of a low, dry wadi, keeping the hot wind away from his horse at least, when his skin started to prickle as if biting insects were suddenly swarming all over him. A sensation welled up inside him at the same time, a feeling of uncontrollable grief. Despite his efforts to forget her he had been thinking about Liv almost the whole way, picturing her face, the *green of her eyes and how her hair had spread bright and golden over the pillow in the sick bay the last time he had seen her. This sadness of leaving her, fuelled by the fever, now spilled out of him and tears rolled down the dry dust on his cheeks. He raised a shaking hand to wipe his face. It came away bloody.*

A blight – *the monk had called it* – a strong smell of oranges followed by a sudden and violent nosebleed.

It's over, he thought, with something close to relief. Now I can lie down.

He steered his horse to an overhang that formed a small oasis of shadow amid the blinding white. This was it, the place his whole life had been heading towards. It looked like a vertical grave.

This was where he would die.

3

Shepherd took a deep breath then let it out slowly, trying not to make a sound as he edged forward, gun first down the dark corridor towards the solitary door. It was open slightly, the splintered timbers around the lock evidence of how many times it had been kicked in over the years. Somewhere above him in the derelict townhouse the Virginia winter wind moaned through a broken window. It was two below outside, probably colder in here, but he was still sweating beneath his body armour.

He stopped a foot short of the door and leaned against the wall, feeling the flex in the plasterboard and timber frame – not much good for stopping bullets. Hunkering down below eye-level, he slipped his scoping mirror from his belt then past the edge of the doorjamb.

Daylight leaked in through high, narrow windows sketching an outline of a room: another door set into the far wall, a table in the centre spilling over with various indistinct items – and a man and a woman standing directly behind it.

The skin tightened on Shepherd's scalp. The man's eyes, framed by safety goggles, were staring straight at him. He saw a hand clamp tighter across the face of the terrified woman, held in front of him like a shield. He saw the other rising up.

He leaped away just as gunfire shattered the cold silence and bullets smacked into the wall where he had been resting. Levelling his gun at the door, he rolled into a new position further down the corridor. 'FBI,' he shouted. 'Drop your weapon and come out slowly with your hands on your head. We have the building surrounded.'

Not true.

He was a lone agent following a cold lead that had just gone volcanic.

Something clattered to the floor inside the room and footsteps scuffed away over floorboards. He moved forward in a crouch, gun just below his line of sight, his free hand reaching for a stun grenade on his belt. He pulled the pin and heaved it round the doorframe.

The grenade clattered across the floor, clanged against the metal leg of the table then detonated with a lightning flash that Shepherd saw even behind his closed eyelids. A sharp, percussive boom shook the flimsy wall and he was up and into the room.

No one there. Door open.

He ran through the white magnesium smoke, performing a flash inventory of the table as he passed it: 9-volt batteries, wire cutters, soldering iron, duct tape, vacuum packs of plastique. The smart move would be to regroup and call for backup, but the suspect knew he was cornered, his bomb-making equipment discovered. He had fired shots and fled, even after Shepherd had identified himself as FBI. He was desperate, and therefore unpredictable.

And he had a hostage.

If Shepherd waited for other units to show, the suspect would probably kill the woman and make a run for it. But right now he was vulnerable, his ears ringing from the pressure wave of the grenade, his eyes useless in the gloom of the basement. Shepherd had the advantage, but it was slight and wouldn't last for more than the next few seconds.

He swept his gun arm round the edge of the doorframe and followed it into the second room. The suspect was in the far corner, backed up against the wall, the hostage still in front of him and terrified.

Shepherd stood square on, maximizing the cover of his body armour, his gun steady in a good two-hand hold, trying to fix the front sight on to what he could see of the suspect's face. With his peripheral vision he sucked in the detail of the room: a single mattress on the floor with disturbed bedding; a low table next to it; a movie poster tacked to the wall with a burnt-orange sun and slashed white lettering. Then it hit him full force, rushing out of his past.

The dank smell . . .

. . . the same sun on the same poster . . .

. . . a room just like this.

Shepherd tried to zone it all out, keeping his eyes on the suspect, his mind on the here and now, but the sun kept pulling at him with something like real gravity, dragging him back to that dark, dark place he had done everything he could to forget.

His hand began to tremble. The suspect was shouting but he couldn't make out what he was saying. Then he saw a hand rise up and there was something in it, some kind of button with a wire trailing from it to the belt bomb wound around the hostage's neck.

Shepherd's world condensed to the end of his gun. He felt weak. He couldn't hold it together. Behind the hostage the sun blazed on the wall like an omen of the explosion to come. The suspect's face came into focus, and so did the words on the movie poster.

Apocalypse Now

He pulled the trigger.

A blur of movement. An explosion of red beyond his gunsight. He adjusted for the recoil – everything muscle memory now, drilled in deep from hours on the range – squeezed off another.

He watched in silence as both suspect and hostage fell in crumpled slow motion to the ground.

In the stillness that followed, Shepherd felt everything drain out of him. His eyes drifted back to the molten sun, his hand dropped to his side, the red-handled gun dangling from his curled trigger finger. He didn't even feel the instructor take it from him, or register the fluorescent lights flickering into life above. He was still back there, staring at the same poster on a different wall – the room where she had found him.

'. . . *Shepherd* . . . !'

The voice seemed to come from very far away.

'*SHEPHERD – YOU OK?*'

The granite face of Special Agent Williams slid into view, obscuring the poster and breaking the spell.

Shepherd blinked. Nodded.

'You made some tactical errors.'

He nodded again.

'Get yourself over to the Biograph for a debrief.' The Practical Applications instructor slapped him on the back with a hand made solid from years of pulling triggers and turned to the two actors, already rising to their feet and tugging wet-wipes from their pockets to clean away the red dye from Shepherd's training pistol. They each had an impact mark on their forehead, just above the eye. Kill shots both.

'Back to initial positions,' Williams barked. 'Next trainee coming through in five.'

4

Liv spent what would later become known as 'Day One – Year Zero' hiding at the top of one of the empty guard towers. She kept to the shadows and out of the heat, shifting her attention between the vast emptiness of the Syrian Desert and what was happening in the drilling compound below.

From time to time arguments flared up in guttural, rapid-fire Arabic that she found she could understand. Most of them were about money and the lack of it now the oil had gone, but some were about her. Angry whispers drifted up like smoke from a kindling fire, calling her names in a variety of languages –

حواء

Hawwāh

Ishtar

Lilith

Some spoke in her defence, but most did not. They declaimed her as a witch who had conjured water where oil had flowed and brought ruin upon them all. Liv remained frozen as she listened to the voices, as if stillness might make her invisible, gripping the scalpel she had stolen from the sick bay and wishing that Gabriel had not gone. She was the only woman in an isolated community of volatile men – and she knew how that tended to work out.

Through the heat-shrunk timbers of the tower walls she studied the desert, her eyes locking on to every flicker of movement and every wisp of dust while she muttered words from the crumpled note she held in her hand:

. . . keep yourself safe – until I find you again.
Gabriel

It was late morning when she heard the first clang of boots climbing the metal ladder. She rolled silently across the floor, her heart jack-hammering, the scalpel slippery in her sweat-slicked grip. She positioned herself by the trapdoor, her legs drawn up tight to her chest, ready to kick hard at whatever appeared in the gap.

The footsteps rose, heavy and loud, then stopped below the trapdoor. 'Hello,' a deep, syrupy voice called up in English.

She didn't reply.

'I bring water and food.' A hand slowly raised the trap and pushed a canteen and a pack of K-rations through the gap, then a pair of eyes appeared. 'No need to fight,' the man said. 'You are safe here. You have my word.'

'And who are you?' Liv replied, now there was no point in keeping silent.

'I am Tariq al Bedu, I rode with Ash'abah – the Ghost. I will watch out for you, in the memory of his name, and you must drink. I will bring more in a while.'

She glanced at the canteen, still wet from being dipped in the pool of fresh water below. 'Thank you,' she said, then – because she had once written an article on victim survival and remembered it was harder to harm someone if you knew their name – added, 'My name is Liv Adamsen.'

The man smiled and she could see the warmth of it spread to his eyes. 'I know who you are,' he said, and was gone.

Liv listened to his steps ringing away down the ladder, melting into the taunting hiss of fresh water spewing out of the ground below her. She dragged the canteen towards her with her foot, still wary of going too close to the trapdoor, unscrewed the cap, sniffed the contents and then took the tiniest of sips. She figured a dilute solution of any kind of knock-out drug wouldn't be able to knock her out, so she sat for as long as her thirst would allow, waiting for something to happen. When nothing did, she took a longer drink and then the rest in thirsty gulps, forcing herself to save a little in case the man did not return.

Within the hour he was back, bringing more water and an apple to eat, then he left her in peace and made sure everyone else did the same. It stayed this way until just before nightfall, when the soldiers came.

They rolled into camp in a cloud of dust and well-drilled purpose, winched the broken helicopter on to a flatbed loader and offered rides back to Al-Hillah for anyone who wanted them. Liv used the distraction of their arrival to steal down the ladder, careful not to make a sound, and ducked into the shade and cover of one of the metal-sided buildings. Much as she wanted to leave behind the hostility she had sensed brewing in the compound, she knew the US military were actively looking for her and, after all that had happened, she wasn't inclined to trust the reasons for their search. And Gabriel had left her here, promising to find her again. What if she went away and he returned only to find her gone? A shadow passed over her as she contemplated this and she turned to discover a stocky man in oily overalls glaring at her.

'A curse be upon you,' he said, spitting on the ground at her feet. He took a step forward, his hand drawing back to strike her. Liv backed away, gripping the scalpel, when Tariq stepped between them. 'Go, if you are going,' he said to the man, 'and take your grudges with you.'

The man's hand dropped to his side. For a moment he looked like he was about to say something but he just spat on the ground again and hurried off towards the American convoy.

'That's Malik,' Tariq said, his eyes fixed on the man. 'He was in charge of transport here until the fuel turned to water and killed all his engines. He thinks you are responsible.' From round the edge of the building Liv watched him join a line waiting to board one of the troop carriers. 'He's leaving, along with all the others who now think this place is cursed.'

458

An American soldier stepped up to the group and ushered them into the vehicle, scanning the compound before hitting the switch to seal the rear hatch. Tariq stayed out of sight. Liv did the same, not quite believing what she was doing.

'I can take you anywhere you want to go,' Tariq said, as if reading her mind, 'or you can stay for a while. For there is much work to be done here, is there not?'

She considered his strange question as the sound of revving diesel engines rumbled through the air. She was still thinking about it when she heard them starting to pull out. She stepped from the cover of the building, figuring she could sprint after them if she chose to, but she didn't. She just stood and watched the dust cloud drift away as the sound of the engines grew quieter.

Most of the men who had stayed behind were riders, those who had ridden with the Ghost and fought to free her and Gabriel. A few were from the compound staff, a couple of drillers, a cook, a member of the transport team whom Malik had clearly failed to poison against her. They gathered around her now, all faces turned towards her. 'What do they want?' Liv whispered.

'They want to know what to do next.'

She smiled at everyone nervously, feeling the expectation coming off them like heat. Strangely, being surrounded by a bunch of strangers like this didn't freak her out as much as she might have imagined. It was as if the soldiers had taken all the anger away with them, leaving just relics of the violence that had erupted here – a few bullet holes in the skin of the buildings, the rust-coloured patches of earth where men had fallen and bled.

'Where are the dead?' she asked, pointing at one of them.

'We put them in a refrigeration truck to keep the flies away,' Tariq replied, 'though with no fuel, the cooler isn't running.'

Liv nodded. 'Then let's bury them,' she said.

5

Shepherd stepped out of the front door of the townhouse into the teeth of a westerly wind straight off the Chesapeake Bay and headed away along Main Street.

Hogan's Alley was a microcosm of any-town America with its own bank, drug store, hotel, gas station – all the institutions that criminals targeted out in the real world. Covering some ten acres of the Marine Base in Quantico, it was used to train FBI, DEA and every other type of law-enforcement in the art of urban tactical deployment. Normally the whole town echoed with radio buzz, shouted orders and the crackle of gunfire, but today it was almost deserted. Like everywhere else, the training facility was winding down for the Christmas holidays.

The streetlights flickered on in response to the steady creep of night. Shepherd hunched his shoulders against the chill and glanced up at the sky out of habit. The evening star had already risen in the west but it was not yet dark enough to see much else. The ancients would have seen omens in its shifting position. Shepherd just saw it as Venus, and drew comfort from the sight of it, like he always had, its brightness a constant, even in his most desperate and lonely nights.

He turned the corner. At the far end of the block, light leaked on to the sidewalk from the foyer of the Biograph, named after the theatre in Chicago where John Dillinger was gunned down in the mid-thirties. The marquee above the entrance advertised *Manhattan Melodrama* starring Clark Gable and Myrna Loy, the last movie Dillinger had ever seen. Shepherd reached the unmanned ticket booth and pushed through the door into the space where the foyer should have been.

The classroom beyond could hold a hundred students seated in concentric rows arranged around a large screen illuminated by a ceiling-mounted projector that could be patched in to a number of audio-visual teaching aids or any combination of the sixty-two security cameras monitoring the town. Right now it showed the basement room of the townhouse with Shepherd in the middle of it, frozen in his two-handed stance, his gun pointing at the crumpled bodies on the floor. A man in a black suit stood before the screen, head to one side as if studying an exhibit in an art gallery. Shepherd had been expecting Agent Franklin to greet him and debrief him on exactly how badly he had done. He was the field agent assigned to his class. The man staring at the screen was not him.

'You see a ghost in there, Shepherd?' the man asked without turning round.

Shepherd didn't look at the screen. He didn't yet trust himself to go back there.

'No, sir, I was just . . . it was a high-pressure situation.'

The man turned and Shepherd experienced a rush of anxiety when he saw who it was. 'They're all high-pressure situations, son – every one of 'em.'

Assistant Director O'Halloran was a thin blade of a man worn sharp by a lifetime spent in the Bureau. Everything about him was hard and precise: the steel rims of his spectacles; the pale grey eyes behind them; the pin holding his narrow tie in place against his starched, white shirt. Even his gunmetal hair appeared to have been parted with a scalpel rather than a comb. Shepherd recognized him from the back page of the recruitment literature he had filled out almost a year ago.

'You have quite the impressive résumé,' O'Halloran said, holding up a thin file with Shepherd's photograph on the cover.

Shepherd swallowed, his throat dry. 'Thank you, sir.'

'Mathematics major with computer science at the University

of Michigan. MSc in Physics from CalTech. Best part of a PhD in Theoretical Cosmology from Cambridge University in England – though you never finished that one, did you? Even so, I imagine you could easily be making six figures and upwards working for any bank in the country, yet you chose to sign up with Uncle Sam at a GS-10 basic starting salary. Why is that, I wonder?'

'Money isn't everything.'

'Really. You a Communist?'

'No, sir – I'm a patriot.'

'OK, Mr Patriot, tell me about your PhD. Why didn't you finish it?'

Shepherd glanced down at the file, recalling the psychiatric evaluations and background checks that had formed part of his recruitment screening. All of it would be in there. At least, everything he had told them. But this was the Assistant Director he was talking to, so there could well be other things now – things he had hoped to keep hidden.

'Timing, sir: 9/11 happened. Homeland defence and the war on terror became the number one priority. Almost the entire space program was shelved, and my studies had been paid for by NASA. I suddenly found myself with no grant and no job to go to. It was . . . like hitting a wall.'

'So you dropped out.'

'I took off and went travelling to clear my head – try and work out what I was going to do with my life now that NASA no longer appeared to be an option.'

'And where did you go, exactly?' O'Halloran held up the file. 'There's a gap of almost two years where you seem to have disappeared off the face of the earth: no social security records, no job history, no credit cards . . .'

'I was off the grid mainly – Europe first then Southeast Asia and eventually Africa, travelling from place to place, working cash jobs in bars and on farms, staying in backpacker hostels that charged by the night. They don't take credit cards in most of those places. I'd been a student for most of my adult life, so I knew how to live cheap.'

'Then what? You saw the light and decided to rejoin society?'

'Something like that. My intention had always been to pay back the money for my education by devoting myself to public service and working for NASA. I came to realize that just because that particular opportunity had been closed to me didn't mean I couldn't pay my dues in other ways.'

'So you signed up for the FBI?'

'It seemed a good way to usefully employ the skill set I had gained at the tax payers' expense.'

O'Halloran pursed his lips and studied Shepherd like a poker player deciding which way to bet. 'I am not in the habit of sending rookies out in the field before they have completed their training or spent at least a year in a field office, but apparently, out of more than thirty thousand currently active Bureau personnel, you are the most uniquely qualified for a situation that has presented itself.'

He reached into his pocket, drew out a leather wallet and handed it over. Inside, Shepherd's photo stared out from a full FBI ID card that expired in a month's time.

'That will *temporarily* entitle you to carry a concealed weapon and transport it on board commercial airlines. You can collect your Roscoe and a box of shells from Agent Williams on your way out. Make no mistake, this is not a free pass. Once your usefulness to the investigation has been exhausted you will report back here to finish your training, understood?'

'Yessir.'

'Good. Now tell me, *Special Agent* Shepherd, what do you know about the Hubble Space Telescope?'

6

They chose a spot a good distance outside the perimeter fence, working by hand now that the earthmovers were no use, breaking through rock and dirt baked hard as brick before carefully placing the bodies at the bottom, enemy next to enemy – all but one. While most had been busy with the communal grave, some of the riders had dug another and into it they laid the body of their leader, the one they called Ash'abah – the Ghost. And when they had filled in all the graves and said their silent prayers, most of the riders left too, melting away into the desert.

Liv stayed by the lone grave for a long time thinking about everything that had brought her to this place. Her previous life seemed like an abstract collection of memories now, something she could as easily have read in a book than experienced in real life. It was no longer possible to imagine herself as that person, flicking through the new IKEA catalogue, subway-surfing through the morning rush hour with a skinny latte in one hand and a smart-phone in the other. It was an existence she had spent a lifetime building, only to have fate dismantle it in a matter of days.

She stared down at the mound of dirt that marked the end of another life and felt a rush of terror at the oblivion of it all. Everything was so fragile and insignificant. She looked around for something to mark the grave, anything that might signify that someone important had died here and the living remembered him. The larger grave was barely marked at all, just a pile of broken rocks taken from the ground during the digging that now served as a sort of cairn. She wanted something more distinct, something that had to have been put there by man, not nature. She tried to think what Gabriel would do and her hand tightened around the note he had left for her as she remembered where she had found it. She sprang from the ground, heading back to the compound.

'*You OK?*' *The voice surprised her and she turned to find Tariq close by.*

'*Yes,*' *she said.* '*Come with me. I'll need your help.*'

The Operations Room was more or less the same as she had last seen it. The large topographical map still filled the back wall, though the laptops were gone along with the smaller maps and anything else deemed portable or valuable enough to take. The solid block of carved black granite containing the Starmap lay where she had left it on the table in the middle of the room, half-buried in discarded paperwork and curled scrolls of seismic data printouts. Liv swept them aside, revealing the carved letter T in the centre of the stone with the smaller symbols surrounding it: the dots of the constellation of Draco; a symbol of a tree; a simple human figure. She grabbed hold of the chipped and broken edges of the stone and hauled it across the table towards her.

'*Let me,*' *Tariq said.*

He took it from her, heaving it up and hugging it to his chest to reveal the carved blocks of text on the back where Gabriel had left the note for her to find, two languages with patterns of dots surrounding them that mapped the stars and had given the tablet its name.

'*This way,*' *Liv said, hurrying back to the gravesite.*

The Starmap thumped onto the Ghost's grave, the weight of it pressing into the loose earth. Liv stared down at it in silence, the deeply carved T-shaped cross standing out in the centre of the broken stone. It seemed appropriate somehow: a cross but not a cross; a religious relic from before the great religions had even been born. And in the strange empty void inside her, where there were echoes of the one she had carried to this dead place, the placing of this stone on the earth made sense to her, like a reminder of an ancient truth she had once known and since forgotten. There would be no mistaking the significance of this grave now.

She stayed like this for a long time, watching the shadows lengthen and the carvings on the stone become more evident. She could almost feel a vibration emanating from it, rippling through the earth and filling her with calm.

'Someone's coming.' The words shook her stillness like a breeze through branches and she looked up, following the line of Tariq's arm. In the far distance a column of dust was rising.

'A horse?' she said, feeling a swell in her chest at the prospect that it might be Gabriel returning to her.

'Horses,' he said, 'many horses.'

'Yours?' Liv stared hard at the distant dust as if her gaze was the only thing capable of keeping it there, clinging to the notion that the riders might have gone looking for Gabriel and now be bringing him back.

Tariq shook his head. 'Wrong direction.' His hand unconsciously gripped the shoulder strap of the AK-47 slung over his back. 'We should get back to the compound,' he said, taking her by the arm and steering her towards the perimeter fence. 'I have a bad feeling about this.'

THE *SUNDAY TIMES* BESTSELLER

WHAT IS THE SECRET OF
SANCTUS?

Liv Adamsen is a New York crime reporter, Kathryn Mann a charity worker. They are very different people, but their fate is bound together by one man's desperate act.

With the world's media watching, a robed man has thrown himself from the top of the oldest inhabited place on earth, an ancient citadel in Turkey. For some it is a sign of great events to come. For Liv and Kathryn it is the start of a race into danger, darkness and the most remarkable secret in the history of humanity.

It is a secret that the fanatical monks in the citadel will kill, torture and break every law, human and divine, to keep hidden…

'A fast-moving, thoroughly enjoyable, adventure – plenty of action, plenty of intrigue … The sort of novel to devour in one sitting'
Kate Mosse

THESANCTI.COM